THE BEETLE

THE BEETLE

Richard Marsh

edited by Julian Wolfreys

broadview editions

National Library of Canada Cataloguing in Publication Data

Marsh, Richard, d. 1915
    The beetle / Richard Marsh ; edited by Julian Wolfreys.

(Broadview editions)
Includes bibliographical references.
ISBN 1-55111-443-7

I. Wolfreys, Julian, 1958-   II. Title.   III. Series.

PR6025.A646B43 2004   823'.912   C2004-900816-1

Broadview Press Ltd. is an independent, international publishing house, incorporated in 1985. Broadview believes in shared ownership, both with its employees and with the general public; since the year 2000 Broadview shares have traded publicly on the Toronto Venture Exchange under the symbol BDP.

We welcome comments and suggestions regarding any aspect of our publications–please feel free to contact us at the addresses below or at broadview@broadviewpress.com.

North America
PO Box 1243, Peterborough, Ontario, Canada K9J 7H5
Tel: (705) 743-8990; Fax: (705) 743-8353
email: customerservice@broadviewpress.com
3576 California Road, Orchard Park, NY, USA 14127

UK, Ireland, and continental Europe
NBN Plymbridge
Estover Road
Plymouth PL6 7PY UK
Tel: 44 (0) 1752 202 301
Fax: 44 (0) 1752 202 331
Fax Order Line: 44 (0) 1752 202 333
Customer Service: cservs@nbnplymbridge.com
Orders: orders@nbnplymbridge.com

Australia and New Zealand
UNIREPS, University of New South Wales
Sydney, NSW, 2052
Tel: 61 2 9664 0999; Fax: 61 2 9664 5420
email: info.press@unsw.edu.au

www.broadviewpress.com

Series editor: Professor L.W. Conolly
Advisory editor for this volume: Michel Pharand

PRINTED IN CANADA

Contents

Acknowledgements • 7

Introduction • 9

Richard Marsh: A Brief Chronology • 35

A Note on the Text • 38

The Beetle • 39

Appendix A: London in the *fin de siècle* • 323
1. From Walter Besant, *All Sorts and Conditions of Men*
   (1882) • 323
2. From Robert Louis Stevenson, *The Strange Case of Dr. Jekyll
   and Mr. Hyde* (1886) • 324
3. From Henry James, "London" (1888) • 325
4. From Arthur Conan Doyle, *The Sign of Four* (1890) • 326
5. From Oscar Wilde, *The Picture of Dorian Gray*
   (1891) • 327
6. From Arthur Machen, *The Three Impostors* (1895) • 327
7. From Arthur Morrison, *A Child of the Jago* (1896) • 328

Appendix B: The New Woman • 330
1. From Ouida, "The New Woman," *North American Review*
   (May 1894) • 330
2. From Sarah Grand, "The New Aspect of the Woman
   Question," *North American Review* (March 1894) • 331
3. From Nat Arling, "What is the Rôle of the 'New Woman?',"
   Westminster Review (November 1898) • 333
4. From Kathleen Caffe, "A Reply from Daughters," *The
   Nineteenth Century* (March 1894) • 337

Appendix C: English Interest and Involvement in Egypt • 340
1. From Georgia Louise Leonard, "The Occult Sciences in the
   Temples of Ancient Egypt," *The Open Court* (1887) • 340

2. From J.Norman Lockyer, "The Astronomy and Mythology of the Ancient Egyptians," *The Nineteenth Century* (July 1892) • 344
3. From "Egypt," *London Quarterly Review* (April 1884) • 348
4. From "Our Position in Egypt," *The Speaker* (19 October 1891) • 351

Appendix D: Mesmerism and Animal Magnetism • 353
1. From Joseph W. Haddock, *Somnolism & Psycheism; or, the Science of the Soul and the Phenomena of Nervation, as Revealed by Vital Magnetism or Mesmerism, Considered Physiologically and Philosophically, with Notes of Mesmeric and Psychical Experience* (1851) • 353
2. From James Esdaile, *Natural and Mesmeric Clairvoyance, with the Practical Application of Mesmerism in Surgery and Medicine* (1852) • 356
3. From "Magic and Mesmerism," *Tait's Edinburgh Magazine*, 50 (1843) • 357
4. From Romulus Katscher, "Mesmerism, Spiritualism and Hypnotism," *The Literary Digest* (21 February 1891) • 358

Works Cited and Recommended Reading • 362

Acknowledgements

I first came across Richard Marsh's odd little novel in 1993; it has mesmerized and haunted me ever since, demanding repeatedly that it be republished; so I would like, therefore, to thank initially Julia Gaunce at Broadview Press for her interest in, enthusiasm for, and support of, this project, by which this obsession of mine can finally be realised. I would also like to thank those anonymous readers for Broadview who responded positively and with some helpful suggestions to the initial proposal for a new edition of *The Beetle*. At the University of Florida, I would like to thank Pamela Gilbert and Chris Snodgrass for their input and comments, discussion and remarks concerning Marsh, *The Beetle*, and the *fin de siècle*. John van Hook, of Smathers Library, University of Florida, discovered some very useful background sources. Ruth Robbins and Jim Kincaid, both of whom know more about this period, degeneration, and the camp dimensions of late Victorian gothic than is good for anyone, deserve, as ever, unending gratitude. Sarah Mallonee's help with research was truly invaluable, and this volume is all the better for her diligence, rigour, and enthusiasm. Finally, I would like to thank those students at the Universities of Luton and Florida whose own enthusiasm for this novel probably says more about them than about one of the stranger volumes of the late nineteenth century.

Julian Wolfreys

Introduction

Richard Heldman, Bernard Heldmann, or Richard Marsh?

Not a great deal is known about Richard Marsh. His given name was Richard Bernard Heldman, though he published from the beginning of his writing career until the early nineties as Bernard Heldmann (making his surname more obviously Germanic through the addition of that extra 'n') and then, afterwards, as Richard Marsh. A Londoner, his family living at the time of his birth in St. John's Wood and subsequently in Isleworth (Taylor 1997, 14),[1] Marsh (as he lived out the last two decades of his life) was born in 1857, and died in 1915 of heart failure or heart disease (the death certificate ambiguously indicates both). Until relatively recently, it had been believed and circulated in brief critical biographies that Heldman had been educated at Eton Public School and Oxford University. For example, in the "Introduction" to *Victorian Villainies*, a collection of four *fin de siècle* detective fictions and mysteries including *The Beetle* (1897), editor Hugh Greene records Marsh's schooling as fact, going on to describe him as "something of a child prodigy" (Greene 1984, 10). However, this now appears merely an embellishment on the part of his grandson, Robert Aickman, a popular and successful writer of what he liked to term "strange stories," who included such spurious details in his own autobiography. What is known of Heldman, though, is that, taking up the profession of journalism, he wrote numerous short stories, boys' adventure tales of a kind similar to those produced by H. Rider Haggard and G.A. Henty, as well as many novels. His short stories were popular enough that they were collected in several editions, continuing to be published after Marsh's death. As Bernard Heldmann, he "had published, between 1881 and 1883, in book form four school stories and one adventure book" (Taylor 1997, 10). Richard Heldman continued to publish as Bernard Heldmann for another decade, at which point he adopted the name Marsh (his mother's maiden name), either late in 1892 or early in 1893, following what some have speculated was a family disgrace, though the details of this remain unknown. However, while he changed his name, he did not impose this change on the repub-

---

[1] Taylor's article provides the most biographical detail of Richard Marsh available, and I gratefully acknowledge the importance of this essay in drawing on it for my introduction.

lication of his earlier works, the popularity of which appeared not to suffer throughout the rest of his life.

While it may be possible to speculate, albeit idly, on the reasons for name change, there is no hard evidence on which to draw, either concerning Marsh's life or in the narrative details of his publications. Certainly, Marsh's writing, from the earliest examples onwards, demonstrates the occasional depiction of somewhat sadistic sexuality or, as in the schoolboy stories, the expression of homoerotic affection. Arguably, however, this is not peculiar to Heldmann/Marsh, the narrative interest in "decadence" being, if not commonplace, at least prevalent in *fin de siècle* fiction. In the school stories published in the 1880s, the boys are given to what would, at the time, have been seen as effeminate behaviour, often crying hysterically or kissing one another; and there are also frequent, sometimes quite explicit homoerotic scenes, along with the occasional instance of sadistic behaviour on the part of some of the school boys towards others.[1] However, it would be dangerous and irresponsible to assert some connection between such fictional instances and either the author's life in general or the alleged disgrace in particular. Marsh's writing as either Heldmann or Marsh gives little if any clue as to the author's life, and on the evidence of his writing it is all but impossible to assign autobiographical influence. If anything, Marsh's anonymity is virtually guaranteed by the fact that his writing is so typical of late Victorian popular melodramatic and sensation fiction. All that is known to be even mildly sensational concerning Heldman's career is that he and G.A. Henty, with whom Heldman had worked regularly in writing for his boys' adventure paper, *The Union Jack*, had a quite public disagreement in 1883, a decade before the name change, leading to Heldman's resignation from *The Union Jack*. It may be the case that Henty, who was editor of the paper, found certain details of Heldman's short stories distasteful, but again there is no evidence of this; and we can be reasonably certain that there is no link to be made between this earlier incident and the unsubstantiated rumour of family disgrace that has been linked tenuously to Heldman's change of name. While, with the name change, Marsh stops writing public school stories and boys' adventures, and begins writing fiction, the principal genres in which he works being detective and supernatural fiction (he also produced a few "New Woman" novels), the interests which drive his narratives, including sexual transgression, remain consistent.

Equally unfounded is the proposal put forward by one critic that

---

[1]   See the discussion of such passages in Taylor (1997, 11).

Richard Heldman's family were of German-Jewish origin, hence the necessity for the transformation of identity. William Baker has suggested that the name change was due to the "xenophobic atmosphere of late Victorian England" (Baker 1994, ix), but, while there may have been undeniable xenophobic or, more accurately, jingoistic and chauvinist tendencies within certain aspects of *fin de siècle* late imperial English culture, there is no evidence that this was ever directed toward either Heldman / Marsh or his family. From the scant records concerning his parents, his siblings— he had a brother, Harry, and a sister, Alice—and his own marriage, there is no evidence as to why Marsh should have been the subject of either xenophobic or, as Baker (in an equally unsubstantiated hypothetical moment) has it, anti-Semitic sentiments, and Marsh's marriage as Heldman in the Church of England hardly lends credence to Baker's claims. Indeed, the continued successful sales of the stories published under the name of Heldmann through the last years of the nineteenth century and through the first two decades of the twentieth appear to give the lie to Baker's speculative, groundless assertions. However, what can be said with reasonable certainty is that "Richard Marsh" was not a pen name merely; it was the name by which Heldman lived for the rest of his life.

Late Imperial England and its Others

While a few of the short stories are still to be found in print, and even though he wrote seventy-six books, including collections of short tales, a number of which proved commercially successful, one work in particular secured Marsh momentary fame, *The Beetle*. *The Beetle* was published in September 1897, just two months after Bram Stoker's *Dracula*, and was, initially at least, even more of a popular success with the reading public than Stoker's now canonical work. There is an apocryphal tale that Stoker and Marsh had a wager to see who could produce the most successful supernatural novel. Whatever the truth of this, it is the case that, while *Dracula* was undeniably a huge commercial success in its own right, sales of *The Beetle* were stronger than those of Stoker's tale of the Transylvanian vampire, *The Beetle* going through fifteen printings by 1913 and reaching its twentieth impression just four years later.[1] Marsh's achievement is perhaps best explained if one does

---

[1]   Given the number of subsequent impressions and editions, the steady commercial success of *The Beetle* is undeniable. A twenty-fourth impression appeared in 1927, and mass-market paperbacks appeared without interruption until 1960 at least.

not seek to understand the novel as idiosyncratic or unusual but as wholly of its time, albeit in a markedly singular fashion. It is a novel in which the various facets of late-Victorian modernity, science, parliamentary democracy, imperial identity, and, most generally expressed, the nineteenth-century investment in the attainability and efficacy of knowledge as a form of power and control are confronted by the non-rational, the inexplicable, the archaic, *the other*. In "the post-Darwinian imperial age that is the late nineteenth century," writes Daniel Bivona, "'knowledge' of the alien Other is being produced on a large scale, and occasioning a crisis in the way England looks at itself" (Bivona 1990, 75). As Bivona's commentary implies, this otherness, this alterity, is never in any simple fashion external to Englishness. It erupts in numerous places from within that national identity, causing that process of self-questioning. Moreover, it is arguable that such potentially ruinous fragmentation of identity through the emergence of the multiple and heterogeneous aspects of alterity come to haunt the very form of the novel itself, as I shall explore in the third part of this introduction.

We might begin by locating such disturbance in the novel's use of mesmerism, the practice of which was widespread throughout the nineteenth century, at least as a form of entertainment.[1] As Alison Winter puts it "[m]esmerism was pervasive in Victorian society. It influenced and was eventually assimilated into several major intellectual enterprises.... Mesmerism was not only ubiquitous but challenging within Victorian intellectual culture, as experiments became catalysts for competing assertions about the nature and seat of intellectual authority" (Winter 1998, 5). While being put to legitimate medical uses from the late eighteenth century, it quickly became accused of being employed for fraudulent purposes, its scientific and medical legitimacy and efficacy being hotly contested, and the mainstream medical profession sought on occasions to distance itself from a practice which, to some, had the patina of a sideshow entertainment, or otherwise suggested non-rational, non-European mysticism. Winter rightly remarks of mesmerism, that, from the 1870s onwards, it "became the occasion for self-conscious reflections about the basis of race inequalities and the natural laws that helped one people to bend another to its will" (Winter 1998, 7). What is truly unsettling, I would suggest, for the

---

[1]   See Alison Winter's fascinating cultural history, *Mesmerized: Powers of Mind in Victorian Britain* (1998). See also, for a specific reading of *The Beetle*, Roger Luckhurst, "Trance-Gothic, 1882–97" (2000, 148–67).

late Victorian reader of *The Beetle*, is that a "science," already seen in a highly ambivalent light by the end of the century, is appropriated by a non-European monstrous other for clearly criminal and sexual purposes, all of which are aimed at undermining any self-reflective certainties about the stability of identity, whether one is speaking of class-position, masculinity, femininity, national identity, or secure belief in one's own position as a subject of empire. That mesmerism is employed to achieve this in the hands of the "degenerate" gothic foreigner,[1] proves all the more efficacious as a narrative device in unleashing the irrational and unconscious fears at the heart of Englishness. As in *Dracula*, mesmerism provides the opportunity for the unscrupulous predatory alien to control and devastate not merely through physical attack and corporeal destruction, but also through the psychic erasure of the boundaries which one imposes on oneself as the necessary limits of self-definition. From this it can be suggested that mesmerism is readable as an act analogous with sexual penetration, an analogy borne out in both *Dracula* and *The Beetle*. Moreover, there is also a threat through the "interpersonal intimacy" of mesmerism to conventional cultural and psychic constructions of gender—men are described in novels such as Marsh's as being "unmanned," while women are psychically, if not physically, violated. Furthermore, the specifically sexual threat of this foreign other taps into what Elaine Showalter has described as the *fin de siècle*'s "syphilophobia" (Showalter 1986, 88-115), the anxiety and fear of widespread transmission of sexually transmitted disease.[2] The analogy between mesmerism's powers over the mind, and its specific ability in *The Beetle* to effect a melodramatic condition of "unbalancing" its subjects, and the effects of syphilis become the more marked, perhaps, if one recalls that the common late-Victorian and Edwardian term for syphilis was "general paralysis of the insane." As Showalter avers, "syphilis was surely the symbolic disease of the fin de

---

[1] Marsh is not alone in exploiting fear of the foreign and racial other in relation to sexuality through the employment of mesmerism. Stoker's Transylvanian count has mesmeric powers, as does the villainous Jew, Svengali, in George Du Maurier's novel, *Trilby*, published two years before *Dracula* and *The Beetle* in 1895. On Stoker, Du Maurier, and Marsh, and their novels' use of mesmerism, see Luckhurst (2000, 148–67).

[2] While not mentioning Marsh's novel, Showalter does discuss the imagery of syphilis in relation to post-Darwinian discourses of degeneration in, amongst other texts, Stoker's *Dracula*, Wilde's *The Picture of Dorian Gray*, H. Rider Haggard's *She*, R.L. Stevenson's *The Strange Case of Dr. Jekyll and Mr. Hyde*, Ibsen's *Ghosts*, Wells's *The Time Machine*, and Thomas Hardy's *Jude the Obscure*.

siècle.... the iconography of syphilis pervades English fiction at the turn of the century.... Syphilis and syphilitic insanity constituted the repressed historical referents for the fantastic mode that dominates so much of late Victorian writing" (Showalter 1986, 88). While, statistically, the incidences of syphilis were dropping in the 1890s, the fear, allied to theories of degeneration and the multiple threats that the other posed to late imperial England, was more rampant than its own narratives of the disease. William Greenslade makes clear the cultural context of the discourse of degeneration, and is worth citing at length: "[t]he idea of degeneration was an important resource of myth for the post-Darwinian world. The late Victorian establishment and the propertied classes generally harboured anxieties about poverty and crime, about public health and national and imperial fitness, about decadent artists, 'new women' and homosexuals." He continues:

> The loose assemblage of beliefs which can now be marked out as 'degenerationism' ... offered a displacement and transference of guilt, and of fear of the uncontrollable and baffling energies of material existence. Degeneration offered boundless scope for both attacking the irrational and sustaining it.... fears at the *fin de siècle* were at work shaping institutional practices.... Degeneration was at the root of what was, in part, an enabling strategy by which the conventional and respectable classes could justify and articulate their hostility to the deviant, the diseased and the subversive. At times when the social order was under particular pressure (London in the mid-1880s is an example...) the pathological element in the discourse of social panic was pressed into service to undermine the intentionality of the oppositional voice, by rendering it as irrational or 'sick'... (1994, 1-2).

Such pathological marking is embodied in the long-fostered myth that British soldiers returning from foreign campaigns, such as those in Egypt and the Sudan throughout the 1880s, would bring with them STDs.

Yet arguably, the greatest perceived threat of the foreign other's application of mesmerism was to the sense of national self, of which the sexual and gendered self were but the most vulnerable facets. Alison Winter remarks that there were "two very strong reasons why mesmerism should have made Europeans uneasy: one was the problem of association between the races; the other was the more profound question of what coming under someone's influence meant in this context" (Winter 1998, 198-99).

Allowing the foreign other control over the Englishman or woman produces an imaginative reversal of colonial relations between master and servant, as there is produced in such a narrative the association of the "vulnerability of the mesmeric *subject* with colonial subservience" (Winter 1998, 199). To extend this a little further, by analogy the fear of the foreign other's presence in England (a fear expressed in various fictions towards Jews, the Irish, and anarchists) is the externalized articulation of the fear of proximity, intimacy, contamination, and penetration that mesmeric invasion of the subject's psyche may be read as figuring. Thus, even as the Egyptian Beetle, that "liminal man-woman-goddess-beetle-Thing" (Luckhurst 2000, 160), is only ever encountered secreted away, largely unobserved, in an unassuming "villa" in West London, the capital of the Empire, and then unnervingly managing to intrude into the private houses of the English ruling classes, so too is it found working its hypnotic way into the minds of the English in a series of what Roger Luckhurst calls trance-gothic encounters. Thus we come to see how, whether externally or internally, the borders of any identity or location are always permeable and always available for haunting in the most uncanny ways imaginable.

Following on from the exemplary figure of mesmerism as that which transgresses boundaries between inner and outer, self and other, proper and improper, and so on, if we are looking for other sites of cultural contestation and disruption, we might also start by acknowledging the novel's oscillation between science and pseudo-science, between its narrative acknowledgement of chemistry and forensics on the one hand, and its address to the discourses of degeneration on the other, prompted by the post-Darwinian theories of Max Nordau, Cesare Lombroso, and Havelock Ellis, amongst others. Degeneration was founded on and promoted notions of psychological deviance and criminal behaviour according to the reading of supposedly typical racial and corporeal features. Nordau, Ellis, and Lombroso all emphasize facial details as being indicative of criminality, deviancy, and degeneracy. For example, Lombroso suggests that "the face of the criminal, like those of most animals, is disproportionate size" (1972, 12), while eyes are shifty, often "Mongolian," or asymmetrical (18). Lips are "fleshy, swollen and protruding, as in negroes… " (31). Chins are small and receding, or flat, "as in apes" (38). Psychologically, the degenerate is prone to cynicism, vanity, vindictiveness, and cruelty (38–39). Ellis makes similar remarks. Also noting the receding chin, along with large ears, and making the comparison once again with apes, he asserts the atavistic nature of the degenerate and criminal, arguing that the "criminal resembles the savage and the prehistoric man" (1973, 61). Ellis claims that the "true degenerative abnormalities … in the lowest human races" are found most often "in Africa … among the indigenous fellaheen, Berbers, and negroes of the Soudan" (70-71). Why should such pseudo-theories abound in the *fin de siècle*? William Greenslade suggests that the "growth of degeneration into fully fledged explanatory myth, with widespread applications, in the latter half of the nineteenth century, is bound up with the huge economic, social, and cultural changes.… Religious belief, moral codes, attitudes to class, to sexual roles, to sexuality itself underwent seismic disturbance and shock, as well as subsidence and erosion" (15).

Thus in Kelly Hurley's words, "a paranoiac text like *The Beetle* serves to reflect and feed into British suspicion of and contempt for Egyptians during a period of heightened British military activity in Egypt," and "it is precisely [the setting of London] which masks the British imperialist project informing and underlying the test" (Hurley 1996, 127). Such a project is further mystified in the novel's focus on the supernatural aspect and the physiological and psychological aspects of the Beetle. In drawing on so-called theories of degeneracy as the basis for representing the creature, the text occludes its historical and ideological fears. Yet with the words of Lombroso and Ellis in mind, we should give close attention to the way the Beetle is imagined. *The Beetle* offers one such "reading" of its creature's face, when, in Chapter III, Robert Holt recounts his first clear sight of the creature:

> I saw someone in front of me lying in a bed. I could not at once decide if it was a man or a woman. Indeed at first I doubted if it was anything human. But, afterwards, I knew it to be a man,—for this reason, if for no other, that it was impossible such a creature could be feminine.…— there was a vitality in his eyes which was startling. It might have been that he had been afflicted by some terrible disease, and it was that which had made him so supernaturally ugly.
>
> There was not a hair upon his face or head, but, to make up for it, the skin, which was a saffron yellow, was an amazing mass of wrinkles. The cranium, and, indeed, the whole skull, was so small as to be disagreeably suggestive of something animal. The nose, on the other hand, was abnormally large; so extravagant were its dimensions, and so peculiar its shape, it resembled the beak of some bird of prey. A characteristic of the face—and an uncomfortable one!—was that, practically, it stopped short at the mouth. The mouth, with its blubber lips, came immediately underneath the

nose, and chin, to all intents and purposes, there was none. This deformity—for the absence of chin amounted to that—it was which gave to the face the appearance of something not human,— that, and the eyes. For so marked a feature of the man were his eyes, that, ere long, it seemed to me that he was nothing but eyes.

His eyes ran, literally, across the whole of the upper portion of his face,—remember, the face was unwontedly small, and the columna of the nose was razor-edged.

The principal features to notice here are the descriptions of the facial details and the wavering uncertainty as to whether to ascribe to such features human or animal origin. Indeed, Holt appears to tend towards a reading of the face as bestial. The blubberiness of the lips and the aquiline nose are both suggestive of the kinds of "racial" and criminal categorization that can be found in both Lombroso and Havelock Ellis. In a more general sense though is the implied "organic" or essentialist connection in the passage between evil, criminality, and inhuman alienness. Arguably, this description would be immediately recognizable to many late Victorian readers as the face of a criminal or degenerate, and quite possibly as foreign also. It does so because it exemplifies and provides, in Judith Halberstam's words, the typical analytical details of "criminal anthropology, [which] quite obviously, as it developed in the nineteenth century focused upon the visual aspects of pathology." She continues: "The attempt to categorize and demonstrate a propensity for degenerative behaviour by reading bodies and faces confirms that racial stereotyping demands that stereotypes be visualizable. And racial degeneracy, with its close ties to a social Darwinist conception of human development, also connects with sexual degeneracy" (Halberstam, 1995, 254). In the previous chapter, there is already a blatant depiction of sexual degeneracy, as the Beetle attempts some form of copulative engagement with Robert Holt, having first mesmerized him into a state of paralysis; but, I would argue, the shift from the dark of Chapter Two to the very visible scene just cited from the following chapter, makes for a certain reader the racial pathology and its "degenerate" qualities undeniable and inescapable. The otherness of the creature is inescapably *there*, on the page as well as in the room, for both Holt and the reader to see. The visible signs render it virtually impossible to apprehend it/him/her as being anything but the most abject and monstrous overdetermined figure of alterity.

Degeneracy is not the only narrative interest. There is also the concern with aspects of the supernatural and late-nineteenth-century understandings of psychology, as articulated through the various states of mind of the various characters. Typical of many late nineteenth-century novels and short stories, *The Beetle* explores what Kate Flint has described as "the uncertain boundaries between fiction of the super-natural and that which dramatizes the workings of the inner mind" (Flint 2000, 252), although, in the case of Marsh's novel, the "inner mind" is as much the national psyche of *fin de siècle* imperial Britain, as it is that of each of its protagonists. It belongs to what Nicholas Daly calls the "romance revival" of the *fin de siècle*, and stands alongside the work of Bram Stoker, H. Rider Haggard, and Arthur Conan Doyle, amongst others, as a text exemplifying, in Daly's words once more, "popular modernism" (Daly 1999, 4-29), a form of popular narrative which seeks to accommodate the anxieties of late imperial English national identity by testing the virility of that identity through the arrival of some threat. Romances such as Marsh's draw on the late-eighteenth and nineteenth-century cultural investment in Gothic narratives, populated with monsters, vampires, foreigners, phantoms, not infrequently Catholics, and, in Marsh's case, an Egyptian priestess, member of the cult of Isis, with the power to transmogrify into a man, a woman, or a Scarab Beetle with mesmeric powers. In common with the other novelists mentioned, Marsh is not merely a gothic story-teller.

To recap briefly, in order to move on, his narrative figures, amongst other things, the late-Victorian English fear of both wayward female sexuality, and also of the colonial and "oriental"[1] other, embodied in

---

[1] I am employing the terms "oriental" and, elsewhere, "Orientalism," in the sense given these words by Edward Said. The Orient, argues Said, is for Europe "one of its deepest and most recurring images of the Other. In addition, the Orient has helped to define Europe (or the West) as its contrasting image, idea, personality, experience…. The Orient is an integral part of the European *material* civilization and culture. Orientalism expresses and represents that part culturally and even ideologically as a mode of discourse with supporting institutions, vocabulary, scholarship, imagery, doctrines, even colonial bureaucracies and colonial styles" (1985, 1). He continues, "Orientalism is a style of thought based upon an ontological and epistemological distinction made between 'the Orient' and (most of the time) 'the Occident' (2). The notion and discourse of Orientalism is defined by Said as beginning roughly in the late eighteenth century, as a means by which the West, particularly European powers controlled its representations. Orientalism is thus the "whole network of interests inevitably brought to bear on (and therefore always involved in) any occasion when that peculiar entity 'the Orient' is in question…. European culture gained in strength and identity by setting itself off against the Orient as a sort of surrogate and even underground self" (3). With Egypt as a particular focal point for the English and the French in the production of Orientalism, "the Orient … existed as a series of values attached, not to its modern realities, but to a series of valorized contacts it had had with a distant European past" (85).

the Beetle, a singularly aggressive and predatory, shadowy revenant who may also be read as a kind of colonial manifestation of what Sigmund Freud terms the "return of the repressed,"[1] otherwise referred to by one of Marsh's narrators, Augustus Champnell, in the final chapter of *The Beetle* as "that awful nightmare from the past" that had made Paul Lessingham a "haunted man."

It is clear that Marsh's beetle-human hybrid provides a powerfully exemplary grotesque embodiment of late Victorian anxieties in so many ways. Not the least part of this "incorporation" is its encrypted, and therefore at least partially repressed, "memory"—of colonial history in the nineteenth century generally and, in particular, the decade or so prior to the publication of *The Beetle*. The body is grotesque because it is unstable, excessive, ambiguously traced by so many fragments of identity. It bears, to cite Judith Halberstam once more, "the marks of the construction of femininity, 'race' and sexuality" (Halberstam 1995, 252). However, the beetle-creature is readable as a disruptive figure, one of prosopopoeia, that rhetorical figure for giving face or voice to what is unrepresentable. *The Beetle* "gives face" to everything that is unstable in late imperial culture. Other characters' reactions during and after their encounters with the creature serve to produce the novel as a site onto which is mapped the cultural concerns of the period, which certain critics are at pains to stress as being intimately interrelated. Sally Ledger remarks that "the recurrent theme of the cultural politics of the *fin de siècle* was instability, and gender was arguably the most destabilizing category" (Ledger 1995, 22). Certainly gender instability is one significant concern in *The Beetle*; whether it is the most destabilizing category is another matter. I would aver that such is the extent of destabilization— or, as I shall go on to argue in the final section of this introduction, the undecidability—that one cannot accord one manifestation of disruption or instability any primacy over any other, whether one is talking of form, content, epistemology or ideology. Kelly Hurley also comments on instability and destabilization but argues for a different emphasis from Ledger's. She writes that "[t]he Beetle-Woman's unspeakability results as much from her racial difference and her species fluctuability as her metamorphic sexuality" (Hurley 1996, 125). What this gives us to understand is that, again in Ledger's words, "the crisis of the *fin de*

---

[1]   Freud presents this psychic principle in his essay "The 'Uncanny,'" in James Strachey, ed., *The Standard Edition of the Complete Psychological Works of Sigmund Freud*, 24 vols. (London: Hogarth Press, 1953–74), vol. 17, 219–56.

siècle centered not just on gender issues, but also on the interconnections between gender roles and contemporary anxieties pertaining to the continuation of the race in the best interests of the British Empire" (Ledger 1995, 31). Such an understanding might open the way to allow us insight into Marsh's choice of the Beetle's Egyptian identity. While *Dracula*'s popularity has been a constant throughout the twentieth century and the vampire remains to this day a potent, mystified symbol of our fear of the other (in *Buffy the Vampire Slayer*'s parallel-universe California, the undead are with us everywhere, all the time threatening to return); and while anti-Semitism and fears of non-white, non-Christian cultures are still today all-too powerful political and cultural forces, so that their particular manifestations in *fin de siècle* fiction require little general introduction, Marsh's exploration of cultural anxiety concerning the occult archaic culture of Egypt requires some brief historical and cultural contextualization beyond the broad, if accurate, thesis concerning the West's production of and attitude towards Orientalism.

English and European, specifically French, interest in Egypt as other has a long history (since the Crusades at least). Such interest manifested itself through colonial, cultural, and commercial activities. In 1798 Napoleon invaded Egypt in order to destroy British trade in the Middle East and Britain's established trade routes through the area. As Edward Said avers, Napoleonic exploits in the Middle East accorded a privileged status to Egyptology (Said 1983, 263), doubtless because Ancient Egypt offered, in its model of a dynastic civilization, a legitimation for Napoleon's own dynastic ambitions. In 1799, French soldiers discovered what has since become known as the Rosetta Stone (named after the village in which it was found), the deciphering of which eventually gave access to the decryption of the hieroglyphs found in temples, tombs, and pyramids. In 1802 the Rosetta Stone was removed to the British Museum in London, where its combination of hieroglyphs, demotic script, and Greek were eventually decoded by Jean François Champollion in 1822. In 1801, the Ottomans, in alliance with the British, forced the withdrawal of Napoleon's troops, the British being able to re-establish commercial and colonial interest in Egypt and surrounding regions. While British cultural interest in Egypt and in all aspects of Egyptology developed throughout the century, the British strengthened their position in Egypt throughout the Victorian period, through such acts as forcing Egypt in 1841 to limit the size of its army.

In 1859 work began on the construction of the Suez Canal, which was completed a decade later and celebrated with the 1871 premiere of Verdi's opera, *Aïda*, set in ancient Egypt. The opening of the canal did not merely serve in the facilitation of trade for the British Empire. It also served as a departure point for an increasing tourist trade, Egypt "combining as it did the advantages of climate, exoticism, monuments of ancient culture and (at this stage still informal) European domination" (Hobsbawm 1996, 205). During the building of the Canal, in 1863, Ismail Pasha became Khedive (the ruler) and began an extensive project of modernizing and rebuilding Egypt. While laudatory, this left the Egyptian economy in a critical position, leaving it vulnerable to further British mercantile and colonial incursions culminating in British Prime Minister Benjamin Disraeli's purchase of the majority interest in the Canal in 1875 (Rubenstein, 1998, 199). This was in turn to lead to Gladstone's Liberal Government becoming increasingly, if unwillingly, "entangled in a series of colonial activities of the most controversial kind, in Egypt and what is now the Sudan" (Rubenstein 1998, 199). British forces removed the Khedive in 1879, putting in his place his son Tewfik (Tawfiq).[1] Tewfik was Khedive in name only, with successive powerful British Administrators having control of the country, though not without resistance and rebellion. As Eric Hobsbawm remarks, the colonial involvement in Egypt was unlike almost any other in colonial history. It not only introduced a British ruling body, but also created a divisive system of rule by placing certain Egyptians in positions of governing power, over both the Egyptians and the Sudanese. There was thereby created a singular situation leading to the nationalist movement: "the unusual exposure of Egypt to the West had created a new elite of landlords, intellectuals, civil functionaries and army officers, which led to the national movement of 1879-82, directed against both the Khedive and the foreigners" (Hobsbawm 1996, 126). Several times, Egyptian army officers attempted uprisings against the British, leading to the prolonged period of struggles between British troops and those Egyptians and Sudanese who rightly resented occupation, domination, and westernization.

A principal figure in the national revolt was Mohammed Ahmed, who, in 1881, declared himself the Mahdi, Allah's chosen one, gathering around himself in the Sudan the forces of resistance, and seeking to overthrow both British presence and Egyptian rule of the Sudan.

---

[1]   On this, on the British interest in the Egyptian occult, and for contemporary discussion of other historical events, refer to Appendix C.

The Mahdi's troops were involved in a number of attacks on British-held positions over the next four years, culminating in the siege of Khartoum. Khartoum had been under the command of General Charles George Gordon, who had arrived there in February 1884, and which he held until 26 January 1885, when the Mahdi and his follow-ers stormed the city, destroying much of it in the process, and Gordon was killed. A singularly significant incident in the crisis perceived by late imperial England, Gordon's death became, in the words of histo-rian K. Theodore Hoppen, "one of the great metaphorical and actual … icons of Late Victorian imperialism" (Hoppen 1998, 663). It is perhaps not too much of an exaggeration to suggest that a result of the symbolic power of Gordon's death to the English, military activ-ity was increased, with the result that, in 1898, one year after the publi-cation of *The Beetle*, the Sudanese were defeated at the battle of Omdurman, and Anglo-Egyptian rule in the Sudan re-established, though not without continued resistance and protest into the twen-tieth century.

Of course, I am not suggesting that it is simply as a result of Gordon's death that Marsh's novel comes to be written. Nor do I wish to over-state the significance of this event in general, even though it does have a powerful effect in the collective national psyche of late Victorian ruling classes, as far as can be judged from contemporary documents. What I do wish to suggest though is that *The Beetle* enjoys its commercial success in part because it channels and exploits a number of fears, anxieties, and obsessions concerning different manifestations of the other in a narra-tive typical of much fiction of the time, one that mediated cultural anxi-ety; and, in part, the success of *The Beetle* occurs because Marsh grounds the anxiety through indirect allusion or reference to recent traumatic historical events and on-going struggle by his choice of Oriental, savage, barbaric, sensual, monstrous other. The Egyptian other is all the more monstrous in Marsh's rendering because it bears few, if any, signs of Egypt's ancient civilization or culture, beyond that reference to what would have been read as an idolatrous and sensuous religion. Daniel Bivona remarks that "notions of the 'barbaric,' the 'uncivilized,' the 'prim-itive'… the alien in time and the alien in space overlap constantly in the Victorian imagination of the late nineteenth century" (Bivona 1990, 77-78). In Marsh's beetle-creature, with its archaic Egyptian, supernat-ural origin, we see this to be so. What gives all the more force to the irrational threat of the beetle is that its foreign, non-European alterity is so intimately enfolded with its ancient and irrational nature, whereby

Marsh mines what Robert Mighall describes as "the major organizing figure of the Gothic," which is its "imputation of anachronism as a source of disorder" (Mighall 1999, 249). Extremity of cultural age, with its hint of the "unnatural" prolongation of life, "disorders" notions of life itself, especially when the sources of this "life" are religious practices so at odds with the transcendent beliefs of late Victorian Christianity. Beyond its strategic topographical and practical economic value, if Egypt's exotic cultural appeal throughout the nineteenth century for the English lay in the remnants of its pre-Christian antiquity—an antiquity suggestive of an empire, a civilization, and a culture comparable with modern imperial identity—then it is that very same archaic identity that is also the source of its perceived threat.

For the archaism of Egyptian civilization is not simply figured as the survival of a single predatory and vengeful figure. This hybrid creature, symbol in Marsh's grotesque and phantasmic narrative of an entire culture, serves as an uncanny reminder that Empires, religions, and dynasties do not last forever, but leave only the material reminders of their own mortality, haunting us because we see in them, as "through a glass darkly" (to recall Paul Lessingham's quotation of the New Testament on his experience in Cairo), our own corporeal, cultural, and historical finitude. Thus the figure of the beetle operates as a singular and disquieting example of the Freudian uncanny, in a number of ways as I have already implied in passing. We should spend a little time on this concept and the ways in which Marsh's text enacts various aspects of the uncanny, as a means of situating the novel's Egyptian obsession in relation to the historical, cultural, and ideological contexts I have sought to sketch. First, it embodies that which "ought to have remained secret and hidden but [which] has come to light" (Freud, 200). Second, drawing on the etymology of the German term for uncanny, *unheimlich* (literally, 'unhomely'), the uncanny is defined by Freud as that which causes feelings of horror and dread in the most familiar places, the places where one should feel the safest; in *The Beetle*, this is both London, the centre and capital of empire, and the houses of the ruling classes, those locations in which the reader should be able to place the surest confidence. Third, the figure of the Beetle causes ontological and epistemological uncertainty, leading again to the experience of the uncanny sensation. All such definitions of the uncanny certainly pertain to the beetle as an individual character. Fourth, the Beetle accords to another of Freud's determinations of the uncanny in that, on the one hand, it doubles, divides, and exchanges a series of selves, while, on the other, its returns and appearances may be read as "the constant recurrence of the same thing" (Freud, 210).

In its doubleness and as representative of a long-vanished culture the Beetle's uncanny resonance is most discomforting and, for the purpose of this reading, most significant. Bearing in mind the doubled, doubling self, the creature is suggestive of both an "assurance of immortality" and "the uncanny harbinger of death" (Freud, 211).[1] More than this, the Beetle is available for a reading of it as trope for that which is neither dead nor alive, but which returns and hovers between either condition as what Jacques Derrida might describe as a "hauntological" trope exceeding any ontology (Derrida, 1994).[2] In this, it has the potential for "awakening uncanny feelings ... created when there is intellectual uncertainty whether an object is alive or not" (Freud, 208). Furthermore, Freud argues, "many people experience the feeling in the highest degree in relation to death ... to the return of the dead, and to spirits and ghosts" (Freud, 218). From this remark, Freud finds it hardly surprising that in modern cities spiritualist shows and related phantasmagorical entertainments abound, promising to bring back the dead, and this is advertised in Marsh's text through the recourse to mesmerism. In our fascination with such processes as telepathy, mesmerism, and spiritualism, Freud sees in modern urban humanity the vestiges of a collective "primitive" fear (Freud, 219); in doing so, he acknowledges that which is other and repressed within ourselves, something archaic and intrinsic to identity, and this is, of course, part of the work of The Beetle. This is unfolded through the Beetle's synecdochic function of standing in for the archaism of Egypt, which, I would contend, offers to impose upon the English of the novel and its English readership an unpleasant recognition concerning the colonial and imperial mission, a recognition which also anticipates in a hauntingly prescient manner the well-known remark of Walter Benjamin: "There is no document of civilization that is not at the same time a document of barbarism. And just as such a document is not free of barbarism, barbarism taints also the manner in which it was transmitted from one owner to another" (Benjamin 1969, 256). To read The Beetle against the grain of its *fin de siècle* fear of the other, where barbarism is located in

---

[1]   Curiously—uncannily?— Freud develops the notion of doubling in relation to death around the example of "the Ancient Egyptians" (210).

[2]   Derrida employs the term occasionally in this book, suggesting something which "haunts" ontology but which exceeds it, and which is irreducible to any ontological definition.

Egypt and civilization in London, it has to be argued that the human-scarab hybrid pursues the politician Paul Lessingham, less from some irrational and barbaric Oriental blood-lust, than out of a sense of injustice for the "barbaric" English defilement of ancient Egypt's sacred locations, where tomb and temple have become defaced as a result of colonial and imperial intrusion, and by colonialism's by-product, tourism. Thus, from such a counter-reading, it can be said that the other, the not-self that returns, arrives not from another location, whether it be Egypt or Transylvania, but from within one's own identity, as a necessary yet repressed mirror of the self that is so much the concern of late imperial English literature.

Narrative Anxieties

From all that has been said so far, it can clearly be argued that *The Beetle* is a novel materially engaged in an imaginative encryption of historical, cultural, and political fears emanating from and mediating particular aspects of the English psyche at the end of the nineteenth century. Such a view is supported by Roger Luckhurst, who comments of *The Beetle* and Stoker's *Dracula* that both are "exemplary texts not so much of the gothic revival as the *fin de siècle itself*" (Luckhurst 2000, 159). *The Beetle* is, moreover, exemplary of a world without a stable centre, as already intimated: it figures a site of anxiety at the dark heart of Englishness in an almost perpetually night-time London, capital of nation and empire, in which the very possibility of agency, whether individually or collectively on the part of the English, is called into question.[1] Faced with what is perceived as the irrational, the Englishmen of Marsh's novel respond in a concerted fashion, calling to their aid the police and the modern technologies of telegraph and public transport. However, despite their modernity and motivation, their actions are marked by the irrational desire for violent retribution and destruction. This is "justified" by the abduction and implied violation of an upper-class Englishwoman, Marjorie Lindon—she is stripped of her clothes by the Beetle, her hair cut off, and re-dressed as a man—the one female figure in the novel who has any agency. Yet the agency of the men is itself ultimately rendered ambivalently. The

---

[1]   On the question of agency and its ethical dimension in *fin de siècle* fiction and culture, see Jil Larson (2001).

precipitation of pursuit leads to the excessively violent moment of a train wreck, as a symbol of modernity comes crashing, quite literally, to an excessive halt. In its relationship to, and as the outcome of, the desire for retribution, the cataclysmic event might seem perhaps more suited to the Old Testament or to some other archaic mythic story in its moral force, despite the narrative vehicle of modern technology violence apparently being justified by an outraged and, again, collective, morality. Thus there is a sense in which we might read the denouement of *The Beetle* as haunted by some anachronistic narrative trace where, once more, anachronism brings about disorder of the most excessive kind. This time, however, the anachronism is not presented through some archaic gothic monster or foreigner, but instead, reading against the grain, is understood to emanate from within the very contours of the narrative's *raison d'être*, the desire for national imperial identity's maintenance. It is thus the novel's protagonists who bring about the disruption of social order.

Amongst the novel's principal protagonists are a politician with an ambiguous incident in his past occurring while in Egypt; a member of the upper classes who designs what are now known as weapons of mass destruction—at one point he describes his work as "legalized murder"; an office worker turned house-breaker, albeit out of the necessity of unemployment; and a member of the aristocracy turned "Confidential Agent" as he is called in the text, or private detective as he would now be known. None could be claimed as exemplars of ideal English manhood, whatever their motivations or histories. And formally there is no single omniscient narrator, but four competing voices. The novel is presented through the four first-person narratives, ordered sequentially in books belonging, in turn, to the homeless and out-of-work clerk just mentioned, Robert Holt, the somewhat pompous inventor Sydney Atherton, Marjorie Lindon (already mentioned), daughter of a Tory Member of Parliament, and the Honourable Augustus Champnell, the Confidential Agent. Of the first three narratives, those of Robert Holt and Marjorie Lindon do not so much end as they come to a halt suggestive of irresolution and an impending crisis. Atherton's is more conclusive, but then this might be expected; as a male member of the ruling classes and a man of science, he is hardly expected to be as vulnerable as an out-or-work clerk and a woman! Champnell's is the final narrative, and as detective it falls on him to draw together the various strands, to decipher the clues and provide a sense of closure, though, as it turns out, this can hardly be said to happen, as I shall discuss shortly.[1] There are two other principal characters already alluded to, the Beetle itself and Paul Lessingham, a fast-rising Member of Parliament (though, unlike Marjorie's father, a Liberal), and fiancé of Marjorie Lindon. With the proposed marriage and, with that, the political alliance of the radical-liberal and a representative of the New Woman (whose narrative purpose is discussed below), the union is unambiguously concerned with the protection of a future for the British ruling classes. Such a future is jeopardized, however, by both the confrontation between the Beetle and Lessingham, and by the Beetle's abduction of Marjorie. While neither the Beetle nor Lessingham have a narrative of their own, the novel's central concern is with the struggle between the two, between the archaic and modern faces of civilization, and it is the task of the reader to understand this dialectic through the partial perspectives of the narrators.

Arguably, the narrators—and unquestionably Sydney and Marjorie, whose romantic tension may be read as a counterpoint of sorts to the principal tussle they are called upon to relate—inadvertently obscure as much as they forward the reader's understanding through the imposition of their personalities on their respective narratives. Certainly, the first three narrations can only ever be partial, given the temporal limits of their adventures. Holt's narrative, with which the novel begins, concerns his encounter with the Beetle, that creature's hypnotic capture of Holt, and Holt's subsequently being made to cross London dressed in nothing but a cloak, to break into the home of Lessingham, in order to confront the politician. Atherton speaks frequently of his inventions, his frustrated desire for Marjorie, and his childish animosity towards Lessingham, while Marjorie Lindon refers repeatedly to her love for Lessingham, her irritation at Atherton's obtuseness concerning her wishes, and her father's dislike of Paul, as well as her own interest in suffragist politics. Marjorie's sense of political frustration on behalf of women, albeit expressed only in shallow and passing ways, and her desire for a degree of independence suggest that Marsh develops her narrative in imitation—or possibly parody—of "New Woman" fiction, Marjorie being shaped in the mould of the New Woman (see Appendix B).

---

[1] Given the novel's Egyptian context, I would like to put forward tentatively a somewhat fanciful speculation concerning Marsh's choice for his detective's name. Champnell's name may echo that of Jean François Champollion, the French linguist and decoder of the Rosetta stone. It is as if one name bore in it the partially encrypted trace of the other, as though there were to be deciphered, around the enigma that goes by the name of Egypt, some connection, however tenuous, between decryption and detection.

Marjorie's status and role in both narrative and novel require brief adumbration in relation to *The Beetle*'s thematics of alterity. As a representative of the New Woman in her ideas and ideals, and as a woman given to liberal political beliefs, while secretly engaged to a Liberal politician of radical opinions, Marjorie challenges her father and all that he represents as a Tory politician, at both public and private levels. As Mr. Lindon himself expresses it to Sydney Atherton:

> She represents me, and it's her duty to represent me adequately—adequately, sir! And what's more ... it's her duty to marry.... My daughter, sir, can marry whom she pleases....Yet ... she actually carries on what I—I can't help calling a—a compromising acquaintance with this man Lessingham! ... as you saw yourself, last night, in—in the face of the assembled House of Commons, after that twaddling clap-trap speech of his.... She positively went away with him.

Beginning with the assumption that Marjorie's purpose is to act as an image or projection of her father's values, that she is in short to embody his ideological notions, Mr. Lindon pursues notions of propriety in relation to duty and property, before turning to and continuing with a critique of Lessingham's political position. His reading of a "compromising acquaintance," coming after the issue of proper representation, in which Lindon seeks to enlist the evidence of Atherton's eyes, indicates the extent to which what the daughter does is expressed as a concern not so much for how she might appear, as how she causes the patriarchal embodiment of Englishness to be seen. And so he continues, veering between an emotional, irrational articulation of ideological distaste for Lessingham's politics, and his daughter's flaunting of what he sees as her proper duty. Though perhaps somewhat comically, if not farcically represented, Marsh employs Marjorie and her father to situate the common anxiety felt amongst the more conservative members of late-nineteenth-century society.

With her ability to move between "public" and "private" spheres and political issues and, in doing so, erasing the boundaries between locations and ideologies, Marjorie as a trope for the New Woman disturbs both novel and its society, through what Sally Ledger terms "an ongoing challenge to the monolithic certainties of mid-Victorian Britain" (Ledger 1995, 22), the very generation to which Marjorie's father belongs. Marjorie is thus figured as a transgressive social element.

Resistant to order, control or being ideologically or ontologically determined or pinned down, she exceeds her normative social use-value,
endangering the assumptions underpinning Late Imperial English hege-
mony. Such elusiveness belongs, as Ledger argues, to the very idea of
the New Woman; to reiterate and develop the argument just presented,
it marks Marjorie unambiguously "as a problem, as a challenge to the
apparently self-identical culture of Victorianism which could not find
a consistent language by which she could be categorized and dealt with.
All that was certain was that she was dangerous, a threat to the status
quo" (Ledger 1995, 24).

While Marjorie is never seen or represented directly as dangerous
exactly, nonetheless Atherton and her father perceive her as willful,
recalcitrant, and therefore, implicitly, the kind of destabilizing force I
have just described. That there is no consistent language to categorize
the New Woman at the *fin de siècle* is intimated in the narrative treatment of Marjorie, both as she is seen by others and also as she speaks
of herself and her beliefs. Moreover, that there *are* four narrators rather
than simply one is, I would contend, indicative of the late Victorian
anxious comprehension that there is no consistent or stable language
with which to address any matter or concern, not least the question and
representation of the New Woman. However, to step back from a sketch
of Marjorie as character and to perceive her function as a figural, ideological, and material device in the structure of the text: more than
merely a representative of the New Woman; more than a mere literary
imitation of New Woman fiction in the form of her narrative,
"Marjorie Lindon" is both destabilizing trope and signifier of otherness—within the late-Victorian sense of cultural and national identity
a relative rather than an absolute other, but an other to be sure.
Arguably, the fear for Victorian masculinity is that the New Woman
presents a form of parodic masculinity, thereby transgressing both the
boundaries of her own supposedly "proper" gendered identity and that
of a certain self-defining Victorian masculinity. If we accept this prem-
ise, it is not so far to go to see the dangerous psychic implications in
the Beetle's transformation of Marjorie into an imitation of a man, by
dressing her in men's clothing and cutting her hair. It may be that the
creature's act is not simply a violation of Marjorie's gender-identity,
even though ostensibly it is that undeniably. More than this, it produces
a potential phantasm of Marjorie already feared in late Victorian masculine imaginary; hence, possibly, the extremity of outrage felt and acted
on by Atherton, Lessingham, and Champnell—for they have made

manifest to them the cultural anxiety presented by the New Woman. And Marjorie's function as other-within, as that image of the not-self troubling to and yet necessary for any ontological, epistemological, or national-cultural determination of the self, is all the more marked if we remind ourselves of the constellated figures that generate anxiety at the close of the nineteenth century. For, as Laura Chrisman recalls, "nineteenth-century British feminist literary identity was inextricable from contemporary ideologies of 'race,' empire and colonialism" (Chrisman 1995, 45). Coming after the accounts by Holt and Atherton, Marjorie Lindon's narrative does nothing to provide comforting resolution for the reader. For, in its provocative reminder that the multi-faceted anxieties of the period—all of which have to do with the erosion of self—are more likely to be found in the most familiar places, at home, than they are abroad, it serves to foreground a troublesome domestic otherness more disruptive than any alien alterity. Fortunately for the men of the novel, after the shocking climax Marjorie retains no memory of her transformation. However, there still remains for the reader that change, mimicking the Beetle's own gender-transmogrification; it aligns her with the archaic Egyptian threat, opening more unanswerable questions than it answers.

The purpose of any detective is of course to answer questions, to provide solution and resolution. As has been argued of the Edwardian detective, in a commentary that provides a telling adjunct to those already directed towards the anxieties of the *fin de siècle*, the purpose of the confidential agent in literature is to assuage those self-same fears: "Detective literature deals with disturbance and destabilization as much as crime *per se*.... New factors influenced the perception of crime: nationalism, anarchism, feminism, labour agitation.... Detective literature ... confronted Edwardian issues such as gender redefinition, capitalism, cosmopolitanism, social class, international diplomacy, race deterioration and imperial policy" (Kestner 2000, 7). A number of these issues are already at stake in *The Beetle* and it is Champnell, of all the narrators—in a narrative in which Marsh is clearly indebted to both Arthur Conan Doyle's stories of Sherlock Holmes and other contemporary fictional detectives—who might present the promise of bringing matters to a conclusion. Yet, as I have already argued, this is doubtful, to the extent that Champnell's final remarks admit to the possibility for uncertainty and indeterminacy at least, in a more conventional reading. Holt's narrative is found to be a composite, not his own first-person report but rather compiled instead "from the statements which Holt made to Atherton, and to Miss Lindon, as she then was, when, a mud-stained derelict he lay at the lady's father's house." Given Atherton and Marjorie's somewhat continually distracted narratives, and the fact of Holt's mental condition being possibly unstable, his having been starved, mesmerized, and fed upon by the Beetle in some variant of vampirism, and subsequently found in a state of delirium (as Champnell reports) it is perhaps not too contentious to suggest that his narration is unreliable, albeit in minor ways.

Furthermore, while Champnell begins Book IV with an assertive statement of fact—"On the afternoon of Friday, June 2, 18__ " —the purpose of which is to suggest precision, attention to detail, and reassuring certainty, he concludes what he calls "the Mystery of the Beetle" with the remark "I do not propose to pronounce a confident opinion. Atherton and I have talked it over many and many a time, and at the end we have got no 'forrader.'"

> So far as I am personally concerned, experience has taught me that there are indeed more things in heaven and earth than are dreamed of in our philosophy, and I am quite prepared to believe that the so-called Beetle, which others saw, but I never, was—or is, for it cannot be certainly shown that the Thing is not still existing—a creature born neither of God nor man.

These remarkable statements, the final words of Marsh's novel, oscillate wildly between recourse to fragile faith and subjective experience, the suspensive modality of belief—what if? asks Champnell—and the absence of empirical data. No amount of discussion can resolve these issues. The confidential agent and the scientist, representatives of the ruling class are forced to confront, thereby experiencing the aporetic, that philosophical impossibility or undecidability, which leads in this narrative not to closure but to an abyssal impasse. Such confrontation and experience is unsettling, causing the late-imperial English mind to reflect on the absolute limit of its inquiry and the impossibility of reaching a solution. The other renders the English helpless, impotent. Invoking Hamlet's attestation of the limits of the imaginative faculty, the detective admits to the boundaries not only of the knowable but also of what can be expressed or represented in language. This is hardly reassuring coming from a representative of the modern science of forensics, whose primary purpose is to interpret the evidence in the name of the Law. It is to be noticed also that the creature is only provisionally named, while, chillingly, there is the implication that it can always return again, and again. And there is that final comment, which registers a radical undecidability concerning the creature, and with that, the failures of analysis, whether grounded in empiricism, forensics, or ontology.

All the more disturbing for the reader perhaps is the fact that the failure of detection and determination on which the Englishman relies—on which, I would argue, national identity is initially and ultimately reliant—is not peculiar either to Champnell's or to Atherton's own abilities or lack thereof, but is a more general condition of the English experience of the foreign other. This is readable in the fragmentary and reiterated use of negation throughout the final chapter: years, we are told, have passed, or else Champnell "should not have felt justified" in recounting the mystery of the Beetle. The detective "declines" to specify the number of years. Marjorie Lindon's recovery was "not merely an affair of weeks or months." Paul Lessingham is not Paul Lessingham; or rather this is the fictional name given to protect the real, though obviously shadowy public figure behind it. Nothing has ever been said to Marjorie about the catastrophic events she underwent at the hands—or should that be pincers—of the Beetle; while "she herself has never alluded to it," her silence is something she has in common with the politician known as Paul Lessingham, now her husband. Champnell also points out that Marjorie may have no memory of what happened and so, "what actually transpired will never, in all human probability, be certainly known." Neither will the fate of the Beetle ever be found out: "to this hour these things are puzzles." Paul Lessingham, the reader is informed, cannot bring himself to speak of beetles. Finally, beyond the immediate details of this narrative, Champnell is compelled to narrate a tale concerning the destruction of a remote location, "some curious subterranean building ... the den of demons described by Paul Lessingham," in the Egyptian desert. Following an explosion, witnesses discover the remains of bodies, which, while neither men nor women, appear, it is alleged—though without "scientific examination" (and thereby open to disbelief and speculation)—to be "of creatures of some monstrous growth." Champnell's final narrative is in ruins, nothing more than so many negative fragments, the negating force of which is cumulative in its effect on the reader as narrative description slides irreversibly into a performative speech act, so that the absence of knowledge spreads like a virus everywhere throughout the narrative, becoming an inextricable part of it. Even the cause of the death of Robert Holt could "never certainly [be] shown." It is not, then, that there is simply uncertainty or indeterminacy. The reader is left, at the conclusion of *The Beetle*, with the signs of undecidability everywhere. Unlike Stoker's *Dracula*, where the Count is firmly dispatched with a stake through the heart—it's almost as if, like a prize butterfly, he were being pinned down, disposed of and defined for all time—Marsh's avenging creature leaves no signs that it has been conclusively, finally destroyed. Not all the forces of modernity, deployed in concerted and co-ordinated fashion, can rid the Empire of this "creature born neither of God nor man," to call up the most haunting line of the text, its very last, in which negation opens, once more, onto an abyssal undecidability, all ontology rejected in the face of this radical other.

Conclusion

Champnell's final words expose the futility of asking the instituting ontological question, "what is...?" so that we are forced to conclude that the book does not so much conclude as it confronts us with just this uncanny experience of the aporetic. The text confronts us with irresolvable contradictions. Nothing can be said for sure, except that one can only admit the impossibility of saying anything other than to bear witness to an undecidable narrative event which nevertheless calls for some response. In this, Richard Marsh's novel is ultimately, like the Beetle, monstrous, a figure of catachresis,[1] having no proper identity as such, being resistant to any single determination. It remains only to suggest that, as a future for reading *The Beetle*, a cultural criticism, such as that which this introduction has pursued, is, in the face of monstrosity, inadequate. Acknowledging this, readings to come of *The Beetle* should seek to pursue what the text does not say, reading for the "ways in which significance can be conjectured despite its apparent absence" (Rand 1976, lii).

In order to attempt this, it might be necessary to understand the Beetle not as a supernatural creature, which we are expected to accept as more or less real within the logic of the novel, but instead to approach it as an effect of perhaps hieroglyphic writing, as a trace irreducible to any particular meaning and yet one which causes a proliferation of interpretation. In order to accept this, one would have to recognize—

---

[1]   Catachresis is the grammatically improper use of a term. In more recent literary theory, the figure operates as a metaphor or trope with no literal referent.

and, I would argue, we are goaded into such a recognition by the unde-cidability of the Beetle —that it is important that one suspends, at least to a degree, one's conventional reading habit—"the naïve opening that once linked the text to *its* thing, referent or reality" (Derrida 1981, 43)— of perceiving an implied empirical object or metaphysical concept beyond the words on the page. Another way to put this is to suggest that we treat the Beetle less as a character in the sense of an anthropo-morphized embodiment of attitudes, rhetorical figures, and descriptive language, beliefs, and other systems of thought, gathered together and animated by work of the proper name, than as a character, in the senses of a mark, inscription or engraving, a graphic symbol, a form or system of writing, or a cipher the purpose of which is to encrypt and there-fore make secret communication. While it is impossible to abandon altogether the phantasmic "reality" that we, as readers, conjure when-ever we read, it is, nonetheless necessary that we attempt to put the breaks on this process as far as possible with regard to the singular instance of the Beetle, if only because there is such an hysterical rush in the novel, in which the unwary reader can be swept away, in the cultural and ideological condemnation of the other given monstrous form. (Recalling Nazi definitions of Jews as "vermin" should act as more than enough of a *caveat* against the too hasty reading.) I am not suggesting that we humanize the Beetle—the novel already engages in just enough anthropomorphization in order to make the creature appear even more monstrous—in some simplistic dialectical opposition to the hegemonic colonial discourse already exposed. Rather, follow-ing J. Hillis Miller (Miller 2002, 123), we should assume a reading habit at once cautious and suspicious of anything that would impose itself on us as logical, inevitable, or—scariest of all—common sense. Treating the Beetle as if it were only a "real" monster would be to succumb to such common sense. If therefore we cannot help reading the Beetle *as* an organism, it has to be comprehended as an organism that, as I have already argued, resolutely resists any final commentary aimed at a firm identification. In coming to terms with this paradox, while holding out the possibility that one can do justice to the Egyptian other in its own terms, it might be necessary, in conclusion, "to consider that organism as a *hieroglyphic text*" (Derrida 1986, xxviii).

Richard Marsh: A Brief Chronology

[Very little is known of Richard Marsh's life, so the biographical details presented here are necessarily sketchy at best. Many of his publications were short stories in magazines and periodicals, subsequently collected and published in single volumes, details of which are given here. There are also novels published after Marsh's death and it appears that so prolific was he, that he left behind him enough manuscripts for John Long, his principal publisher at the time of Marsh's death, to continue to bring out "new" works by the author until 1920. While the majority of Marsh's publications were under the name of Marsh, a few early collections and novels were published under the name Bernard Heldmann (and were subsequently reprinted, often frequently, throughout the rest of Marsh's life in the name under which they had been originally published), and are indicated here by "(BH)" following the title.]

1857   Richard Bernard Heldman born, St. John's Wood, London; two siblings, Harry and Alice.
1880-83 Heldman publishes short stories about life in public schools in the boys' periodical, *The Union Jack*, edited by W. H. G. Kingston and novelist G.A. Henty.
1881   *Boxall School: A Tale of Schoolboy Life* (BH) published.
1881   *Dorrincourt* (BH) published.
1882   (October) Made associate editor of *The Union Jack* with Henty.
1882   *Expelled: Being the Story of a Young Gentleman* (BH) published.
1882   *The Mutiny on Board the Ship "Leander": A Story of the Sea* (BH) published.
1882   *The Belton Scholarship: A Chapter from the Life of George Denton* (BH) published.
1883   *Daintree* (BH) published.
1883   Public disagreement with Henty. A brief notice is published in *The Union Jack* (5th June), stating that Heldman is no longer associated with the periodical.
1886   Marsh marries Ada Kate, the daughter of a stone carver from Walworth; no other details known. Marsh's wife gives birth to six children between 1887 and 1895, 4 sons and 2 daughters.

1887   Marsh and Ada live in Richmond, West London. Marsh is earning a meagre living as a journalist.

1888   Marsh's mother dies; in her will leaves Richard £25, the rest of the estate being divided equally between Harry and Alice.

1890   Evidence of Marsh's family living in Fulham, West London, with Marsh's financial conditions being in somewhat better state than previously.

1891-95   Marsh and family living in Three Bridges, Sussex.

1892   Changes name to Richard Marsh.

1893   *The Mahatma's Pupil*; *The Devil's Diamond* published.

1895   *Mrs Musgrave and Her Husband* published.

1897   *The Beetle*; *Crime and the Criminal*; *The Duke and the Damsel*; *The Mystery of Philip Bennion's Death* published.

1898   *The House of Mystery, Curios: Some Strange Adventures of Two Bachelors*; *The Datchet Diamonds*; *A First Night*; *A Prophet*; *The Philosopher's Stone*; *Tom Ossington's Ghost* published.

1899   *In Full Cry*; *Frivolities: Especially Addressed to Those Tired of Being Serious*; *The Woman with One Hand*; *Mr Ely's Engagement* published.

1900   *Marvels and Mysteries*; *A Hero of Romance*; *The Goddess: A Demon*; *An Aristocratic Detective*; *The Chase of the Ruby*; *A Second Coming*; *The Seen and the Unseen* published.

1901   *The Joss: A Reversion*; *Amusement Only (Tales)*; *Both Sides of the Veil* published.

1902   *The Adventures of Augustus Short*; *Between the Dark and the Daylight*; *The Twickenham Peerage* published.

1903   *A Metamorphosis*; *The Magnetic Girl*; *The Death Whistle* published.

1904   *Miss Arnott's Marriage*; *A Duel*; *Garnered (Tales)* published.

1905   *A Spoiler of Men*; *The Marquis of Putney*; *The Confessions of a Young Lady: Her Doings and Misdoings* published.

1906   *In the Service of Love*; *The Garden of Mystery* published.

1907   *The Girl and the Miracle*; *The Romance of a Maid of Honour*; *A Woman Perfected*; *Who Killed Lady Poynder?* published.

1908   *The Coward behind the Curtain*; *The Surprising Husband*; *Under One Flag* published.

1909   *The Girl in the Blue Dress*; *A Royal Indiscretion* published.

1910   *The Lovely Mrs Blake* published.

1911   *Live Men's Shoes; The Interrupted Kiss; Ada Vernham; Actress; A Drama of the Telephone and Other Tales* published.

1912   *Judith Lee: Some Pages from her Life; Violet Forster's Lover* published.

1913   *A Master of Deception; Justice Suspended; If It Please You* published.

1914   *Molly's Husband; Margot and Her Judges; Twin Sisters; The Woman in the Car* published.

1915   Marsh dies, either of heart failure or heart disease. *A Man with Nine Lives, Love in Fetters, The Flying Girl, His Love or His Life: A Romance; Sam Briggs: His Book* published.

1916   *The Great Temptation; The Adventures of Judith Lee; Coming of Age* published.

1917   *The Deacon's Daughter* published.

1918   *On the Jury; Orders to Marry (Tales)* published.

1919   *Outwitted* published.

1920   *Apron-Strings* published.

A Note on the Text

Richard Marsh made no apparent changes to *The Beetle* after its initial publication by Skeffington and Sons in 1897. A very few typographical errors are corrected between the first British and first American editions, on the latter (third impression, 1917) of which the present edition is based.

BOOK I

THE HOUSE WITH THE OPEN WINDOW

THE SURPRISING NARRATION
OF ROBERT HOLT

CHAPTER 1

OUTSIDE

"NO room!—Full up!"

He banged the door in my face.

That was the final blow.

To have tramped about all day looking for work; to have begged even for a job which would give me money enough to buy a little food; and to have tramped and to have begged in vain,—that was bad. But sick at heart depressed in mind and in body, exhausted by hunger and fatigue, to have been compelled to pocket any little pride I might have left, and solicit, as the penniless, homeless tramp which indeed I was, a night's lodging in the casual ward,[1]—and to solicit it in vain!—that was worse. Much worse. About as bad as bad could be.

I stared, stupidly, at the door which had just been banged in my face. I could scarcely believe that the thing was possible. I had hardly expected to figure as a tramp; but, supposing it conceivable that I could become a tramp that I should be refused admission to that abode of all ignominy, the tramps' ward, was to have attained a depth of misery of which never even in nightmares I had dreamed.

As I stood wondering what I should do, a man slouched towards me out of the shadow of the wall.

"Won't 'e let yer in?"

"He says it's full."

---

[1] Casual Wards or District Asylums were first built in England for vagrants, the homeless, and the poor following the Poor Law Act of 1844. The Act attempted to ensure temporary provision for the poor by forcing parishes to combine to provide shelter and food where traditional workhouses did not. Parish relief, which made local parishes responsible for support of the poor, orphans, and the elderly, was instituted by the 1601 Poor Law Act, which allowed for the indigent to live at home. While Parishes built workhouses from the seventeenth to the nineteenth centuries, it was as a result of the Poor Law Amendment Act (1834) that those receiving parish relief were forced to live in the workhouse. Marsh seems to have in mind the Nightly Asylums of London, which admitted vagrants such as Holt on a nightly basis.

"Says it's full, does 'e? That's the lay[1] at Fulham,[2]—they always says it's full. They wants to keep the number down."

I looked at the man askance. His head hung forward; his hands were in his trouser pockets; his clothes were rags; his tone was husky.

"Do you mean that they say it's full when it isn't,—that they won't let me in although there's room?"

"That's it,—bloke's a-kiddin' yer."

"But, if there's room, aren't they bound to let me in?"

"Course they are,—and, blimey,[3] if I was you I'd make 'em. Blimey I would!"

He broke into a volley of execrations.

"But what am I to do?"

"Why, give 'em another rouser—let 'em know as you won't be kidded!"

I hesitated; then, acting on his suggestion, for the second time I rang the bell. The door was flung wide open, and the grizzled pauper, who had previously responded to my summons, stood in the open doorway. Had he been the Chairman of the Board of Guardians[4] himself he could not have addressed me with greater scorn.

"What, here again! What's your little game? Think I've nothing better to do than to wait upon the likes of you?"

"I want to be admitted."

"Then you won't be admitted!"

"I want to see someone in authority."

"Ain't yer seein' someone in authority?"

"I want to see someone beside you,—I want to see the master."

"Then you won't see the master!"

He moved the door swiftly to; but, prepared for such a manœuvre, I thrust my foot sufficiently inside to prevent his shutting it. I continued to address him.

"Are you sure that the ward is full?"

"Full two hours ago!"

"But what am I to do?"

"I don't know what you're to do!"

---

[1] Slang, meaning either the 'score' or the way things are done, or a line of business or procedure.

[2] Borough in South-West London. Throughout *The Beetle*, Marsh refers to a number of districts and boroughs, as well as streets, in London.

[3] Mild curse, a contraction of "God blind me."

[4] The Board of Guardians consisted of those prominent members of a parish responsible for the governance of the workhouse.

"Which is the next nearest workhouse?"

"Kensington."[1]

Suddenly opening the door, as he answered me, putting out his arm he thrust me backwards. Before I could recover the door was closed. The man in rags had continued a grim spectator of the scene. Now he spoke.

"Nice bloke, ain't he?"

"He's only one of the paupers,—has he any right to act as one of the officials?"

"I tell yer some of them paupers is wuss than the orficers,—a long sight wuss! They thinks they owns the 'ouses, blimey they do. Oh it's a—fine world, this is!"

He paused. I hesitated. For some time there had been a suspicion of rain in the air. Now it was commencing to fall in a fine but soaking drizzle. It only needed that to fill my cup to overflowing. My companion was regarding me with a sort of sullen curiosity.

"Ain't you got no money?"

"Not a farthing." [2]

"Done much of this sort of thing?"

"It's the first time I've been to a casual ward,—and it doesn't seem as if I'm going to get in now."

"I thought you looked as if you was a bit fresh.—What are yer goin' to do?"

"How far is it to Kensington?"

"Work'us?[3]—about three mile;—but, if I was you, I'd try St. George's."[4]

"Where's that?"

"In the Fulham Road. Kensington's only a small place, they do you well there, and it's always full as soon as the door's opened;—you'd 'ave more chawnce at St. George's."

---

[1]   London borough, made a "Royal" borough in 1901 on the death of Queen Victoria, who was born in Kensington Palace (1819) and lived there until her accession to the throne (1837).

[2]   One of the coins in the British duodecimal monetary system, worth 1/4 penny. The duodecimal system was not abandoned until the end of the 1960s in Britain. The pound, the principal unit of currency, was made up of twelve shillings. There were twelve pennies to each shilling, and, therefore, 144 pence to the pound.

[3]   Phonetic spelling of London dialect pronunciation of workhouse. Marsh imitates London working-class dialect throughout the novel for the speech of minor characters.

[4]   St. George's Workhouse, built on the south side of the Fulham Road, was opened in 1858, on the site of an asylum for children and the insane, built in 1786-88. A new infirmary, capable of housing 830 patients, was built in 1878.

He was silent. I turned his words over in my mind, feeling as little disposed to try the one place as the other. Presently he began again.

"I've travelled from Reading[1] this—day, I 'ave,—tramped every—foot!—and all the way as I come along, I'll 'ave a shakedown[2] at 'Ammersmith,[3] I says,—and now I'm as fur off from it as ever! This is a—fine country, this is,—I wish every—soul in it was swept into the—sea, blimey, I do! But I ain't goin' to go no further,—I'll 'ave a bed in 'Ammersmith or I'll know the reason why."

"How are you going to manage it,—have you got any money?"

"Got any money?—My crikey![4]—I look as though I 'ad,—I sound as though I 'ad too! I ain't 'ad no brads,[5] 'cept now and then a brown,[6] this larst six months."

"How are you going to get a bed then?"

"'Ow am I going to?—why, like this way." He picked up two stones, one in either hand. The one in his left he flung at the glass which was over the door of the casual ward. It crashed through it, and through the lamp beyond. "That's 'ow I'm goin' to get a bed."

The door was hastily opened. The grizzled pauper reappeared. He shouted as he peered at us in the darkness.

"Who done that?"

"I done it, guvnor,—and, if you like, you can see me do the other. It might do your eyesight good."

Before the grizzled pauper could interfere, he had hurled the stone in his right hand through another pane. I felt that it was time for me to go. He was earning a night's rest at a price which, even in my extremity, I was not disposed to pay.

When I left two or three other persons had appeared upon the scene, and the man in rags was addressing them with a degree of frankness which, in that direction, left little to be desired. I slunk away unnoticed. But had not gone far before I had almost decided that I might as well have thrown in my fortune with the bolder wretch, and smashed a

---

[1] Town in the county of Berkshire, west of London, and approximately midway between London and Oxford.

[2] Originally, a bed made by throwing straw on the ground, but here any makeshift bed.

[3] Hammersmith, south west London borough.

[4] An exclamation of surprise or astonishment. The *Oxford English Dictionary* suggests that, being alliterative with "Christ," its use may have originated as an alternative expression to avoid profanity.

[5] Slang for coins or money in general.

[6] Any of the smaller denominations of money, such as pennies, halfpennies, or farthings, referred to as browns or coppers because of their colour.

window too. Indeed, more than once my feet faltered, as I all but returned to do the feat which I had left undone.

A more miserable night for an out-of-door excursion I could hardly have chosen. The rain was like a mist, and was not only drenching me to the skin, but it was rendering it difficult to see more than a little distance in any direction. The neighbourhood was badly lighted. It was one in which I was a stranger. I had come to Hammersmith as a last resource. It had seemed to me that I had tried to find some occupation which would enable me to keep body and soul together in every other part of London, and that now only Hammersmith was left. And, at Hammersmith, even the workhouse would have none of me!

Retreating from the inhospitable portal of the casual ward, I had taken the first turning to the left,—and, at the moment, had been glad to take it. In the darkness and the rain, the locality which I was entering appeared unfinished. I seemed to be leaving civilization behind me. The path was unpaved; the road rough and uneven, as if it had never been properly made. Houses were few and far between. Those which I did encounter, seemed, in the imperfect light, amid the general desolation, to be cottages which were crumbling to decay.

Exactly where I was I could not tell. I had a faint notion that, if I only kept on long enough, I should strike some part of Walham Green.[1] How long I should have to keep on I could only guess. Not a creature seemed to be about of whom I could make inquiries. It was as if I was in a land of desolation. *—ve call to adventure*

I suppose it was between eleven o'clock and midnight. I had not given up my quest for work till all the shops were closed,—and in Hammersmith, that night, at any rate, they were not early closers. Then I had lounged about dispiritedly, wondering what was the next thing I could do. It was only because I feared that if I attempted to spend the night in the open air, without food, when the morning came I should be broken up, and fit for nothing, that I sought a night's free board and lodging. It was really hunger which drove me to the workhouse door. That was Wednesday. Since the Sunday night preceding nothing had passed my lips save water from the public fountains,—with the exception of a crust of bread which a man had given me whom I had found crouching at the root of a tree in Holland Park.[2] For three days I had been fasting,—practically all the time upon my feet. It seemed to me

---

[1] District in the London borough of Hammersmith and Fulham.
[2] District in the London borough of Kensington and Chelsea.

that if I had to go hungry till the morning I should collapse—there would be an end. Yet, in that strange and inhospitable place, where was I to get food at that time of night, and how?

I do not know how far I went. Every yard I covered, my feet dragged more. I was dead beat, inside and out. I had neither strength nor courage left. And within there was that frightful craving, which was as though it shrieked aloud. I leant against some palings, dazed and giddy. If only death had come upon me quickly, painlessly, how true a friend I should have thought it! It was the agony of dying inch by inch which was so hard to bear.

It was some minutes before I could collect myself sufficiently to withdraw from the support of the railings, and to start afresh. I stumbled blindly over the uneven road. Once, like a drunken man, I lurched forward, and fell upon my knees. Such was my backboneless state that for some seconds I remained where I was, half disposed to let things slide, accept the good the gods had sent me, and make a night of it just there. A long night, I fancy, it would have been, stretching from time unto eternity.

Having regained my feet, I had gone perhaps another couple of hundred yards along the road—Heaven knows that it seemed to me just then a couple of miles!—when there came over me again that overpowering giddiness which, I take it, was born of my agony of hunger. I staggered, helplessly, against a low wall which, just there, was at the side of the path. Without it, I should have fallen in a heap. The attack appeared to last for hours, I suppose it was only seconds; and, when I came to myself, it was as though I had been aroused from a swoon of sleep,—aroused, to an extremity of pain. I exclaimed aloud,

"For a loaf of bread what wouldn't I do!"

I looked about me, in a kind of frenzy. As I did so I for the first time became conscious that behind me was a house. It was not a large one. It was one of those so-called villas which are springing up in multitudes all round London and which are let at rentals of from twenty-five to forty pounds a year. It was detached. So far as I could see, in the imperfect light, there was not another building within twenty or thirty yards of either side of it. It was in two storeys. There were three windows in the upper storey. Behind each the blinds were closely drawn. The hall door was on my right. It was approached by a little wooden gate.

The house itself was so close to the public road that by leaning over the wall I could have touched either of the windows on the lower floor. There were two of them. One of them was a bow window. The bow window was open. The bottom centre sash was raised about six inches.

call to adventure

CHAPTER 2

INSIDE

I realised, and, so to speak, mentally photographed all the little details of the house in front of which I was standing with what almost amounted to a gleam of preternatural perception. An instant before, the world swam before my eyes. I saw nothing. Now I saw everything, with a clearness which, as it were, was shocking.

Above all, I saw the open window. I stared at it, conscious, as I did so, of a curious catching of the breath. It was so near to me; so very near. I had but to stretch out my hand to thrust it through the aperture. Once inside, my hand would at least be dry. How it rained out there! My scanty clothing was soaked; I was wet to the skin! I was shivering. And, each second, it seemed to rain still faster. My teeth were chattering. The damp was liquefying the very marrow in my bones.

And, inside that open window, it was, it must be, so warm, so dry!

There was not a soul in sight. Not a human being anywhere near. I listened; there was not a sound. I alone was at the mercy of the sodden night. Of all God's creatures the only one unsheltered from the fountains of Heaven which He had opened. There was not one to see what I might do; not one to care. I need fear no spy.

Perhaps the house was empty; nay, probably. It was my plain duty to knock at the door, rouse the inmates, and call attention to their oversight,—the open window. The least they could do would be to reward me for my pains. But suppose the place was empty, what would be the use of knocking? It would be to make a useless clatter. Possibly to disturb the neighbourhood, for nothing. And, even if the people were at home, I might go unrewarded. I had learned, in a hard school, the world's ingratitude. To have caused the window to be closed—the inviting window, the tempting window, the convenient window!—and then to be no better for it after all, but still to be penniless, hopeless, hungry, out in the cold and the rain—better anything than that. In such a situation, too late, I should say to myself that mine had been the conduct of a fool. And I should say it justly too. To be sure.

Leaning over the low wall I found that I could very easily put my hand inside the room. How warm it was in there! I could feel the difference of temperature in my finger-tips. Very quietly I stepped right over the wall. There was just room to stand in comfort between the window and the wall. The ground felt to the foot as if it were cemented. Stooping down, I peered through the opening. I could see nothing. It was black as pitch inside. The blind was drawn right up; it seemed incredible that anyone could be at home and have gone to bed, leaving the blind up, and the window open. I placed my ear to the crevice. How still it was! Beyond doubt, the place was empty.

I decided to push the window up another inch or two, so as to enable me to reconnoitre. If anyone caught me in the act, then there would be an opportunity to describe the circumstances, and to explain how I was just on the point of giving the alarm. Only, I must go carefully. In such damp weather it was probable that the sash would creak.

Not a bit of it. It moved as readily and as noiselessly as if it had been oiled. This silence of the sash so emboldened me that I raised it more than I intended. In fact, as far as it would go. Not by a sound did it betray me. Bending over the sill I put my head and half my body into the room. But I was no forwarder. I could see nothing. Not a thing. For all I could tell the room might be unfurnished. Indeed, the likelihood of such an explanation began to occur to me. I might have chanced upon an empty house. In the darkness there was nothing to suggest the contrary. What was I to do?

Well, if the house was empty, in such a plight as mine I might be said to have a moral, if not a legal, right, to its bare shelter. Who, with a heart in his bosom, would deny it me? Hardly the most punctilious landlord. Raising myself by means of the sill I slipped my legs into the room.

The moment I did so I became conscious that, at any rate, the room was not entirely unfurnished. The floor was carpeted. I have had my feet on some good carpets in my time; I know what carpets are; but never did I stand upon a softer one than that. It reminded me, somehow, even then, of the turf in Richmond Park,[1]—it caressed my instep, and sprang beneath my tread. To my poor, travel-worn feet, it was luxury after the puddly, uneven road. Should I, now I had ascertained that the room was, at least, partially furnished, beat a retreat? Or should I push my researches further? It would have been rapture to have thrown off my clothes, and to have sunk down, on the carpet, then and there, to sleep. But,—I was so hungry; so famine-goaded, what would I not have given to have lighted on something good to eat!

---

[1] Now one of London's royal parks, the 2,500 acres to the south-west of London was originally enclosed by Charles I in 1637 for the purpose of deer hunting. The public were not admitted until 1758.

I moved a step or two forward, gingerly, reaching out with my hands, lest I struck, unawares, against some unseen thing. When I had taken three or four such steps, without encountering an obstacle, or, indeed anything at all, I began, all at once, to wish I had not seen the house; that I had passed it by; that I had not come through the window; that I were safely out of it again. I became, on a sudden, aware, that something was with me in the room. There was nothing, ostensible, to lead me to such a conviction; it may be that my faculties were unnaturally keen; but, all at once, I knew that there was something there. What was more, I had a horrible persuasion that, though unseeing, I was seen; that my every movement was being watched.

What it was that was with me I could not tell; I could not even guess. It was as though something in my mental organization had been stricken by a sudden paralysis. It may seem childish to use such language; but I was overwrought, played out; physically speaking, at my last counter; and, in an instant without the slightest warning, I was conscious of a very curious sensation the like of which I had never felt before, and the like of which I pray that I never may feel again—a sensation of panic fear. I remained rooted to the spot on which I stood, not daring to move, fearing to draw my breath. I felt that the presence with me in the room was something strange, something evil.

I do not know how long I stood there, spellbound, but certainly for some considerable space of time. By degrees, as nothing moved, nothing was seen, nothing was heard and nothing happened, I made an effort to better play the man. I knew that, at the moment, I played the cur. And endeavoured to ask myself of what it was I was afraid. I was shivering at my own imaginings. What could be in the room, to have suffered me to open the window and to enter unopposed? Whatever it was, was surely to the full as great a coward as I was or why permit, unchecked, my burglarious entry. Since I had been allowed to enter the probability was that I should be at liberty to retreat,—and I was sensible of a much keener desire to retreat than I had ever had to enter.

I had to put the greatest amount of pressure upon myself before I could summon up sufficient courage to enable me to even turn my head upon my shoulders,—and the moment I did so I turned it back again. What constrained me, to save my soul I could not have said,—but I was constrained. My heart was palpitating in my bosom; I could hear it beat. I was trembling so that I could scarcely stand. I was overwhelmed by a fresh flood of terror. I stared in front of me with eyes in which, had it been light, would have been seen the frenzy of unreasoning fear. My ears were strained so that I listened with an acuteness of tension which was painful.

Something moved. Slightly, with so slight a sound, that it would scarcely have been audible to other ears save mine. But I heard. I was looking in the direction from which the movement came, and, as I looked, I saw in front of me two specks of light. They had not been there a moment before, that I would swear. They were there now. They were eyes,—I told myself they were eyes. I had heard how cats' eyes gleam in the dark, though I had never seen them, and I said to myself that these were cats' eyes; that the thing in front of me was nothing but a cat. But I knew I lied. I knew that these were eyes, and I knew they were not cats' eyes, but what eyes they were I did not know,—nor dared to think.

They moved,—towards me. The creature to which the eyes belonged was coming closer. So intense was my desire to fly that I would much rather have died than stood there still; yet I could not control a limb; my limbs were as if they were not mine. The eyes came on,—noiselessly. At first they were between two and three feet from the ground; but, on a sudden, there was a squelching sound, as if some yielding body had been squashed upon the floor. The eyes vanished,—to reappear, a moment afterwards, at what I judged to be a distance of some six inches from the floor. And they again came on.

So it seemed that the creature, whatever it was to which the eyes belonged was, after all, but small. Why I did not obey the frantic longing which I had to flee from it, I cannot tell; I only know, I could not. I take it that the stress and privations which I had lately undergone, and which I was, even then, still undergoing, had much to do with my conduct at that moment, and with the part I played in all that followed. Ordinarily I believe that I have as high a spirit as the average man, and as solid a resolution; but when one has been dragged through the Valley of Humiliation, and plunged, again and again into the Waters of Bitterness and Privation,[1] a man can be constrained to a course of action of which, in his happier moments, he would have deemed himself incapable. I know this of my own knowledge.

Slowly the eyes came on, with a strange slowness, and as they came they moved from side to side as if their owner walked unevenly. Nothing could have exceeded the horror with which I awaited their approach,—except my incapacity to escape them. Not for an instant

---

[1]   Marsh is alluding to John Bunyan's *The Pilgrim's Progress* (pt. 1 1678, pt. 2 1684).

did my glance pass from them,—I could not have shut my eyes for all the gold the world contains!—so that as they came closer I had to look right down to what seemed to be almost the level of my feet. And at last, they reached my feet. They never paused. On a sudden I felt something on my boot, and, with a sense of shrinking, horror, nausea, rendering me momentarily more helpless, I realized that the creature was beginning to ascend my legs, to climb my body. Even then what it was I could not tell,—it mounted me, apparently, with as much ease as if I had been horizontal instead of perpendicular. It was as though it were some gigantic spider,—a spider of the nightmares; a monstrous conception of some dreadful vision. It pressed lightly against my clothing with what might, for all the world, have been spider's legs. There was an amazing host of them,—I felt the pressure of each separate one. They embraced me softly, stickily, as if the creature glued and unglued them, each time it moved.

Higher and higher! It had gained my loins. It was moving towards the pit of my stomach. The helplessness with which I suffered its invasion was not the least part of my agony,—it was that helplessness which we know in dreadful dreams. I understood, quite well, that if I did but give myself a hearty shake, the creature would fall off; but I had not a muscle at my command.

As the creature mounted its eyes began to play the part of two small lamps; they positively emitted rays of light. By their rays I began to perceive faint outlines of its body. It seemed larger than I had supposed. Either the body itself was slightly phosphorescent, or it was of a peculiar yellow hue. It gleamed in the darkness. What it was there was still nothing to positively show, but the impression grew upon me that it was some member of the spider family, some monstrous member, of the like of which I had never heard or read. It was heavy, so heavy indeed, that I wondered how, with so slight a pressure, it managed to retain its hold,—that it did so by the aid of some adhesive substance at the end of its legs I was sure,—I could feel it stick. Its weight increased as it ascended,—and it smelt! I had been for some time aware that it emitted an unpleasant, fœtid odour; as it neared my face it became so intense as to be unbearable.

It was at my chest. I became more and more conscious of an uncomfortable wobbling motion, as if each time it breathed its body heaved. Its forelegs touched the bare skin about the base of my neck; they stuck to it,—shall I ever forget the feeling? I have it often in my dreams. While it hung on with those in front it seemed to draw its other legs up after it. It crawled up my neck, with hideous slowness, a quarter of an inch at a time, its weight compelling me to brace the muscles of my back. It reached my chin, it touched my lips,—and I stood still and bore it all, while it enveloped my face with its huge, slimy, evil-smelling body, and embraced me with its myriad legs. The horror of it made me mad. I shook myself like one stricken by the shaking ague.[1] I shook the creature off. It squashed upon the floor. Shrieking like some lost spirit, turning, I dashed towards the window. As I went, my foot, catching in some obstacle, I fell headlong to the floor.

Picking myself up as quickly as I could I resumed my flight,—rain or no rain, oh to get out of that room! I already had my hand upon the sill, in another instant I should have been over it,—then, despite my hunger, my fatigues, let anyone have stopped me if they could!—when someone behind me struck a light.

CHAPTER 3

THE MAN IN THE BED

The illumination which instantly followed was unexpected. It startled me causing a moment's check, from which I was just recovering when a voice said,

"Keep still!"

There was a quality in the voice which I cannot describe. Not only an accent of command, but a something malicious, a something saturnine.[2] It was a little guttural, though whether it was a man speaking I could not have positively said; but I had no doubt it was a foreigner. It was the most disagreeable voice I had ever heard, and it had on me the most disagreeable effect; for when it said, "Keep still!" I kept still. It was as though there was nothing else for me to do.

"Turn round!"

I turned round, mechanically, like an automaton. Such passivity was worse than undignified, it was galling, I knew that well. I resented it with secret rage. But in that room, in that presence I was invertebrate.

---

[1] A fever marked by alternate chills and sweating.
[2] Morose, taciturn, or gloomy.

When I turned I found myself confronting someone who was lying in bed. At the head of the bed was a shelf. On the shelf was a small lamp which gave the most brilliant light I had ever seen. It caught me full in the eyes, having on me such a blinding effect that for some seconds I could see nothing. Throughout the whole of that strange interview I cannot affirm that I saw clearly; the dazzling glare caused dancing specks to obscure my vision. Yet after an interval of time, I did see something; and what I did see I had rather have left unseen.

I saw someone in front of me lying in a bed. I could not at once decide if it was a man or a woman. Indeed at first I doubted if it was anything human. But, afterwards, I knew it to be a man,—for this reason, if for no other, that it was impossible such a creature could be feminine. The bedclothes were drawn up to his shoulders; only his head was visible. He lay on his left side, his head resting on his left hand; motionless, eyeing me as if he sought to read my inmost soul. And, in very truth, I believe he read it. His age I could not guess; such a look of age I had never imagined. Had he asserted that he had been living through the ages, I should have been forced to admit that, at least, he looked it. And yet I felt that it was quite within the range of possibility that he was no older than myself,—there was a vitality in his eyes which was startling. It might have been that he had been afflicted by some terrible disease, and it was that which had made him so supernaturally ugly.

There was not a hair upon his face or head, but, to make up for it, the skin, which was a saffron yellow, was an amazing mass of wrinkles. The cranium, and, indeed, the whole skull, was so small as to be disagreeably suggestive of something animal. The nose, on the other hand, was abnormally large; so extravagant were its dimensions, and so peculiar its shape, it resembled the beak of some bird of prey. A characteristic of the face—and an uncomfortable one!—was that, practically, it stopped short at the mouth. The mouth, with its blubber lips, came immediately underneath the nose, and chin, to all intents and purposes, there was none. This deformity—for the absence of chin amounted to that—it was which gave to the face the appearance of something not human,— that, and the eyes. For so marked a feature of the man were his eyes, that, ere long, it seemed to me that he was nothing but eyes.

His eyes ran, literally, across the whole of the upper portion of his face,—remember, the face was unwontedly small, and the columna of the nose was razor-edged. They were long, and they looked out of narrow windows, and they seemed to be lighted by some internal radiance, for they shone out like lamps in a lighthouse tower. Escape them

I could not, while, as I endeavoured to meet them, it was as if I shrivelled into nothingness. Never before had I realized what was meant by the power of the eye. They held me enchained, helpless, spell-bound. I felt that they could do with me as they would; and they did. Their gaze was unfaltering, having the bird-like trick of never blinking; this man could have glared at me for hours and never moved an eyelid.

It was he who broke the silence. I was speechless.

"Shut the window." I did as he bade me. "Pull down the blind." I obeyed. "Turn round again." I was still obedient. "What is your name?"

Then I spoke,—to answer him. There was this odd thing about the words I uttered, that they came from me, not in response to my will power, but in response to his. It was not I who willed that I should speak; it was he. What he willed that I should say, I said. Just that, and nothing more. For the time I was no longer a man; my manhood was merged in his. I was, in the extremest sense, an example of passive obedience.

"Robert Holt."

"What are you?"

"A clerk."

"You look as if you were a clerk." There was a flame of scorn in his voice which scorched me even then. "What sort of a clerk are you?"

"I am out of a situation."

"You look as if you were out of a situation." Again the scorn. "Are you the sort of clerk who is always out of a situation? You are a thief."

"I am not a thief."

"Do clerks come through the window?" I was still,—he putting no constraint on me to speak. "Why did you come through the window?"

"Because it was open."

"So!—Do you always come through a window which is open?"

"No."

"Then why through this?"

"Because I was wet—and cold—and hungry—and tired."

The words came from me as if he had dragged them one by one,—which, in fact, he did.

"Have you no home?"

"No."

"Money?"

"No."

"Friends?"

"No."

"Then what sort of a clerk are you?"

I did not answer him,—I did not know what it was he wished me to say. I was the victim of bad luck, nothing else,—I swear it. Misfortune had followed hard upon misfortune. The firm by whom I had been employed for years suspended payment. I obtained a situation with one of their creditors at a lower salary. They reduced their staff, which entailed my going. After an interval I obtained a temporary engagement; the occasion which required my services passed, and I with it. After another, and a longer interval, I again found temporary employment, the pay for which was but a pittance. When that was over I could find nothing. That was nine months ago, and since then I had not earned a penny. It is so easy to grow shabby, when you are on the everlasting tramp, and are living on your stock of clothes. I had trudged all over London in search of work,—work of any kind would have been welcome so long as it would have enabled me to keep body and soul together. And I had trudged in vain. Now I had been refused admittance as a casual,—how easy is the descent! But I did not tell the man lying on the bed all this. He did not wish to hear,—had he wished he would have made me tell him.

It may be that he read my story, unspoken though it was,—it is conceivable. His eyes had powers of penetration which were peculiarly their own,—that I know.

"Undress!"

When he spoke again that was what he said, in those guttural tones of his in which there was a reminiscence of some foreign land. I obeyed, letting my sodden, shabby clothes fall anyhow upon the floor. A look came on his face, as I stood naked in front of him, which, if it was meant for a smile, was a satyr's[1] smile, and which filled me with a sensation of shuddering repulsion.

"What a white skin you have,—how white! What would I not give for a skin as white as that,—ah yes!" He paused, devouring me with his glances; then continued. "Go to the cupboard; you will find a cloak; put it on."

I went to a cupboard which was in a corner of the room, his eyes following me as I moved. It was full of clothing,—garments which might have formed the stock-in-trade of a costumier whose speciality was providing costumes for masquerades. A long dark cloak hung on a peg. My hand moved towards it, apparently of its own volition. I put it on, its ample folds falling to my feet.

---

[1] Ancient Greek deity, part man and part horse, a follower of Bacchus, god of wine.

"In the other cupboard you will find meat, and bread, and wine. Eat and drink."

On the opposite side of the room, near the head of his bed, there was a second cupboard. In this, upon a shelf, I found what looked like pressed beef, several round cakes of what tasted like rye bread, and some thin, sour wine, in a straw-covered flask. But I was in no mood to criticize; I crammed myself, I believe, like some famished wolf, he watching me, in silence, all the time. When I had done, which was when I had eaten and drunk as much as I could hold, there returned to his face that satyr's grin.

"I would that I could eat and drink like that,—ah yes!—Put back what is left." I put it back,—which seemed an unnecessary exertion, there was so little to put. "Look me in the face."

I looked him in the face,—and immediately became conscious, as I did so, that something was going from me,—the capacity, as it were, to be myself. His eyes grew larger and larger, till they seemed to fill all space—till I became lost in their immensity. He moved his hand, doing something to me, I know not what, as it passed through the air—cutting the solid ground from underneath my feet, so that I fell headlong to the ground. Where I fell, there I lay, like a log.

And the light went out.

CHAPTER 4

A LONELY VIGIL

I knew that the light went out. For not the least singular, nor, indeed, the least distressing part of my condition was the fact that, to the best of my knowledge and belief, I never once lost consciousness during the long hours which followed. I was aware of the extinction of the lamp, and of the black darkness which ensued. I heard a rustling sound, as if the man in the bed was settling himself between the sheets. Then all was still. And throughout that interminable night I remained, my brain awake, my body dead, waiting, watching, for the day. What had happened to me I could not guess. That I probably wore some of the external evidences of death my instinct told me,—I knew I did. Paradoxical though it may sound, I felt as a man might feel who had actually died,—

as, in moments of speculation, in the days gone by, I had imagined it as quite possible that he would feel. It is very far from certain that feeling necessarily expires with what we call life. I continually asked myself if I could be dead,—the inquiry pressed itself on me with awful iteration. Does the body die, and the brain—the I, the ego—still live on? God only knows. But, then! The agony of the thought.

The hours passed. By slow degrees, the silence was eclipsed. Sounds of traffic, of hurrying footsteps,—life!—were ushers of the morn. Outside the window sparrows twittered,—a cat mewed, a dog barked—there was the clatter of a milk can. Shafts of light stole past the blind, increasing in intensity. It still rained, now and again it pattered against the pane. The wind must have shifted, because, for the first time, there came, on a sudden, the clang of a distant clock striking the hour,—seven. Then, with the interval of a lifetime between each chiming, eight,—nine,—ten.

So far, in the room itself there had not been a sound. When the clock had struck ten, as it seemed to me, years ago, there came a rustling noise, from the direction of the bed. Feet stepped upon the floor,—moving towards where I was lying. It was, of course, now broad day, and I, presently, perceived that a figure, clad in some queer coloured garment, was standing at my side, looking down at me. It stooped, then knelt. My only covering was unceremoniously thrown off me, so that I lay there in my nakedness. Fingers prodded me then and there, as if I had been some beast ready for the butcher's stall. A face looked into mine, and, in front of me, were those dreadful eyes. Then, whether I was dead or living, I said to myself that this could be nothing human,—nothing fashioned in God's image could wear such a shape as that. Fingers were pressed into my cheeks, they were thrust into my mouth, they touched my staring eyes, shut my eyelids, then opened them again, and—horror of horrors!—the blubber lips were pressed to mine—the soul of something evil entered into me in the guise of a kiss.

Then this travesty of manhood reascended to his feet, and said, whether speaking to me or to himself I could not tell.

"Dead!—dead!—as good as dead!—and better! We'll have him buried."

He moved away from me. I heard a door open and shut, and knew that he was gone.

And he continued gone throughout the day. I had no actual knowledge of his issuing out into the street, but he must have done so, because the house appeared deserted. What had become of the dreadful creature of the night before I could not guess. My first fear was that he had left it behind him in the room with me,—it might be, as a sort of watch-dog. But, as the minutes and the hours passed and there was still no sign or sound of anything living, I concluded that, if the thing was there, it was, possibly, as helpless as myself, and that during its owner's absence, at any rate, I had nothing to fear from its too pressing attentions.

That, with the exception of myself, the house held nothing human, I had strong presumptive proof more than once in the course of the day. Several times, both in the morning and the afternoon, people without endeavoured to attract the attention of whoever was within. Vehicles— probably tradesmen's carts—drew up in front, their stopping being followed by more or less assiduous assaults upon the knocker and the bell. But in every case their appeals remained unheeded. Whatever it was they wanted, they had to go unsatisfied away. Lying there, torpid, with noth-ing to do but listen, I was, possibly, struck by very little, but it did occur to me that one among the callers was more persistent than the rest.

The distant clock had just struck noon when I heard the gate open, and someone approached the front door. Since nothing but silence followed, I supposed that the occupant of the place had returned, and had chosen to do so as silently as he had gone. Presently, however, there came from the doorstep a slight but peculiar call, as if a rat was squeak-ing. It was repeated three times, and then there was the sound of foot-steps quietly retreating, and the gate re-closing. Between one and two the caller came again; there was a repetition of the same signal,—that it was a signal I did not doubt; followed by the same retreat. About three the mysterious visitant returned. The signal was repeated, and, when there was no response, fingers tapped softly against the panels of the front door. When there was still no answer footsteps stole softly round the side of the house, and there came the signal from the rear,—and then, again, tapping of fingers against what was, apparently the back door. No notice being taken of these various proceedings the footsteps returned the way they went, and, as before, the gate was closed.

Shortly after darkness had fallen this assiduous caller returned, to make a fourth and more resolute attempt to call attention to his pres-ence. From the peculiar character of his manœuvres it seemed that he suspected that whoever was within had particular reasons for ignoring him without. He went through the familiar pantomime of the three squeaky calls both at the front door and the back,—followed by the tapping of the fingers on the panels. This time, however, he also tried the window panes,—I could hear, quite distinctly, the clear, yet distinct, noise of what seemed like knuckles rapping against the windows behind.

Disappointed there, he renewed his efforts at the front. The curiously quiet footsteps came round the house, to pause before the window of the room in which I lay,—and then something singular occurred.

While I waited for the tapping, there came, instead, the sound of someone or something, scrambling on to the window-sill,—as if some creature, unable to reach the window from the ground, was endeavouring to gain the vantage of the sill. Some ungainly creature, unskilled in surmounting such an obstacle as a perpendicular brick wall. There was the noise of what seemed to be the scratching of claws, as if it experienced considerable difficulty in obtaining a hold on the unyielding surface. What kind of creature it was I could not think,—I was astonished to find that it was a creature at all. I had taken it for granted that the persevering visitor was either a woman or a man. If, however, as now seemed likely, it was some sort of animal, the fact explained the squeaking sounds,—though what, except a rat did squeak like that was more than I could say—and the absence of any knocking or ringing.

Whatever it was, it had gained the summit of its desires,—the window-sill. It panted as if its efforts at climbing had made it short of breath. Then began the tapping. In the light of my new discovery, I perceived, clearly enough, that the tapping was hardly that which was likely to be the product of human fingers,—it was sharp and definite, rather resembling the striking of the point of a nail against the glass. It was not loud, but in time—it continued with much persistency—it became plainly vicious. It was accompanied by what I can only describe as the most extraordinary noises. There were squeaks, growing angrier and shriller as the minutes passed; what seemed like gaspings for breath; and a peculiar buzzing sound like, yet unlike, the purring of a cat.

The creature's resentment at its want of success in attracting attention was unmistakable. The tapping became like the clattering of hailstones; it kept up a continuous noise with its cries and pantings; there was the sound as of some large body being rubbed against the glass, as if it were extending itself against the window, and endeavouring, by force of pressure, to gain an entrance through the pane. So violent did its contortions become that I momentarily anticipated the yielding of the glass, and the excited assailant coming crashing through. Considerably to my relief the window proved more impregnable than seemed at one time likely. The stolid resistance proved, in the end, to be too much either for its endurance or its patience. Just as I was looking for some fresh manifestation of fury, it seemed rather to tumble than to spring off the sill; then came, once more, the same sound of quietly retreating footsteps; and what, under the circumstances, seemed odder still, the same closing of the gate.

During the two or three hours which immediately ensued nothing happened at all out of the way,—and then took place the most surprising incident of all. The clock had struck ten some time before. Since before the striking of the hour nothing and no one had passed along what was evidently the little frequented road in front of that uncanny house. On a sudden two sounds broke the stillness without,—of someone running, and of cries. Judging from his hurrying steps someone seemed to be flying for his life,—to the accompaniment of curious cries. It was only when the runner reached the front of the house that, in the cries, I recognized the squeaks of the persistent caller. I imagined that he had returned, as before, alone, to renew his attacks upon the window,—until it was made plain, as it quickly was, that, with him, was some sort of a companion. Immediately there arose, from without, the noise of battle. Two creatures, whose cries were, to me, of so unusual a character, that I found it impossible to even guess at their identity, seemed to be waging war to the knife upon the doorstep. After a minute or two of furious contention, victory seemed to rest with one of the combatants, for the other fled, squeaking as with pain. While I listened, with strained attention, for the next episode in this queer drama, expecting that now would come another assault upon the window, to my unbounded surprise I heard a key thrust in the keyhole, the lock turned, and the front door thrown open with a furious bang. It was closed as loudly as it was opened. Then the door of the room in which I was, was dashed open, with the same display of excitement, and of clamour, footsteps came hurrying in, the door was slammed to with a force which shook the house to its foundations, there was a rustling as of bed-clothes, the brilliant illumination of the night before, and a voice, which I had only too good reason to remember said,

"Stand up."

I stood up, automatically, at the word of command, facing towards the bed.

There, between the sheets, with his head resting on his hand in the attitude in which I had seen him last, was the being I had made acquaintance with under circumstances which I was never likely to forget,—the same, yet not the same.[1]

---

[1] This phrase, "the same, yet not the same," echoes a line from Tennyson's *In Memoriam A. H. H.*: "the same, but not the same" (LXXXVII, 14).

CHAPTER 5

AN INSTRUCTION TO COMMIT BURGLARY

That the man in the bed was the one whom, to my cost, I had suffered myself to stumble on the night before, there could, of course, not be the faintest doubt. And yet, directly I saw him, I recognized that some astonishing alteration had taken place in his appearance. To begin with, he seemed younger,—the decrepitude of age had given place to something very like the fire of youth. His features had undergone some subtle change. His nose, for instance, was not by any means so grotesque; its beak-like quality was less conspicuous. The most part of his wrinkles had disappeared, as if by magic. And, though his skin was still as yellow as saffron, his contours had rounded,—he had even come into possession of a modest allowance of chin. But the most astounding novelty was that about the face there was something which was essentially feminine; so feminine, indeed, that I wondered if I could by any possibility have blundered, and mistaken a woman for a man; some ghoulish example of her sex, who had so yielded to her depraved instincts as to have become nothing but a ghastly reminiscence of womanhood.

The effect of the changes which had come about in his appearance—for, after all, I told myself that it was impossible that I could have been such a simpleton as to have been mistaken on such a question as gender—was heightened by the self-evident fact that, very recently, he had been engaged in some pitched battle; some hand to hand, and, probably, discreditable encounter, from which he had borne away uncomfortable proofs of his opponent's prowess. His antagonist could hardly have been a chivalrous fighter, for his countenance was marked by a dozen different scratches which seemed to suggest that the weapons used had been someone's finger-nails. It was, perhaps, because the heat of the battle was still in his veins that he was in such a state of excitement. He seemed to be almost overwhelmed by the strength of his own feelings. His eyes seemed literally to flame with fire. The muscles of his face were working as if they were wholly beyond his own control. When he spoke his accent was markedly foreign; the words rushed from his lips in an inarticulate torrent; he kept repeating the same thing over and over again in a fashion which was not a little suggestive of insanity.

"So you're not dead!—you're not dead:—you're alive!—you're alive! Well,—how does it feel to be dead? I ask you!—Is it not good to be dead? To keep dead is better,—it is the best of all! To have made an end of all things, to cease to strive and to cease to weep, to cease to want and to cease to have, to cease to annoy and to cease to long, to no more care,—no!—not for anything, to put from you the curse of life,—forever!—is that not the best? Oh yes!—I tell you!—do I not know? But for you such knowledge is not yet. For you there is the return to life, the coming out of death,—you shall live on!—for me!—Live on!"

He made a movement with his hand, and, directly he did so, it happened as on the previous evening, that a metamorphosis took place in the very abysses of my being. I woke from my torpor, as he put it, I came out of death, and was alive again. I was far, yet, from being my own man; I realized that he exercised on me a degree of mesmeric force[1] which I had never dreamed that one creature could exercise on another; but, at least, I was no longer in doubt as to whether I was or was not dead. I knew I was alive.

He lay, watching me, as if he was reading the thoughts which occupied my brain,—and, for all I know, he was.

"Robert Holt, you are a thief."

"I am not."

My own voice, as I heard it, startled me,—it was so long since it had sounded in my ears.

"You are a thief! Only thieves come through windows,—did you not come through the window?" I was still,—what would my contradiction have availed me? "But it is well that you came through the window—well you are a thief,—well for me! for me! It is you that I am wanting,—at the happy moment you have dropped yourself into my hands,—in the nick of time. For you are my slave,—at my beck and call,—my familiar spirit, to do with as I will,—you know this,—eh?"

I did know it, and the knowledge of my impotence was terrible. I felt that if I could only get away from him; only release myself from the bonds with which he had bound me about; only remove myself from the horrible glamour of his near neighbourhood; only get one or two square meals and have an opportunity of recovering from the enervating stress of

---

[1]   Mesmerism, another name for hypnotism and named after eighteenth-century physician Franz Anton Mesmer, was for the Victorians a fascinating subject, and mesmeric séances as forms of both public and private entertainment were widespread throughout the nineteenth century.

mental and bodily fatigue;—I felt that then I might be something like his match, and that a second time, he would endeavour in vain to bring me within the compass of his magic. But, as it was, I was conscious that I was helpless, and the consciousness was agony. He persisted in reiterating his former falsehood.

"I say you are a thief!—a thief, Robert Holt, a thief! You came through a window for your own pleasure, now you will go through a window for mine,—not this window, but another." Where the jest lay I did not perceive; but it tickled him, for a grating sound came from his throat which was meant for laughter. "This time it is as a thief that you will go—oh yes, be sure."

He paused as it seemed, to transfix me with his gaze. His unblinking eyes never for an instant quitted my face. With what a frightful fascination they constrained me,—and how I loathed them!

When he spoke again there was a new intonation in his speech,—something bitter, cruel, unrelenting.

"Do you know Paul Lessingham?"

He pronounced the name as if he hated it,—and yet as if he loved to have it on his tongue.

"What Paul Lessingham?"

"There is only one Paul Lessingham! *The* Paul Lessingham,—the *great* Paul Lessingham!"

He shrieked, rather than said this, with an outburst of rage so frenzied that I thought, for the moment, that he was going to spring on me and rend me. I shook all over. I do not doubt that, as I replied, my voice was sufficiently tremulous.

"All the world knows Paul Lessingham,—the politician,—the statesman."

As he glared at me his eyes dilated. I still stood in expectation of a physical assault. But, for the present, he contented himself with words.

"To-night you are going through his window like a thief!"

I had no inkling of his meaning,—and, apparently, judging from his next words, I looked something of the bewilderment I felt.

"You do not understand?—no!—it is simple!—what could be simpler? I say that to-night—to-night!—you are going through his window like a thief. You came through my window,—why not through the window of Paul Lessingham, the politician—the statesman."

He repeated my words as if in mockery. I am—I make it my boast!—of that great multitude which regards Paul Lessingham as the greatest living force in practical politics; and which looks to him, with confidence, to carry through that great work of constitutional and social reform which he has set himself to do. I daresay that my tone, in speaking of him, savoured of laudation,—which, plainly, the man in the bed resented. What he meant by his wild words about my going through Paul Lessingham's window like a thief, I still had not the faintest notion. They sounded like the ravings of a madman.

As I continued silent, and he yet stared, there came into his tone another note,—a note of tenderness,—a note of which I had not deemed him capable.

"He is good to look at, Paul Lessingham,—is he not good to look at?"

I was aware that, physically, Mr. Lessingham was a fine specimen of manhood, but I was not prepared for the assertion of the fact in such a quarter,—nor for the manner in which the temporary master of my fate continued to harp and enlarge upon the theme.

"He is straight,—straight as the mast of a ship,—he is tall,—his skin is white; he is strong—do I not know that he is strong—how strong!— oh yes! Is there a better thing than to be his wife? his well-beloved? the light of his eyes? Is there for a woman a happier chance? Oh no, not one! His wife!—Paul Lessingham!"

As, with soft cadences, he gave vent to these unlooked-for sentiments, the fashion of his countenance was changed. A look of longing came into his face—of savage, frantic longing—which, unalluring though it was, for the moment transfigured him. But the mood was transient.

"To be his wife,—oh yes!—the wife of his scorn! the despised and rejected!"

The return to the venom of his former bitterness was rapid,—I could not but feel that this was the natural man. Though why a creature such as he was should go out of his way to apostrophize, in such a manner, a publicist of Mr. Lessingham's eminence, surpassed my comprehension. Yet he stuck to his subject like a leech,—as if it had been one in which he had an engrossing personal interest.

"He is a devil,—hard as the granite rock,—cold as the snows of Ararat. In him there is none of life's warm blood,—he is accursed! He is false,— ay, false as the fables of those who lie for love of lies,—he is all treachery. Her whom he has taken to his bosom he would put away from him as if she had never been,—he would steal from her like a thief in the night,— he would forget she ever was! But the avenger follows after, lurking in the shadows, hiding among the rocks, waiting, watching, till his time shall come. And it shall come!—the day of the avenger!—ay, the day!"

Raising himself to a sitting posture, he threw his arms above his head, and shrieked with a demoniac fury. Presently he became a trifle calmer. Reverting to his recumbent position, resting his head upon his hand, he eyed me steadily; then asked me a question which struck me as being, under the circumstances, more than a little singular.

"You know his house,—the house of the great Paul Lessingham,—the politician,—the statesman?"

"I do not."

"You lie!—you do!"

The words came from him with a sort of snarl,—as if he would have lashed me across the face with them.

"I do not. Men in my position are not acquainted with the residences of men in his. I may, at some time, have seen his address in print; but, if so, I have forgotten it."

He looked at me intently, for some moments, as if to learn if I spoke the truth and apparently, at last, was satisfied that I did.

"You do not know it?—Well! I will show it you,—I will show the house of the great Paul Lessingham."

What he meant I did not know; but I was soon to learn—an astounding revelation it proved to be. There was about his manner something hardly human; something which, for want of a better phrase, I would call vulpine. In his tone there was a mixture of mockery and bitterness, as if he wished his words to have the effect of corrosive sublimate, and to sear me as he uttered them.

"Listen with all your ears. Give me your whole attention. Hearken to my bidding, so that you may do as I bid you. Not that I fear your obedience,—oh no!"

He paused,—as if to enable me to fully realize the picture of my helplessness conjured up by his jibes.

"You came through my window, like a thief. You will go through my window, like a fool. You will go to the house of the great Paul Lessingham. You say you do not know it? Well, I will show it you. I will be your guide. Unseen, in the darkness and the night, I will stalk beside you, and will lead you to where I would have you go.—You will go just as you are, with bare feet, and head uncovered, and with but a single garment to hide your nakedness. You will be cold, your feet will be cut and bleeding,—but what better does a thief deserve? If any see you, at the least they will take you for a madman, there will be trouble. But have no fear; bear a bold heart. None shall see you while I stalk at your side. I will cover you with the cloak of invisibility,—so that you may come in safety to the house of the great Paul Lessingham."

He paused again. What he said, wild and wanton though it was, was beginning to fill me with a sense of the most extreme discomfort. His sentences, in some strange, indescribable way, seemed, as they came from his lips, to warp my limbs; to enwrap themselves about me; to confine me, tighter and tighter, within, as it were, swaddling clothes; to make me more and more helpless. I was already conscious that whatever mad freak he chose to set me on I should have no option but to carry it through.

"When you come to the house, you will stand, and look, and seek for a window convenient for entry. It may be that you will find one open, as you did mine; if not, you will open one. How,—that is your affair, not mine. You will practise the arts of a thief to steal into his house."

The monstrosity of his suggestion fought against the spell which he again was casting upon me, and forced me into speech,—endowed me with the power to show that there still was in me something of a man; though every second the strands of my manhood, as it seemed, were slipping faster through the fingers which were strained to clutch them.

"I will not."

He was silent. He looked at me. The pupils of his eyes dilated,—until they seemed all pupil.

"You will.—Do you hear?—I say you will."

"I am not a thief, I am an honest man,—why should I do this thing?"

"Because I bid you."

"Have mercy!"

"On whom—on you, or on Paul Lessingham?—Who, at any time, has shown mercy unto me, that I should show mercy unto any?"

He stopped, and then again went on,—reiterating his former incredible suggestion with an emphasis which seemed to eat its way into my brain.

"You will practise the arts of a thief to steal into his house and being in will listen. If all be still, you will make your way to the room he calls his study."

"How shall I find it? I know nothing of his house."

The question was wrung from me; I felt that the sweat was standing in great drops upon my brow.

"I will show it you."

"Shall you go with me?"

"Ay,—I shall go with you. All the time I shall be with you. You will not see me, but I shall be there. Be not afraid."

His claim to supernatural powers, for what he said amounted to nothing less, was, on the face of it, preposterous, but, then, I was in no condition to even hint at its absurdity. He continued.

"When you have gained the study, you will go to a certain drawer, which is in a certain bureau, in a corner of the room—I see it now; when you are there you shall see it too—and you will open it."

"Should it be locked?"

"You still will open it."

"But how shall I open it if it is locked?"

"By those arts in which a thief is skilled. I say to you again that that is your affair, not mine."

I made no attempt to answer him. Even supposing that he forced me, by the wicked, and unconscionable exercise of what, I presumed, were the hypnotic powers with which nature had to such a dangerous degree endowed him, to carry the adventure to a certain stage, since he could hardly, at an instant's notice, endow me with the knack of picking locks, should the drawer he alluded to be locked—which might Providence permit!—nothing serious might issue from it after all. He read my thoughts.

"You will open it,—though it be doubly and trebly locked, I say that you will open it.—In it you will find—" he hesitated, as if to reflect—"some letters; it may be two or three,—I know not just how many,—they are bound about by a silken ribbon. You will take them out of the drawer, and, having taken them, you will make the best of your way out of the house, and bear them back to me."

"And should anyone come upon me while engaged in these nefarious proceedings,—for instance, should I encounter Mr. Lessingham himself, what then?"

"Paul Lessingham?—You need have no fear if you encounter him."

"I need have no fear!—If he finds me, in his own house, at dead of night, committing burglary!"

"You need have no fear of him."

"On your account, or on my own?—At least he will have me hauled to gaol."

"I say you need have no fear of him. I say what I mean."

"How, then, shall I escape his righteous vengeance? He is not the man to suffer a midnight robber to escape him scatheless,—shall I have to kill him?"

"You will not touch him with a finger,—nor will he touch you."

"By what spell shall I prevent him?"

"By the spell of two words."

"What words are they?"

"Should Paul Lessingham chance to come upon you, and find you in his house, a thief, and should seek to stay you from whatever it is you may be at, you will not flinch nor flee from him, but you will stand still, and you will say——"

Something in the crescendo accents of his voice, something weird and ominous, caused my heart to press against my ribs, so that when he stopped, in my eagerness I cried out,

"What?"

"THE BEETLE!"

As the words came from him in a kind of screech, the lamp went out, and the place was all in darkness, and I knew, so that the knowledge filled me with a sense of loathing, that with me, in the room, was the evil presence of the night before. Two bright specks gleamed in front of me; something flopped from off the bed on to the ground; the thing was coming towards me across the floor. It came slowly on, and on, and on. I stood still, speechless in the sickness of my horror. Until, on my bare feet, it touched me with slimy feelers, and my terror lest it should creep up my naked body lent me voice, and I fell shrieking like a soul in agony. | Dante's Inferno

It may be that my shrieking drove it from me. At least, it went. I knew it went. And all was still. Until, on a sudden, the lamp flamed out again, and there, lying, as before, in bed, glaring at me with his baleful eyes, was the being whom, in my folly, or in my wisdom,—whichever it was!—I was beginning to credit with the possession of unhallowed, unlawful powers.

"You will say that to him; those two words; they only; no more. And you will see what you will see. But Paul Lessingham is a man of resolution. Should he still persist in interference, or seek to hinder you, you will say those two words again. You need do no more. Twice will suffice, I promise you.—Now go.—Draw up the blind; open the window, climb through it. Hasten to do what I have bidden you. I wait here for your return,—and all the way I shall be with you."

CHAPTER 6

A SINGULAR FELONY

I went to the window; I drew up the blind, unlatching the sash, I threw it open, and clad, or, rather, unclad as I was, I clambered through it into the open air. I was not only incapable of resistance, I was incapable of distinctly formulating the desire to offer resistance. Some compelling influence moved me hither and thither, with completest disregard of whether I would or would not.

And yet, when I found myself without, I was conscious of a sense of exultation at having escaped from the miasmic atmosphere of that room of unholy memories. And a faint hope began to dawn within my bosom that, as I increased the distance between myself and it, I might shake off something of the nightmare helplessness which numbed and tortured me. I lingered for a moment by the window; then stepped over the short dividing wall into the street; and then again I lingered.

My condition was one of dual personality,—while, physically, I was bound, mentally to a considerable extent, I was free. But this measure of freedom on my mental side made my plight no better. For, among other things, I realized what a ridiculous figure I must be cutting, bare-footed and bareheaded, abroad, at such an hour of the night, in such a boisterous breeze,—for I quickly discovered that the wind amounted to something like a gale. Apart from all other considerations, the notion of parading the streets in such a condition filled me with profound disgust. And I do believe that if my tyrannical oppressor had only permitted me to attire myself in my own garments, I should have started with a comparatively light heart on the felonious mission on which he apparently was sending me. I believe, too, that the consciousness of the incongruity of my attire increased my sense of helplessness, and that, had I been dressed as Englishmen are wont to be, who take their walks abroad, he would not have found in me, on that occasion, the facile instrument, which, in fact, he did.

There was a moment, in which the gravelled pathway first made itself known to my naked feet, and the cutting wind to my naked flesh, when I think it possible that, had I gritted my teeth, and strained my every nerve, I might have shaken myself free from the bonds which shackled me and bade defiance to the ancient sinner who, for all I knew, was peeping at me through the window. But so depressed was I by the knowledge of the ridiculous appearance I presented that, before I could take advantage of it the moment passed,—not to return again that night.

I did catch, as it were, at its fringe, as it was flying past me, making a hurried movement to one side,—the first I had made, of my own initiative, for hours. But it was too late. My tormentor,—as if, though unseen, he saw—tightened his grip, I was whirled round, and sped hastily onwards in a direction in which I certainly had no desire of travelling.

All the way I never met a soul. I have since wondered whether in that respect my experience was not a normal one; whether it might not have happened to any. If so, there are streets in London, long lines of streets which, at a certain period of the night, in a certain sort of weather—probably the weather had something to do with it—are clean deserted; in which there is neither foot-passenger nor vehicle—not even a policeman. The greater part of the route along which I was driven—I know no juster word—was one with which I had some sort of acquaintance. It led, at first, through what, I take it, was some part of Walham Green; then along the Lillie Road, through Brompton, across the Fulham Road, through the network of streets leading to Sloane Street, across Sloane Street into Lowndes Square.[1] Who goes that way goes some distance, and goes through some important thoroughfares; yet not a creature did I see, nor, I imagine, was there a creature who saw me. As I crossed Sloane Street, I fancied that I heard the distant rumbling of a vehicle along the Knightsbridge Road, but that was the only sound I heard.

It is painful even to recollect the plight in which I was when I was stopped,—for stopped I was, as shortly and as sharply, as the beast of burden, with a bridle in its mouth, whose driver puts a period to his career. I was wet,—intermittent gusts of rain were borne on the scurrying wind; in spite of the pace at which I had been brought, I was chilled to the bone; and—worst of all!—my mud-stained feet, all cut and bleeding, were so painful—for unfortunately, I was still susceptible enough to pain—that it was agony to have them come into contact with the cold and the slime of the hard, unyielding pavement.

I had been stopped on the opposite side of the square,—that nearest to the hospital; in front of a house which struck me as being somewhat smaller than the rest. It was a house with a portico; about the pillars of this portico was trelliswork, and on the trelliswork was trained some climbing plant. As I stood, shivering, wondering what would happen

---

[1]   Holt is moving east across London.

next, some strange impulse mastered me, and, immediately, to my own unbounded amazement, I found myself scrambling up the trellis towards the verandah above. I am no gymnast, either by nature or by education; I doubt whether, previously, I had ever attempted to climb anything more difficult than a step ladder. The result was, that, though the impulse might be given me, the skill could not, and I had only ascended a yard or so when, losing my footing, I came slithering down upon my back. Bruised and shaken though I was, I was not allowed to inquire into my injuries. In a moment I was on my feet again, and again I was impelled to climb,—only, however, again to come to grief. This time the demon, or whatever it was, that had entered into me, seeming to appreciate the impossibility of getting me to the top of that verandah, directed me to try another way. I mounted the steps leading to the front door, got on to the low parapet which was at one side, thence on to the sill of the adjacent window,—had I slipped then I should have fallen a sheer descent of at least twenty feet to the bottom of the deep area down below. But the sill was broad, and—if it is proper to use such language in connection with a transaction of the sort in which I was engaged—fortune favoured me. I did not fall. In my clenched fist I had a stone. With this I struck the pane of glass, as with a hammer. Through the hole which resulted, I could just insert my hand, and reach the latch within. In another minute the sash was raised, and I was in the house,—I had committed burglary.

As I look back and reflect upon the audacity of the whole proceeding, even now I tremble. Hapless slave of another's will although in very truth I was, I cannot repeat too often that I realized to the full just what it was that I was being compelled to do—a fact which was very far from rendering my situation less distressful!—and every detail of my involuntary actions was projected upon my brain in a series of pictures, whose clear-cut outlines, so long as memory endures, will never fade. Certainly no professional burglar, nor, indeed, any creature in his senses, would have ventured to emulate my surprising rashness. The process of smashing the pane of glass—it was plate glass—was anything but a noiseless one. There was, first, the blow itself, then the shivering of the glass, then the clattering of fragments into the area beneath. One would have thought that the whole thing would have made din enough to have roused the Seven Sleepers.[1] But, here, again the weather was on

---

[1] The Seven Sleepers of Ephesus, all subsequently canonized, who, according to legend, sought refuge from the Christian persecutions of Decius (c. 250 AD) by hiding in a cave in Mount Pion, Turkey. Waking up again in the reign of the emperor Theodosius (either the Great, c. 4th century, or the Younger, 5th century), the sleepers restored Theodosius' wavering faith.

my side. About that time the wind was howling wildly,—it came shrieking across the square. It is possible that the tumult which it made deadened all other sounds.

Anyhow, as I stood within the room which I had violated, listening for signs of someone being on the alert, I could hear nothing. Within the house there seemed to be the silence of the grave. I drew down the window, and made for the door.

It proved by no means easy to find. The windows were obscured by heavy curtains, so that the room inside was dark as pitch. It appeared to be unusually full of furniture,—an appearance due, perhaps, to my being a stranger in the midst of such Cimmerian blackness.[1] I had to feel my way, very gingerly indeed, among the various impedimenta. As it was I seemed to come into contact with most of the obstacles there were to come into contact with, stumbling more than once over footstools, and over what seemed to be dwarf chairs. It was a miracle that my movements still continued to be unheard,—but I believe that the explanation was, that the house was well built; that the servants were the only persons in it at the time; that their bedrooms were on the top floor; that they were fast asleep; and that they were little likely to be disturbed by anything that might occur in the room which I had entered.

Reaching the door at last, I opened it,—listening for any promise of being interrupted—and—to adapt a hackneyed phrase—directed by the power which shaped my end,[2] I went across the hall and up the stairs. I passed up the first landing, and, on the second, moved to a door upon the right. I turned the handle, it yielded, the door opened, I entered, closing it behind me. I went to the wall just inside the door, found a handle, jerked it, and switched on the electric light,—doing, I make no doubt, all these things, from a spectator's point of view, so naturally, that a judge and jury would have been with difficulty persuaded that they were not the product of my own volition.

In the brilliant glow of the electric light I took a leisurely survey of the contents of the room. It was, as the man in the bed had said it would be, a study,—a fine, spacious apartment, evidently intended rather for work than for show. There were three separate writing-tables, one very large and two smaller ones, all covered with an orderly array of manuscripts

---

[1] The Cimmerii were a legendary ancient people reputed to have lived in perpetual darkness, hence the adjectival qualification to suggest dense gloom or night-time.

[2] Holt is alluding to—and incorrectly paraphrasing—a line from *Hamlet*: "There's a divinity that shapes our ends, / Rough-hew them how we will" (V.ii.10-11).

and papers. A typewriter stood at the side of one. On the floor, under and about them, were piles of books, portfolios, and official-looking documents. Every available foot of wall space on three sides of the room was lined with shelves, full as they could hold with books. On the fourth side, facing the door, was a large lock-up oak bookcase, and, in the further corner, a quaint old bureau. So soon as I saw this bureau I went for it, straight as an arrow from a bow,—indeed, it would be no abuse of metaphor to say that I was propelled towards it like an arrow from a bow.

It had drawers below, glass doors above, and between the drawers and the doors was a flap to let down. It was to this flap my attention was directed. I put out my hand to open it; it was locked at the top. I pulled at it with both hands; it refused to budge.

So this was the lock I was, if necessary, to practise the arts of a thief to open. I was no picklock; I had flattered myself that nothing, and no one, could make me such a thing. Yet now that I found myself confronted by that unyielding flap, I found that pressure, irresistible pressure, was being put upon me to gain, by any and every means, access to its interior. I had no option but to yield. I looked about me in search of some convenient tool with which to ply the felon's trade. I found it close beside me. Leaning against the wall, within a yard of where I stood, were examples of various kinds of weapons—among them, spear-heads. Taking one of these spear-heads, with much difficulty I forced the point between the flap and the bureau. Using the leverage thus obtained, I attempted to prise it open. The flap held fast; the spear-head snapped in two. I tried another, with the same result; a third, to fail again. There were no more. The most convenient thing remaining was a queer, heavy-headed sharp-edged hatchet. This I took, brought the sharp edge down with all my force upon the refractory flap. The hatchet went through—before I had done with it, it was open with a vengeance.

But I was destined on the occasion of my first—and, I trust, last—experience of the burglar's calling, to carry the part completely through. I had gained access to the flap itself only to find that at the back were several small drawers, on one of which my observation was brought to bear in a fashion which it was quite impossible to disregard. As a matter of course it was locked, and, once more, I had to search for something which would serve as a rough-and-ready substitute for the missing key.

There was nothing at all suitable among the weapons,—I could hardly for such a purpose use the hatchet; the drawer in question was such a little one that to have done so would have been to shiver it to splinters. On the mantelshelf, in an open leather case, were a pair of revolvers. Statesmen, nowadays, sometimes stand in actual peril of their lives.[1] It is possible that Mr. Lessingham, conscious of continually threatened danger, carried them about with him as a necessary protection. They were serviceable weapons, large, and somewhat weighty,—of the type which, I believe, upon occasion the police are armed. Not only were all the barrels loaded, but, in the case itself there was a supply of cartridges more than sufficient to charge them all again.

I was handling the weapons, wondering—if, in my condition, the word was applicable—what use I could make of them to enable me to gain admission to that drawer, when there came, on a sudden, from the street without, the sound of approaching wheels. There was a whirring within my brain, as if someone was endeavouring to explain to me to what service to apply the revolvers, and I, perforce, strained every nerve to grasp the meaning of my invisible mentor. While I did so, the wheels drew rapidly nearer, and, just as I was expecting them to go whirling by, stopped,—in front of the house. My heart leapt in my bosom. In a convulsion of frantic terror, again, during the passage of one frenzied moment, I all but burst the bonds that held me, and fled, haphazard, from the imminent peril. But the bonds were stronger than I,—it was as if I had been rooted to the ground.

A key was inserted in the keyhole of the front door, the lock was turned, the door thrown open, firm footsteps entered the house. If I could I would not have stood upon the order of my going,[2] but gone at once, anywhere, anyhow; but, at that moment, my comings and goings were not matters in which I was consulted. Panic fear raging within, outwardly I was calm as possible, and stood, turning the revolvers over and over, asking myself what it could be that I was intended to do with them. All at once it came to me in an illuminating flash,—I was to fire at the lock of the drawer, and blow it open.

A madder scheme it would have been impossible to hit upon. The servants had slept through a good deal, but they would hardly sleep through the discharge of a revolver in a room below them,—not to speak of the person who had just entered the premises, and whose footsteps were

---

[1] At the end of the nineteenth century throughout Europe there was a fear, often fostered and exaggerated, if not on occasions generated, by the media, of violent attacks on politicians and other prominent figures by revolutionary and anarchist groups. Other novels, roughly contemporary with Marsh's, dealing with the perception of such threats and their fictionalized occurrence, include Henry James's *The Princess Casamassima* (1886) and Joseph Conrad's *The Secret Agent* (1907).

[2] "Stand not upon the order of your going, / But go at once" *Macbeth* (III.iv.119).

already audible as he came up the stairs. I struggled to make a dumb protest against the insensate folly which was hurrying me to infallible destruction, without success. For me there was only obedience. With a revolver in either hand I marched towards the bureau as unconcernedly as if I would not have given my life to have escaped the dénouement[1] which I needed but a slight modicum of common sense to be aware was close at hand. I placed the muzzle of one of the revolvers against the keyhole of the drawer to which my unseen guide had previously directed me, and pulled the trigger. The lock was shattered, the contents of the drawer were at my mercy. I snatched up a bundle of letters, about which a pink ribbon was wrapped. Startled by a noise behind me immediately following the report of the pistol, I glanced over my shoulder.

The room door was open, and Mr. Lessingham was standing with the handle in his hand.

CHAPTER 7

THE GREAT PAUL LESSINGHAM

He was in evening dress. He carried a small portfolio in his left hand. If the discovery of my presence startled him, as it could scarcely have failed to do, he allowed no sign of surprise to escape him. Paul Lessingham's impenetrability is proverbial. Whether on platforms addressing excited crowds, or in the midst of heated discussion in the House of Commons, all the world knows that his coolness remains unruffled. It is generally understood that he owes his success in the political arena in no slight measure to the adroitness which is born of his invulnerable presence of mind. He gave me a taste of its quality then. Standing in the attitude which has been familiarized to us by caricaturists, his feet apart, his broad shoulders well set back, his handsome head a little advanced, his keen blue eyes having in them something suggestive of a bird of prey considering just when, where, and how to pounce, he regarded me for some seconds in perfect silence,—whether outwardly I flinched I cannot say; inwardly I know I did. When he spoke, it was without moving from where he stood, and in the calm,

---

[1]   *Dénouement*: the unravelling or disclosure of a mystery in a plot.

airy tones in which he might have addressed an acquaintance who had just dropped in.

"May I ask, sir, to what I am indebted for the pleasure of your company?"

He paused, as if waiting for my answer. When none came, he put his question in another form.

"Pray, sir, who are you, and on whose invitation do I find you here?"

As I still stood speechless, motionless, meeting his glance without a twitching of an eyebrow, nor a tremor of the hand, I imagine that he began to consider me with an even closer intentness than before. And that the—to say the least of it—peculiarity of my appearance, caused him to suspect that he was face to face with an adventure of a peculiar kind. Whether he took me for a lunatic I cannot certainly say; but, from his manner, I think it possible he did. He began to move towards me from across the room, addressing me with the utmost suavity and courtesy.

"Be so good as to give me the revolver, and the papers you are holding in your hand."

As he came on, something entered into me, and forced itself from between my lips, so that I said, in a low, hissing voice, which I vow was never mine, *Serpent motif*

"THE BEETLE!"

Whether it was, or was not, owing, in some degree, to a trick of my imagination, I cannot determine, but, as the words were spoken, it seemed to me that the lights went low, so that the place was all in darkness, and I again was filled with the nauseous consciousness of the presence of something evil in the room. But if, in that matter, my abnormally strained imagination played me a trick, there could be no doubt whatever as to the effect which the words had on Mr. Lessingham. When the mist of the blackness—real or supposititious—had passed from before my eyes, I found that he had retreated to the extremest limits of the room, and was crouching his back against the bookshelves, clutching at them, in the attitude of a man who has received a staggering blow, from which, as yet, he has had no opportunity of recovering. A most extraordinary change had taken place in the expression of his face; in his countenance amazement, fear, and horror seemed struggling for the mastery. I was filled with a most discomforting qualm as I gazed at the frightened figure in front of me, and realized that it was that of the great Paul Lessingham, the god of my political idolatry.

"Who are you?—In God's name, who are you?"

His very voice seemed changed; his frenzied, choking accents would hardly have been recognized by either friend or foe.

"Who are you?—Do you hear me ask, who are you? In the name of God, I bid you say!"

As he perceived that I was still, he began to show a species of excitement which it was unpleasant to witness, especially as he continued to crouch against the bookshelf, as if he was afraid to stand up straight. So far from exhibiting the impassivity for which he was renowned, all the muscles in his face and all the limbs in his body seemed to be in motion at once; he was like a man afflicted with the shivering ague,—his very fingers were twitching aimlessly, as they were stretched out on either side of him, as if seeking for support from the shelves against which he leaned.

"Where have you come from? what do you want? who sent you here? what concern have you with me? is it necessary that you should come and play these childish tricks with me? why? why?"

The questions came from him with astonishing rapidity. When he saw that I continued silent, they came still faster, mingled with what sounded to me like a stream of inchoate abuse.

"Why do you stand there in that extraordinary garment,—it's worse than nakedness, yes, worse than nakedness! For that alone I could have you punished, and I will!—and try to play the fool? Do you think I am a boy to be bamboozled by every bogey[1] a blunderer may try to conjure up? If so, you're wrong, as whoever sent you might have had sense enough to let you know. If you tell me who you are, and who sent you here, and what it is you want, I will be merciful; if not, the police shall be sent for, and the law shall take its course,—to the bitter end!—I warn you.—Do you hear? You fool! tell me who you are?"

The last words came from him in what was very like a burst of childish fury. He himself seemed conscious, the moment after, that his passion was sadly lacking in dignity, and to be ashamed of it. He drew himself straight up. With a pocket-handkerchief which he took from an inner pocket of his coat, he wiped his lips. Then, clutching it tightly in his hand, he eyed me with a fixedness which, under any other circumstances, I should have found unbearable.

"Well, sir, is your continued silence part of the business of the rôle you have set yourself to play?"

---

[1]   An object of terror; a goblin; something fearful; also spelt bogle.

His tone was firmer, and his bearing more in keeping with his character.

"If it be so, I presume that I at least have liberty to speak. When I find a gentleman, even one gifted with your eloquence of silence, playing the part of burglar, I think you will grant that a few words on my part cannot justly be considered to be out of place."

Again he paused. I could not but feel that he was employing the vehicle of somewhat cumbrous sarcasm to gain time, and to give himself the opportunity of recovering, if the thing was possible, his pristine courage. That, for some cause wholly hidden from me, the mysterious utterance had shaken his nature to its deepest foundation, was made plainer by his endeavour to treat the whole business with a sort of cynical levity.

"To commence with, may I ask if you have come through London, or through any portion of it, in that costume,—or rather, in that want of costume? It would seem out of place in a Cairene[1] street,—would it not?—even in the Rue de Rabagas,—was it not the Rue de Rabagas?"

He asked the question with an emphasis the meaning of which was wholly lost on me. What he referred to either then, or in what immediately followed, I, of course, knew no more than the man in the moon,—though I should probably have found great difficulty in convincing him of my ignorance.

"I take it that you are a reminiscence of the Rue de Rabagas,—that, of course;—is it not of course? The little house with the blue-grey venetians, and the piano with the F sharp missing? Is there still the piano? With the tinny treble—indeed, the whole atmosphere, was it not tinny?—You agree with me?—I have not forgotten. I am not even afraid to remember,—you perceive it?"

A new idea seemed to strike him,—born, perhaps, of my continued silence.

"You look English,—is it possible that you are not English? What are you then—French? We shall see!"

He addressed me in a tongue which I recognized as French, but with which I was not sufficiently acquainted to understand. Although, I flatter myself that,—as the present narrative should show—I have not made an ill-use of the opportunities which I have had to improve my, originally, modest education, I regret that I have never had so much as a ghost of a chance to acquire an even rudimentary knowledge of any language except my own. Recognizing, I suppose, from my looks, that

---

[1]   A street in Cairo.

he was addressing me in a tongue to which I was a stranger, after a time he stopped, added something with a smile, and then began to talk to me in a lingo to which, in a manner of speaking, I was even stranger, for this time I had not the faintest notion what it was,—it might have been gibberish for all that I could tell. Quickly perceiving that he had succeeded no better than before, he returned to English.

"You do not know French?—nor the *patois*[1] of the Rue de Rabagas? Very good,—then what is it that you do know? Are you under a vow of silence, or are you dumb,—except upon occasion? Your face is English,—what can be seen of it, and I will take it, therefore, that English spoken words convey some meaning to your brain. So listen, sir, to what I have to say,—do me the favour to listen carefully."

He was becoming more and more his former self. In his clear, modulated tones there was a ring of something like a threat,—a something which went very far beyond his words.

"You know something of a period which I choose to have forgotten,—that is plain; you come from a person who, probably, knows still more. Go back to that person and say that what I have forgotten I have forgotten; nothing will be gained by anyone by an endeavour to induce me to remember,—be very sure upon that point, say that nothing will be gained by anyone. That time was one of mirage, of delusion, of disease. I was in a condition, mentally and bodily, in which pranks could have been played upon me by any trickster. Such pranks were played. I know that now quite well. I do not pretend to be proficient in the *modus operandi*[2] of the hankey-pankey man,[3] but I know that he has a method, all the same,—one susceptible, too, of facile explanation. Go back to your friend, and tell him that I am not again likely to be made the butt of his old method,—nor of his new one either.—You hear me, sir?"

I remained motionless and silent,—an attitude which, plainly he resented.

"Are you deaf and dumb? You certainly are not dumb, for you spoke to me just now. Be advised by me, and do not compel me to resort to measures which will be the cause to you of serious discomfort.—You hear me, sir?"

Still, from me, not a sign of comprehension,—to his increased annoyance.

---

[1] A dialect particular to a region or district; occasionally used in English as a pejorative term for dialect.
[2] Method of working.
[3] Juggling or legerdemain, but also referring to deceit or underhand dealings.

"So be it. Keep your own counsel, if you choose. Yours will be the bitterness not mine. You may play the lunatic, and play it excellently well, but that you do understand what is said to you is clear.—Come to business, sir. Give me that revolver, and the packet of letters which you have stolen from my desk."

He had been speaking with the air of one who desired to convince himself as much as me,—and about his last words there was almost a flavour of braggadocio.[1] I remained unheeding.

"Are you going to do as I require, or are you insane enough to refuse?—in which case I shall summon assistance, and there will quickly be an end of it. Pray do not imagine that you can trick me into supposing that you do not grasp the situation. I know better.—Once more, are you going to give me that revolver and those letters?"

Yet no reply. His anger was—growing momentarily greater,—and his agitation too. On my first introduction to Paul Lessingham I was not destined to discover in him any one of those qualities of which the world held him to be the undisputed possessor. He showed himself to be as unlike the statesman I had conceived, and esteemed, as he easily could have done.

"Do you think I stand in awe of you?—you!—of such a thing as you! Do as I tell you, or I myself will make you,—and, at the same time, teach you a much-needed lesson."

He raised his voice. In his bearing there was a would-be defiance. He might not have been aware of it, but the repetitions of the threats were, in themselves, confessions of weakness. He came a step or two forward,—then, stopping short, began to tremble. The perspiration broke out upon his brow; he made spasmodic little dabs at it with his crumpled-up handkerchief. His eyes wandered hither and thither, as if searching for something which they feared to see yet were constrained to seek. He began to talk to himself, out loud, in odd disconnected sentences,—apparently ignoring me entirely.

"What was that?—It was nothing.—It was my imagination.—My nerves are out of order.—I have been working too hard.—I am not well.—*What's that?*"

This last inquiry came from him in a half-stifled shriek,—as the door opened to admit the head and body of an elderly man in a state of considerable undress. He had the tousled appearance of one who had been unexpectedly roused out of slumber, and unwillingly dragged from bed.

---

[1] Someone who brags or swaggers.

Mr. Lessingham stared at him as if he had been a ghost, while he stared back at Mr. Lessingham as if he found a difficulty in crediting the evidence of his own eyes. It was he who broke the silence,—stutteringly.

"I am sure I beg your pardon, sir, but one of the maids thought that she heard the sound of a shot, and we came down to see if there was anything the matter,—I had no idea, sir, that you were here." His eyes travelled from Mr. Lessingham towards me,—suddenly increasing, when they saw me, to about twice their previous size. "God save us!—who is that?"

The man's self-evident cowardice possibly impressed Mr. Lessingham with the conviction that he himself was not cutting the most dignified of figures. At any rate, he made a notable effort to, once more, assume a bearing of greater determination.

"You are quite right, Matthews, quite right. I am obliged by your watchfulness. At present you may leave the room—I propose to deal with this fellow myself,—only remain with the other men upon the landing, so that, if I call, you may come to my assistance."

Matthews did as he was told, he left the room,—with, I fancy, more rapidity than he had entered it. Mr. Lessingham returned to me, his manner distinctly more determined, as if he found his resolution reinforced by the near neighbourhood of his retainers.

"Now, my man, you see how the case stands, at a word from me you will be overpowered and doomed to undergo a long period of imprisonment. Yet I am still willing to listen to the dictates of mercy. Put down that revolver, give me those letters,—you will not find me disposed to treat you hardly."

For all the attention I paid him, I might have been a graven image. He misunderstood, or pretended to misunderstand, the cause of my silence.

"Come, I see that you suppose my intentions to be harsher than they really are,—do not let us have a scandal, and a scene,—be sensible!—give me those letters!"

Again he moved in my direction; again, after he had taken a step or two, to stumble and stop, and look about him with frightened eyes; again to begin to mumble to himself aloud.

"It's a conjurer's trick!—Of course!—Nothing more.—What else could it be?—I am not to be fooled.—I'm older than I was. I've been overdoing it,—that's all."

Suddenly he broke into cries.

"Matthews! Matthews!—Help! help!"

Matthews entered the room, followed by three other men, younger than himself. Evidently all had slipped into the first articles of clothing they could lay their hands upon, and each carried a stick, or some similar rudimentary weapon.

Their master spurred them on.

"Strike the revolver out of his hand, Matthews!—knock him down!—take the letters from him!—don't be afraid!—I'm not afraid!"

In proof of it, he rushed at me, as it seemed half blindly. As he did so I was constrained to shout out, in tones which I should not have recognized as mine,

"THE BEETLE!"

And that moment the room was all in darkness, and there were screams as of someone in an agony of terror or of pain. I felt that something had come into the room, I knew not whence nor how,—something of horror. And the next action of which I was conscious was, that under cover of the darkness, I was flying from the room, propelled by I knew not what.

CHAPTER 8

THE MAN IN THE STREET

Whether anyone pursued I cannot say. I have some dim recollection, as I came out of the room, of women being huddled against the wall upon the landing, and of their screaming as I went past. But whether any effort was made to arrest my progress I cannot tell. My own impression is that not the slightest attempt to impede my headlong flight was made by anyone.

In what direction I was going I did not know. I was like a man flying through the phantasmagoric[1] happenings of a dream, knowing neither how nor whither. I tore along what I suppose was a broad passage, through a door at the end into what, I fancy, was a drawing-room. Across this room I dashed helter-skelter, bringing down, in the gloom, unseen articles of furniture, with myself sometimes on top, and sometimes under them. In a trice, each time I fell, I was on my feet again,—

---

[1]   By the end of the eighteenth century phantasmagoria or magic lantern shows featuring images of spectres and phantoms were a highly popular form of entertainment, both in Europe and in Great Britain. By the time Marsh is writing, the term has become largely metaphorical, as in this example, referring to the phantasms produced by the mind.

until I went crashing against a window which was concealed by curtains. It would not have been strange had I crashed through it,—but I was spared that. Thrusting aside the curtains, I fumbled for the fastening of the window. It was a tall French casement extending, so far as I could judge, from floor to ceiling. When I had it open I stepped through it on to the verandah without—to find that I was on the top of the portico which I had vainly essayed to ascend from below.

I tried the road down which I had tried up,—proceeding with a breakneck recklessness of which now I shudder to think. It was, probably, some thirty feet above the pavement, yet I rushed at the descent with as much disregard for the safety of life and limb as if it had been only three. Over the edge of the parapet I went, obtaining, with my naked feet, a precarious foothold on the latticework,—then down I commenced to scramble. I never did get a proper hold, and when I had descended, perhaps, rather more than half the distance,—scraping, as it seemed to me, every scrap of skin off my body in the process—I lost what little hold I had. Down to the bottom I went tumbling, rolling right across the pavement into the muddy road. It was a miracle I was not seriously injured,—but in that sense, certainly, that night the miracles were on my side. Hardly was I down, than I was up again,—mud and all.

Just as I was getting on to my feet I felt a firm hand grip me by the shoulder. Turning I found myself confronted by a tall, slenderly built man, with a long drooping moustache, and an overcoat buttoned up to the chin, who held me with a grasp of steel. He looked at me,—and I looked back at him.

"After the ball,—eh?"

Even then I was struck by something pleasant in his voice, and some quality as of sunshine in his handsome face.

Seeing that I said nothing he went on,—with a curious, half mocking smile.

"Is that the way to come slithering down the Apostle's pillar?—Is it simple burglary, or simpler murder?—Tell me the glad tidings that you've killed St. Paul, and I'll let you go."

Whether he was mad or not I cannot say,—there was some excuse for thinking so. He did not look mad, though his words and actions alike were strange.

"Although you have confined yourself to gentle felony, shall I not shower blessings on the head of him who has been robbing Paul?—Away with you!"

He removed his grip, giving me a gentle push as he did so,—and I was away. I neither stayed nor paused.

I know little of records, but if anyone has made a better record than I did that night between Lowndes Square and Walham Green I should like to know just what it was,—I should, too, like to have seen it done.

In an incredibly short space of time I was once more in front of the house with the open window,—the packet of letters—which were like to have cost me so dear—gripped tightly in my hand.

CHAPTER 9

THE CONTENTS OF THE PACKET

I pulled up sharply,—as if a brake had been suddenly, and even mercilessly applied to bring me to a standstill. In front of the window I stood shivering. A shower had recently commenced,—the falling rain was being blown before the breeze. I was in a terrible sweat,—yet tremulous as with cold; covered with mud; bruised, and cut, and bleeding,—as piteous an object as you would care to see. Every limb in my body ached; every muscle was exhausted; mentally and physically I was done; had I not been held up, willy nilly, by the spell which was upon me, I should have sunk down, then and there, in a hopeless, helpless, hapless heap.

But my tormentor was not yet at an end with me.

As I stood there, like some broken and beaten hack, waiting for the word of command, it came. It was as if some strong magnetic current had been switched on to me through the window to draw me into the room. Over the low wall I went, over the sill,—once more I stood in that chamber of my humiliation and my shame. And once again I was conscious of that awful sense of the presence of an evil thing. How much of it was fact, and how much of it was the product of imagination I cannot say; but, looking back, it seems to me that it was as if I had been taken out of the corporeal body to be plunged into the inner chambers of all nameless sin. There was the sound of something flopping from off the bed on to the ground, and I knew that the thing was coming at me across the floor. My stomach quaked, my heart melted within me,—the very anguish of my terror gave me strength to scream,—and scream! Sometimes, even now, I seem to hear those screams of mine ringing through the night, and I bury my face in the pillow, and it is as though I was passing through the very Valley of the Shadow.[1]

The thing went back,—I could hear it slipping and sliding across the floor. There was silence. And, presently, the lamp was lit, and the room was all in brightness. There, on the bed, in the familiar attitude between the sheets, his head resting on his hand, his eyes blazing like living coals, was the dreadful cause of all my agonies. He looked at me with his unpitying, unblinking glance.

"So!—Through the window again!—like a thief!—Is it always through that door that you come into a house?"

He paused,—as if to give me time to digest his gibe.

"You saw Paul Lessingham,—well?—the great Paul Lessingham!—Was he, then, so great?"

His rasping voice, with its queer foreign twang, reminded me, in some uncomfortable way, of a rusty saw,—the things he said, and the manner in which he said them, were alike intended to add to my discomfort. It was solely because the feat was barely possible that he only partially succeeded.

"Like a thief you went into his house,—did I not tell you that you would? Like a thief he found you,—were you not ashamed? Since, like a thief he found you, how comes it that you have escaped,—by what robber's artifice have you saved yourself from gaol?"

His manner changed,—so that, all at once, he seemed to snarl at me.

"Is he great?—well!—is he great,—Paul Lessingham? You are small, but he is smaller,—your great Paul Lessingham!—Was there ever a man so less than nothing?"

With the recollection fresh upon me of Mr. Lessingham as I had so lately seen him I could not but feel that there might be a modicum of truth in what, with such an intensity of bitterness, the speaker suggested. The picture which, in my mental gallery, I had hung in the place of honour, seemed, to say the least, to have become a trifle smudged.

As usual, the man in the bed seemed to experience not the slightest difficulty in deciphering what was passing through my mind.

"That is so,—you and he, you are a pair,—the great Paul Lessingham is as great a thief as you—and greater—for, at least, than you he has more courage."

For some moments he was still; then exclaimed, with sudden fierceness,

"Give me what you have stolen!"

---

[1] Psalm 23: 4; the valley of the shadow of death.

I moved towards the bed—most unwillingly—and held out to him the packet of letters which I had abstracted from the little drawer. Perceiving my disinclination to his near neighbourhood, he set himself to play with it. Ignoring my outstretched hand, he stared me straight in the face.

"What ails you? Are you not well? Is it not sweet to stand close at my side? You, with your white skin, if I were a woman, would you not take me for a wife?"

There was something about the manner in which this was said which was so essentially feminine that once more I wondered if I could possibly be mistaken in the creature's sex. I would have given much to have been able to strike him across the face,—or, better, to have taken him by the neck, and thrown him through the window, and rolled him in the mud.

He condescended to notice what I was holding out to him.

"So!—that is what you have stolen! That is what you have taken from the drawer in the bureau—the drawer which was locked—and which you used the arts in which a thief is skilled to enter. Give it to me,—thief!"

He snatched the packet from me, scratching the back of my hand as he did so, as if his nails had been talons. He turned the packet over and over, glaring at it as he did so,—it was strange what a relief it was to have his glance removed from off my face.

"You kept it in your inner drawer, Paul Lessingham, where none but you could see it,—did you? You hid it as one hides treasure. There should be something here worth having, worth seeing, worth knowing,—yes, worth knowing!—since you found it worth your while to hide it up so closely."

As I have said, the packet was bound about by a string of pink-ribbon,—a fact on which he presently began to comment.

"With what a pretty string you have encircled it,—and how neatly it is tied! Surely only a woman's hand could tie a knot like that,—who would have guessed yours were such agile fingers?—So! An endorsement on the cover! What's this?—let's see what's written!—'The letters of my dear love, Marjorie Lindon.'"

As he read these words, which, as he said, were endorsed upon the outer sheet of paper which served as a cover for the letters which were enclosed within, his face became transfigured. Never did I suppose that rage could have so possessed a human countenance. His jaw dropped open so that his yellow fangs gleamed through his parted lips,—he held his breath so long that each moment I looked to see him fall down in a fit; the veins stood out all over his face and head like seams of blood. I know not how long he continued speechless. When his breath returned, it was with chokings and gaspings in the midst of which he hissed out his words, as if their mere passage through his throat brought him near to strangulation.

"The letters of his dear love!—of his dear love!—his!—Paul Lessingham's!—So!—It is as I guessed,—as I knew,—as I saw!— Marjorie Lindon!—Sweet Marjorie!—His dear love!—Paul Lessingham's dear love!—She with the lily face, the corn-hued hair!—What is it his dear love has found in her fond heart to write Paul Lessingham?"

Sitting up in bed he tore the packet open. It contained, perhaps, eight or nine letters,—some mere notes, some long epistles. But, short or long, he devoured them with equal appetite, each one over and over again, till I thought he never would have done re-reading them. They were on thick white paper, of a peculiar shade of whiteness, with untrimmed edges. On each sheet a crest and an address were stamped in gold, and all the sheets were of the same shape and size. I told myself that if anywhere, at any time, I saw writing paper like that again, I should not fail to know it. The caligraphy was, like the paper, unusual, bold, decided, and, I should have guessed, produced by a J pen.[1]

All the time that he was reading he kept emitting sounds, more resembling yelps and snarls than anything more human,—like some savage beast nursing its pent-up rage. When he had made an end of reading,—for the season,—he let his passion have full vent.

"So!—That is what his dear love has found it in her heart to write Paul Lessingham!—Paul Lessingham!"

Pen cannot describe the concentrated frenzy of hatred with which the speaker dwelt upon the name,—it was demoniac.

"It is enough!—it is the end!—it is his doom! He shall be ground between the upper and the nether stones in the towers of anguish, and all that is left of him shall be cast on the accursed stream of the bitter waters, to stink under the blood-grimed sun! And for her—for Marjorie Lindon!—for his dear love!—it shall come to pass that she shall wish that she was never born,—nor he!—and the gods of the shadows shall smell the sweet incense of her suffering!—It shall be! it shall be! It is I that say it,—even I!"

---

[1] A steel nibbed pen produced by C. Brandauer & Co., Birmingham, England, in the nineteenth century, and favoured by cartoonists and calligraphers.

In the madness of his rhapsodical frenzy I believe that he had actually forgotten I was there. But, on a sudden, glancing aside, he saw me, and remembered,—and was prompt to take advantage of an opportunity to wreak his rage upon a tangible object.

"It is you!—you thief!—you still live!—to make a mock of one of the children of the gods!"

He leaped, shrieking, off the bed, and sprang at me, clasping my throat with his horrid hands, bearing me backwards on to the floor; I felt his breath mingle with mine and then God, in His mercy, sent oblivion.

BOOK II

THE HAUNTED MAN

THE STORY ACCORDING TO·
SYDNEY ATHERTON, ESQUIRE

CHAPTER 10

REJECTED

It was after our second waltz I did it. In the usual quiet corner,—which, that time, was in the shadow of a palm in the hall. Before I had got into my stride she checked me,—touching my sleeve with her fan, turning towards me with startled eyes.

"Stop, please!"

But I was not to be stopped. Cliff Challoner passed, with Gerty Cazel. I fancy that, as he passed, he nodded. I did not care, I was wound up to go, and I went it. No man knows how he can talk till he does talk,—to the girl he wants to marry. It is my impression that I gave her recollections of the Restoration poets. She seemed surprised,—not having previously detected in me the poetic strain, and insisted on cutting in.

"Mr. Atherton, I am so sorry."

Then I did let fly.

"Sorry that I love you!—why? Why should you be sorry that you have become the one thing needful in any man's eyes,—even in mine? The one thing precious,—the one thing to be altogether esteemed! Is it so common for a woman to come across a man who would be willing to lay down his life for her that she should be sorry when she finds him?"

"I did not know that you felt like this, though I confess that I have had my—my doubts."

"Doubts!—I thank you."

"You are quite aware, Mr. Atherton, that I like you very much."

"Like me!—Bah!"

"I cannot help liking you, —though it may be 'bah.'"

"I don't want you to like me,—I want you to love me."

"Precisely,—that is your mistake."

"My mistake!—in wanting you to love me!—when I love you—"

"Then you shouldn't,—though I can't help thinking that you are mistaken even there."

"Mistaken!—in supposing that I love you! —when I assert and reassert it with the whole force of my being! What do you want me to do to prove I love you,—take you in my arms and crush you to my bosom, and make a spectacle of you before every creature in the place?"

"I'd rather you wouldn't, and perhaps you wouldn't mind not talking quite so loud. Mr. Challoner seems to be wondering what you're shouting about."

"You shouldn't torture me."

She opened and shut her fan,—as she looked down at it I am disposed to suspect that she smiled.

"I am glad we have had this little explanation, because, of course, you are my friend."

"I am not your friend."

"Pardon me, you are."

"I say I'm not,—if I can't be something else, I'll be no friend."

She went on,—calmly ignoring me,—playing with her fan.

"As it happens, I am, just now, in rather a delicate position, in which a friend is welcome."

"What's the matter? Who's been worrying you,—your father?"

"Well,—he has not,—as yet; but he may be soon."

"What's in the wind?"

"Mr. Lessingham."

She dropped her voice,—and her eyes. For the moment I did not catch her meaning.

"What?"

"Your friend, Mr. Lessingham."

"Excuse me, Miss Lindon, but I am by no means sure that anyone is entitled to call Mr. Lessingham a friend of mine."

"What!—Not when I am going to be his wife?"

That took me aback. I had had my suspicions that Paul Lessingham was more with Marjorie than he had any right to be, but I had never supposed that she could see anything desirable in a stick of a man like that. Not to speak of a hundred and one other considerations,—Lessingham on one side of the House, and her father on the other;[1] and old Lindon girding

---

[1]   The Houses of Parliament are divided into two houses, the Commons, where Paul Lessingham and Marjorie's father sit with other elected Members of Parliament, and the Lords, occupied by unelected peers. At the time of the novel, in the Commons, the Liberal Party, of which Lessingham is a member, occupies one side of the House, while the Conservative party occupies the other. The side on which the parties sit is determined by which party is in power.

at him anywhere and everywhere—with his high-dried Tory notions of his family importance,—to say nothing of his fortune.

I don't know if I looked what I felt,—if I did, I looked uncommonly blank.

"You have chosen an appropriate moment, Miss Lindon, to make to me such a communication."

She chose to disregard my irony.

"I am glad you think so, because now you will understand what a difficult position I am in."

"I offer you my hearty congratulations."

"And I thank you for them, Mr. Atherton, in the spirit in which they are offered, because from you I know they mean so much."

I bit my lip,—for the life of me I could not tell how she wished me to read her words.

"Do I understand that this announcement has been made to me as one of the public?"

"You do not. It is made to you, in confidence, as my friend,—as my greatest friend; because a husband is something more than friend." My pulses tingled. "You will be on my side?"

She had paused,—and I stayed silent.

"On your side,—or Mr. Lessingham's?"

"His side is my side, and my side is his side;—you will be on our side?"

"I am not sure that I altogether follow you."

"You are the first I have told. When papa hears it is possible that there will be trouble,—as you know. He thinks so much of you and of your opinion; when that trouble comes I want you to be on our side,— on my side."

"Why should I?—what does it matter? You are stronger than your father,—and it is just possible that Lessingham is stronger than you; together, from your father's point of view, you will be invincible."

"You are my friend,—are you not my friend?"

"In effect, you offer me the Apple of Sodom."[1]

"Thank you;—I did not think you so unkind."

"And you,—are you kind? I make you an avowal of my love, and, straightway, you ask me to act as chorus to the love of another."

---

[1] A mythical tree found in Medieval Christian narrative, reputed to stand on the site of the city of Sodom and Gomorrah. According to the myth any apple picked from the tree will turn to dust and ashes in the hand. Sidney is saying that, in effect, Marjorie's friendship is worthless.

"How could I tell you loved me,—as you say! I had no notion. You have known me all your life, yet you have not breathed a word of it till now."

"If I had spoken before?"

I imagine that there was a slight movement of her shoulders,— almost amounting to a shrug.

"I do not know that it would have made any difference.—I do not pretend that it would. But I do know this, I believe that you yourself have only discovered the state of your own mind within the last half-hour."

If she had slapped my face she could not have startled me more. I had no notion if her words were uttered at random, but they came so near the truth they held me breathless. It was a fact that only during the last few minutes had I really realised how things were with me,— only since the end of that first waltz that the flame had burst out in my soul which was now consuming me. She had read me by what seemed so like a flash of inspiration that I hardly knew what to say to her. I tried to be stinging.

"You flatter me, Miss Lindon, you flatter me at every point. Had you only discovered to me the state of your mind a little sooner I should not have discovered to you the state of mine at all."

"We will consider it *terra incognita*."[1]

"Since you wish it." Her provoking calmness stirred me,—and the suspicion that she was laughing at me in her sleeve. I gave her a glimpse of the cloven hoof. "But, at the same time, since you assert that you have so long been innocent, I beg that you will continue so no more. At least, your innocence shall be without excuse. For I wish you to understand that I love you, that I have loved you, that I shall love you. Any understanding you may have with Mr. Lessingham will not make the slightest difference. I warn you, Miss Lindon, that, until death, you will have to write me down your lover."

She looked at me, with wide open eyes,—as if I almost frightened her. To be frank, that was what I wished to do.

"Mr. Atherton!"

"Miss Lindon?"

"That is not like you at all."

"We seem to be making each other's acquaintance for the first time."

She continued to gaze at me with her big eyes,—which, to be candid, I found it difficult to meet. On a sudden her face was lighted by a smile,—which I resented.

---

[1] Unknown or secret ground.

"Not after all these years,—not after all these years! I know you, and though I daresay you're not flawless, I fancy you'll be found to ring pretty true."

Her manner was almost sisterly,—elder-sisterly. I could have shaken her. Hartridge coming to claim his dance gave me an opportunity to escape with such remnants of dignity as I could gather about me. He dawdled up,—his thumbs, as usual, in his waistcoat pockets.

"I believe, Miss Lindon, this is our dance."

She acknowledged it with a bow, and rose to take his arm. I got up and left her, without a word.

As I crossed the hall I chanced on Percy Woodville. He was in his familiar state of fluster, and was gaping about him as if he had mislaid the Koh-i-noor,[1] and wondered where in thunder it had got to. When he saw it was I he caught me by the arm.

"I say, Atherton, have you seen Miss Lindon?"

"I have."

"No!—Have you?—By Jove!—Where? I've been looking for her all over the place, except in the cellars and the attics,—and I was just going to commence on them. This is our dance."

"In that case, she's shunted you."

"No!—Impossible!" His mouth went like an O,—and his eyes ditto, his eyeglass clattering down on to his shirt front. "I expect the mistake's mine. Fact is, I've made a mess of my programme. It's either the last dance, or this dance, or the next, that I've booked with her, but I'm hanged if I know which. Just take a squint at it, there's a good chap, and tell me which one you think it is."

I "took a squint"—since he held the thing within an inch of my nose I could hardly help it; one "squint," and that was enough—and more. Some men's ball programmes are studies in impressionism, Percy's seemed to me to be a study in madness. It was covered with hiero-glyphics, but what they meant, or what they did there anyhow, it was absurd to suppose that I could tell,—I never put them there!—Proverbially, the man's a champion hasher.[2]

---

[1]   Its name meaning "mountain of light," the Koh-i-noor diamond was found by British colonial officials in 1849 upon the annexation of the Punjab. It was found in the city of Lahore and presented to Queen Victoria in the following year by Lord Dalhousie. The stone was subsequently placed in a crown made for Elizabeth, the late Queen Mother, for her coronation as Queen Consort and Empress of India. The story of the Koh-i-noor served as a source for Wilkie Collins' novel, *The Moonstone* (1868).

[2]   Someone who makes a mess of something.

"I regret, my dear Percy, that I am not an expert in cuneiform[1] writing. If you have any doubt as to which dance is yours you'd better ask the lady,—she'll feel flattered."

Leaving him to do his own addling I went to find my coat,—I panted to get into the open air; as for dancing I felt that I loathed it. Just as I neared the cloak-room someone stopped me. It was Dora Grayling.

"Have you forgotten that this is our dance?"

I had forgotten,—clean. And I was not obliged by her remembering. Though as I looked at her sweet, grey eyes, and at the soft contours of her gentle face, I felt that I deserved well kicking. She is an angel,—one of the best!—but I was in no mood for angels. Not for a very great deal would I have gone through that dance just then, nor, with Dora Grayling, of all women in the world, would I have sat it out.—So I was a brute and blundered.

"You must forgive me, Miss Grayling, but—I am not feeling very well, and—I don't think I'm up to any more dancing.—Good-night."

CHAPTER 11

A MIDNIGHT EPISODE

The weather out of doors was in tune with my frame of mind,—I was in a deuce of a temper, and it was a deuce of a night. A keen north-east wind, warranted to take the skin right off you, was playing catch-who-catch-can with intermittent gusts of blinding rain. Since it was not fit for a dog to walk, none of your cabs for me,—nothing would serve but pedestrian exercise.

So I had it.

I went down Park Lane,—and the wind and rain went with me, — also, thoughts of Dora Grayling. What a bounder[2] I had been,—and was! If there is anything in worse taste than to book a lady for a dance, and then to leave her in the lurch, I should like to know what that thing

---

[1] A type of writing composed of wedge-shaped or arrow-headed elements. The term is used to describe the ancient writings of Persia, Assyria, and other civilizations with similar forms of inscription.

[2] Someone who behaves improperly or rudely.

is,—when found it ought to be made a note of. If any man of my acquaintance allowed himself to be guilty of such a felony in the first degree, I should cut him. I wished someone would try to cut me,—I should like to see him at it.

It was all Marjorie's fault,—everything! past, present, and to come! I had known that girl when she was in long frocks,—I had, at that period of our acquaintance, pretty recently got out of them; when she was advanced to short ones; and when, once more, she returned to long. And all that time,—well, I was nearly persuaded that the whole of the time I had loved her. If I had not mentioned it, it was because I had suffered my affection, "like the worm, to lie hidden in the bud,"[1] —or whatever it is the fellow says.

At any rate, I was perfectly positive that if I had had the faintest notion that she would ever seriously consider such a man as Lessingham I should have loved her long ago. Lessingham! Why, he was old enough to be her father,—at least he was a good many years older than I was. And a wretched Radical! It is true that on certain points I, also, am what some people would call a Radical,—but not a radical of the kind he is. Thank heaven, no! No doubt I have admired traits in his character, until I learnt this thing of him. I am even prepared to admit that he is a man of ability,—in his way! which is, emphatically, not mine. But to think of him in connection with such a girl as Marjorie Lindon,—preposterous! Why, the man's as dry as a stick,—drier! And cold as an iceberg. Nothing but a politician, absolutely. He a lover!—how I could fancy such a stroke of humour setting all the benches in a roar. Both by education, and by nature, he was incapable of even playing such a part; as for being the thing,—absurd! If you were to sink a shaft from the crown of his head to the soles of his feet, you would find inside him nothing but the dry bones of parties and politics.

What my Marjorie—if everyone had his own, she is mine, and, in that sense, she always will be mine—what my Marjorie could see in such a dry-as-dust out of which even to construct the rudiments of a husband was beyond my fathoming.

Suchlike agreeable reflections were fit company for the wind and the wet, so they bore me company all down the lane. I crossed at the corner, going round the hospital towards the square. This brought me to the

---

[1] Atherton gets the quotation from *Twelfth Night* wrong. Viola, responding to the Duke, remarks, "She never told her love, / But let concealment, like a worm i' the bud, / Feed on her damask cheek" (II.iv.110-12).

abiding-place of Paul the Apostle. Like the idiot I was, I went out into the middle of the street, and stood awhile in the mud to curse him and his house,—on the whole, when one considers that that is the kind of man I can be, it is, perhaps, not surprising that Marjorie disdained me.

"May your following," I cried,—and it is an absolute fact that the words were shouted!—"both in the House and out of it, no longer regard you as a leader! May your party follow after other gods! May your political aspirations wither, and your speeches be listened to by empty benches! May the Speaker persistently and strenuously refuse to allow you to catch his eye, and, at the next election, may your constituency reject you!— Jehoram![1] —what's that?"

I might well ask. Until that moment I had appeared to be the only lunatic at large, either outside the house or in it, but, on a sudden, a second lunatic came on the scene, and that with a vengeance. A window was crashed open from within,—the one over the front door, and someone came plunging through it on to the top of the portico. That it was a case of intended suicide I made sure, —and I began to be in hopes that I was about to witness the suicide of Paul. But I was not so assured of the intention when the individual in question began to scramble down the pillar of the porch in the most extraordinary fashion I ever witnessed,—I was not even convinced of a suicidal purpose when he came tumbling down, and lay sprawling in the mud at my feet.

I fancy if I had performed that portion of the act I should have lain quiet for a second or two, to consider whereabouts I was, and which end of me was uppermost. But there was no nonsense of that sort about that singularly agile stranger,—if he was not made of indiarubber[2] he ought to have been. So to speak, before he was down he was up,—it was all I could do to grab at him before he was off like a rocket.

Such a figure as he presented is seldom seen,—at least, in the streets of London. What he had done with the rest of his apparel I am not in a position to say,—all that was left of it was a long, dark cloak which he strove to wrap round him. Save for that,—and mud!—he was bare as the palm of my hand. Yet it was his face that held me. In my time I have

---

[1]   According to 2 Kings 8:16, Jehoram, the son of Jehoshaphat, became King of Judah in the fifth year of the reign of Joram, King of Israel.

[2]   Later shortened to rubber, indiarubber is the coagulated juice of trees, useful for the production of a number of different products. What is interesting, and perhaps significant, about this and other fleeting references and allusions throughout the novel is their colonial context relating to the principal narrative concerning the Beetle's desire for vengeance against Paul Lessingham.

seen strange expressions on men's faces, but never before one such as I saw on his. He looked like a man might look who, after living a life of undiluted crime, at last finds himself face to face with the devil. It was not the look of a madman,—far from it; it was something worse.

It was the expression on the man's countenance, as much as anything else, which made me behave as I did. I said something to him,—some nonsense, I know not what. He regarded me with a silence which was supernatural. I spoke to him again;—not a word issued from those rigid lips; there was not a tremor of those awful eyes,—eyes which I was tolerably convinced saw something which I had never seen, or ever should. Then I took my hand from off his shoulder, and let him go. I know not why,—I did.

He had remained as motionless as a statue while I held him,—indeed, for any evidence of life he gave, he might have been a statue; but, when my grasp was loosed, how he ran! He had turned the corner and was out of sight before I could say, "How do!"

It was only then,—when he had gone, and I had realised the extra-double-express-flash-of-lightning rate at which he had taken his departure—that it occurred to me of what an extremely sensible act I had been guilty in letting him go at all. Here was an individual who had been committing burglary, or something very like it, in the house of a budding cabinet minister, and who had tumbled plump into my arms, so that all I had to do was to call a policeman and get him quodded,[1]— and all that I had done was something of a totally different kind.

"You're a nice type of an ideal citizen!" I was addressing myself. "A first chop[2] specimen of a low-down idiot,—to connive at the escape of the robber who's been robbing Paul. Since you've let the villain go, the least you can do is to leave a card on the Apostle, and inquire how he's feeling."

I went to Lessingham's front door and knocked,—I knocked once, I knocked twice, I knocked thrice, and the third time, I give you my word, I made the echoes ring,—but there was still not a soul that answered.

"If this is a case of a seven or seventy-fold murder, and the gentleman in the cloak has made a fair clearance of every living creature the house contains, perhaps it's just as well I've chanced upon the scene,—still I do think that one of the corpses might get up to answer the door. If it is possible to make noise enough to waken the dead, you bet I'm on to it."

---

[1]   Slang, to quod someone is to put them in gaol.
[2]   Of Anglo-Indian origin, meaning first rate or high quality.

And I was,—I punished that knocker! until I warrant the pounding I gave it was audible on the other side of Green Park.[I] And, at last, I woke the dead,—or, rather, I roused Matthews to a consciousness that something was going on.

Opening the door about six inches, through the interstice he protruded his ancient nose.

"Who's there?"

"Nothing, my dear sir, nothing and no one. It must have been your vigorous imagination which induced you to suppose that there was,— you let it run away with you."

Then he knew me,—opened the door about two feet.

"Oh, it's you, Mr. Atherton. I beg your pardon, sir,—I thought it might have been the police."

"What then? Do you stand in terror of the minions of the law,—at last?"

A most discreet servant, Matthews,—just the fellow for a budding cabinet minister. He glanced over his shoulder,—I had suspected the presence of a colleague at his back, now I was assured. He put his hand up to his mouth,—and I thought how exceedingly discreet he looked, in his trousers and his stockinged feet, and with his hair all rumpled, and his braces dangling behind, and his nightshirt creased.

"Well, sir, I have received instructions not to admit the police."

"The deuce you have!—From whom?"

Coughing behind his hand, leaning forward, he addressed me with an air which was flatteringly confidential.

"From Mr. Lessingham, sir."

"Possibly Mr. Lessingham is not aware that a robbery has been committed on his premises, that the burglar has just come out of his drawing-room window with a hop, skip, and a jump, bounded out of the window like a tennis-ball, flashed round the corner like a rocket."

Again Matthews glanced over his shoulder, as if not clear which way discretion lay, whether fore or aft.

"Thank you, sir. I believe that Mr. Lessingham is aware of something of the kind." He seemed to come to a sudden resolution, dropping his voice to a whisper. "The fact is, sir, that I fancy Mr. Lessingham's a good deal upset."

"Upset?" I stared at him. There was something in his manner I did not understand. "What do you mean by upset? Has the scoundrel attempted violence?"

[I]   The smallest of London's Royal Parks, close to Buckingham Palace.

"Who's there?"

The voice was Lessingham's, calling to Matthews from the staircase, though, for an instant, I hardly recognised it, it was so curiously petulant. Pushing past Matthews, I stepped into the hall. A young man, I suppose a footman, in the same undress as Matthews, was holding a candle,—it seemed the only light about the place. By its glimmer I perceived Lessingham standing half-way up the stairs. He was in full war paint,—as he is not the sort of man who dresses for the House, I took it that he had been mixing pleasure with business.

"It's I, Lessingham,—Atherton. Do you know that a fellow has jumped out of your drawing-room window?"

It was a second or two before he answered. When he did, his voice had lost its petulance.

"Has he escaped?"

"Clean,—he's a mile away by now."

It seemed to me that in his tone, when he spoke again, there was a note of relief.

"I wondered if he had. Poor fellow! more sinned against than sinning![1] Take my advice, Atherton, and keep out of politics. They bring you into contact with all the lunatics at large. Good night! I am much obliged to you for knocking us up. Matthews, shut the door."

Tolerably cool, on my honour,—a man who brings news big with the fate of Rome does not expect to receive such treatment. He expects to be listened to with deference, and to hear all that there is to hear, and not to be sent to the right-about before he has had a chance of really opening his lips. Before I know it—almost!—the door was shut, and I was on the doorstep. Confound the Apostle's impudence! Next time he might have his house burnt down—and him in it! before I took the trouble to touch his dirty knocker.

What did he mean by his allusion to lunatics in politics,—did he think to fool me? There was more in the business than met the eye,—and a good deal more than he wished to meet mine,—hence his insolence. The creature.

What Marjorie Lindon could see in such an opusculum[2] surpassed my comprehension; especially when there was a man of my sort walking about, who adored the very ground she trod upon.

---

[1] "I am a man / More sinn'd against than sinning" *King Lear* (III.iii.58–59).

[2] A little or insignificant piece of work.

CHAPTER 12

A MORNING VISITOR

All through the night, waking and sleeping, and in my dreams, I wondered what Marjorie could see in him! In those same dreams I satisfied myself that she could, and did, see nothing in him, but everything in me,—oh the comfort! The misfortune was that when I awoke I knew it was the other way round, so that it was a sad awakening. An awakening to thoughts of murder.

So swallowing a mouthful and a peg,[1] I went into my laboratory to plan murder—legalised murder—on the biggest scale it ever has been planned. I was on the track of a weapon which would make war not only an affair of a single campaign, but of a single half-hour. It would not want an army to work it either. Once let an individual, or two or three at most, in possession of my weapon-that-was-to-be, get within a mile or so of even the largest body of disciplined troops that ever yet a nation put into the field, and —pouf!—in about the time it takes you to say that they would all be dead men. If weapons of precision, which may be relied upon to slay, are preservers of the peace—and the man is a fool who says that they are not!—then I was within reach of the finest preserver of the peace imagination had ever yet conceived.

What a sublime thought to think that in the hollow of your own hand lies the life and death of nations,—and it was almost in mine.

I had in front of me some of the finest destructive agents you could wish to light upon—carbon-monoxide, chlorine-trioxide, mercuric-oxide, conine, potassimide, potassium-carboxide, cyanogens[2]—when Edwards entered, I was wearing a mask of my own invention, a thing that covered ears and head and everything, something like a diver's helmet—I was dealing with gases a sniff of which meant death; only a few days before, unmasked, I had been doing some fool's trick with a couple of acids —sulphuric and cyanide of potassium—when, somehow, my hand slipped, and, before I knew it, minute portions of them combined. By the mercy of Providence I fell backwards instead of

---

[1] Another term with a colonial context, it can either mean a segment of citrus fruit or, as is more likely in this case, a drink of Brandy and water; this latter use is of Anglo-Indian origin.
[2] All are poisonous gasses.

forwards; sequel, about an hour afterwards Edwards found me on the floor, and it took me the remainder of the day, and most of the doctors in town, to bring me back to life again.

Edwards announced his presence by touching me on the shoulder,—when I am wearing that mask it isn't always easy to make me hear.

"Someone wishes to see you, sir."

"Then tell someone that I don't wish to see him."

Well-trained servant, Edwards,—he walked off with the message as decorously as you please. And then I thought there was an end,—but there wasn't.

I was regulating the valve of a cylinder in which I was fusing some oxides when, once more, someone touched me on the shoulder. Without turning I took it for granted it was Edwards back again.

"I have only to give a tiny twist to this tap, my good fellow, and you will be in the land where the bogies bloom. Why will you come where you're not wanted?" Then I looked round. "Who the devil are you?"

For it was not Edwards at all, but quite a different class of character.

I found myself confronting an individual who might almost have sat for one of the bogies I had just alluded to. His costume was reminiscent of the "Algerians"[1] whom one finds all over France, and who are the most persistent, insolent and amusing of pedlars. I remember one who used to haunt the *répétitions* at the Alcazar at Tours,[2]—but there! This individual was like the originals, yet unlike,—he was less gaudy, and a good deal dingier, than his Gallic prototypes are apt to be. Then he wore a burnoose,[3]—the yellow, grimy-looking article of the Arab of the Soudan, not the spick and span Arab of the boulevard. Chief difference of all, his face was clean shaven,—and whoever saw an Algerian of Paris whose chiefest glory was not his well-trimmed moustache and beard?

I expected that he would address me in the lingo which these gentlemen call French,—but he didn't.

"You are Mr. Atherton?"

"And you are Mr.—Who?—how did you come here? Where's my servant?"

---

[1] While, because of colonial occupation of Algeria by France, Algerians would be found in France, Atherton intends the phrase as derogatory and racist, referring to any itinerant travelling vendor of North African origin.

[2] "Répétitions" refers to theatrical rehearsals; while there was an Alcazar theatre in Marseilles, I have been unable to find evidence of a theatre with this name in Tours.

[3] An Arab or Moorish hooded cloak.

The fellow held up his hand. As he did so, as if in accordance with a pre-arranged signal, Edwards came into the room looking excessively startled. I turned to him.

"Is this the person who wished to see me?"

"Yes, sir."

"Didn't I tell you to say that I didn't wish to see him?"

"Yes, sir."

"Then why didn't you do as I told you?"

"I did, sir."

"Then how comes he here?"

"Really, sir,"—Edwards put his hand up to his head as if he was half asleep—"I don't quite know."

"What do you mean by you don't know? Why didn't you stop him?"

"I think, sir, that I must have had a touch of sudden faintness, because I tried to put out my hand to stop him, and—I couldn't."

"You're an idiot,—Go!" And he went. I turned to the stranger. "Pray, sir, are you a magician?"

He replied to my question with another.

"You, Mr. Atherton,—are you also a magician?"

He was staring at my mask with an evident lack of comprehension.

"I wear this because, in this place, death lurks in so many subtle forms, that, without it, I dare not breathe." He inclined his head,—though I doubt if he understood.

"Be so good as to tell me, briefly, what it is you wish with me."

He slipped his hand into the folds of his burnoose, and, taking out a slip of paper, laid it on the shelf by which we were standing. I glanced at it, expecting to find on it a petition, or a testimonial, or a true statement of his sad case; instead it contained two words only,—"Marjorie Lindon." The unlooked-for-sight of that well-loved name brought the blood into my cheeks.

"You come from Miss Lindon?"

He narrowed his shoulders, brought his finger-tips together, inclined his head, in a fashion which was peculiarly Oriental,[1] but not particularly explanatory,—so I repeated my question.

---

[1] Atherton uses the word here and elsewhere in *The Beetle* in a general sense to refer to Eastern, non-European cultures or, more specifically, discourses constructing representations of those cultures from a Western perspective. For an extended critical exploration of the concept of Orientalism and its discursive production in Western culture and literature over several centuries, see Edward Said's *Orientalism* (1978).

"Do you wish me to understand that you do come from Miss Lindon?"

Again he slipped his hand into his burnoose, again he produced a slip of paper, again he laid it on the shelf, again I glanced at it, again nothing was written on it but a name,—"Paul Lessingham."

"Well?—I see,—Paul Lessingham.—What then?"

"She is good,—he is bad,—is it not so?"

He touched first one scrap of paper, then the other. I stared.

"Pray how do you happen to know?"

"He shall never have her,—eh?"

"What on earth do you mean?"

"Ah!—what do I mean!"

"Precisely, what do you mean? And also, and at the same time, who the devil are you?"

"It is as a friend that I come to you."

"Then in that case you may go; I happen to be over-stocked in that line just now."

"Not with the kind of friend I am!"

"The saints forefend!"

"You love her,—you love Miss Lindon! Can you bear to think of him in her arms?"

I took off my mask,—feeling that the occasion required it. As I did so he brushed aside the hanging folds of the hood of his burnoose, so that I saw more of his face. I was immediately conscious that in his eyes there was, in an especial degree, what, for want of a better term, one may call the mesmeric quality. That his was one of those morbid organisations which are oftener found, thank goodness, in the east than in the west, and which are apt to exercise an uncanny influence over the weak and foolish folk with whom they come in contact,—the kind of creature for whom it is always just as well to keep a seasoned rope handy. I was, also, conscious that he was taking advantage of the removal of my mask to try his strength on me,—than which he could not have found a tougher job. The sensitive something which is found in the hypnotic subject happens, in me, to be wholly absent.

"I see you are a mesmerist."

He started.

"I am nothing,—a shadow!"

"And I'm a scientist. I should like, with your permission—or without it!—to try an experiment or two on you."

He moved further back. There came a gleam into his eyes which suggested that he possessed his hideous power to an unusual degree,—

that, in the estimation of his own people, he was qualified to take his standing as a regular evil-doctor.

"We will try experiments together, you and I,—on Paul Lessingham."

"Why on him?"

"You do not know?"

"I do not."

"Why do you lie to me?"

"I don't lie to you,—I haven't the faintest notion what is the nature of your interest in Mr. Lessingham."

"My interest?—that is another thing; it is your interest of which we are speaking."

"Pardon me,—it is yours."

"Listen!—you love her,—and he! But at a word from you he shall not have her,—never! It is I who say it,—I!"

"And, once more, sir, who are you?"

"I am of the children of Isis!"[1]

"Is that so?—it occurs to me that you have made a slight mistake,— this is London, not a dog-hole in the desert."

"Do I not know?—what does it matter?—you shall see! There will come a time when you will want me,—you will find that you cannot bear to think of him in her arms, her whom you love! You will call to me, and I shall come, and of Paul Lessingham there shall be an end."

While I was wondering whether he was really as mad as he sounded, or whether he was some impudent charlatan who had an axe of his own to grind, and thought that he had found in me a grindstone, he had vanished from the room. I moved after him.

"Hang it all!—stop!" I cried.

He must have made pretty good travelling, because, before I had a foot in the hall, I heard the front door slam, and, when I reached the

---

[1] The Cult of Isis centered on Osiris and Isis, Egyptian deities. The practices of the cult developed around the myth of the death and rebirth of Osiris, who is both husband and brother to Isis. The cult's rituals remain for the most part a mystery (as Paul Lessingham's remarks further on in this chapter make clear), though it is known that initiation into the cult involved a symbolic death and rebirth, by which new members would be purified by Isis. Forms of material sacrifice linked to symbolic death and rebirth were of great importance. Spreading throughout the Hellenic world from c. 4th century BC, the cult was brought back to the Roman Empire during the Egyptian campaigns of the Second Triumvirate, and enjoyed a popular following until challenged by the rise of Christianity. It seems certain that the worship of the Virgin Mary in early Christianity develops and is influenced by worship of Isis.

street, intent on calling him back, neither to the right nor to the left was there a sign of him to be seen.

CHAPTER 13

THE PICTURE

"I wonder what that nice-looking beggar really means, and who he happens to be?" That was what I said to myself when I returned to the laboratory. "If it is true that, now and again, Providence does write a man's character on his face, then there can't be the slightest shred of a doubt that a curious one's been written on his. I wonder what his connection has been with the Apostle,—or if it's only part of his game of bluff."

I strode up and down,—for the moment my interest in the experiments I was conducting had waned.

"If it was all bluff I never saw a better piece of acting,—and yet what sort of finger can such a precisian[1] as St Paul have in such a pie? The fellow seemed to squirm at the mere mention of the rising-hope-of-the-Radicals' name. Can the objection be political? Let me consider,—what has Lessingham done which could offend the religious or patriotic susceptibilities of the most fanatical of Orientals? Politically, I can recall nothing. Foreign affairs, as a rule, he has carefully eschewed. If he has offended—and if he hasn't the seeming was uncommonly good!—the cause will have to be sought upon some other track. But, then, what track?"

The more I strove to puzzle it out, the greater the puzzlement grew.

"Absurd!—The rascal has had no more connection with St Paul than St Peter. The probability is that he's a crack-pot; and if he isn't, he has some little game on foot—in close association with the hunt of the oof-bird!—my Marjorie! —only she isn't mine, confound it!—if I had had my senses about me, I should have broken his head in several places for daring to allow her name to pass his lips,—the unbaptised Mohammedan!—Now to return to the chase of splendid murder!"

I snatched up my mask—one of the most ingenious inventions, by the way, of recent years; if the armies of the future wear my mask they

---

[1] Someone strict in the observance of rules or protocol, or one who is precise in religious observance.

will defy my weapon!—and was about to re-adjust it in its place, when someone knocked at the door.

"Who's there?—Come in!"

It was Edwards. He looked round him as if surprised.

"I beg your pardon, sir,—I thought you were engaged. I didn't know that— that gentleman had gone."

"He went up the chimney, as all that kind of gentlemen do.—Why the deuce did you let him in when I told you not to?"

"Really, sir, I don't know. I gave him your message, and—he looked at me, and—that is all I remember till I found myself standing in this room."

Had it not been Edwards I might have suspected him of having had his palm well greased,—but, in his case, I knew better. It was as I thought,—my visitor was a mesmerist of the first class; he had actually played some of his tricks, in broad daylight, on my servant, at my own front door,—a man worth studying. Edwards continued.

"There is someone else, sir, who wishes to see you,—Mr. Lessingham."

"Mr. Lessingham!" At that moment the juxtaposition seemed odd, though I daresay it was so rather in appearance than in reality. "Show him in."

Presently in came Paul.

I am free to confess,—I have owned it before!—that, in a sense, I admire that man,—so long as he does not presume to thrust himself into a certain position. He possesses physical qualities which please my eye—speaking as a mere biologist, I like the suggestion conveyed by his every pose, his every movement, of a tenacious hold on life,—of reserve force, of a repository of bone and gristle on which he can fall back at pleasure. The fellow's lithe and active; not hasty, yet agile; clean built, well hung,—the sort of man who might be relied upon to make a good recovery. You might beat him in a sprint,—mental or physical—though to do that you would have to be spry!—but in a staying race he would see you out. I do not know that he is exactly the kind of man whom I would trust,—unless I knew that he was on the job,—which knowledge, in his case, would be uncommonly hard to attain. He is too calm; too self-contained; with the knack of looking all round him even in moments of extremist peril,—and for whatever he does he has a good excuse. He has the reputation, both in the House and out of it, of being a man of iron nerve,—and with some reason; yet I am not so sure. Unless I read him wrongly his is one of those individualities which, confronted by certain eventualities, collapse,—to rise, the moment of trial having passed, like Phoenix from her ashes.[1] However it might be with his adherents, he would show no trace of his disaster.

And this was the man whom Marjorie loved. Well, she could show some cause. He was a man of position,—destined, probably, to rise much higher; a man of parts,—with capacity to make the most of them; not ill-looking; with agreeable manners,—when he chose; and he came within the lady's definition of a gentleman, "he always did the right thing, at the right time, in the right way." And yet —! Well, I take it that we are all cads, and that we most of us are prigs; for mercy's sake do not let us all give ourselves away.

He was dressed as a gentleman should be dressed,—black frock coat, black vest, dark grey trousers, stand-up collar, smartly-tied bow, gloves of the proper shade, neatly brushed hair, and a smile, which if it was not childlike, at any rate was bland.

"I am not disturbing you?"

"Not at all."

"Sure?—I never enter a place like this, where a man is matching himself with nature, to wrest from her her secrets, without feeling that I am crossing the threshold of the unknown. The last time I was in this room was just after you had taken out the final patents for your System of Telegraphy at Sea,[2] which the Admiralty purchased,—wisely—What is it, now?"

"Death."

"No?—really?—what do you mean?"

"If you are a member of the next government, you will possibly learn; I may offer them the refusal of a new wrinkle in the art of murder."

"I see,—a new projectile. How long is this race to continue between attack and defence?"

"Until the sun grows cold."

"And then?"

"There'll be no defence,—nothing to defend."

He looked at me with his calm, grave eyes.

---

[1]   A mythical bird attributed to Assyrian, Egyptian, Arabian, and other cultures. The earliest known reference to the myth of the phoenix is found in Hesiod (8th century BC). The bird is supposed to live for approximately 500 years before dying by self-immolation. After three days, a new phoenix is born from the ashes of the old bird.

[2]   Atherton's device is a little ahead of its time, as the earliest use of wireless marine telegraphy was in 1907, when the Marconi coastal station in Halifax began broadcasting to ships at sea and in 1908, when a ship responded to a telegraphic SOS, which saved over 1500 lives following the collision of two ships off Nantucket.

"The theory of the Age of Ice[1] towards which we are advancing is not a cheerful one." He began to finger a glass retort which lay upon a table. "By the way, it was very good of you to give me a look in last night. I am afraid you thought me peremptory,—I have come to apologise."

"I don't know that I thought you peremptory; I thought you—queer."

"Yes." He glanced at me with that expressionless look upon his face which he could summon at will, and which is at the bottom of the superstition about his iron nerve. "I was worried, and not well. Besides, one doesn't care to be burgled, even by a maniac."

"Was he a maniac?"

"Did you see him?"

"Clearly?"

"Where?"

"In the street."

"How close were you to him?"

"Closer than I am to you."

"Indeed. I didn't know you were so close to him as that. Did you try to stop him?"

"Easier said than done,—he was off at such a rate."

"Did you see how he was dressed,—or, rather, undressed?"

"I did."

"In nothing but a cloak on such a night. Who but a lunatic would have attempted burglary in such a costume?"

"Did he take anything?"

"Absolutely nothing."

"It seems to have been a curious episode."

He moved his eyebrows,—according to members of the House the only gesture in which he has been known to indulge.

"We become accustomed to curious episodes. Oblige me by not mentioning it to anyone,—to anyone." He repeated the last two words, as if to give them emphasis. I wondered if he was thinking of Marjorie. "I am communicating with the police. Until they move I don't want it to get into the papers,—or to be talked about. It's a worry,—you understand?"

I nodded. He changed the theme.

"This that you've engaged upon,—is it a projectile or a weapon?"

"If you are a member of the next government you will possibly know; if you aren't you possibly won't."

---

[1] There was some scientific speculation that the world was in an interglacial period and that another ice age would eventually occur.

"I suppose you have to keep this sort of thing secret?"

"I do. It seems that matters of much less moment you wish to keep secret."

"You mean that business of last night? If a trifle of that sort gets into the papers, or gets talked about,—which is the same thing!—you have no notion how we are pestered. It becomes an almost unbearable nuisance. Jones the Unknown can commit murder with less inconvenience to himself than Jones the Notorious can have his pocket picked,—there is not so much exaggeration in that as there sounds.— Good-bye,—thanks for your promise." I had given him no promise, but that was by the way. He turned as to go,—then stopped. "There's another thing,—I believe you're a specialist on questions of ancient superstitions and extinct religions."

"I am interested in such subjects, but I am not a specialist."

"Can you tell me what were the exact tenets of the worshippers of Isis?"

"Neither I nor any man,—with scientific certainty. As you know, she had a brother; the cult of Osiris and Isis was one and the same. What, precisely, were its dogmas, or its practices, or anything about it, none, now, can tell. The Papyri, hieroglyphics, and so on, which remain are very far from being exhaustive, and our knowledge of those which do remain, is still less so."

"I suppose that the marvels which are told of it are purely legendary?"

"To what marvels do you particularly refer?"

"Weren't supernatural powers attributed to the priests of Isis?"

"Broadly speaking, at that time, supernatural powers were attributed to all the priests of all the creeds."

"I see." Presently he continued. "I presume that her cult is long since extinct,—that none of the worshippers of Isis exist to-day."

I hesitated,—I was wondering why he had hit on such a subject; if he really had a reason, or if he was merely asking questions as a cover for something else,—you see, I knew my Paul.

"That is not so sure."

He looked at me with that passionless, yet searching glance of his.

"You think that she still is worshipped?"

"I think it possible, even probable, that, here and there, in Africa—Africa is a large order!—homage is paid to Isis, quite in the good old way."[1]

"Do you know that as a fact?"

---

[1] This is probably an indirect allusion to H. Rider Haggard's enormously successful *She* (1886).

"Excuse me, but do you know it as a fact?—Are you aware that you are treating me as if I was on the witness stand?—Have you any special purpose in making these inquiries?"

He smiled.

"In a kind of way I have. I have recently come across rather a curious story; I am trying to get to the bottom of it."

"What is the story?"

"I am afraid that at present I am not at liberty to tell it you; when I am I will. You will find it interesting,—as an instance of a singular survival.—Didn't the followers of Isis believe in transmigration?"

"Some of them,—no doubt."

"What did they understand by transmigration?"

"Transmigration."

"Yes, but of the soul or of the body?"

"How do you mean?—transmigration is transmigration. Are you driving at something in particular? If you tell me fairly and squarely what it is I'll do my best to give you the information you require; as it is, your questions are a bit perplexing."

"Oh, it doesn't matter,—as you say, 'transmigration is transmigration.'" I was eyeing him keenly; I seemed to detect in his manner an odd reluctance to enlarge on the subject he himself had started. He continued to trifle with the retort upon the table. "Hadn't the followers of Isis a—what shall I say?—a sacred emblem?"

"How?"

"Hadn't they an especial regard for some sort of a—wasn't it some sort of a—beetle?"

"You mean *Scarabaeus sacer*,[1]—according to Latreille,[2] *Scarabaeus Egyptiorum*? Undoubtedly,—the scarab was venerated throughout Egypt,—indeed, speaking generally, most things that had life, for instance, cats; as you know, Osiris continued among men in the figure of Apis, the bull."[3]

---

[1] Sacred scarab beetle. The Egyptians believed that the scarab beetle represented the sun god, Ra.

[2] Pierre-André Latreille (1762–1833), zoologist and entomologist, considered the father of modern entomology.

[3] The Apis bull cult was widespread in ancient Egypt, considered amongst the most sacred. According to Herodotus the Apis was the "calf of a cow which is never afterwards able to have another. The Egyptian belief is that a flash of lightning descends upon the cow from heaven, and this causes her to receive Apis." While Apis came to be known as an incarnation of Osiris, as Lessingham asserts, the bull was first thought to be an incarnation of Ptah, creator of the universe. The Apis bull could be recognized by particular markings including an image of a scarab under its tongue.

"Weren't the priests of Isis,—or some of them—supposed to assume, after death, the form of a—scarabaeus?"

"I never heard of it."

"Are you sure?—think!"

"I shouldn't like to answer such a question positively, offhand, but I don't, on the spur of the moment, recall any supposition of the kind."

"Don't laugh at me—I'm not a lunatic!—but I understand that recent researches have shown that even in some of the most astounding of the ancient legends there was a substratum of fact. Is it absolutely certain that there could be no shred of truth in such a belief?"

"In what belief?"

"In the belief that a priest of Isis—or anyone—assumed after death the form of a scarabeus?"

"It seems to me, Lessingham, that you have lately come across some uncommonly interesting data, of a kind, too, which it is your bounden duty to give to the world,—or, at any rate, to that portion of the world which is represented by me. Come,—tell us all about it!—what are you afraid of?"

"I am afraid of nothing,—and some day you shall be told,—but not now. At present, answer my question."

"Then repeat your question,—clearly."

"Is it absolutely certain that there could be no foundation of truth in the belief that a priest of Isis—or anyone—assumed after death the form of a beetle?"

"I know no more than the man in the moon,—how the dickens should I? Such a belief may have been symbolical. Christians believe that after death the body takes the shape of worms—and so, in a sense, it does—and, sometimes, eels."

"That is not what I mean."

"Then what do you mean?"

"Listen. If a person, of whose veracity there could not be a vestige of a doubt, assured you that he had seen such a transformation actually take place, could it conceivably be explained on natural grounds?"

"Seen a priest of Isis assume the form of a beetle?"

"Or a follower of Isis?"

"Before, or after death?"

He hesitated. I had seldom seen him wear such an appearance of interest,—to be frank, I was keenly interested too!—but, on a sudden there came into his eyes a glint of something that was almost terror. When he spoke, it was with the most unwonted awkwardness.

"In—in the very act of dying."

"In—in the very act of dying?"

"If—he had seen a follower of Isis in—the very act of dying, assume the form of a—a beetle, on any conceivable grounds would such transformation be susceptible of a natural explanation?"

I stared,—as who would not? Such an extraordinary question was rendered more extraordinary by coming from such a man,—yet I was almost beginning to suspect that there was something behind it more extraordinary still.

"Look here, Lessingham, I can see you've a capital tale to tell,—so tell it, man! Unless I'm mistaken, it's not the kind of tale in which ordinary scruples can have any part or parcel,—anyhow, it's hardly fair of you to set my curiosity all agog, and then to leave it unappeased."

He eyed me steadily, the appearance of interest fading more and more, until, presently, his face assumed its wonted expressionless mask,—somehow I was conscious that what he had seen in my face was not altogether to his liking, His voice was once more bland and self-contained.

"I perceive you are of opinion that I have been told a taradiddle.[1] I suppose I have."

"But what is the taradiddle?—don't you see I'm burning?"

"Unfortunately, Atherton, I am on my honour. Until I have permission to unloose it, my tongue is tied." He picked up his hat and umbrella from where he had placed them on the table. Holding them in his left hand, he advanced to me with his right outstretched. "It is very good of you to suffer my continued interruption; I know, to my sorrow, what such interruptions mean,—believe me, I am not ungrateful. What is this?"

On the shelf, within a foot or so of where I stood, was a sheet of paper,—the size and shape of half a sheet of post note. At this he stooped to glance. As he did so, something surprising occurred. On the instant a look came on to his face which, literally, transfigured him. His hat and umbrella fell from his grasp on to the floor. He retreated, gibbering, his hands held out as if to ward something off from him, until he reached the wall on the other side of the room. A more amazing spectacle than he presented I never saw.

"Lessingham!" I exclaimed. "What's wrong with you?"

My first impression was that he was struck by a fit of epilepsy,—though anyone less like an epileptic subject it would be hard to find. In

---

[1]   Slang for a lie or falsehood.

my bewilderment I looked round to see what could be the immediate cause. My eye fell upon the sheet of paper. I stared at it with considerable surprise. I had not noticed it there previously, I had not put it there,—where had it come from? The curious thing was that, on it, produced apparently by some process of photogravure,[1] was an illustration of a species of beetle with which I felt that I ought to be acquainted, and yet was not. It was of a dull golden green; the colour was so well brought out,—even to the extent of seeming to scintillate, and the whole thing was so dexterously done that the creature seemed alive. The semblance of reality was, indeed, so vivid that it needed a second glance to be assured that it was a mere trick of the reproducer. Its presence there was odd,—after what we had been talking about it might seem to need explanation; but it was absurd to suppose that that alone could have had such an effect on a man like Lessingham.

With the thing in my hand, I crossed to where he was,—pressing his back against the wall, he had shrunk lower inch by inch till he was actually crouching on his haunches.

"Lessingham!—come, man, what's wrong with you?"

Taking him by the shoulder, I shook him with some vigour. My touch had on him the effect of seeming to wake him out of a dream, of restoring him to consciousness as against the nightmare horrors with which he was struggling. He gazed up at me with that look of cunning on his face which one associates with abject terror.

"Atherton? Is it you?—It's all right,—quite right.—I'm well,—very well."

As he spoke, he slowly drew himself up, till he was standing erect.

"Then, in that case, all I can say is that you have a queer way of being very well." He put his hand up to his mouth, as if to hide the trembling of his lips.

"It's the pressure of overwork,—I've had one or two attacks like this,—but it's nothing, only—a local lesion."

I observed him keenly; to my thinking there was something about him which was very odd indeed.

"Only a local lesion!—if you take my strongly-urged advice you'll get a medical opinion without delay,—if you haven't been wise enough to have done so already."

---

[1] A process of photographic engraving, by transferring a photographic negative of an image to a metal plate, and then etching it in; also the term refers to any image produced by this process.

"I'll go to-day;—at once; but I know it's only mental over-strain."

"You're sure it's nothing to do with this?"

I held out in front of him the photogravure of the beetle. As I did so he backed away from me, shrieking, trembling as with palsy.

"Take it away! take it away!" he screamed.

I stared at him, for some seconds, astonished into speechlessness. Then I found my tongue.

"Lessingham!—it's only a picture! are you stark mad?"

He persisted in his ejaculations.

"Take it away! take it away!—Tear it up!—Burn it!"

His agitation was so unnatural,—from whatever cause it arose!—that, fearing the recurrence of the attack from which he had just recovered, I did as he bade me. I tore the sheet of paper into quarters, and, striking a match, set fire to each separate piece. He watched the process of incineration as if fascinated. When it was concluded, and nothing but ashes remained, he gave a gasp of relief.

"Lessingham," I said, "you're either mad already, or you're going mad,—which is it?"

"I think it's neither. I believe I am as sane as you. It's—it's that story of which I was speaking; it—it seems curious, but I'll tell you all about it—some day. As I observed, I think you will find it an interesting instance of a singular survival." He made an obvious effort to become more like his usual self. "It is extremely unfortunate, Atherton, that I should have troubled you with such a display of weakness,—especially as I am able to offer you so scant an explanation. One thing I would ask of you,—to observe strict confidence. What has taken place has been between ourselves. I am in your hands, but you are my friend, I know I can rely on you not to speak of it to anyone,—and, in particular, not to breathe a hint of it to Miss Lindon."

"Why, in particular, not to Miss Lindon."

"Can you not guess?"

I hunched my shoulder.

"If what I guess is what you mean is not that a cause the more why silence would be unfair to her?"

"It is for me to speak, if for anyone. I shall not fail to do what should be done.—Give me your promise that you will not hint a word to her of what you have so unfortunately seen?"

I gave him the promise he required.

★ ★ ★

There was no more work for me that day. The Apostle, his divagations, his examples of the coleoptera, his Arabian friend,—these things were as microbes which, acting on a system already predisposed for their reception, produced high fever; I was in a fever,—of unrest. Brain in a whirl!—Marjorie, Paul, Isis, beetle, mesmerism, in delirious jumble. Love's upsetting!—in itself a sufficiently severe disease; but when complications intervene, suggestive of mystery and novelties, so that you do not know if you are moving in an atmosphere of dreams or of frozen facts,—if, then, your temperature does not rise, like that rocket of M. Verne's,[1]—which reached the moon, then you are a freak of an entirely genuine kind, and if the surgeons do not preserve you, and place you on view, in pickle, they ought to, for the sake of historical doubters, for no one will believe that there ever was a man like you, unless you yourself are somewhere around to prove them Thomases.[2]

Myself,—I am not that kind of man. When I get warm I grow heated, and when I am heated there is likely to be a variety show of a gaudy kind. When Paul had gone I tried to think things out, and if I had kept on trying something would have happened—so I went on the river instead.

CHAPTER 14

THE DUCHESS' BALL

That night was the Duchess of Datchet's ball—the first person I saw as I entered the dancing-room was Dora Grayling.

I went straight up to her.

"Miss Grayling, I behaved very badly to you last night. I have come to make to you my apologies,—to sue for your forgiveness!"

"My forgiveness?" Her head went back,—she has a pretty bird-like trick of cocking it a little on one side. "You were not well. Are you better?"

---

[1] Jules Verne (1828-1905), author of numerous adventure novels, including *From the Earth to the Moon* (1865).

[2] The reference is to Thomas, one of the twelve disciples, popularly referred to as doubting Thomas because he could not believe that Jesus had been resurrected.

"Quite.—You forgive me? Then grant me plenary absolution by giving me a dance for the one I lost last night."

She rose. A man came up,—a stranger to me; she's one of the best hunted women in England,—there's a million with her.

"This is my dance, Miss Grayling."

She looked at him.

"You must excuse me. I am afraid I have made a mistake. I had forgotten that I was already engaged."

I had not thought her capable of it. She took my arm, and away we went, and left him staring.

"It's he who's the sufferer now," I whispered, as we went round, she can waltz!

"You think so? It was I last night,—I did not mean, if I could help it, to suffer again. To me a dance with you means something." She went all red,—adding, as an after-thought, "Nowadays, so few men really dance. I expect it's because you dance so well."

"Thank you."

We danced the waltz right through, then we went to an impromptu shelter which had been rigged up on a balcony. And we talked. There's something sympathetic about Miss Grayling which leads one to talk about one's self,—before I was half aware of it I was telling her of all my plans and projects,—actually telling her of my latest notion which, ultimately, was to result in the destruction of whole armies as by a flash of lightning. She took an amount of interest in it which was surprising.

"What really stands in the way of things of this sort is not theory but practice,—one can prove one's facts on paper, or on a small scale in a room; what is wanted is proof on a large scale, by actual experiment. If, for instance, I could take my plant to one of the forests of South America, where there is plenty of animal life but no human, I could demonstrate the soundness of my position then and there."

"Why don't you?"

"Think of the money it would cost."

"I thought I was a friend of yours."

"I had hoped you were."

"Then why don't you let me help you?"

"Help me?—How?"

"By letting you have the money for your South American experiment;—it would be an investment on which I should expect to receive good interest."

I fidgeted.

"It is very good of you, Miss Grayling, to talk like that."

She became quite frigid.

"Please don't be absurd!—I perceive quite clearly that you are snubbing me, and that you are trying to do it as delicately as you know how."

"Miss Grayling!"

"I understand that it was an impertinence on my part to volunteer assistance which was unasked; you have made that sufficiently plain."

"I assure you——"

"Pray don't. Of course, if it had been Miss Lindon it would have been different; she would at least have received a civil answer. But we are not all Miss Lindon."

I was aghast. The outburst was so uncalled for,—I had not the faintest notion what I had said or done to cause it; she was in such a surprising passion—and it suited her!—I thought I had never seen her look prettier,—I could do nothing else but stare. So she went on,—with just as little reason.

"Here is someone coming to claim this dance,—I can't throw all my partners over. Have I offended you so irremediably that it will be impossible for you to dance with me again?"

"Miss Grayling!—I shall be only too delighted." She handed me her card. "Which may I have?"

"For your own sake you had better place it as far off as you possibly can."

"They all seem taken."

"That doesn't matter; strike off any name you please, anywhere, and put your own instead."

It was giving me an almost embarrassingly free hand. I booked myself for the next waltz but two,—who it was who would have to give way to me I did not trouble to inquire.

"Mr. Atherton!—Is that you?"

It was,—it was also she. It was Marjorie! And so soon as I saw her I knew that there was only one woman in the world for me,—the mere sight of her sent the blood tingling through my veins. Turning to her attendant cavalier, she dismissed him with a bow.

"Is there an empty chair?"

She seated herself in the one Miss Grayling had just vacated. I sat down beside her. She glanced at me, laughter in her eyes. I was all in a stupid tremblement.

"You remember that last night I told you that I might require your friendly services in diplomatic intervention?" I nodded,—I felt that the allusion was unfair. "Well, the occasion's come,—or, at least, it's very near." She was still,—and I said nothing to help her. "You know how unreasonable papa can be."

I did,—never a more pig-headed man in England than Geoffrey Lindon,—or, in a sense, a duller. But, just then, I was not prepared to admit it to his child.

"You know what an absurd objection he has to—Paul."

There was an appreciative hesitation before she uttered the fellow's Christian name,—when it came it was with an accent of tenderness which stung me like a gadfly. To speak to me—of all men,—of the fellow in such a tone was—like a woman.

"Has Mr. Lindon no notion of how things stand between you?"

"Except what he suspects. That is just where you are to come in, papa thinks so much of you—I want you to sound Paul's praises in his ear—to prepare him for what must come." Was ever rejected lover burdened with such a task? Its enormity kept me still. "Sydney, you have always been my friend,—my truest, dearest friend. When I was a little girl you used to come between papa and me, to shield me from his wrath. Now that I am a big girl I want you to be on my side once more, and to shield me still."

Her voice softened. She laid her hand upon my arm. How, under her touch, I burned.

"But I don't understand what cause there has been for secrecy,— why should there have been any secrecy from the first?"

"It was Paul's wish that papa should not be told."

"Is Mr. Lessingham ashamed of you?"

"Sydney!"

"Or does he fear your father?"

"You are unkind. You know perfectly well that papa has been prejudiced against him all along, you know that his political position is just now one of the greatest difficulty, that every nerve and muscle is kept on the continual strain, that it is in the highest degree essential that further complications of every and any sort should be avoided. He is quite aware that his suit will not be approved of by papa, and he simply wishes that nothing shall be said about it till the end of the session, that is all."

"I see! Mr. Lessingham is cautious even in love-making,—politician first, and lover afterwards."

"Well!—and why not?—would you have him injure the cause he has at heart for the want of a little patience?"

"It depends what cause it is he has at heart."

"What is the matter with you?—why do you speak to me like that?—it is not like you at all." She looked at me shrewdly, with flashing eyes. "Is it possible that you are—jealous?—that you were in earnest in what you said last night?—I thought it was the sort of thing you said to every girl."

I would have given a great deal to take her in my arms, and press her to my bosom then and there,—to think that she should taunt me with having said to her the sort of thing I said to every girl.

"What do you know of Mr. Lessingham?"

"What all the world knows,—that history will be made by him."

"There are kinds of history in the making of which one would not desire to be associated. What do you know of his private life,—it was to that that I was referring."

"Really,—you go too far. I know that he is one of the best, just as he is one of the greatest, of men; for me, that is sufficient."

"If you do know that, it is sufficient."

"I do know it,—all the world knows it. Everyone with whom he comes in contact is aware—must be aware, that he is incapable of a dishonourable thought or action."

"Take my advice, don't appreciate any man too highly. In the book of every man's life there is a page which he would wish to keep turned down."

"There is no such page in Paul's—there may be in yours; I think that probable."

"Thank you. I fear it is more than probable. I fear that, in my case, the page may extend to several. There is nothing Apostolic about me,—not even the name."

"Sydney!—you are unendurable!—It is the more strange to hear you talk like this since Paul regards you as his friend."

"He flatters me."

"Are you not his friend?"

"Is it not sufficient to be yours?"

"No,—who is against Paul is against me."

"That is hard."

"How is it hard? Who is against the husband can hardly be for the wife,—when the husband and wife are one."

"But as yet you are not one.—Is my cause so hopeless?"

"What do you call your cause?—are you thinking of that nonsense you were talking about last night?"

She laughed!

"You call it nonsense.—You ask for sympathy, and give—so much!"

"I will give you all the sympathy you stand in need of,—I promise it! My poor, dear Sydney!—don't be so absurd! Do you think that I don't know you? You're the best of friends, and the worst of lovers,—as the one, so true; so fickle as the other. To my certain knowledge, with how many girls have you been in love,—and out again. It is true that, to the best of my knowledge and belief, you have never been in love with me before,—but that's the merest accident. Believe me, my dear, dear Sydney, you'll be in love with someone else tomorrow,—if you're not half-way there tonight. I confess, quite frankly, that, in that direction, all the experience I have had of you has in nowise strengthened my prophetic instinct. Cheer up!—one never knows!—Who is this that's coming?"

It was Dora Grayling who was coming,—I went off with her without a word,—we were half-way through the dance before she spoke to me.

"I am sorry that I was cross to you just now, and—disagreeable. Somehow I always seem destined to show to you my most unpleasant side."

"The blame was mine,—what sort of side do I show you? You are far kinder to me than I deserve, now, and always."

"That is what you say."

"Pardon me, it's true,—else how comes it that, at this time of day, I'm without a friend in all the world?"

"You!—without a friend!—I never knew a man who had so many!—I never knew a person of whom so many men and women join in speaking well!"

"Miss Grayling!"

"As for never having done anything worth doing, think of what you have done. Think of your discoveries, think of your inventions, think of—but never mind! The world knows you have done great things, and it confidently looks to you to do still greater. You talk of being friendless, and yet when I ask, as a favour—as a great favour!—to be allowed to do something to show my friendship, you—well, you snub me."

"I snub you!"

"You know you snubbed me."

"Do you really mean that you take an interest in—in my work?"

"You know I mean it."

She turned to me, her face all glowing,—and I did know it.

"Will you come to my laboratory to-morrow morning?"

"Will I!—won't I!"

"With your aunt?"

"Yes, with my aunt."

"I'll show you round, and tell you all there is to be told, and then if you still think there's anything in it, I'll accept your offer about that South American experiment,—that is, if it still holds good."

"Of course it still holds good."

"And we'll be partners."

"Partners?—Yes,—we will be partners."

"It will cost a terrific sum."

"There are some things which never can cost too much."

"That's not my experience."

"I hope it will be mine."

"It's a bargain?"

"On my side, I promise you that it's a bargain."

When I got outside the room I found that Percy Woodville was at my side. His round face was, in a manner of speaking, as long as my arm. He took his glass out of his eye, and rubbed it with his handkerchief, and directly he put it back he took it out and rubbed it again. I believe that I never saw him in such a state of fluster, and, when one speaks of Woodville, that means something.

"Atherton, I am in a devil of a stew." He looked it. "All of a heap!—I've had a blow which I shall never get over!"

"Then get under."

Woodville is one of those fellows who will insist on telling me their most private matters,—even to what they owe their washerwomen for the ruination of their shirts. Why, goodness alone can tell, heaven knows I'm not sympathetic.

"Don't be an idiot!—you don't know what I'm suffering!—I'm as nearly as possible stark mad."

"That's all right, old chap,—I've seen you that way more than once before."

"Don't talk like that,—you're not a perfect brute!"

"I bet you a shilling that I am."

"Don't torture me, you're not. Atherton!" He seized me by the lapels of my coat, seeming half beside himself,—fortunately he had drawn me into a recess, so that we were noticed by few observers. "What do you think has happened?"

"My dear chap, how on earth am I to know?"

"She's refused me!"

"Has she!—Well I never!—Buck up,—try some other address,—there are quite as good fish in the sea as ever came out of it."

"Atherton, you're a blackguard."

He had crumpled his handkerchief into a ball, and was actually bobbing at his eyes with it,—the idea of Percy Woodville being dissolved in tears was excruciatingly funny,—but, just then, I could hardly tell him so.

"There's not a doubt of it,—it's my way of being sympathetic. Don't be so down, man,—try her again!"

"It's not the slightest use—I know it isn't—from the way she treated me."

"Don't be so sure—women often say what they mean least. Who's the lady?"

"Who?—Is there more women in the world than one for me, or has there ever been? You ask me who! What does that word mean to me but Marjorie Lindon!"

"Marjorie Lindon?"

I fancy that my jaw dropped open,—that, to use his own vernacular, I was "all of a heap." I felt like it.

I strode away—leaving him mazed—and all but ran into Marjorie's arms.

"I'm just leaving. Will you see me to the carriage, Mr. Atherton?" I saw her to the carriage. "Are you off?—Can I give you a lift?"

"Thank you,—I am not thinking of being off."

"I'm going to the House of Commons,—won't you come?"

"What are you going there for?"

Directly she spoke of it I knew why she was going, and she knew that I knew, as her words showed.

"You are quite well aware of what the magnet is. You are not so ignorant as not to know that the Agricultural Amendment Act is on tonight, and that Paul is to speak. I always try to be there when Paul is to speak, and I mean to always keep trying."

"He is a fortunate man."

"Indeed,—and again indeed. A man with such gifts as his is inadequately described as fortunate.—But I must be off. He expected to be up before, but I heard from him a few minutes ago that there has been a delay, but that he will be up within half-an-hour.—Till our next meeting."

As I returned into the house, in the hall I met Percy Woodville. He had his hat on.

"Where are you off to?"

"I'm off to the House."

"To hear Paul Lessingham?"

"Damn Paul Lessingham!"

"With all my heart!"

"There's a division expected,—I've got to go."

"Someone else has gone to hear Paul Lessingham,—Marjorie Lindon."

"No!—you don't say so!—by Jove!—I say, Atherton, I wish I could make a speech,—I never can. When I'm electioneering I have to have my speeches written for me, and then I have to read 'em. But, by Jove, if I knew Miss Lindon was in the gallery, and if I knew anything about the thing, or could get someone to tell me something, hang me if I wouldn't speak,—I'd show her I'm not the fool she thinks I am!"

"Speak, Percy, speak!—you'd knock 'em silly, sir!—I tell you what I'll do,—I'll come with you! I'll to the House as well! —Paul Lessingham shall have an audience of three."

CHAPTER 15

MR. LESSINGHAM SPEAKS

The House was full. Percy and I went upstairs,—to the gallery which is theoretically supposed to be reserved for what are called "distinguished strangers,"[1]—those curious animals. Trumperton was up, hammering out those sentences which smell, not so much of the lamp as of the dunderhead. Nobody was listening,—except the men in the Press Gallery; where is the brain of the House, and ninety per cent of its wisdom.

It was not till Trumperton had finished that I discovered Lessingham. The tedious ancient resumed his seat amidst a murmur of sounds which, I have no doubt, some of the press-men interpreted next day as "loud and continued applause." There was movement in the House, possibly expressive of relief; a hum of voices; men came flocking in. Then, from the Opposition benches, there rose a sound which was applause,—and I perceived that, on a cross bench close to the gangway, Paul Lessingham was standing up bareheaded.

I eyed him critically,—as a collector might eye a valuable specimen, or a pathologist a curious subject. During the last four and twenty hours my interest in him had grown apace. Just then, to me, he was the most interesting man the world contained.

---

[1] Both of the Houses of Parliament have strangers' galleries, to which the public is permitted access.

When I remembered how I had seen him the same morning, a nerveless, terror-stricken wretch, grovelling, like some craven cur, upon the floor, frightened, to the verge of imbecility, by a shadow, and less than a shadow, I was confronted by two hypotheses. Either I had exaggerated his condition then, or I exaggerated his condition now. So far as appearance went, it was incredible that this man could be that one.

I confess that my feeling rapidly became one of admiration. I love the fighter. I quickly recognised that here we had him in perfection. There was no seeming about him then,—the man was to the manner born. To his finger-tips a fighting man. I had never realised it so clearly before. He was coolness itself. He had all his faculties under complete command. While never, for a moment, really exposing himself, he would be swift in perceiving the slightest weakness in his opponents' defence, and, so soon as he saw it, like lightning, he would slip in a telling blow. Though defeated, he would hardly be disgraced; and one might easily believe that their very victories would be so expensive to his assailant, that, in the end, they would actually conduce to his own triumph.

"Hang me!" I told myself, "if, after all, I am surprised if Marjorie does see something in him." For I perceived how a clever and imaginative young woman, seeing him at his best, holding his own, like a gallant knight, against overwhelming odds, in the lists in which he was so much at home, might come to think of him as if he were always and only there, ignoring altogether the kind of man he was when the joust was finished.

It did me good to hear him, I do know that,—and I could easily imagine the effect he had on one particular auditor who was in the Ladies' Cage.[1] It was very far from being an "oration" in the American sense; it had little or nothing of the fire and fury of the French Tribune; it was marked neither by the ponderosity nor the sentiment of the eloquent German; yet it was as satisfying as are the efforts of either of the three, producing, without doubt, precisely the effect which the speaker intended. His voice was clear and calm, not exactly musical, yet distinctly pleasant, and it was so managed that each word he uttered was as audible to every person present as if it had been addressed particularly to him. His sentences were short and crisp; the words which he used were not big ones, but they came from him with an agreeable ease; and he spoke just fast enough to keep one's interest alert without involving a strain on the attention.

---

[1]   Part of the gallery reserved for women.

He commenced by making, in the quietest and most courteous manner, sarcastic comments on the speeches and methods of Trumperton and his friends which tickled the House amazingly. But he did not make the mistake of pushing his personalities too far. To a speaker of a certain sort nothing is easier than to sting to madness. If he likes, his every word is barbed. Wounds so given fester; they are not easily forgiven;—it is essential to a politician that he should have his firmest friends among the fools; or his climbing days will soon be over. Soon his sarcasms were at an end. He began to exchange them for sweet-sounding phrases. He actually began to say pleasant things to his opponents; apparently to mean them. To put them in a good conceit with themselves. He pointed out how much truth there was in what they said; and then, as if by accident, with what ease and at how little cost, amendments might be made. He found their arguments, and took them for his own, and flattered them, whether they would or not, by showing how firmly they were founded upon fact; and grafted other arguments upon them, which seemed their natural sequelae;[1] and transformed them, and drove them hither and thither; and brought them—their own arguments!—to a round, irrefragable conclusion, which was diametrically the reverse of that to which they themselves had brought them. And he did it all with an aptness, a readiness, a grace, which was incontestable. So that, when he sat down, he had performed that most difficult of all feats, he had delivered what, in a House of Commons' sense, was a practical, statesmanlike speech, and yet one which left his hearers in an excellent humour.

It was a great success,—an immense success. A parliamentary triumph of almost the highest order. Paul Lessingham had been coming on by leaps and bounds. When he resumed his seat, amidst applause which, this time, really was applause, there were, probably, few who doubted that he was destined to go still farther. How much farther it is true that time alone could tell; but, so far as appearances went, all the prizes, which are as the crown and climax of a statesman's career, were well within his reach.

For my part I was delighted. I had enjoyed an intellectual exercise, a species of enjoyment not so common as might be. The Apostle had almost persuaded me that the political game was one worth playing, and that its triumphs were things to be desired. It is something, after all, to be able to appeal successfully to the passions and aspirations of your peers;

---

[1] A medical term, referring to condition or disease as a result of a previous disease; more generally, as in this example, a consequence or sequence of consequences.

to gain their plaudits; to prove your skill at the game you yourself have chosen; to be looked up to and admired. And when a woman's heart beats time with yours,—each man to his own temperament, but when that woman is the woman whom you love, to know that your triumph means her glory, and her gladness, to me that would be the best part of it all.

In that hour,—the Apostle's hour!—I almost wished that I were a politician too!

The division was over. The business of the night was practically done. I was back again in the lobby! The theme of conversation was the Apostle's speech,—on every side they talked of it.

Suddenly Marjorie was at my side. Her face was glowing. I never saw her look more beautiful,—or happier. She seemed to be alone.

"So you have come, after all!—Wasn't it splendid?—wasn't it magnificent? Isn't it grand to have such great gifts, and to use them to such good purpose?—Speak, Sydney! Don't feign a coolness which is foreign to your nature!"

I saw that she was hungry for me to praise the man whom she delighted to honour. But, somehow, her enthusiasm cooled mine.

"It was not a bad speech, of a kind."

"Of a kind!" How her eyes flashed fire! With what disdain she treated me! "What do you mean by 'of a kind?' My dear Sydney, are you not aware that it is an attribute of small minds to attempt to belittle those which are greater? Even if you are conscious of inferiority, it's unwise to show it. Mr. Lessingham's was a great speech, of any kind; your incapacity to recognise the fact simply reveals your lack of the critical faculty."

"It is fortunate for Mr. Lessingham that there is at least one person in whom the critical faculty is so bountifully developed. Apparently, in your judgement, he who discriminates is lost."

I thought she was going to burst into passion. But, instead, laughing, she placed her hand upon my shoulder.

"Poor Sydney!—I understand!—It is so sad!—Do you know you are like a little boy who, when he is beaten, declares that the victor has cheated him. Never mind! as you grow older, you will learn better."

She stung me almost beyond bearing,—I cared not what I said.

"You, unless I am mistaken, will learn better before you are older."

"What do you mean?"

Before I could have told her—if I had meant to tell; which I did not—Lessingham came up.

"I hope I have not kept you waiting; I have been delayed longer than I expected."

"Not at all,—though I am quite ready to get away; it's a little tiresome waiting here."

This with a mischievous glance towards me,—a glance which compelled Lessingham to notice me.

"You do not often favour us."

"I don't. I find better employment for my time."

"You are wrong. It's the cant of the day to underrate the House of Commons, and the work which it performs; don't you suffer yourself to join in the chorus of the simpletons. Your time cannot be better employed than in endeavouring to improve the body politic."

"I am obliged to you.—I hope you are feeling better than when I saw you last."

A gleam came into his eyes, fading as quickly as it came. He showed no other sign of comprehension, surprise, or resentment.

"Thank you.—I am very well."

But Marjorie perceived that I meant more than met the eye, and that what I meant was meant unpleasantly.

"Come,—let us be off. It is Mr. Atherton to-night who is not well."

She had just slipped her arm through Lessingham's when her father approached. Old Lindon stared at her on the Apostle's arm, as if he could hardly believe that it was she.

"I thought that you were at the Duchess'?"

"So I have been, papa; and now I'm here."

"Here!" Old Lindon began to stutter and stammer, and to grow red in the face, as is his wont when at all excited.

"W—what do you mean by here?—wh—where's the carriage?"

"Where should it be, except waiting for me outside, unless the horses have run away."

"I—I—I'll take you down to it. I—I don't approve of y—your w—w—waiting in a place like this."

"Thank you, papa, but Mr. Lessingham is going to take me down.—I shall see you afterwards.—Good-bye."

Anything cooler than the way in which she walked off I do not think I ever saw. This is the age of feminine advancement. Young women think nothing of twisting their mothers round their fingers, let alone their fathers; but the fashion in which that young woman walked off, on the Apostle's arm, and left her father standing there, was, in its way, a study.

Lindon seemed scarcely able to realise that the pair of them had gone. Even after they had disappeared in the crowd he stood staring after them, growing redder and redder, till the veins stood out upon his face, and I thought that an apoplectic seizure threatened. Then, with a gasp, he turned to me.

"Damned scoundrel!" I took it for granted that he alluded to the gentleman, even though his following words hardly suggested it. "Only this morning I forbade her to have anything to do with him, and n— now he's w-walked off with her! C—confounded adventurer! That's what he is, an adventurer, and before many hours have passed I'll take the liberty to tell him so!"

Jamming his fists into his pockets, and puffing like a grampus[1] in distress, he took himself away, and it was time he did, for his words were as audible as they were pointed, and already people were wondering what the matter was. Woodville came up as Lindon was going,—just as sorely distressed as ever.

"She went away with Lessingham, did you see her?"

"Of course I saw her. When a man makes a speech like Lessingham's any girl would go away with him,—and be proud to. When you are endowed with such great powers as he is, and use them for such lofty purposes, she'll walk away with you,—but, till then, never."

He was at his old trick of polishing his eyeglass.

"It's bitter hard. When I knew that she was there, I'd half a mind to make a speech myself, upon my word I had, only I didn't know what to speak about, and I can't speak anyhow,—how can a fellow speak when he's shoved into the gallery?"

"As you say, how can he? he can't stand on the railing and shout,— even with a friend holding him behind."

"I know I shall speak one day,—bound to; and then she won't be there."

"It'll be better for you if she isn't."

"Think so?—Perhaps you're right. I'd be safe to make a mess of it, and then, if she were to see me at it, it'd be the devil! 'Pon my word, I've been wishing, lately, I was clever."

He rubbed his nose with the rim of his eyeglass, looking the most comically disconsolate figure.

"Put black care behind you, Percy!—buck up, my boy! The division's over—you are free—now we'll go 'on the fly.'"[2]

And we did "go on the fly."

---

[1] The popular name for whales, dolphins, and other aquatic animals which have blow-holes, the term becomes used for anyone noted for puffing and blowing.

[2] To be on the move, to be active. Here, the sense is to go on the town, to have a good time.

CHAPTER 16

ATHERTON'S MAGIC VAPOUR

I bore him off to supper at the Helicon. All the way in the cab he was trying to tell me the story of how he proposed to Marjorie, and he was very far from being through with it when we reached the club. There was the usual crowd of supperites, but we got a little table to ourselves, in a corner of the room, and before anything was brought for us to eat he was at it again. A good many of the people were pretty near to shouting, and as they seemed to be all speaking at once, and the band was playing, and as the Helicon supper band is not piano, Percy did not have it quite all to himself, but, considering the delicacy of his subject, he talked as loudly as was decent,—getting more so as he went on. But Percy is peculiar.

"I don't know how many times I've tried to tell her,—over and over again."

"Have you now?"

"Yes, pretty near every time I met her,—but I never seemed to get quite to it, don't you know."

"How was that?"

"Why, just as I was going to say, 'Miss Lindon, may I offer you the gift of my affection—'"

"Was that how you invariably intended to begin?"

"Well, not always—one time like that, another time another way. Fact is, I got off a little speech by heart, but I never got a chance to reel it off, so I made up my mind to just say anything."

"And what did you say?"

"Well, nothing,—you see, I never got there. Just as I was feeling my way, she'd ask if I preferred big sleeves to little ones, or top hats to billycocks, or some nonsense of the kind."

"Would she now?"

"Yes,—of course I had to answer, and by the time I'd answered the chance was lost." Percy was polishing his eye-glass. "I tried to get there so many times, and she choked me off so often, that I can't help thinking that she suspected what it was that I was after."

"You think she did?"

"She must have done. Once I followed her down Piccadilly, and chivvied her into a glove shop in the Burlington Arcade.[1] I meant to propose to her in there,—I hadn't had a wink of sleep all night through dreaming of her, and I was just about desperate."

"And did you propose?"

"The girl behind the counter made me buy a dozen pairs of gloves instead. They turned out to be three sizes too large for me when they came home. I believe she thought I'd gone to spoon the glove girl,— she went out and left me there. That girl loaded me with all sorts of things when she was gone, I couldn't get away. She held me with her blessed eye. I believe it was a glass one."

"Miss Lindon's?—or the glove girl's?"

"The glove girl's. She sent me home a whole cartload of green ties, and declared I'd ordered them. I shall never forget that day. I've never been up the Arcade since, and never mean to."

"You gave Miss Lindon a wrong impression."

"I don't know. I was always giving her wrong impressions. Once she said that she knew I was not a marrying man, that I was the sort of chap who never would marry, because she saw it in my face."

"Under the circumstances, that was trying."

"Bitter hard." Percy sighed again. "I shouldn't mind if I wasn't so gone. I'm not a fellow who does get gone, but when I do get gone, I get so beastly gone."

"I tell you what, Percy,—have a drink!"

"I'm a teetotaller,[2]—you know I am."

"You talk of your heart being broken, and of your being a teetotaller in the same breath,—if your heart were really broken you'd throw teetotalism to the winds."

"Do you think so,—why?"

"Because you would,—men whose hearts are broken always do,— you'd swallow a magnum[3] at the least."

Percy groaned.

"When I drink I'm always ill,—but I'll have a try."

He had a try,—making a good beginning by emptying at a draught the glass which the waiter had just now filled. Then he relapsed into melancholy.

---

[1] Nineteenth-century shopping arcade in Piccadilly, central London, built in 1819 for Lord Cavendish.

[2] Someone who abstains from alcohol; a member of a temperance society; such societies were common in the nineteenth century.

[3] A bottle containing two quarts or four pints; also the amount of liquid.

"Tell me, Percy,—honest Indian!—do you really love her?"

"Love her?" His eyes grew round as saucers. "Don't I tell you that I love her?"

"I know you tell me, but that sort of thing is easy telling. What does it make you feel like, this love you talk so much about?"

"Feel like?—just anyhow,—and nohow. You should look inside me, and then you'd know."

"I see.—It's like that, is it?—Suppose she loved another man, what sort of feeling would you feel towards him?"

"Does she love another man?"

"I say, suppose."

"I dare say she does. I expect that's it.—What an idiot I am not to have thought of that before." He sighed,—and refilled his glass. "He's a lucky chap, whoever he is. I'd—I'd like to tell him so."

"You'd like to tell him so?"

"He's such a jolly lucky chap, you know."

"Possibly,—but his jolly good luck is your jolly bad luck. Would you be willing to resign her to him without a word?"

"If she loves him."

"But you say you love her."

"Of course I do."

"Well then?"

"You don't suppose that, because I love her, I shouldn't like to see her happy?—I'm not such a beast!—I'd sooner see her happy than anything else in all the world."

"I see.—Even happy with another?—I'm afraid that my philosophy is not like yours. If I loved Miss Lindon, and she loved, say, Jones, I'm afraid I shouldn't feel like that towards Jones at all."

"What would you feel like?"

"Murder.—Percy, you come home with me,—we've begun the night together, let's end it together,—and I'll show you one of the finest notions for committing murder on a scale of real magnificence you ever dreamed of. I should like to make use of it to show my feelings towards the supposititious Jones,—he'd know what I felt for him when once he had been introduced to it."

Percy went with me without a word. He had not had much to drink, but it had been too much for him, and he was in a condition of maundering sentimentality. I got him into a cab. We dashed along Piccadilly.

He was silent, and sat looking in front of him with an air of vacuous sullenness which ill-became his cast of countenance. I bade the cabman pass though Lowndes Square. As we passed the Apostle's I pulled him up. I pointed out the place to Woodville.

"You see, Percy, that's Lessingham's house!—that's the house of the man who went away with Marjorie!"

"Yes." Words came from him slowly, with a quite unnecessary stress on each. "Because he made a speech.—I'd like to make a speech.—One day I'll make a speech."

"Because he made a speech,—only that, and nothing more! When a man speaks with an Apostle's tongue, he can witch any woman in the land.—Hallo, who's that?—Lessingham, is that you?"

I saw, or thought I saw, someone, or something, glide up the steps, and withdraw into the shadow of the doorway, as if unwilling to be seen. When I hailed no one answered. I called again.

"Don't be shy, my friend!"

I sprang out of the cab, ran across the pavement, and up the steps. To my surprise, there was no one in the doorway. It seemed incredible, but the place was empty. I felt about me with my hands, as if I had been playing at blind man's buff, and grasped at vacancy. I came down a step or two.

"Ostensibly, there's a vacuum,—which nature abhors.—I say, driver, didn't you see someone come up the steps?"

"I thought I did, sir,—I could have sworn I did."

"So could I.—It's very odd."

"Perhaps whoever it was has gone into the 'ouse, sir."

"I don't see how. We should have heard the door open, if we hadn't seen it,—and we should have seen it, it's not so dark as that.—I've half a mind to ring the bell and inquire."

"I shouldn't do that if I was you, sir,—you jump in, and I'll get along. This is Mr. Lessingham's,—the great Mr. Lessingham's."

I believe the cabman thought that I was drunk,—and not respectable enough to claim acquaintance with the great Mr. Lessingham.

"Wake up, Woodville! Do you know I believe there's some mystery about this place,—I feel assured of it. I feel as if I were in the presence of something uncanny,—something which I can neither see, nor touch, nor hear."

The cabman bent down from his seat, wheedling me.

"Jump in, sir, and we'll be getting along."

I jumped in, and we got along,—but not far. Before we had gone a dozen yards, I was out again, without troubling the driver to stop. He pulled up, aggrieved.

"Well, sir, what's the matter now? You'll be damaging yourself before you've done, and then you'll be blaming me."

I had caught sight of a cat crouching in the shadow of the railings,— a black one. That cat was my quarry. Either the creature was unusually sleepy, or slow, or stupid, or it had lost its wits—which a cat seldom does lose!—anyhow, without making an attempt to escape it allowed me to grab it by the nape of the neck.

So soon as we were inside my laboratory, I put the cat into my glass box. Percy stared.

"What have you put it there for?"

"That, my dear Percy, is what you are shortly about to see. You are about to be the witness of an experiment which, to a legislator—such as you are!—ought to be of the greatest possible interest. I am going to demonstrate, on a small scale, the action of the force which, on a large scale, I propose to employ on behalf of my native land."

He showed no signs of being interested. Sinking into a chair, he recommenced his wearisome reiteration.

"I hate cats!—Do let it go!—I'm always miserable when there's a cat in the room."

"Nonsense,—that's your fancy! What you want's a taste of whisky— you'll be as chirpy as a cricket."

"I don't want anything more to drink!—I've had too much already!"

I paid no heed to what he said. I poured two stiff doses into a couple of tumblers. Without seeming to be aware of what it was that he was doing he disposed of the better half of the one I gave him at a draught. Putting his glass upon the table, he dropped his head upon his hands, and groaned.

"What would Marjorie think of me if she saw me now?"

"Think?—nothing. Why should she think of a man like you, when she has so much better fish to fry?"

"I'm feeling frightfully ill!—I'll be drunk before I've done!"

"Then be drunk!—only, for gracious sake, be lively drunk, not deadly doleful.—Cheer up, Percy!" I clapped him on the shoulder,—almost knocking him off his seat on to the floor. "I am now going to show you that little experiment of which I was speaking!—You see that cat?"

"Of course I see it!—the beast!—I wish you'd let it go!"

"Why should I let it go?—Do you know whose cat that is? That cat's Paul Lessingham's."

"Paul Lessingham's?"

"Yes, Paul Lessingham's,—the man who made the speech,—the man whom Marjorie went away with."

"How do you know it's his?"

"I don't know it is, but I believe it is,—I choose to believe it is!—I intend to believe it is!—It was outside his house, therefore it's his cat,—that's how I argue. I can't get Lessingham inside that box, so I get his cat instead."

"Whatever for?"

"You shall see—you observe how happy it is?"

"It don't seem happy."

"We've all our ways of seeming happy,—that's its way."

The creature was behaving like a cat gone mad, dashing itself against the sides of its glass prison, leaping to and fro, and from side to side, squealing with rage, or with terror, or with both. Perhaps it foresaw what was coming,—there is no fathoming the intelligence of what we call the lower animals.

"It's a funny way."

"We some of us have funny ways, beside cats. Now, attention! Observe this little toy,—you've seen something of its kind before. It's a spring gun; you pull the spring—drop the charge into the barrel—release the spring—and the charge is fired. I'll unlock this safe, which is built into the wall. It's a letter lock, the combination just now, is 'whisky,'—you see, that's a hint to you. You'll notice the safe is strongly made,—it's airtight, fire-proof, the outer casing is of triple-plated drill-proof steel,—the contents are valuable—to me!—and devilish dangerous,—I'd pity the thief who, in his innocent ignorance, broke in to steal. Look inside,—you see it's full of balls,—glass balls, each in its own little separate nest; light as feathers; transparent,—you can see right through them. Here are a couple, like tiny pills. They contain neither dynamite, nor cordite, nor anything of the kind, yet, given a fair field and no favour, they'll work more mischief than all the explosives man has fashioned. Take hold of one—you say your heart is broken!—squeeze this under your nose—it wants but a gentle pressure—and in less time than no time you'll be in the land where they say there are no broken hearts."

He shrunk back.

"I don't know what you're talking about.—I don't want the thing.—Take it away."

"Think twice,—the chance may not recur."

"I tell you I don't want it."

"Sure?—Consider!"

"Of course I'm sure!"

"Then the cat shall have it."

"Let the poor brute go!"

"The poor brute's going,—to the land which is so near, and yet so far. Once more, if you please, attention. Notice what I do with this toy gun. I pull back the spring; I insert this small glass pellet; I thrust the muzzle of the gun through the opening in the glass box which contains the Apostle's cat,—you'll observe it fits quite close, which, on the whole, is perhaps as well for us.—I am about to release the spring.—Close attention, please.—Notice the effect."

"Atherton, let the brute go!"

"The brute's gone! I've released the spring—the pellet has been discharged—it has struck against the roof of the glass box—it has been broken by the contact,—and, hey presto! the cat lies dead,—and that in face of its nine lives. You perceive how still it is,—how still! Let's hope that, now, it's really happy. The cat which I choose to believe is Paul Lessingham's has received its quietus;[1] in the morning I'll send it back to him, with my respectful compliments. He'll miss it if I don't.—Reflect! think of a huge bomb, filled with what we'll call Atherton's Magic Vapour, fired, say, from a hundred and twenty ton gun, bursting at a given elevation over the heads of an opposing force. Properly managed, in less than an instant of time, a hundred thousand men,—quite possibly more!—would drop down dead, as if smitten by the lightning of the skies. Isn't that something like a weapon, sir?"

"I'm not well!—I want to get away!—I wish I'd never come!"

That was all Woodville had to say.

"Rubbish!—You're adding to your stock of information every second, and, in these days, when a member of Parliament is supposed to know all about everything, information's the one thing wanted. Empty your glass, man,—that's the time of day for you!"

I handed him his tumbler. He drained what was left of its contents, then, in a fit of tipsy, childish temper he flung the tumbler from him. I had placed—carelessly enough—the second pellet within a foot of the edge of the table. The shock of the heavy beaker striking the board close to it, set it rolling. I was at the other side. I started forward to stop its motion, but I was too late. Before I could reach the crystal globule, it had fallen off the edge of the table on to the floor at Woodville's feet, and smashed in falling. As it smashed, he was looking down, wondering, no doubt, in his stupidity, what the pother[2] was about,—for I was shouting,

---

[1] A final settlement, an ending; a release from duty; something causing death.
[2] A fuss or disturbance.

and making something of a clatter in my efforts to prevent the catastrophe which I saw was coming. On the instant, as the vapour secreted in the broken pellet gained access to the air, he fell forward on to his face. Rushing to him, I snatched his senseless body from the ground, and dragged it, staggeringly, towards the door which opened on to the yard. Flinging the door open, I got him into the open air.

As I did so, I found myself confronted by someone who stood outside. It was Lessingham's mysterious Egypto-Arabian friend,—my morning's visitor.

CHAPTER 17

MAGIC?—OR MIRACLE?

The passage into the yard from the electrically lit laboratory was a passage from brilliancy to gloom. The shrouded figure, standing in the shadow, was like some object in a dream. My own senses reeled. It was only because I had resolutely held my breath, and kept my face averted that I had not succumbed to the fate which had overtaken Woodville. Had I been a moment longer in gaining the open air, it would have been too late. As it was, in placing Woodville on the ground, I stumbled over him. My senses left me. Even as they went I was conscious of exclaiming,—remembering the saying about the engineer being hoist by his own petard.[1]

"Atherton's Magic Vapour!"

My sensations on returning to consciousness were curious. I found myself being supported in someone's arms, a stranger's face was bending over me, and the most extraordinary pair of eyes I had ever seen were looking into mine.

"Who the deuce are you?" I asked.

Then, understanding that it was my uninvited visitor, with scant ceremony I drew myself away from him. By the light which was streaming through the laboratory door I saw that Woodville was lying dose beside me,—stark and still.

---

[1] A metal bell-shaped container or wooden box, filled with gun-powder, employed in the early modern period to blow open a door or holes in walls. The phrase "hoist with his own petard" is taken from *Hamlet* (III.iv.207).

"Is he dead?" I cried. "Percy!—speak, man!—it's not so bad with you as that!"

But it was pretty bad,—so bad that, as I bent down and looked at him, my heart beat uncomfortably fast lest it was as bad as it could be. His heart seemed still,—the vapour took effect directly on the cardiac centres. To revive their action, and that instantly, was indispensable. Yet my brain was in such a whirl that I could not even think of how to set about beginning. Had I been alone, it is more than probable Woodville would have died. As I stared at him, senselessly, aimlessly, the stranger, passing his arms beneath his body, extended himself at full length upon his motionless form. Putting his lips to Percy's, he seemed to be pumping life from his own body into the unconscious man's. As I gazed bewildered, surprised, presently there came a movement of Percy's body.

His limbs twitched, as if he was in pain. By degrees, the motions became convulsive,—till on a sudden he bestirred himself to such effect that the stranger was rolled right off him. I bent down,—to find that the young gentleman's condition still seemed very far from satisfactory. There was a rigidity about the muscles of his face, a clamminess about his skin, a disagreeable suggestiveness about the way in which his teeth and the whites of his eyes were exposed, which was uncomfortable to contemplate.

The stranger must have seen what was passing through my mind,— not a very difficult thing to see. Pointing to the recumbent Percy, he said, with that queer foreign twang of his, which, whatever it had seemed like in the morning, sounded musical enough just then.

"All will be well with him."

"I am not so sure."

The stranger did not deign to answer. He was kneeling on one side of the victim of modern science, I on the other. Passing his hand to and fro in front of the unconscious countenance, as if by magic all semblance of discomfort vanished from Percy's features, and, to all appearances, he was placidly asleep.

"Have you hypnotised him?"

"What does it matter?"

If it was a case of hypnotism, it was very neatly done. The conditions were both unusual and trying, the effect produced seemed all that could be desired,—the change brought about in half a dozen seconds was quite remarkable. I began to be aware of a feeling of quasi-respect for Paul Lessingham's friend. His morals might be peculiar, and manners he might have none, but in this case, at any rate, the end seemed to have justified the means. He went on.

"He sleeps. When he awakes he will remember nothing that has been. Leave him,—the night is warm,—all will be well."

As he said, the night was warm,—and it was dry. Percy would come to little harm by being allowed to enjoy, for a while, the pleasant breezes. So I acted on the stranger's advice, and left him lying in the yard, while I had a little interview with the impromptu physician.

CHAPTER 18

THE APOTHEOSIS OF THE BEETLE

The laboratory door was closed. The stranger was standing a foot or two away from it. I was further within the room, and was subjecting him to as keen a scrutiny as circumstances permitted. Beyond doubt he was conscious of my observation, yet he bore himself with an air of indifference, which was suggestive of perfect unconcern. The fellow was oriental to the finger-tips,—that much was certain; yet in spite of a pretty wide personal knowledge of oriental people I could not make up my mind as to the exact part of the cast from which he came. He was hardly an Arab, he was not a fellah,[1]—he was not, unless I erred, a Mohammedan at all. There was something about him which was distinctly not Mussulmanic. So far as looks were concerned, he was not a flattering example of his race, whatever his race might be. The portentous size of his beak-like nose would have been, in itself, sufficient to damn him in any court of beauty. His lips were thick and shapeless,—and this, joined to another peculiarity in his appearance, seemed to suggest that, in his veins there ran more than a streak of negro blood. The peculiarity alluded to was his semblance of great age. As one eyed him one was reminded of the legends told of people who have been supposed to have retained something of their pristine vigour after having lived for centuries. As, however, one continued to gaze, one began to wonder if he really was so old as he seemed,—if, indeed, he was exceptionally old at all. Negroes, and especially negresses, are apt to age with extreme rapidity. Among "coloured folk" one sometimes encounters women whose faces seem to have been lined by the passage of centuries, yet whose actual tale of years would entitle them to regard

---

[1] Egyptian or Arabic-speaking peasant or labourer.

themselves, here in England, as in the prime of life. The senility of the fellow's countenance, besides, was contradicted by the juvenescence[1] of his eyes. No really old man could have had eyes like that. They were curiously shaped, reminding me of the elongated, faceted eyes of some queer creature with whose appearance I was familiar, although I could not, at the instant, recall its name. They glowed not only with the force and fire, but, also with the frenzy of youth. More uncanny-looking eyes I had never encountered,—their possessor could not be, in any sense of the word, a clubbable person.[2] Owing, probably, to some peculiar formation of the optic-nerve one felt, as one met his gaze, that he was looking right through you. More obvious danger signals never yet were placed in a creature's head. The individual who, having once caught sight of him, still sought to cultivate their owner's acquaintance, had only himself to thank if the very worst results of frequenting evil company promptly ensued.

It happens that I am myself endowed with an unusual tenacity of vision. I could, for instance, easily outstare any man I ever met. Yet, as I continued to stare at this man, I was conscious that it was only by an effort of will that I was able to resist a baleful something which seemed to be passing from his eyes to mine. It might have been imagination, but, in that sense, I am not an imaginative man; and, if it was, it was imagination of an unpleasantly vivid kind. I could understand how, in the case of a nervous, or a sensitive temperament, the fellow might exercise, by means of the peculiar quality of his glance alone, an influence of a most disastrous sort, which given an appropriate subject in the manifestation of its power might approach almost to the supernatural. If ever man was endowed with the traditional evil eye, in which Italians, among modern nations, are such profound believers, it was he.

When we had stared at each other for, I daresay, quite five minutes, I began to think I had had about enough of it. So, by way of breaking the ice, I put to him a question.

"May I ask how you found your way into my back yard?"

He did not reply in words, but, raising his hands, he lowered them, palms downward, with a gesture which was peculiarly oriental.

"Indeed?—Is that so?—Your meaning may be lucidity itself to you, but, for my benefit, perhaps you would not mind translating it into words. Once more I ask, how did you find your way into my back yard?"

Again nothing but the gesture.

---

[1] Youthfulness.
[2] Someone who is sociable or who enjoys company.

"Possibly you are not sufficiently acquainted with English manners and customs to be aware that you have placed yourself within reach of the pains and penalties of the law. Were I to call in the police you would find yourself in an awkward situation,—and, unless you are presently more explanatory, called in they will be."

By way of answer he indulged in a distortion of the countenance which might have been meant for a smile,—and which seemed to suggest that he regarded the police with a contempt which was too great for words.

"Why do you laugh—do you think that being threatened with the police is a joke? You are not likely to find it so.—Have you suddenly been bereft of the use of your tongue?"

He proved that he had not by using it.

"I have still the use of my tongue."

"That, at least, is something. Perhaps, since the subject of how you got into my back yard seems to be a delicate one, you will tell me why you got there."

"You know why I have come."

"Pardon me if I appear to flatly contradict you, but that is precisely what I do not know."

"You do know."

"Do I?—Then, in that case, I presume that you are here for the reason which appears upon the surface,—to commit a felony."

"You call me thief?"

"What else are you?"

"I am no thief.—You know why I have come."

He raised his head a little. A look came into his eyes which I felt that I ought to understand, yet to the meaning of which I seemed, for the instant, to have mislaid the key. I shrugged my shoulders.

"I have come because you wanted me."

"Because I wanted you!—On my word!—That's sublime!"

"All night you have wanted me,—do I not know? When she talked to you of him, and the blood boiled in your veins; when he spoke, and all the people listened, and you hated him, because he had honour in her eyes."

I was startled. Either he meant what it appeared incredible that he could mean, or—there was confusion somewhere.

"Take my advice, my friend, and don't try to come the bunco-steerer[1] over me,—I'm a bit in that line myself, you know."

---

[1] North American slang for a swindler, bunco came to mean con-trick or swindle, and might have been a corruption of the Spanish "banca," a card game.

This time the score was mine,—he was puzzled.

"I know not what you talk of."

"In that case, we're equal,—I know not what you talk of either."

His manner, for him, was childlike and bland.

"What is it you do not know? This morning did I not say,—if you want me, then I come?"

"I fancy I have some faint recollection of your being so good as to say something of the kind, but—where's the application?"

"Do you not feel for him the same as l?"

"Who's the him?"

"Paul Lessingham."

It was spoken quietly, but with a degree of—to put it gently—spitefulness which showed that at least the will to do the Apostle harm would not be lacking.

"And, pray, what is the common feeling which we have for him?"

"Hate."

Plainly, with this gentleman, hate meant hate,—in the solid oriental sense. I should hardly have been surprised if the mere utterance of the words had seared his lips.

"I am by no means prepared to admit that I have this feeling which you attribute to me, but, even granting that I have, what then?"

"Those who hate are kin."

"That, also, I should be slow to admit; but—to go a step farther— what has all this to do with your presence on my premises at this hour of the night?"

"You love her." This time I did not ask him to supply the name,— being unwilling that it should be soiled by the traffic of his lips. "She loves him,—that is not well. If you choose, she shall love you,—that will be well."

"Indeed.—And pray how is this consummation which is so devoutly to be desired to be brought about?"

"Put your hand into mine. Say that you wish it. It shall be done."

Moving a step forward, he stretched out his hand towards me. I hesitated. There was that in the fellow's manner which, for the moment, had for me an unwholesome fascination. Memories flashed through my mind of stupid stories which have been told of compacts made with the devil. I almost felt as if I was standing in the actual presence of one of the powers of evil. I thought of my love for Marjorie,—which had revealed itself after all these years; of the delight of holding her in my arms, of feeling the pressure of her lips to mine. As my gaze met his, the lower side of what the conquest of this fair lady would mean, burned in my brain; fierce imaginings blazed before my eyes. To win her,—only to win her!

What nonsense he was talking! What empty brag it was! Suppose, just for the sake of the joke, I did put my hand in his, and did wish, right out, what it was plain he knew. If I wished, what harm would it do! It would be the purest jest. Out of his own mouth he would be confounded, for it was certain that nothing would come of it. Why should I not do it then?

I would act on his suggestion,—I would carry the thing right through. Already I was advancing towards him, when—I stopped. I don't know why. On the instant, my thoughts went off at a tangent.

What sort of a blackguard did I call myself that I should take a woman's name in vain for the sake of playing fool's tricks with such scum of the earth as the hideous vagabond in front of me,—and that the name of the woman whom I loved? Rage took hold of me.

"You hound!" I cried.

In my sudden passage from one mood to another, I was filled with the desire to shake the life half out of him. But so soon as I moved a step in his direction, intending war instead of peace, he altered the position of his hand, holding it out towards me as if forbidding my approach. Directly he did so, quite involuntarily, I pulled up dead,—as if my progress had been stayed by bars of iron and walls of steel.

For the moment, I was astonished to the verge of stupefaction. The sensation was peculiar. I was as incapable of advancing another inch in his direction as if I had lost the use of my limbs,—I was even incapable of attempting to attempt to advance. At first I could only stare and gape. Presently I began to have an inkling of what had happened.

The scoundrel had almost succeeded in hypnotising me.

That was a nice thing to happen to a man of my sort at my time of life. A shiver went down my back,—what might have occurred if I had not pulled up in time! What pranks might a creature of that character not have been disposed to play. It was the old story of the peril of playing with edged tools; I had made the dangerous mistake of underrating the enemy's strength. Evidently, in his own line, the fellow was altogether something out of the usual way.

I believe that even as it was he thought he had me. As I turned away, and leaned against the table at my back, I fancy that he shivered,—as if this proof of my being still my own master was unexpected. I was silent,—it took some seconds to enable me to recover from the shock of the discovery of the peril in which I had been standing. Then I resolved that I would endeavour to do something which should make me equal to this gentleman of many talents.

"Take my advice, my friend, and don't attempt to play that hankey pankey off on to me again."

"I don't know what you talk of."

"Don't lie to me,—or I'll burn you into ashes."

Behind me was an electrical machine, giving an eighteen inch spark. It was set in motion by a lever fitted into the table, which I could easily reach from where I sat. As I spoke the visitor was treated to a little exhibition of electricity. The change in his bearing was amusing. He shook with terror. He salaamed down to the ground.

"My lord!—my lord!—have mercy, oh my lord!"

"Then you be careful, that's all. You may suppose yourself to be something of a magician, but it happens, unfortunately for you, that I can do a bit in that line myself,—perhaps I'm a trifle better at the game than you are. Especially as you have ventured into my stronghold, which contains magic enough to make a show of a hundred thousand such as you.

Taking down a bottle from a shelf, I sprinkled a drop or two of its contents on the floor. Immediately flames arose, accompanied by a blinding vapour. It was a sufficiently simple illustration of one of the qualities of phosphorous-bromide, but its effect upon my visitor was as startling as it was unexpected. If I could believe the evidence of my own eyesight, in the very act of giving utterance to a scream of terror he disappeared, how, or why, or whither, there was nothing to show,—in his place, where he had been standing, there seemed to be a dim object of some sort in a state of frenzied agitation on the floor. The phosphorescent vapour was confusing; the lights appeared to be suddenly burning low; before I had sense enough to go and see if there was anything there, and, if so, what, the flames had vanished, the man himself had reappeared, and, prostrated on his knees, was salaaming in a condition of abject terror.

"My lord! my lord!" he whined. "I entreat you, my lord, to use me as your slave!"

"I'll use you as my slave!" Whether he or I was the more agitated it would have been difficult to say,—but, at least, it would not have done to betray my feelings as he did his. "Stand up!"

He stood up. I eyed him as he did with an interest which, so far as I was concerned, was of a distinctly new and original sort. Whether or not I had been the victim of an ocular delusion I could not be sure. It was incredible to suppose that he could have disappeared as he had seemed to disappear,—it was also incredible that I could have imagined his disappearance. If the thing had been a trick, I had not the faintest notion how it had been worked; and, if it was not a trick, then what was it? Was it something new in scientific marvels? Could he give me as much instruction in the qualities of unknown forces as I could him?

In the meanwhile he stood in an attitude of complete submission, with downcast eyes, and hands crossed upon his breast. I started to cross-examine him.

"I am going to ask you some questions. So long as you answer them promptly, truthfully, you will be safe. Otherwise you had best beware."

"Ask, oh my lord."

"What is the nature of your objection to Mr. Lessingham?"

"Revenge."

"What has he done to you that you should wish to be revenged on him?"

"It is the feud of the innocent blood."

"What do you mean by that?"

"On his hands is the blood of my kin. It cries aloud for vengeance."

"Who has he killed?"

"That, my lord, is for me,—and for him."

"I see.—Am I to understand that you do not choose to answer me, and that I am again to use my—magic?"

I saw that he quivered.

"My lord, he has spilled the blood of her who has lain upon his breast."

I hesitated. What he meant appeared clear enough. Perhaps it would be as well not to press for further details. The words pointed to what it might be courteous to call an Eastern Romance,—though it was hard to conceive of the Apostle figuring as the hero of such a theme. It was the old tale retold, that to the life of every man there is a background,— that it is precisely in the unlikeliest cases that the background's darkest. What would that penny-plain-and-two-pence-coloured bogey, the Nonconformist Conscience,[1] make of such a story if it were blazoned through the land. Would Paul not come down with a run?

"'Spilling blood' is a figure of speech; pretty, perhaps, but vague. If you mean that Mr. Lessingham has been killing someone, your surest and—most effectual revenge would be gained by an appeal to the law."

---

[1] Nineteenth-century Protestant sects such as Baptists, Calvinistic Methodists, Quakers, Unitarians, and Congregationalists, which established themselves as separatist churches critical of the Church of England, were referred to as nonconformist or, otherwise, dissenters. While Atherton is referring to a publication, it appears to be fictitous.

"What has the Englishman's law to do with me?"

"If you can prove that he has been guilty of murder it would have a great deal to do with you. I assure you that at any rate, in that sense, the Englishman's law is no respecter of persons. Show him to be guilty, and it would hang Paul Lessingham as indifferently, and as cheerfully, as it would hang Bill Brown."

"Is that so?"

"It is so, as, if you choose, you will be easily able to prove to your own entire satisfaction."

He had raised his head, and was looking at something which he seemed to see in front of him with a maleficent glare in his sensitive eyes which it was not nice to see.

"He would be shamed?"

"Indeed he would be shamed."

"Before all men?"

"Before all men,—and, I take it, before all women too."

"And he would hang?"

"If shown to have been guilty of wilful murder,—yes."

His hideous face was lighted up by a sort of diabolical exultation which made it, if that were possible, more hideous still. I had apparently given him a wrinkle which pleased him most consummately.

"Perhaps I will do that in the end,—in the end!" He opened his eyes to their widest limits, then shut them tight,—as if to gloat on the picture which his fancy painted. Then reopened them. "In the meantime I will have vengeance in my own fashion. He knows already that the avenger is upon him,—he has good reason to know it. And through the days and the nights the knowledge shall be with him still, and it shall be to him as the bitterness of death,—aye, of many deaths. For he will know that escape there is none, and that for him there shall be no more sun in the sky, and that the terror shall be with him by night and by day, at his rising up and at his lying down, wherever his eyes shall turn it shall be there,—yet, behold, the sap and the juice of my vengeance is in this, in that though he shall be very sure that the days that are, are as the days of his death, yet shall he know that THE DEATH, THE GREAT DEATH, is coming—coming—and shall be on him—when I will!"

The fellow spoke like an inspired maniac. If he meant half what he said,—and if he did not then his looks and his tones belied him!—then a promising future bade fair to be in store for Mr. Lessingham,—and, also, circumstances being as they were, for Marjorie. It was this latter reflection which gave me pause. Either this imprecatory fanatic would have to be disposed of, by Lessingham himself, or by someone acting on his behalf, and, so far as their power of doing mischief went, his big words proved empty windbags, or Marjorie would have to be warned that there was at least one passage in her suitor's life, into which, ere it was too late, it was advisable that inquiry should be made. To allow Marjorie to irrevocably link her fate with the Apostle's, without being first of all made aware that he was, to all intents and purposes, a haunted man—that was not to be thought of.

"You employ large phrases."

My words cooled the other's heated blood. Once more his eyes were cast down, his hands crossed upon his breast.

"I crave my lord's pardon. My wound is ever new."

"By the way, what was the secret history, this morning, of that little incident of the cockroach?"

He glanced up quickly.

"Cockroach?—I know not what you say."

"Well,—was it beetle, then?"

"Beetle!"

He seemed, all at once, to have lost his voice,—the word was gasped.

"After you went we found, upon a sheet of paper, a capitally executed drawing of a beetle, which, I fancy, you must have left behind you,—*Scarabaeus sacer,* wasn't it?"

"I know not what you talk of."

"Its discovery seemed to have quite a singular effect on Mr. Lessingham. Now, why was that?"

"I know nothing."

"Oh yes you do,—and, before you go, I mean to know something too."

The man was trembling, looking this way and that, showing signs of marked discomfiture. That there was something about that ancient scarab, which figures so largely in the still unravelled tangles of the Egyptian mythologies, and the effect which the mere sight of its cartouche[1]—for the drawing had resembled something of the kind—had had on such a seasoned vessel as Paul Lessingham, which might be well worth my finding out, I felt convinced,—the man's demeanour, on my recurring to the matter, told its own plain tale. I made up my mind, if possible, to probe the business to the bottom, then and there.

---

[1] In Egyptology, an elongated oval with a straight bar at the end containing the hieroglyphs of the names and titles of pharaohs.

"Listen to me, my friend. I am a plain man, and I use plain speech,—it's a kind of hobby I have. You will give me the information I require, and that at once, or I will pit my magic against yours,—in which case I think it extremely probable that you will come off worst from the encounter."

I reached out for the lever, and the exhibition of electricity recommenced. Immediately his tremors were redoubled.

"My lord, I know not of what you talk."

"None of your lies for me.—Tell me why, at the sight of the thing on that sheet of paper, Paul Lessingham went green and yellow."

"Ask him, my lord."

"Probably, later on, that is what I shall do. In the meantime, I am asking you. Answer,—or look out for squalls."

The electrical exhibition was going on. He was glaring at it as if he wished that it would stop. As if ashamed of his cowardice, plainly, on a sudden, he made a desperate effort to get the better of his fears,—and succeeded better than I had expected or desired. He drew himself up with what, in him, amounted to an air of dignity.

"I am a child of Isis!"

It struck me that he made this remark, not so much to impress me, as with a view of elevating his own low spirits.

"Are you?—Then, in that case, I regret that I am unable to congratulate the lady on her offspring."

When I said that, a ring came into his voice which I had not heard before.

"Silence!—You know not of what you speak!—I warn you, as I warned Paul Lessingham, be careful not to go too far. Be not like him,—heed my warning."

"What is it I am being warned against,—the beetle?"

"Yes,—the beetle!"

Were I upon oath, and this statement being made, in the presence of witnesses, say, in a solicitor's office, I standing in fear of pains and penalties, I think that, at this point, I should leave the paper blank. No man likes to own himself a fool, or that he ever was a fool,—and ever since I have been wondering whether, on that occasion, that "child of Isis" did, or did not, play the fool with me. His performance was realistic enough at the time, heaven knows. But, as it gets farther and farther away, I ask myself, more and more confidently, as time effluxes, whether, after all, it was not clever juggling,—superhumanly clever juggling, if you will; that, and nothing more. If it was something more, then, with a vengeance! there is more in heaven and earth than is dreamed of in *Hamlet* our philosophy. The mere possibility opens vistas which the sane mind fears to contemplate.

Since, then, I am not on oath, and, should I fall short of verbal accuracy, I do not need to fear the engines of the law, what seemed to happen was this.

He was standing within about ten feet of where I leaned against the edge of the table. The light was full on, so that it was difficult to suppose that I could make a mistake as to what took place in front of me. As he replied to my mocking allusion to the beetle by echoing my own words, he vanished,—or, rather, I saw him taking a different shape before my eyes. His loose draperies all fell off him, and, as they were in the very act of falling, there issued, or there seemed to issue out of them, a monstrous creature of the beetle tribe,—the man himself was gone. On the point of size I wish to make myself clear. My impression, when I saw it first, was that it was as large as the man had been, and that it was, in some way, standing up on end, the legs towards me. But, the moment it came in view, it began to dwindle, and that so rapidly that, in a couple of seconds at most, a little heap of drapery was lying on the floor, on which was a truly astonishing example of the coleoptera.[1] It appeared to be a beetle. It was, perhaps, six or seven inches high, and about a foot in length. Its scales were of a vivid golden green. I could distinctly see where the wings were sheathed along the back, and, as they seemed to be slightly agitated. I looked, every moment, to see them opened, and the thing take wing.

I was so astonished,—as who would not have been?—that for an appreciable space of time I was practically in a state of stupefaction. I could do nothing but stare. I was acquainted with the legendary transmigrations of Isis, and with the story of the beetle which issues from the woman's womb through all eternity, and with the other pretty tales, but this, of which I was an actual spectator, was something new, even in legends. If the man, with whom I had just been speaking, was gone, where had he gone to? If this glittering creature was there, in his stead, whence had it come?

I do protest this much, that, after the first shock of surprise had passed, I retained my presence of mind. I felt as an investigator might feel, who has stumbled, haphazard, on some astounding, some epoch-making, discovery. I was conscious that I should have to make the best use of my mental faculties if I was to take full advantage of so

---

[1] Winged beetles.

astonishing an accident. I kept my glance riveted on the creature, with the idea of photographing it on my brain. I believe that if it were possible to take a retinal print—which it some day will be—you would have a perfect picture of what it was I saw. Beyond doubt it was a lamellicorn,[1] one of the *Copridæ*. With the one exception of its monstrous size, there were the characteristics in plain view;—the convex body, the large head, the projecting clypeus.[2] More, its smooth head and throat seemed to suggest that it was a female. Equally beyond a doubt, apart from its size, there were unusual features present too. The eyes were not only unwontedly conspicuous, they gleamed as if they were lighted by internal flames,—in some indescribable fashion they reminded me of my vanished visitor. The colouring was superb, and the creature appeared to have the chameleon-like faculty of lightening and darkening the shades at will. Its not least curious feature was its restlessness. It was in a state of continual agitation; and, as if it resented my inspection, the more I looked at it the more its agitation grew. As I have said, I expected every moment to see it take wing and circle through the air.

All the while I was casting about in my mind as to what means I could use to effect its capture. I did think of killing it, and, on the whole, I rather wish that I had at any rate attempted slaughter,—there were dozens of things, lying ready to my hand, any one of which would have severely tried its constitution;—but, on the spur of the moment, the only method of taking it alive which occurred to me, was to pop over it a big tin canister which had contained soda-lime. This canister was on the floor to my left. I moved towards it, as nonchalantly as I could, keeping an eye on that shining wonder all the time. Directly I moved, its agitation perceptibly increased,—it was, so to speak, all one whirr of tremblement; it scintillated, as if its coloured scales had been so many prisms; it began to unsheath its wings, as if it had finally decided that it would make use of them. Picking up the tin, disembarrassing it of its lid, I sprang towards my intended victim. Its wings opened wide; obviously it was about to rise; but it was too late. Before it had cleared the ground, the tin was over it.

It remained over it, however, for an instant only. I had stumbled, in my haste, and, in my effort to save myself from falling face foremost on to the floor, I was compelled to remove my hands from the tin. Before I was able to replace them, the tin was sent flying, and, while I was still partially recumbent, within eighteen inches of me, that beetle swelled

---

[1] A type of beetle, typically with antennae.
[2] A protective plate on an insect's head.

and swelled, until it had assumed its former portentous dimensions, when, as it seemed, it was enveloped by a human shape, and in less time than no time, there stood in front of me, naked from top to toe, my truly versatile oriental friend. One startling fact nudity revealed,—that I had been egregiously mistaken on the question of sex. My visitor was not a man, but a woman, and, judging from the brief glimpse which I had of her body, by no means old or ill-shaped either.

If that transformation was not a bewildering one, then two and two make five. The most level-headed scientist would temporarily have lost his mental equipoise on witnessing such a quick change as that within a span or two of his own nose. I was not only witless, I was breathless too,—I could only gape. And, while I gaped, the woman, stooping down, picking up her draperies, began to huddle them on her anyhow,—and, also, to skedaddle towards the door which led into the yard. When I observed this last manoeuvre, to some extent I did rise to the requirements of the situation. Leaping up, I rushed to stay her flight.

"Stop!" I shouted.

But she was too quick for me. Ere I could reach her, she had opened the door, and was through it,—and, what was more, she had slammed it in my face. In my excitement, I did some fumbling with the handle. When, in my turn, I was in the yard, she was out of sight. I did fancy I saw a dim form disappearing over the wall at the further side, and I made for it as fast as I knew how. I clambered on to the wall, looking this way and that, but there was nothing and no one to be seen. I listened for the sound of retreating footsteps, but all was still. Apparently I had the entire neighbourhood to my own sweet self. My visitor had vanished. Time devoted to pursuit I felt would be time ill-spent.

As I returned across the yard, Woodville, who still was taking his rest under the open canopy of heaven, sat up. Seemingly my approach had roused him out of slumber. At sight of me he rubbed his eyes, and yawned, and blinked.

"I say," he remarked, not at all unreasonably, "where am I?"

"You're on holy—or on haunted ground,—hang me if I quite know which!—but that's where you are, my boy."

"By Jove!—I am feeling queer!—I have got a headache, don't you know."

"I shouldn't be in the least surprised at anything you have, or haven't,—I'm beyond surprise. It's a drop of whisky you are wanting,—and what I'm wanting too,—only, for goodness sake, drop me none of your drops! Mine is a case for a bottle at the least."

I put my arm through his, and went with him into the laboratory. And, when we were in, I shut, and locked, and barred the door.

CHAPTER 19

THE LADY RAGES

Dora Grayling stood in the doorway.

"I told your servant he need not trouble to show me in,—and I've come without my aunt. I hope I'm not intruding."

She was—confoundedly; and it was on the tip of my tongue to tell her so. She came into the room, with twinkling eyes, looking radiantly happy,— that sort of look which makes even a plain young woman prepossessing.

"Am I intruding?—I believe I am."

She held out her hand, while she was still a dozen feet away, and when I did not at once dash forward to make a clutch at it, she shook her head and made a little mouth at me.

"What's the matter with you?—Aren't you well?"

I was not well,—I was very far from well. I was as unwell as I could be without being positively ill, and any person of common discernment would have perceived it at a glance. At the same time I was not going to admit anything of the kind to her.

"Thank you,—I am perfectly well."

"Then, if I were you, I would endeavour to become imperfectly well; a little imperfection in that direction might make you appear to more advantage."

"I am afraid that I am not one of those persons who ever do appear to much advantage,—did I not tell you so last night?"

"I believe you did say something of the kind,—it's very good of you to remember. Have you forgotten something else which you said to me last night?"

"You can hardly expect me to keep fresh in my memory all the follies of which my tongue is guilty."

"Thank you.—That is quite enough.—Good-day."

She turned as if to go.

"Miss Grayling!"

"Mr. Atherton?"

"What's the matter?—What have I been saying now?"

"Last night you invited me to come and see you this morning,—is that one of the follies of which your tongue was guilty?"

The engagement had escaped my recollection—it is a fact!—and my face betrayed me.

"You had forgotten?" Her cheeks flamed; her eyes sparkled. "You must pardon my stupidity for not having understood that the invitation was of that general kind which is never meant to be acted on."

She was half way to the door before I stopped her,—I had to take her by the shoulder to do it.

"Miss Grayling!—You are hard on me."

"I suppose I am.—Is anything harder than to be intruded on by an undesired, and unexpected, guest?"

"Now you are harder still.—If you knew what I have gone through since our conversation of last night, in your strength you would be merciful."

"Indeed?—What have you gone through?"

I hesitated. What I actually had gone through I certainly did not propose to tell her. Other reasons apart I did not desire to seem madder than I admittedly am,—and I lacked sufficient plausibility to enable me to concoct, on the spur of the moment, a plain tale of the doings of my midnight visitor which would have suggested that the narrator was perfectly sane. So I fenced,—or tried to.

"For one thing,—I have had no sleep."

I had not,—not one single wink. When I did get between the sheets, "all night I lay in agony," I suffered from that worst form of nightmare,— the nightmare of the man who is wide awake. There was continually before my fevered eyes the strange figure of that Nameless Thing. I had often smiled at tales of haunted folk,—here was I one of them. My feelings were not rendered more agreeable by a strengthening conviction that if I had only retained the normal attitude of a scientific observer I should, in all probability, have solved the mystery of my oriental friend, and that his example of the genus of *copridæ* might have been pinned,—by a very large pin!—on a piece—a monstrous piece!—of cork. It was galling to reflect that he and I had played together a game of bluff,—a game at which civilisation was once more proved to be a failure.

She could not have seen all this in my face; but she saw something— because her own look softened.

"You do look tired." She seemed to be casting about in her own mind for a cause. "You have been worrying." She glanced round the big laboratory. "Have you been spending the night in this—wizard's cave?"

"Pretty well."

"Oh!"

The monosyllable, as she uttered it, was big with meaning. Uninvited, she seated herself in an arm-chair, a huge old thing, of shagreen leather, which would have held half a dozen of her. Demure in it she looked, like an agreeable reminiscence, alive, and a little up-to-date, of the women of long ago. Her dove grey eyes seemed to perceive so much more than they cared to show.

"How is it that you have forgotten that you asked me to come?—didn't you mean it?"

"Of course I meant it."

"Then how is it you've forgotten?"

"I didn't forget."

"Don't tell fibs.—Something is the matter,—tell me what it is.—Is it that I am too early?"

"Nothing of the sort,—you couldn't be too early."

"Thank you.—When you pay a compliment, even so neat a one as that, sometimes, you should look as if you meant it.—It is early,—I know it's early, but afterwards I want you to come to lunch. I told aunt that I would bring you back with me."

"You are much better to me than I deserve."

"Perhaps." A tone came into her voice which was almost pathetic. "I think that to some men women are almost better than they deserve. I don't know why. I suppose it pleases them. It is odd." There was a different intonation,—a dryness. "Have you forgotten what I came for?"

"Not a bit of it,—I am not quite the brute I seem. You came to see an illustration of that pleasant little fancy of mine for slaughtering my fellows. The fact is, I'm hardly in a mood for that just now,—I've been illustrating it too much already."

"What do you mean?"

"Well, for one thing it's been murdering Lessingham's cat."

"Mr. Lessingham's cat?"

"Then it almost murdered Percy Woodville."

"Mr. Atherton!—I wish you wouldn't talk like that."

"It's a fact. It was a question of a little matter in a wrong place, and, if it hadn't been for something very like a miracle, he'd be dead."

"I wish you wouldn't have anything to do with such things—I hate them."

I stared.

"Hate them?—I thought you'd come to see an illustration."

"And pray what was your notion of an illustration?"

"Well, another cat would have had to be killed, at least."

"And do you suppose that I would have sat still while a cat was being killed for my—edification?"

"It needn't necessarily have been a cat, but something would have had to be killed,—how are you going to illustrate the death-dealing propensities of a weapon of that sort without it?"

"Is it possible that you imagine that I came here to see something killed?"

"Then for what did you come?"

I do not know what there was about the question which was startling, but as soon as it was out, she went a fiery red.

"Because I was a fool."

I was bewildered. Either she had got out of the wrong side of bed, or I had,—or we both had. Here she was, assailing me, hammer and tongs, so far as I could see, for absolutely nothing.

"You are pleased to be satirical at my expense."

"I should not dare. Your detection of me would be so painfully rapid."

I was in no mood for jangling. I turned a little away from her. Immediately she was at my elbow.

"Mr. Atherton?"

"Miss Grayling."

"Are you cross with me?"

"Why should I be? If it pleases you to laugh at my stupidity you are completely justified."

"But you are not stupid."

"No?—Nor you satirical."

"You are not stupid,—you know you are not stupid; it was only stupidity on my part to pretend that you were."

"It is very good of you to say so.—But I fear that I am an indifferent host. Although you would not care for an illustration, there may be other things which you might find amusing."

"Why do you keep on snubbing me?"

"I keep on snubbing you!"

"You are always snubbing me,—you know you are. Sometimes I feel as if I hated you."

"Miss Grayling!"

"I do! I do! I do!"

"After all, it is only natural."

"That is how you talk,—as if I were a child, and you were,—oh I don't know what.—Well, Mr. Atherton, I am sorry to be obliged to leave you. I have enjoyed my visit very much. I only hope I have not seemed too intrusive."

She flounced—"flounce" was the only appropriate word!—out of the room before I could stop her. I caught her in the passage.

"Miss Grayling, I entreat you—"

"Pray do not entreat me, Mr. Atherton." Standing still she turned to me. "I would rather show myself to the door as I showed myself in, but, if that is impossible, might I ask you not to speak to me between this and the street?"

The hint was broad enough, even for me. I escorted her through the hall without a word,—in perfect silence she shook the dust of my abode from off her feet.

I had made a pretty mess of things. I felt it as I stood on the top of the steps and watched her going,—she was walking off at four miles an hour; I had not even ventured to ask to be allowed to call a hansom.

It was beginning to occur to me that this was a case in which another blow upon the river might be, to say the least of it, advisable—and I was just returning into the house with the intention of putting myself into my flannels, when a cab drew up, and old Lindon got out of it.

CHAPTER 20

A HEAVY FATHER

Mr. Lindon was excited,—there is no mistaking it when he is, because with him excitement means perspiration, and as soon as he was out of the cab he took off his hat and began to wipe the lining.

"Atherton, I want to speak to you—most particularly—somewhere in private."

I took him into my laboratory. It is my rule to take no one there; it is a workshop, not a playroom,—the place is private; but, recently, my rules had become dead letters. Directly he was inside, Lindon began puffing and stewing, wiping his forehead, throwing out his chest, as if he were oppressed by a sense of his own importance. Then he started off talking at the top of his voice,—and it is not a low one either.

"Atherton, I—I've always looked on you as a—a kind of a son."

"That's very kind of you."

"I've always regarded you as a—a level-headed fellow; a man from whom sound advice can be obtained when sound advice—is—is most to be desired."

"That also is very kind of you."

"And therefore I make no apology for coming to you at—at what may be regarded as a—a strictly domestic crisis; at a moment in the history of the Lindons when delicacy and common sense are—are essentially required."

This time I contented myself with nodding. Already I perceived what was coming; somehow, when I am with a man I feel so much more clear-headed than I do when I am with a woman,—realise so much better the nature of the ground on which I am standing.

"What do you know of this man Lessingham?"

I knew it was coming.

"What all the world knows."

"And what does all the world know of him?—I ask you that! A flashy, plausible, shallow-pated, carpet-bagger,[1]—that is what all the world knows of him. The man's a political adventurer,—he snatches a precarious, and criminal, notoriety by trading on the follies of his fellow countrymen. He is devoid of decency, destitute of principle,— and impervious to all the feelings of a gentleman. What do you know of him besides this?"

"I am not prepared to admit that I do know that."

"Oh yes you do!—don't talk nonsense!—you choose to screen the fellow! I say what I mean,—I always have said, and I always shall say.— What do you know of him outside politics,—of his family—of his private life?"

"Well,—not very much."

"Of course you don't!—nor does anybody else! The man's a mush-room,—or a toadstool, rather!—sprung up in the course of a single night, apparently out of some dirty ditch.—Why, sir, not only is he without ordinary intelligence, he is even without a Brummagen[2] substitute for manners."

---

[1] American term for someone seeking political success in a place with which he has no connection.

[2] Dialect version of "Birmingham," a major industrial city in the English midlands. Presumably the use here is intended as an insult.

He had worked himself into a state of heat in which his countenance presented a not too agreeable assortment of scarlets and purples. He flung himself into a chair, threw his coat wide open, and his arms too, and started off again.

"The family of the Lindons is, at this moment, represented by a—a young woman,—by my daughter, sir. She represents me, and it's her duty to represent me adequately—adequately, sir! And what's more, between ourselves, sir, it's her duty to marry. My property's my own, and I would-n't have it pass to either of my confounded brothers on any account. They're next door to fools, and—and they don't represent me in any possible sense of the word. My daughter, sir, can marry whom she pleases,—whom she pleases! There's no one in England, peer or commoner, who would not esteem it an honour to have her for his wife—I've told her so,—yes, sir, I've told her, though you—you'd think that she, of all people in the world, wouldn't require telling. Yet what do you think she does? She—she actually carries on what I—I can't help calling a—a compromising acquaintance with this man Lessingham!"

"No!"

"But I say yes!—and I wish to heaven I didn't. I—I've warned her against the scoundrel more than once; I—I've told her to cut him dead. And yet, as—as you saw yourself, last night, in—in the face of the assembled House of Commons, after that twaddling clap-trap speech of his, in which there was not one sound sentiment, nor an idea which—which would hold water, she positively went away with him, in—in the most ostentatious and—and disgraceful fashion, on—on his arm, and—and actually snubbed her father.—It is monstrous that a parent—a father!—should be subjected to such treatment by his child."

The poor old boy polished his brow with his pocket-handkerchief.

"When I got home I—I told her what I thought of her, I promise you that,—and I told her what I thought of him,—I didn't mince my words with her. There are occasions when plain speaking is demanded,—and that was one. I positively forbade her to speak to the fellow again, or to recognise him if she met him in the street. I pointed out to her, with perfect candour, that the fellow was an infernal scoundrel,—that and nothing else!—and that he would bring disgrace on whoever came into contact with him, even with the end of a barge pole.—And what do you think she said?"

"She promised to obey you, I make no doubt."

"Did she, sir!—By gad, did she!—That shows how much you know her!—She said, and, by gad, by her manner, and—and the way she went on, you'd—you'd have thought that she was the parent and I was the child—she said that I—I grieved her, that she was disappointed in me, that times have changed,—yes, sir, she said that times have changed!—that, nowadays, parents weren't Russian autocrats—no, sir, not Russian autocrats!—that—that she was sorry. she couldn't oblige me,—yes, sir, that was how she put it,—she was sorry she couldn't oblige me, but it was altogether out of the question to suppose that she could put a period to a friendship which she valued, simply on account of—of my unreasonable prejudices,—and—and—and, in short, she—she told me to go to the devil, sir!"

"And did you—"

I was on the point of asking him if he went,—but I checked myself in time.

"Let us look at the matter as men of the world. What do you know against Lessingham, apart from his politics?"

"That's just it,—I know nothing."

"In a sense, isn't that in his favour?"

"I don't see how you make that out. I—I don't mind telling you that I—I've had inquiries made. He's not been in the House six years—this is his second Parliament—he's jumped up like a jack-in-the-box. His first constituency was Harwich—they've got him still, and much good may he do 'em!—but how he came to stand for the place,—or who, or what, or where he was before he stood for the place, no one seems to have the faintest notion."

"Hasn't he been a great traveller?"

"I never heard of it."

"Not in the East?"

"Has he told you so?"

"No,—I was only wondering. Well, it seems to me that to find out that nothing is known against him is something in his favour!"

"My dear Sydney, don't talk nonsense. What it proves is simply,—that he's a nothing and a nobody. Had he been anything or anyone, something would have been known about him, either for or against. I don't want my daughter to marry a man who—who—who's shot up through a trap, simply because nothing is known against him. Ha-hang me, if I wouldn't ten times sooner she should marry you."

When he said that, my heart leaped in my bosom. I had to turn away.

"I am afraid that is out of the question."

He stopped in his tramping, and looked at me askance.

"Why?"

I felt that, if I was not careful, I should be done for,—and, probably, in his present mood, Marjorie too.

"My dear Lindon, I cannot tell you how grateful I am to you for your suggestion, but I can only repeat that—unfortunately, anything of the kind is out of the question."

"I don't see why."

"Perhaps not."

"You—you're a pretty lot, upon my word!"

"I'm afraid we are."

"I—I want you to tell her that Lessingham is a damned scoundrel."

"I see.—But I would suggest that if I am to use the influence with which you credit me to the best advantage, or to preserve a shred of it, I had hardly better state the fact quite so bluntly as that."

"I don't care how you state it,—state it as you like. Only—only I want you to soak her mind with a loathing of the fellow; I—I—I want you to paint him in his true colours; in—in—in fact, I—I want you to choke him off."

While he still struggled with his words, and with the perspiration on his brow, Edwards entered. I turned to him.

"What is it?"

"Miss Lindon, sir, wishes to see you particularly, and at once."

At that moment I found the announcement a trifle perplexing,—it delighted Lindon. He began to stutter and to stammer.

"T-the very thing!—c-couldn't have been better!—show her in here! H-hide me somewhere,—I don't care where,—behind that screen! Y-you use your influence with her;—g-give her a good talking to;—t-tell her what I've told you; and at—at the critical moment I'll come in, and then—then if we can't manage her between us, it'll be a wonder."

The proposition staggered me.

"But, my dear Mr. Lindon—I fear that I cannot—"

He cut me short.

"Here she comes!"

Ere I could stop him he was behind the screen,—I had not seen him move with such agility before!—and before I could expostulate Marjorie was in the room. Something which was in her bearing, in her face, in her eyes, quickened the beating of my pulses,—she looked as if something had come into her life, and taken the joy clean out of it.

CHAPTER 21

THE TERROR IN THE NIGHT

"Sydney!" she cried, "I'm so glad that I can see you!"

She might be,—but, at that moment, I could scarcely assert that I was a sharer of her joy.

"I told you that if trouble overtook me I should come to you, and—I'm in trouble now. Such strange trouble."

So was I,—and in perplexity as well. An idea occurred to me,—I would outwit her eavesdropping father.

"Come with me into the house,—tell me all about it there."

She refused to budge.

"No,—I will tell you all about it here." She looked about her,—as it struck me queerly. "This is just the sort of place in which to unfold a tale like mine. It looks uncanny."

"But—"

"'But me no buts!' Sydney, don't torture me,—let me stop here where I am,—don't you see I'm haunted?"

She had seated herself. Now she stood up, holding her hands out in front of her in a state of extraordinary agitation, her manner as wild as her words.

"Why are you staring at me like that? Do you think I'm mad?—I wonder if I'm going mad.—Sydney, do people suddenly go mad? You're a bit of everything, you're a bit of a doctor too, feel my pulse,—there it is!—tell me if I'm ill!"

I felt her pulse,—it did not need its swift beating to inform me that fever of some sort was in her veins. I gave her something in a glass. She held it up to the level of her eyes.

"What's this?"

"It's a decoction of my own. You might not think it, but my brain sometimes gets into a whirl. I use it as a sedative. It will do you good."

She drained the glass.

"It's done me good already,—I believe it has; that's being something like a doctor.—Well, Sydney, the storm has almost burst. Last night papa forbade me to speak to Paul Lessingham—by way of a prelude."

"Exactly. Mr. Lindon—"

"Yes, Mr. Lindon,—that's papa. I fancy we almost quarrelled. I know papa said some surprising things,—but it's a way he has,—he's apt to say surprising things. He's the best father in the world, but—it's not in his nature to like a really clever person; your good high dried old Tory never can;—I've always thought that that's why he's so fond of you."

"Thank you. I presume that is the reason, though it had not occurred to me before."

Since her entry, I had, to the best of my ability, been turning the position over in my mind. I came to the conclusion that, all things considered, her father had probably as much right to be a sharer of his daughter's confidence as I had, even from the vantage of the screen,— and that for him to hear a few home truths proceeding from her lips might serve to clear the air. From such a clearance the lady would not be likely to come off worst. I had not the faintest inkling of what was the actual purport of her visit.

She started off, as it seemed to me, at a tangent.

"Did I tell you last night about what took place yesterday morning,—about the adventure of my finding the man?"

"Not a word."

"I believe I meant to,—I'm half disposed to think he's brought me trouble. Isn't there some superstition about evil befalling whoever shelters a homeless stranger?"

"We'll hope not, for humanity's sake."

"I fancy there is,—I feel sure there is.—Anyhow, listen to my story. Yesterday morning, before breakfast,—to be accurate, between eight and nine, I looked out of the window, and I saw a crowd in the street. I sent Peter out to see what was the matter. He came back and said there was a man in a fit. I went out to look at the man in the fit. I found, lying on the ground, in the centre of the crowd, a man who, but for the tattered remnants of what had apparently once been a cloak, would have been stark naked. He was covered with dust, and dirt, and blood,—a dreadful sight. As you know, I have had my smattering of instruction in First Aid to the Injured, and that kind of thing, so, as no one else seemed to have any sense, and the man seemed as good as dead, I thought I would try my hand. Directly I knelt down beside him, what do you think he said?"

"Thank you."

"Nonsense.—He said, in such a queer, hollow, croaking voice, 'Paul Lessingham.' I was dreadfully startled. To hear a perfect stranger, a man in his condition, utter that name in such a fashion—to me, of all people in the world!—took me aback. The policeman who was holding his head remarked, 'That's the first time he's opened his mouth. I thought he was dead.' He opened his mouth a second time. A convulsive movement went all over him, and he exclaimed, with the strangest earnestness, and so loudly that you might have heard him at the other end of the street, 'Be warned, Paul Lessingham, be warned!' It was very silly of me, perhaps, but I cannot tell you how his words, and his manner—the two together—affected me.—Well, the long and the short of it was, that I had him taken into the house, and washed, and put to bed,—and I had the doctor sent for. The doctor could make nothing of it at all. He reported that the man seemed to be suffering from some sort of cataleptic seizure[1]—I could see that he thought it likely to turn out most as interesting a case as I did."

"Did you acquaint your father with the addition to his household?"

She looked at me, quizzically.

"You see, when one has such a father as mine one cannot tell him everything, at once. There are occasions on which one requires time."

I felt that this would be wholesome hearing for old Lindon.

"Last night, after papa and I had exchanged our little courtesies,—which, it is to be hoped, were to papa's satisfaction, since they were not to mine—I went to see the patient. I was told that he had neither eaten nor drunk, moved nor spoken. But, so soon as I approached his bed, he showed signs of agitation. He half raised himself upon his pillow, and he called out, as if he had been addressing some large assembly—I can't describe to you the dreadful something which was in his voice, and on his face,—'Paul Lessingham!—Beware!—The Beetle!'"

When she said that, I was startled.

"Are you sure those were the words he used?"

"Quite sure. Do you think I could mistake them,—especially after what has happened since? I hear them singing in my ears,—they haunt me all the time."

She put her hands up to her face, as if to veil something from her eyes. I was becoming more and more convinced that there was something about the Apostle's connection with his Oriental friend which needed probing to the bottom.

"What sort of a man is he to look at, this patient of yours?"

I had my doubts as to the gentleman's identity,—which her words dissolved; only, however, to increase my mystification in another direction.

"He seems to be between thirty and forty. He has light hair, and straggling sandy whiskers. He is so thin as to be nothing but skin and bone,—the doctor says it's a case of starvation."

---

[1] A trance-like condition, where consciousness or sensation is suspended.

"You say he has light hair, and sandy whiskers. Are you sure the whiskers are real?"

She opened her eyes.

"Of course they're real. Why shouldn't they be real?"

"Does he strike you as being a—foreigner?"

"Certainly not. He looks like an Englishman, and he speaks like one, and not, I should say, of the lowest class. It is true that there is a very curious, a weird, quality in his voice, what I have heard of it, but it is not un-English. If it is catalepsy he is suffering from, then it is a kind of catalepsy I never heard of. Have you ever seen a clairvoyant?" I nodded. "He seems to me to be in a state of clairvoyance. Of course the doctor laughed when I told him so, but we know what doctors are, and I still believe that he is in some condition of the kind. When he said that last night he struck me as being under what those sort of people call 'influence,' and that whoever had him under influence was forcing him to speak against his will, for the words came from his lips as if they had been wrung from him in agony."

Knowing what I did know, that struck me as being rather a remarkable conclusion for her to have reached, by the exercise of her own unaided powers of intuition,—but I did not choose to let her know I thought so.

"My dear Marjorie!—you who pride yourself on having your imagination so strictly under control!—on suffering it to take no errant flights!"

"Is not the fact that I do so pride myself proof that I am not likely to make assertions wildly,—proof, at any rate, to you? Listen to me. When I left that unfortunate creature's room,—I had had a nurse sent for, I left him in her charge—and reached my own bedroom, I was possessed by a profound conviction that some appalling, intangible, but very real danger, was at that moment threatening Paul."

"Remember,—you had had an exciting evening; and a discussion with your father. Your patient's words came as a climax."

"That is what I told myself,—or, rather, that was what I tried to tell myself, because, in some extraordinary fashion, I had lost the command of my powers of reflection."

"Precisely."

"It was not precisely,—or, at least, it was not precisely in the sense you mean. You may laugh at me, Sydney, but I had an altogether indescribable feeling, a feeling which amounted to knowledge, that I was in the presence of the supernatural."

"Nonsense!"

"It was not nonsense,—I wish it had been nonsense. As I have said, I was conscious, completely conscious, that some frightful peril was assailing Paul. I did not know what it was, but I did know that it was something altogether awful, of which merely to think was to shudder. I wanted to go to his assistance, I tried to, more than once; but I couldn't, and I knew that I couldn't,—I knew that I couldn't move as much as a finger to help him.—Stop,—let me finish!—I told myself that it was absurd, but it wouldn't do; absurd or not, there was the terror with me in the room. I knelt down, and I prayed, but the words wouldn't come. I tried to ask God to remove this burden from my brain, but my longings wouldn't shape themselves into words, and my tongue was palsied. I don't know how long I struggled, but, at last, I came to understand that, for some cause, God had chosen to leave me to fight the fight alone. So I got up, and undressed, and went to bed,—and that was the worst of all. I had sent my maid away in the first rush of my terror, afraid, and, I think, ashamed, to let her see my fear. Now I would have given anything to summon her back again, but I couldn't do it, I couldn't even ring the bell. So, as I say, I got into bed."

She paused, as if to collect her thoughts. To listen to her words, and to think of the suffering which they meant to her, was almost more than I could endure. I would have thrown away the world to have been able to take her in my arms, and soothe her fears. I knew her to be, in general, the least hysterical of young women; little wont to become the prey of mere delusions; and, incredible though it sounded, I had an innate conviction that, even in its wildest periods, her story had some sort of basis in solid fact. What that basis amounted to, it would be my business, at any and every cost, quickly to determine.

"You know how you have always laughed at me because of my objection to—cockroaches, and how, in spring, the neighbourhood of May-bugs has always made me uneasy. As soon as I got into bed I felt that something of the kind was in the room."

"Something of what kind?"

"Some kind of—beetle. I could hear the whirring of its wings; I could hear its droning in the air; I knew that it was hovering above my head; that it was coming lower and lower, nearer and nearer. I hid myself; I covered myself all over with the clothes,—then I felt it bumping against the coverlet. And, Sydney!" She drew closer. Her blanched cheeks and frightened eyes made my heart bleed. Her voice became but an echo of itself. "It followed me."

"Marjorie!"

"It got into the bed."

"You imagined it."

"I didn't imagine it. I heard it crawl along the sheets, till it found a way between them, and then it crawled towards me. And I felt it—against my face.—And it's there now."

"Where?"

She raised the forefinger of her left hand.

"There!—Can't you hear it droning?"

She listened, intently. I listened too. Oddly enough, at that instant the droning of an insect did become audible.

"It's only a bee, child, which has found its way through the open window."

"I wish it were only a bee, I wish it were.—Sydney, don't you feel as if you were in the presence of evil? Don't you want to get away from it, back into the presence of God?"

"Marjorie!"

"Pray, Sydney, pray!—I can't!—I don't know why, but I can't!"

She flung her arms about my neck, and pressed herself against me in paroxysmal agitation. The violence of her emotion bade fair to unman me too. It was so unlike Marjorie,—and I would have given my life to save her from a toothache. She kept repeating her own words,—as if she could not help it.

"Pray, Sydney, pray!"

At last I did as she wished me. At least, there is no harm in praying,—I never heard of its bringing hurt to anyone. I repeated aloud the Lord's Prayer,—the first time for I know not how long. As the divine sentences came from my lips, hesitatingly enough, I make no doubt, her tremors ceased. She became calmer. Until, as I reached the last great petition, "Deliver us from evil," she loosed her arms from about my neck, and dropped upon her knees, close to my feet. And she joined me in the closing words, as a sort of chorus.

"For Thine is the Kingdom, the Power, and the Glory, for ever and ever. Amen."

When the prayer was ended, we both of us were still. She with her head bowed, and her hands clasped; and I with something tugging at my heart-strings which I had not felt there for many and many a year, almost as if it had been my mother's hand,—I daresay that sometimes she does stretch out her hand, from her place among the angels, to touch my heart-strings, and I know nothing of it all the while.

As the silence still continued, I chanced to glance up, and there was old Lindon peeping at us from his hiding-place behind the screen. The look of amazed perplexity which was on his big red face struck me with such a keen sense of the incongruous that it was all I could do to keep from laughter. Apparently the sight of us did nothing to lighten the fog which was in his brain, for he stammered out, in what was possibly intended for a whisper,

"Is—is she m-mad?"

The whisper,—if it was meant for a whisper—was more than sufficiently audible to catch his daughter's ears. She started—raised her head—sprang to her feet—turned—and saw her father.

"Papa!"

Immediately her sire was seized with an access of stuttering.

"W-w-what the d-devil's the—the m-m-meaning of this?"

Her utterance was clear enough,—I fancy her parent found it almost painfully clear.

"Rather it is for me to ask, what is the meaning of this! Is it possible, that, all the time, you have actually been concealed behind that—screen?"

Unless I am mistaken the old gentleman cowered before the directness of his daughter's gaze,—and endeavoured to conceal the fact by an explosion of passion.

"Do-don't you s-speak to me li-like that, you un-undutiful girl! I—I'm your father!"

"You certainly are my father; though I was unaware until now that my father was capable of playing the part of eavesdropper."

Rage rendered him speechless,—or, at any rate, he chose to let us believe that that was the determining cause of his continuing silent. So Marjorie turned to me,—and, on the whole, I had rather she had not. Her manner was very different from what it had been just now,—it was more than civil, it was freezing.

"Am I to understand, Mr. Atherton, that this has been done with your cognisance? That while you suffered me to pour out my heart to you unchecked, you were aware, all the time, that there was a listener behind the screen?"

I became keenly aware, on a sudden, that I had borne my share in playing her a very shabby trick,—I should have liked to throw old Lindon through the window.

"The thing was not of my contriving. Had I the opportunity I would have compelled Mr. Lindon to face you when you came in. But your distress caused me to lose my balance. And you will do me the justice—

to remember that I endeavoured to induce you to come with me into another room."

"But I do not seem to remember your hinting at there being any particular reason why I should have gone."

"You never gave me a chance."

"Sydney!—I had not thought you would have played me such a trick!"

When she said that—in such a tone!—the woman whom I loved! – I could have hammered my head against the wall. The hound I was to have treated her so scurvily!

Perceiving I was crushed she turned again to face her father, cool, calm, stately;—she was, on a sudden, once more, the Marjorie with whom I was familiar. The demeanour of parent and child was in striking contrast. If appearances went for aught, the odds were heavy that in any encounter which might be coming the senior would suffer.

"I hope, papa, that you are going to tell me that there has been some curious mistake, and that nothing was farther from your intention than to listen at a keyhole. What would you have thought—and said—if I had attempted to play the spy on you? And I have always understood that men were so particular on points of honour."

Old Lindon was still hardly fit to do much else than splutter,— certainly not qualified to chop phrases with this sharp-tongued maiden.

"D-don't talk to me li-like that, girl!—I—I believe you're s-stark mad!" He turned to me. "W-what was that tomfoolery she was talking to you about?"

"To what do you allude?"

"About a rub-rubbishing b-beetle, and g-goodness alone knows what, d-diseased and m-morbid imagination,—r-reared on the literature of the gutter!—I never thought that a child of mine could have s-sunk to such a depth!—Now, Atherton, I ask you to t-tell me frankly,—what do you think of a child who behaves as she has done? Who makes a nameless vagabond into the house and con-conceals his presence from her father? And m-mark the sequel! even the vagabond warns her against the r-rascal Lessingham!—Now, Atherton, tell me what you think of a girl who behaves like that?" I shrugged my shoulders. "I—I know very well what you d-do think of her,—don't be afraid to say it out because she's present."

"No; Sydney, don't be afraid."

I saw that her eyes were dancing,—in a manner of speaking, her looks brightened under the sunshine of her father's displeasure.

"Let's hear what you think of her as a—as a m-man of the world!"

"Pray, Sydney, do!"

"What you feel for her in your—your heart of hearts!"

"Yes, Sydney, what do you feel for me in your heart of hearts?"

The baggage beamed with heartless sweetness,—she was making a mock of me. Her father turned as if he would have rent her.

"D-don't you speak until you're spoken to! Atherton, I—I hope I'm not deceived in you; I—I hope you're the man I—I took you for; that you're willing and—and ready to play the part of a-a-an honest friend to this mis-misguided simpleton. T-this is not the time for mincing words, it—it's the time for candid speech. Tell this—this weak-minded young woman, right out, whether this man Lessingham is, or is not, a damned scoundrel."

"Papa!—Do you really think that Sydney's opinion, or your opinion, is likely to alter facts?"

"Do you hear, Atherton, tell this wretched girl the truth!"

"My dear Mr. Lindon, I have already told you that I know nothing either for or against Mr. Lessingham except what is known to all the world."

"Exactly,—and all the world knows him to be a miserable adventurer who is scheming to entrap my daughter."

"I am bound to say, since you press me, that your language appears to me to be unnecessarily strong."

"Atherton, I—I'm ashamed of you!"

"You see, Sydney, even papa is ashamed of you; now you are outside the pale.—My dear papa, if you will allow me to speak, I will tell you what I know to be the truth, the whole truth, and nothing but the truth.—That Mr. Lessingham is a man with great gifts goes without saying,—permit me, papa! He is a man of genius. He is a man of honour. He is a man of the loftiest ambitions, of the highest aims. He has dedicated his whole life to the improvement of the conditions amidst which the less fortunate of his fellow countrymen are at present compelled to exist. That seems to me to be an object well worth having. He has asked me to share his lifework, and I have told him that I will; when, and where, and how, he wants me to. And I will. I do not suppose his life has been free from peccadilloes. I have no delusion on the point. What man's life has? Who among men can claim to be without sin? Even the members of our highest families sometimes hide behind screens. But I know that he is, at least, as good a man as I ever met, I am persuaded that I shall never meet a better; and I thank God that I have found favour in his eyes.—Goodbye, Sydney.—I suppose I shall see you again, papa."

With the merest inclination of her head to both of us she straightway left the room. Lindon would have stopped her.

"S-stay, y-y-y-you—" he stuttered.

But I caught him by the arm.

"If you will be advised by me, you will let her go. No good purpose will be served by a multiplication of words."

"Atherton, I—I'm disappointed in you. You—you haven't behaved as I expected. I—I haven't received from you the assistance which I looked for."

"My dear Lindon, it seems to me that your method of diverting the young lady from the path which she has set herself to tread is calculated to send her furiously along it."

"C-confound the women! c-confound the women! I don't mind telling you, in c-confidence, that at—at times, her mother was the devil, and I'll be—I'll be hanged if her daughter isn't worse.—What was the tomfoolery she was talking to you about? Is she mad?"

"No,—I don't think she's mad."

"I never heard such stuff, it made my blood run cold to bear her. What's the matter with the girl?"

"Well,—you must excuse my saying that I don't fancy you quite understand women."

"I—I don't,—and I—I—I don't want to either."

I hesitated; then resolved on a taradiddle—in Marjorie's interest.

"Marjorie is high-strung,—extremely sensitive. Her imagination is quickly aflame. Perhaps, last night, you drove her as far as was safe. You heard for yourself how, in consequence, she suffered. You don't want people to say you have driven her into a lunatic asylum."

"I—good heavens, no! I—I'll send for the doctor directly I get home,—I—I'll have the best opinion in town."

"You'll do nothing of the kind,—you'll only make her worse. What you have to do is to be patient with her, and let her have peace.—As for this affair of Lessingham's, I have a suspicion that it may not be all such plain sailing as she supposes."

"What do you mean?"

"I mean nothing. I only wish you to understand that until you hear from me again you had better let matters slide. Give the girl her head."

"Give the girl her head! H-haven't I—I g-given the g-girl her h-head all her l-life!" He looked at his watch. "Why, the day's half gone!" He began scurrying towards the front door, I following at his heels. "I've got a committee meeting on at the club,—m-most important! For weeks they've been giving us the worst food you ever tasted in your life,—p-played havoc with my digestion, and I—I'm going to tell them if—things aren't changed, they—they'll have to pay my doctor's bills.—As for that man, Lessingham—"

As he spoke, he himself opened the hall door, and there, standing on the step was "that man Lessingham" himself. Lindon was a picture. The Apostle was as cool as a cucumber. He held out his hand.

"Good morning, Mr. Lindon. What delightful weather we are having."

Lindon put his hand behind his back,—and behaved as stupidly as he very well could have done.

"You will understand, Mr. Lessingham, that, in future, I don't know you, and that I shall decline to recognise you anywhere; and that what I say applies equally to any member of my family."

With his hat very much on the back of his head he went down the steps like an inflated turkeycock.

CHAPTER 22

THE HAUNTED MAN

To have received the cut discourteous from his future father-in-law might have been the most commonplace of incidents,—Lessingham evinced not a trace of discomposure. So far as I could judge, he took no notice of the episode whatever, behaving exactly as if nothing had happened. He merely waited till Mr. Lindon was well off the steps; then, turning to me, he placidly observed,

"Interrupting you again, you see.—May I?"

The sight of him had set up such a turmoil in my veins, that, for the moment, I could not trust myself to speak. I felt, acutely, that an explanation with him was, of all things, the thing most to be desired,—and that quickly. Providence could not have thrown him more opportunely in the way. If, before he went away, we did not understand each other a good deal more clearly, upon certain points, the fault should not be mine. Without a responsive word, turning on my heels, I led the way into the laboratory.

Whether he noticed anything peculiar in my demeanour, I could not tell. Within he looked about him with that purely facial smile, the sight of which had always engendered in me a certain distrust of him.

"Do you always receive visitors in here?"

"By no means."

"What is this?"

Stooping down, he picked up something from the floor. It was a lady's purse—a gorgeous affair, of crimson leather and gleaming gold. Whether it was Marjorie's or Miss Grayling's I could not tell. He watched me as I examined it.

"Is it yours?"

"No. It is not mine."

Placing his hat and umbrella on one chair, he placed himself upon another,—very leisurely. Crossing his legs, laying his folded hands upon his knees, he sat and looked at me. I was quite conscious of his observation; but endured it in silence, being a little wishful that he should begin.

Presently he had, as I suppose, enough of looking at me, and spoke.

"Atherton, what is the matter with you?—Have I done something to offend you too?"

"Why do you ask?"

"Your manner seems a little singular."

"You think so?"

"I do."

"What have you come to see me about?"

"Just now, nothing.—I like to know where I stand."

His manner was courteous, easy, even graceful. I was out-manoeuvred. I understood the man sufficiently well to be aware that when once he was on the defensive, the first blow would have to come from me. So I struck it.

"I, also, like to know where I stand.—Lessingham, I am aware, and you know that I am aware, that you have made certain overtures to Miss Lindon. That is a fact in which I am keenly interested."

"As—how?"

"The Lindons and the Athertons are not the acquaintances of one generation only. Marjorie Lindon and I have been friends since childhood. She looks upon me as a brother—"

"As a brother?"

"As a brother."

"Yes."

"Mr. Lindon regards me as a son. He has given me his confidence; as I believe you are aware, Marjorie has given me hers; and now I want you to give me yours."

"What do you want to know?"

"I wish to explain my position before I say what I have to say, because I want you to understand me clearly.—I believe, honestly, that the thing I most desire in this world is to see Marjorie Lindon happy. If I thought she would be happy with you, I should say, God speed you both! and I should congratulate you with all my heart, because I think that you would have won the best girl in the whole world to be your wife."

"I think so too."

"But, before I did that, I should have to see, at least, some reasonable probability that she would be happy with you."

"Why should she not?"

"Will you answer a question?"

"What is the question?"

"What is the story in your life of which you stand in such hideous terror?"

There was a perceptible pause before he answered.

"Explain yourself."

"No explanation is needed,—you know perfectly well what I mean."

"You credit me with miraculous acumen."

"Don't juggle, Lessingham,—be frank!"

"The frankness should not be all on one side.—There is that in your frankness, although you may be unconscious of it, which some men might not unreasonably resent."

"Do you resent it?"

"That depends. If you are arrogating to yourself the right to place yourself between Miss Lindon and me, I do resent it, strongly."

"Answer my question!"

"I answer no question which is addressed to me in such a tone."

He was as calm as you please. I recognised that already I was in peril of losing my temper,—which was not at all what I desired. I eyed him intently, he returning me look for look. His countenance betrayed no sign of a guilty conscience; I had not seen him more completely at his ease. He smiled,—facially, and also, as it seemed to me, a little derisively. I am bound to admit that his bearing showed not the faintest shadow of resentment, and that in his eyes there was a gentleness, a softness, which I had not observed in them before,—I could almost have suspected him of being sympathetic.

"In this matter, you must know, I stand in the place of Mr. Lindon."

"Well?"

"Surely you must understand that before anyone is allowed to think of marriage with Marjorie Lindon he will have to show that his past, as the advertisements have it, will bear the fullest investigation."

"Is that so?—Will your past bear the fullest investigation?"

I winced.

"At any rate, it is known to all the world."

"Is it?—Forgive me if I say, I doubt it. I doubt if, of any wise man, that can be said with truth. In all our lives there are episodes which we keep to ourselves."

I felt that that was so true that, for the instant, I hardly knew what to say.

"But there are episodes and episodes, and when it comes to a man being haunted one draws the line."

"Haunted?"

"As you are."

He got up.

"Atherton, I think that I understand you, but I fear that you do not understand me." He went to where a self-acting mercurial air-pump was standing on a shelf. "What is this curious arrangement of glass tubes and bulbs?"

"I do not think that you do understand me, or you would know that I am in no mood to be trifled with."

"Is it some kind of an exhauster?"

"My dear Lessingham, I am entirely at your service. I intend to have an answer to my question before you leave this room, but, in the meanwhile, your convenience is mine. There are some very interesting things here which you might care to see."

"Marvellous, is it not, how the human intellect progresses,—from conquest unto conquest."

"Among the ancients the progression had proceeded farther than with us."

"In what respect?"

"For instance, in the affair of the Apotheosis of the Beetle;—I saw it take place last night."

"Where?"

"Here,—within a few feet of where you are standing."

"Are you serious?"

"Perfectly."

"What did you see?"

"I saw the legendary Apotheosis of the Beetle performed, last night, before my eyes, with a gaudy magnificence at which the legends never hinted."

"That is odd. I once thought that I saw something of the kind myself."

"So I understand."

"From whom?"

"From a friend of yours."

"From a friend of mine?—Are you sure it was from a friend of mine?"

The man's attempt at coolness did him credit,—but it did not deceive me. That he thought I was endeavouring to bluff him out of his secret I perceived quite clearly; that it was a secret which he would only render with his life I was beginning to suspect. Had it not been for Marjorie, I should have cared nothing,—his affairs were his affairs; though I realised perfectly well that there was something about the man which, from the scientific explorer's point of view, might be well worth finding out. Still, as I say, if it had not been for Marjorie, I should have let it go; but, since she was so intimately concerned in it, I wondered more and more what it could be.

My attitude towards what is called the supernatural is an open one. That all things are possible I unhesitatingly believe,—I have, even in my short time, seen so many so-called impossibilities proved possible. That we know everything, I doubt;—that our great-great-great-greatgrand-sires, our forebears of thousands of years ago, of the extinct civilisations, knew more on some subjects than we do, I think is, at least, probable. All the legends can hardly be false.

Because men claimed to be able to do things in those days which we cannot do, and which we do not know how they did, we profess to think that their claims are finally dismissed by exclaiming—lies! But it is not so sure.

For my part, what I had seen I had seen. I had seen some devil's trick played before my very eyes. Some trick of the same sort seemed to have been played upon my Marjorie,—I repeat that I write "my Marjorie" because, to me, she will always be "my" Marjorie! It had driven her half out of her senses. As I looked at Lessingham, I seemed to see her at his side, as I had seen her not long ago, with her white, drawn face, and staring eyes, dumb with an agony of fear. Her life was bidding fair to be knit with his,—what Upas tree[1] of horror was rooted in his very bones? The thought that her sweet purity was likely to be engulfed in a devil's slough in which he was wallowing was not to be endured. As I realised that the man was more than my match at the game which I was playing—in which such vital interests were at stake!—my hands itched to clutch him by the throat, and try another way.

---

[1] Southeast Asian tree, also known as the poison tree, and belonging the mulberry family, with a poisonous latex used for arrows; legend has it that it is reputed to kill all who fall asleep under it.

Doubtless my face revealed my feelings, because, presently, he said,

"Are you aware how strangely you are looking at me, Atherton? Were my countenance a mirror I think you would be surprised to see in it your own."

I drew back from him,—I daresay, sullenly.

"Not so surprised as, yesterday morning, you would have been to have seen yours,—at the mere sight of a pictured scarab."

"How easily you quarrel."

"I do not quarrel."

"Then perhaps it's I. If that is so, then, at once, the quarrel's ended,— pouf! it's done. Mr. Lindon, I fear, because, politically, we differ, regards me as anathema. Has he put some of his spirit into you?—You are a wiser man."

"I am aware that you are an adept with words. But this is a case in which words only will not serve."

"Then what will serve?"

"I am myself beginning to wonder."

"And I."

"As you so courteously suggest, I believe I am wiser than Lindon. I do not care for your politics, or for what you call your politics, one fig. I do not care if you are as other men are, as I am,—not unspotted from the world! But I do care if you are leprous. And I believe you are."

"Atherton!"

"Ever since I have known you I have been conscious of there being something about you which I found it difficult to diagnose;—in an unwholesome sense, something out of the common, non-natural; an atmosphere of your own. Events, so far as you are concerned, have, during the last few days moved quickly. They have thrown an uncomfortably lurid light on that peculiarity of yours which I have noticed. Unless you can explain them to my satisfaction, you will withdraw your pretensions to Miss Lindon's hand, or I shall place certain facts before that lady, and, if necessary, publish them to the world."

He grew visibly paler but he smiled—facially.

"You have your own way of conducting a conversation, Mr. Atherton.—What are the events to whose rapid transit you are alluding?"

"Who was the individual, practically stark naked, who came out of your house, in such singular fashion, at dead of night?"

"Is that one of the facts with which you propose to tickle the public ear?"

"Is that the only explanation which you have to offer?"

"Proceed, for the present, with your indictment."

"I am not so unobservant as you appear to imagine. There were features about the episode which struck me forcibly at the time, and which have struck me more forcibly since. To suggest, as you did yesterday morning, that it was an ordinary case of burglary, or that the man was a lunatic, is an absurdity!"

"Pardon me,—I did nothing of the kind."

"Then what do you suggest?"

"I suggested, and do suggest, nothing. All the suggestions come from you."

"You went very much out of your way to beg me to keep the matter quiet. There is an appearance of suggestion about that."

"You take a jaundiced view of all my actions, Mr. Atherton. Nothing, to me, could seem more natural.—However,—proceed."

He had his hands behind his back, and rested them on the edge of the table against which he was leaning. He was undoubtedly ill at ease; but so far I had not made the impression on him, either mentally or morally, which I desired.

"Who is your Oriental friend?"

"I do not follow you."

"Are you sure?"

"I am certain. Repeat your question."

"Who is your Oriental friend?"

"I was not aware that I had one."

"Do you swear that?"

He laughed, a strange laugh.

"Do you seek to catch me tripping? You conduct your case with too much animus. You must allow me to grasp the exact purport of your inquiry before I can undertake to reply to it on oath."

"Are you not aware that at present there is in London an individual who claims to have had a very close, and a very curious, acquaintance with you in the East?"

"I am not."

"That you swear?"

"That I do swear."

"That is singular."

"Why is it singular?"

"Because I fancy that that individual haunts you."

"Haunts me?"

"Haunts you."

"You jest."

"You think so?—You remember that picture of the scarabaeus which, yesterday morning, frightened you into a state of semi-idiocy!"

"You use strong language.—I know what you allude to."

"Do you mean to say that you don't know that you were indebted for that to your Oriental friend?"

"I don't understand you."

"Are you sure?"

"Certainly I am sure.—It occurs to me, Mr. Atherton, that an explanation is demanded from you rather than from me. Are you aware that the purport of my presence here is to ask you how that picture found its way into your room?"

"It was projected by the Lord of the Beetle."

The words were chance ones,—but they struck a mark.

"The Lord—." He faltered,—and stopped. He showed signs of discomposure. "I will be frank with you,—since frankness is what you ask." His smile, that time, was obviously forced. "Recently I have been the victim of delusions," there was a pause before the word, "of a singular kind. I have feared that they were the result of mental overstrain. Is it possible that you can enlighten me as to their source?"

I was silent. He was putting a great strain upon himself, but the twitching of his lips betrayed him. A little more, and I should reach the other side of Mr. Lessingham,—the side which he kept hidden from the world.

"Who is this—individual whom you speak of as my—Oriental friend?"

"Being your friend, you should know better than I do."

"What sort of man is he to look at?"

"I did not say it was a man."

"But I presume it is a man."

"I did not say so."

He seemed, for a moment, to hold his breath,—and he looked at me with eyes which were not friendly. Then, with a display of self-command which did him credit, he drew himself upright, with an air of dignity which well became him.

"Atherton, consciously, or unconsciously, you are doing me a serious injustice. I do not know what conception it is which you have formed of me, or on what the conception is founded, but I protest that, to the best of my knowledge and belief, I am as reputable, as honest, and as clean a man as you are."

"But you're haunted."

"Haunted?" He held himself erect, looking me straight in the face. Then a shiver went all over him; the muscles of his mouth twitched; and, in an instant, he was livid. He staggered against the table. "Yes, God knows it's true,—I'm haunted."

"So either you're mad, and therefore unfit to marry; or else you've done something which places you outside the tolerably generous boundaries of civilised society, and are therefore still more unfit to marry. You're on the horns of a dilemma."

"I—I'm the victim of a delusion."

"What is the nature of the delusion? Does it take the shape of a—beetle?"

"Atherton!"

Without the slightest warning, he collapsed,—was transformed; I can describe the change which took place in him in no other way. He sank in a heap on the floor; he held up his hands above his head; and he gibbered,—like some frenzied animal. A more uncomfortable spectacle than he presented it would be difficult to find. I have seen it matched in the padded rooms of lunatic asylums, but nowhere else. The sight of him set every nerve of my body on edge.

"In Heaven's name, what is the matter with you, man? Are you stark, staring mad? Here,—drink this!"

Filling a tumbler with brandy, I forced it between his quivering fingers. Then it was some moments before I could get him to understand what it was I wanted him to do. When he did get the glass to his lips, he swallowed its contents as if they were so much water. By degrees his senses returned to him. He stood up. He looked about him, with a smile which was positively ghastly.

"It's—it's a delusion."

"It's a very queer kind of a delusion, if it is."

I eyed him, curiously. He was evidently making the most strenuous efforts to regain his self-control,—all the while with that horrible smile about his lips.

"Atherton, you—you take me at an advantage." I was still. "Who—who's your Oriental friend?"

"My Oriental friend?—you mean yours. I supposed, at first, that the individual in question was a man; but it appears that she's a woman."

"A woman?—Oh.—How do you mean?"

"Well, the face is a man's—of an uncommonly disagreeable type, of which the powers forbid that there are many!—and the voice is a man's,—also of a kind!—but the body, as, last night, I chanced to discover, is a woman's."

"That sounds very odd." He closed his eyes. I could see that his cheeks were clammy. "Do you—do you believe in witchcraft?"

"That depends."

"Have you heard of Obi?"

"I have."

"I have been told that an Obeah man[1] can put a spell upon a person which compels a person to see whatever he—the Obeah man—may please. Do you think that's possible?"

"It is not a question to which I should be disposed to answer either yes or no."

He looked at me out of his half-closed eyes. It struck me that he was making conversation,—saying anything for the sake of gaining time.

"I remember reading a book entitled 'Obscure Diseases of the Brain.'[2] It contained some interesting data on the subject of hallucinations."

"Possibly."

"Now, candidly, would you recommend me to place myself in the hands of a mental pathologist?"

"I don't think that you're insane, if that's what you mean."

"No?—That is good hearing. Of all diseases insanity is the most to be dreaded.—Well, Atherton, I'm keeping you. The truth is that, insane or not, I am very far from well. I think I must give myself a holiday."

He moved towards his hat and umbrella.

"There is something else which you must do."

"What is that?"

"You must resign your pretensions to Miss Lindon's hand."

"My dear Atherton, if my health is really failing me, I shall resign everything,—everything!"

He repeated his own word with a little movement of his hands which was pathetic.

"Understand me, Lessingham. What else you do is no affair of mine. I am concerned only with Miss Lindon. You must give me your definite promise, before you leave this room, to terminate your engagement with her before to-night."

---

[1] Obeah or Obi is a form of shamanistic witchcraft or sorcery practiced originally in Africa, and carried to Jamaica. Its origins are obscure, and the word translates, very loosely, as "occult power."

[2] The reference could be to Forbes Winslow, *On the Obscure Diseases of the Brain, and Disorders of the Mind* (1860), one of the first studies of neuropsychiatry.

His back was towards me.

"There will come a time when your conscience will prick you because of your treatment of me; when you will realise that I am the most unfortunate of men."

"I realise that now. It is because I realise it that I am so desirous that the shadow of your evil fortune shall not fall upon an innocent girl."

He turned.

"Atherton, what is your actual position with reference to Marjorie Lindon?"

"She regards me as her brother."

"And do you regard her as a sister? Are your sentiments towards her purely fraternal?"

"You know that I love her."

"And do you suppose that my removal will clear the path for you?"

"I suppose nothing of the kind. You may believe me or not, but my one desire is for her happiness, and surely, if you love her, that is your desire too."

"That is so." He paused. An expression of sadness stole over his face of which I had not thought it capable. "That is so to an extent of which you do not dream. No man likes to have his hand forced, especially by one whom he regards—may I say it?—as a possible rival. But I will tell you this much. If the blight which has fallen on my life is likely to continue, I would not wish,—God forbid that I should wish to join her fate with mine,—not for all that the world could offer me."

He stopped. And I was still. Presently he continued.

"When I was younger I was subject to a—similar delusion. But it vanished,—I saw no trace of it for years,—I thought that I had done with it for good. Recently, however, it has returned,—as you have witnessed. I shall institute inquiries into the cause of its reappearance; if it seems likely to be irremovable, or even if it bids fair to he prolonged, I shall not only, as you phrase it, withdraw my pretensions to Miss Lindon's hand, but to all my other ambitions. In the interim, as regards Miss Lindon I shall be careful to hold myself on the footing of a mere acquaintance."

"You promise me?"

"I do.—And on your side, Atherton, in the meantime, deal with me more gently. Judgment in my case has still to be given. You will find that I am not the guilty wretch you apparently imagine. And there are few things more disagreeable to one's self-esteem than to learn, too late, that one has persisted in judging another man too harshly. Think of all that the world has, at this moment, to offer me, and what it will mean if I have to turn my back on it,—owing to a mischievous twist of fortune's wheel."

He turned, as if to go. Then stopped, and looked round, in an attitude of listening.

"What's that?"

There was a sound of droning,—I recalled what Marjorie had said of her experiences of the night before, it was like the droning of a beetle. The instant the Apostle heard it, the fashion of his countenance began to change,—it was pitiable to witness. I rushed to him.

"Lessingham!—don't be a fool!—play the man!"

He gripped my left arm with his right hand till it felt as if it were being compressed in a vice.

"Then—I shall have to have some more brandy."

Fortunately the bottle was within reach from where I stood, otherwise I doubt if he would have released my arm to let me get at it. I gave him the decanter and the glass. He helped himself to a copious libation. By the time that he had swallowed it the droning sound had gone. He put down the empty tumbler.

"When a man has to resort to alcohol to keep his nerves up to concert pitch, things are in a bad way with him, you may be sure of that,—but then you have never known what it is to stand in momentary expectation of a tête-à-tête with the devil."

Again he turned to leave the room,—and this time he actually went. I let him go alone. I heard his footsteps passing along the passage, and the hall-door close. Then I sat in an arm-chair, stretched my legs out in front of me, thrust my hands in my trouser pockets, and—I wondered.

I had been there, perhaps, four or five minutes, when there was a slight noise at my side. Glancing round, I saw a sheet of paper come fluttering through the open window. It fell almost at my feet. I picked it up. It was a picture of a beetle,—a facsimile of the one which had had such an extraordinary effect on Mr. Lessingham the day before.

"If this was intended for St Paul, it's a trifle late;—unless—"

I could hear that someone was approaching along the corridor. I looked up, expecting to see the Apostle reappear;—in which expectation I was agreeably disappointed. The new-comer was feminine. It was Miss Grayling. As she stood in the open doorway, I saw that her cheeks were red as roses.

"I hope I am not interrupting you again, but—I left my purse here." She stopped; then added, as if it were an afterthought, "And—I want you to come and lunch with me."

I locked the picture of the beetle in the drawer,—and I lunched with Dora Grayling.

BOOK III

THE TERROR BY NIGHT
AND THE TERROR BY DAY

CHAPTER 23

THE WAY HE TOLD HER

I am the happiest woman in the world! I wonder how many women have said that of themselves in their time,—but I am. Paul has told me that he loves me. How long I have made inward confession of my love for him, I should be ashamed to say. It sounds prosaic, but I believe it is a fact that the first stirring of my pulses was caused by the report of a speech of his which I read in the Times. It was on the Eight Hours' Bill.[1] Papa was most unflattering. He said that he was an oily spouter, an ignorant agitator, an irresponsible fire-brand, and a good deal more to the same effect. I remember very well how papa fidgeted with the paper, declaring that it read even worse than it had sounded, and goodness knew that it had sounded bad enough. He was so very emphatic that when he had gone I thought I would see what all the pother was about, and read the speech for myself. So I read it. It affected me quite differently. The speaker's words showed such knowledge, charity, and sympathy that they went straight to my heart.

After that I read everything of Paul Lessingham's which I came across. And the more I read the more I was impressed. But it was some time before we met. Considering what papa's opinions were, it was not likely that he would go out of his way to facilitate a meeting. To him, the mere mention of the name was like a red rag to a bull. But at last we did meet. And then I knew that he was stronger, greater, better even than his words. It is so often the other way; one finds that men, and women too, are so apt to put their best, as it were, into their shop windows, that the discovery was as novel as it was delightful.

---

[1]   Though fictitious, like the Agricultural Amendment Bill, referred to elsewhere in the novel, Marsh's reference is to the demand for a legislated universal eight-hour work day. The nine-hour day was widely in practice by the 1870s, but there were still huge discrepancies.

When the ice was once broken, we often met. I do not know how it was. We did not plan our meetings,—at first, at any rate. Yet we seemed always meeting. Seldom a day passed on which we did not meet,—sometimes twice or thrice. It was odd how we were always coming across each other in the most unlikely places. I believe we did not notice it at the time, but looking back I can see that we must have managed our engagements so that somewhere, somehow, we should be certain to have an opportunity of exchanging half a dozen words. Those constant encounters could not have all been chance ones.

But I never supposed he loved me,—never. I am not even sure that, for some time, I was aware that I loved him. We were great on friendship, both of us.—I was quite aware that I was his friend,—that he regarded me as his friend; he told me so more than once.

"I tell you this," he would say, referring to this, that, or the other, "because I know that, in speaking to you, I am speaking to a friend."

With him those were not empty words. All kinds of people talk to one like that,—especially men; it is a kind of formula which they use with every woman who shows herself disposed to listen. But Paul is not like that. He is chary of speech; not by any means a woman's man. I tell him that is his weakest point. If legend does not lie more even than is common, few politicians have achieved prosperity without the aid of women. He replies that he is not a politician; that he never means to be a politician. He simply wishes to work for his country; if his country does not need his services—well, let it be. Papa's political friends have always so many axes of their own to grind, that, at first, to hear a member of Parliament talk like that was almost disquieting. I had dreamed of men like that; but I never encountered one till I met Paul Lessingham.

Our friendship was a pleasant one. It became pleasanter and pleasanter. Until there came a time when he told me everything; the dreams he dreamed; the plans which he had planned; the great purposes which, if health and strength were given him, he intended to carry to a great fulfilment. And, at last, he told me something else.

It was after a meeting at a Working Women's Club[1] in Westminster. He had spoken, and I had spoken too. I don't know what papa would

---

[1]   The period in which Marsh is writing, and, indeed, all of the second half of the nineteenth century, is one of great political agitation on the part of women, and the reference to a working women's club in Westminster reflects this. As merely one example of such activity, one might cite the London Society for Women's Suffrage, Kensington, which had been founded in 1868. A branch was subsequently opened in Hastings, Sussex, which later became the basis in 1903 for the Women's Social and Political Union. From the 1850s at

have said, if he had known, but I had. A formal resolution had been proposed, and I had seconded it,—in perhaps a couple of hundred words; but that would have been quite enough for papa to have regarded me as an Abandoned Wretch,—papa always puts those sort of words into capitals.[1] Papa regards a speechifying woman as a thing of horror,—I have known him look askance at a Primrose Dame.[2]

The night was fine. Paul proposed that I should walk with him down the Westminster Bridge Road, until we reached the House, and then he would see me into a cab. I did as he suggested. It was still early, not yet ten, and the streets were alive with people. Our conversation, as we went, was entirely political. The Agricultural Amendment Act was then before the Commons, and Paul felt very strongly that it was one of those measures which give with one hand, while taking with the other. The committee stage was at hand, and already several amendments were threatened, the effect of which would be to strengthen the landlord at the expense of the tenant. More than one of these, and they not the most moderate, were to be proposed by papa. Paul was pointing out how it would be his duty to oppose these tooth and nail, when, all at once, he stopped.

"I sometimes wonder how you really feel upon this matter."

"What matter?"

"On the difference of opinion, in political matters, which exists between your father and myself. I am conscious that Mr. Lindon regards my action as a personal question, and resents it so keenly, that I am sometimes moved to wonder if at least a portion of his resentment is not shared by you."

"I have explained; I consider papa the politician as one person, and papa the father as quite another."

---

least, the *Westminster Review*, edited by philosopher and political economist John Stuart Mill, regularly published articles advocating equal rights for women. In 1856, a petition initiated by Barbara Leigh Smith (later Bodichon) in Hastings, and consisting of 26,000 signatures gathered nationwide, was presented to Parliament, urging legal recognition of women's property rights in marriage. This lead, eventually, in the following year, to the Matrimonial Causes Act. Bodichon was also a member of the Kensington society.

1   Marsh provides a nice moment of self-conscious verisimiltude for Marjorie here. Given her reference to "Papa's" practice, and the example of this practice in the sentence, Marsh perhaps intends here, as elsewhere, for his readers to assume that Marjorie Lindon's account is taken from her journals.

2   A woman associated with the Primrose League, a Conservative political association founded in 1883 in memory of Benjamin Disraeli, Earl of Beaconsfield, and espousing his political principles. The society was so named because of the association of the flower with the memory of Disraeli.

"You are his daughter."

"Certainly I am;—but would you, on that account, wish me to share his political opinions, even though I believe them to be wrong."

"You love him."

"Of course I do,—he is the best of fathers."

"Your defection will be a grievous disappointment."

I looked at him out of the corner of my eye. I wondered what was passing through his mind. The subject of my relations with papa was one which, without saying anything at all about it, we had consented to taboo.

"I am not so sure. I am permeated with a suspicion that papa has no politics."

"Miss Lindon!—I fancy that I can adduce proof to the contrary."

"I believe that if papa were to marry again, say, a Home Ruler,[1] within three weeks his wife's politics would be his own."

Paul thought before he spoke; then he smiled.

"I suppose that men sometimes do change their coats to please their wives,—even their political ones."

"Papa's opinions are the opinions of those with whom he mixes. The reason why he consorts with Tories of the crusted school is because he fears that if he associated with anybody else—with Radicals, say,—before he knew it, he would be a Radical too. With him, association is synonymous with logic."

Paul laughed outright. By this time we had reached Westminster Bridge. Standing, we looked down upon the river. A long line of lanterns was gliding mysteriously over the waters; it was a tug towing a string of barges. For some moments neither spoke. Then Paul recurred to what I had just been saying.

"And you,—do you think marriage would colour your convictions?"

"Would it yours?"

"That depends." He was silent. Then he said, in that tone which I had learned to look for when he was most in earnest, "It depends on whether you would marry me."

I was still. His words were so unexpected that they took my breath away. I knew not what to make of them. My head was in a whirl. Then he addressed to me a monosyllabic interrogation.

"Well?"

---

[1] Someone advocating political self-determination and autonomy for Ireland. Political debate over Irish Home Rule reached a pitch during Gladstone's government in 1885–86.

I found my voice,—or a part of it.

"Well?—to what?"

He came a little closer.

"Will you be my wife?"

The part of my voice which I had found, was lost again. Tears came into my eyes. I shivered. I had not thought that I could be so absurd. Just then the moon came from behind a cloud; the rippling waters were tipped with silver. He spoke again, so gently that his words just reached my ears.

"You know that I love you."

Then I knew that I loved him too. That what I had fancied was a feeling of friendship was something very different. It was as if somebody, in tearing a veil from before my eyes, had revealed a spectacle which dazzled me. I was speechless. He misconstrued my silence.

"Have I offended you?"

"No."

I fancy that he noted the tremor which was in my voice, and read it rightly. For he too was still. Presently his hand stole along the parapet, and fastened upon mine, and held it tight.

And that was how it came about. Other things were said; but they were hardly of the first importance. Though I believe we took some time in saying them. Of myself I can say with truth, that my heart was too full for copious speech; I was dumb with a great happiness. And, I believe, I can say the same of Paul. He told me as much when we were parting.

It seemed that we had only just come there when Paul started. Turning, he stared up at Big Ben.

"Midnight!—The House up!—Impossible!"

But it was more than possible, it was fact. We had actually been on the Bridge two hours, and it had not seemed ten minutes. Never had I supposed that the flight of time could have been so entirely unnoticed. Paul was considerably taken aback. His legislative conscience pricked him. He excused himself—in his own fashion.

"Fortunately, for once in a way, my business in the House was not so important as my business out of it."

He had his arm through mine. We were standing face to face.

"So you call this business!"

He laughed.

He not only saw me into a cab, but he saw me home in it. And in the cab he kissed me. I fancy I was a little out of sorts that night. My nervous system was, perhaps, demoralised. Because, when he kissed me, I did a thing which I never do,—I have my own standard of behaviour, and that sort of thing is quite outside of it; I behaved like a sentimental chit.[1] I cried. And it took him all the way to my father's door to comfort me.

I can only hope that, perceiving the singularity of the occasion, he consented to excuse me.

CHAPTER 24

A WOMAN'S VIEW

Sydney Atherton has asked me to be his wife. It is not only annoying; worse, it is absurd.

This is the result of Paul's wish that our engagement should not be announced. He is afraid of papa;—not really, but for the moment. The atmosphere of the House is charged with electricity. Party feeling runs high. They are at each other, hammer and tongs, about this Agricultural Amendment Act. The strain on Paul is tremendous. I am beginning to feel positively concerned. Little things which I have noticed about him lately convince me that he is being overwrought. I suspect him of having sleepless nights. The amount of work which he has been getting through lately has been too much for any single human being, I care not who he is. He himself admits that he shall be glad when the session is at an end. So shall I.

In the meantime, it is his desire that nothing shall be said about our engagement until the House rises. It is reasonable enough. Papa is sure to be violent,—lately, the barest allusion to Paul's name has been enough to make him explode. When the discovery does come, he will be unmanageable,—I foresee it clearly. From little incidents which have happened recently I predict the worst. He will be capable of making a scene within the precincts of the House. And, as Paul says, there is some truth in the saying that the last straw breaks the camel's back. He will be better able to face papa's wild wrath when the House has risen.

So the news is to bide a wee.[2] Of course Paul is right. And what he wishes I wish too. Still, it is not all such plain sailing for me as he perhaps

---

[1]   A derogatory term for a young, inexperienced woman.
[2]   Wait a while (Scottish dialect).

thinks. The domestic atmosphere is almost as electrical as that in the House. Papa is like the terrier who scents a rat,—he is always sniffing the air. He has not actually forbidden me to speak to Paul,—his courage is not quite at the sticking point; but he is constantly making uncomfortable allusions to persons who number among their acquaintance "political adventurers," "grasping carpet-baggers," "Radical riff-raff," and that kind of thing. Sometimes I venture to call my soul my own; but such a tempest invariably follows that I become discreet again as soon as I possibly can. So, as a rule, I suffer in silence.

Still, I would with all my heart that the concealment were at an end. No one need imagine that I am ashamed of being about to marry Paul,—papa least of all. On the contrary, I am as proud of it as a woman can be. Sometimes, when he has said or done something unusually wonderful, I fear that my pride will out,—I do feel it so strong within me. I should be delighted to have a trial of strength with papa; anywhere, at any time,—I should not be so rude to him as he would be to me. At the bottom of his heart papa knows that I am the more sensible of the two; after a pitched battle or so he would understand it better still. I know papa! I have not been his daughter for all these years in vain. I feel like hot-blooded soldiers must feel, who, burning to attack the enemy in the open field, are ordered to skulk behind hedges, and be shot at.

One result is that Sydney has actually made a proposal of marriage,—he of all people! It is too comical. The best of it was that he took himself quite seriously. I do not know how many times he has confided to me the sufferings which he has endured for love of other women—some of them, I am sorry to say, decent married women too; but this is the first occasion on which the theme has been a personal one. He was so frantic, as he is wont to be, that, to calm him, I told him about Paul,—which, under the circumstances, to him I felt myself at liberty to do. In return, he was melodramatic; hinting darkly at I know not what. I was almost cross with him.

He is a curious person, Sydney Atherton. I suppose it is because I have known him all my life, and have always looked upon him, in cases of necessity, as a capital substitute for a brother, that I criticise him with so much frankness. In some respects, he is a genius; in others—I will not write fool, for that he never is, though he has often done some extremely foolish things. The fame of his inventions is in the mouths of all men; though the half of them has never been told. He is the most extraordinary mixture. The things which most people would like to have proclaimed in the street, he keeps tightly locked in his own bosom;

while those which the same persons would be only too glad to conceal, he shouts from the roofs. A very famous man once told me that if Mr. Atherton chose to become a specialist, to take up one branch of inquiry, and devote his life to it, his fame, before he died, would bridge the spheres. But sticking to one thing is not in Sydney's line at all. He prefers, like the bee, to roam from flower to flower.

As for his being in love with me; it is ridiculous. He is as much in love with the moon. I cannot think what has put the idea into his head. Some girl must have been ill-using him, or he imagines that she has. The girl whom he ought to marry, and whom he ultimately will marry, is Dora Grayling. She is young, charming, immensely rich, and over head and ears in love with him;—if she were not, then he would be over head and ears in love with her. I believe he is very near it as it is,— sometimes he is so very rude to her. It is a characteristic of Sydney's, that he is apt to be rude to a girl whom he really likes. As for Dora, I suspect she dreams of him. He is tall, straight, very handsome, with a big moustache, and the most extraordinary eyes;—I fancy that those eyes of his have as much to do with Dora's state as anything. I have heard it said that he possesses the hypnotic power to an unusual degree, and that, if he chose to exercise it, he might become a danger to society. I believe he has hypnotised Dora.

He makes an excellent brother. I have gone to him, many and many a time, for help,—and some excellent advice I have received. I daresay I shall consult him still. There are matters of which one would hardly dare to talk to Paul. In all things he is the great man. He could hardly condescend to chiffons.[1] Now Sydney can and does. When he is in the mood on the vital subject of trimmings a woman could not appeal to a sounder authority. I tell him, if he had been a dressmaker, he would have been magnificent. I am sure he would.

---

[1] A light material but referring in the plural to ornamental "details" of women's dress. The use of the term was extended to refer colloquially to discussion of such details in inconsequential conversation. Here, Marjorie is both alluding to the discussion of such "trimmings" as she puts it shortly afterwards but also, more generally, to Sydney's willingness to speak about trivia, when the mood takes him.

CHAPTER 25

THE MAN IN THE STREET

This morning I had an adventure.

I was in the breakfast-room. Papa, as usual, was late for breakfast, and I was wondering whether I should begin without him, when, chancing to look round, something caught my eye in the street. I went to the window to see what it was. A small crowd of people was in the middle of the road, and they were all staring at something which, apparently, was lying on the ground. What it was I could not see.

The butler happened to be in the room. I spoke to him.

"Peter, what is the matter in the street? Go and see."

He went and saw; and, presently, he returned. Peter is an excellent servant; but the fashion of his speech, even when conveying the most trivial information, is slightly sesquipedalian.[1] He would have made a capital cabinet minister at question time,—he wraps up the smallest portions of meaning in the largest possible words. "An unfortunate individual appears to have been the victim of a catastrophe. I am informed that he is dead. The constable asserts that he is drunk."

"Drunk?—dead? Do you mean that he is dead drunk?—at this hour!"

"He is either one or the other. I did not behold the individual myself. I derived my information from a bystander."

That was not sufficiently explicit for me. I gave way to a, seemingly, quite causeless impulse of curiosity, I went out into the street, just as I was, to see for myself. It was, perhaps, not the most sensible thing I could have done, and papa would have been shocked; but I am always shocking papa. It had been raining in the night, and the shoes which I had on were not so well suited as they might have been for an encounter with the mud.

I made my way to the point of interest.

"What's the matter?" I asked.

A workman, with a bag of tools over his shoulder, answered me.

"There's something wrong with someone. Policeman says he's drunk, but he looks to me as if he was something worse."

"Will you let me pass, please?"

---

[1]   A word containing many syllables, or someone given to using long words.

When they saw I was a woman, they permitted me to reach the centre of the crowd.

A man was lying on his back, in the grease and dirt of the road. He was so plastered with mud, that it was difficult, at first, to be sure that he really was a man. His head and feet were bare. His body was partially covered by a long ragged cloak. It was obvious that that one wretched, dirt-stained, sopping wet rag was all the clothing he had on. A huge constable was holding his shoulders in his hands, and was regarding him as if he could not make him out at all. He seemed uncertain as to whether it was or was not a case of shamming.

He spoke to him as if he had been some refractory child.

"Come, my lad, this won't do!—Wake up!—What's the matter?"

But he neither woke up, nor explained what was the matter. I took hold of his hand. It was icy cold. Apparently the wrist was pulseless. Clearly this was no ordinary case of drunkenness.

"There is something seriously wrong, officer. Medical assistance ought to be had at once."

"Do you think he's in a fit, miss?"

"That a doctor should be able to tell you better than I can. There seems to be no pulse. I should not be surprised to find that he was—"

The word "dead" was actually on my lips, when the stranger saved me from making a glaring exposure of my ignorance by snatching his wrist away from me, and sitting up in the mud. He held out his hands in front of him, opened his eyes, and exclaimed, in a loud, but painfully raucous tone of voice, as if he was suffering from a very bad cold,

"Paul Lessingham!"

I was so surprised that I all but sat down in the mud. To hear Paul—my Paul!—apostrophised by an individual of his appearance, in that fashion, was something which I had not expected. Directly the words were uttered, he closed his eyes again, sank backward, and seemingly relapsed into unconsciousness,—the constable gripping him by the shoulder just in time to prevent him banging the back of his head against the road.

The officer shook him,—scarcely gently.

"Now, my lad, it's plain that you're not dead!—What's the meaning of this?—Move yourself!"

Looking round I found that Peter was close behind. Apparently he had been struck by the singularity of his mistress' behaviour, and had followed to see that it did not meet with the reward which it deserved. I spoke to him.

"Peter, let someone go at once for Dr. Cotes!"

Dr. Cotes lives just round the corner, and since it was evident that the man's lapse into consciousness had made the policeman sceptical as to his case being so serious as it seemed, I thought it might be advisable that a competent opinion should be obtained without delay.

Peter was starting, when again the stranger returned to consciousness,—that is, if it really was consciousness, as to which I was more than a little in doubt. He repeated his previous pantomime; sat up in the mud, stretched out his arms, opened his eyes unnaturally wide,—and yet they appeared unseeing!—a sort of convulsion went all over him, and he shrieked—it really amounted to shrieking—as a man might shriek who was in mortal terror.

"Be warned, Paul Lessingham—be warned!"

For my part, that settled it. There was a mystery here which needed to be unravelled. Twice had he called upon Paul's name,—and in the strangest fashion! It was for me to learn the why and the wherefore; to ascertain what connection there was between this lifeless creature and Paul Lessingham. Providence might have cast him there before my door. I might be entertaining an angel unawares. My mind was made up on the instant.

"Peter, hasten for Dr. Cotes." Peter passed the word, and immediately a footman started running as fast as his legs would carry him. "Officer, I will have this man taken into my father's house.—Will some of you men help to carry him?"

There were volunteers enough, and to spare. I spoke to Peter in the hall.

"Is papa down yet?"

"Mr. Lindon has sent down to say that you will please not wait for him for breakfast. He has issued instructions to have his breakfast conveyed to him upstairs."

"That's all right." I nodded towards the poor wretch who was being carried through the hall. "You will say nothing to him about this unless he particularly asks. You understand?"

Peter bowed. He is discretion itself. He knows I have my vagaries,[1] and it is not his fault if the savour of them travels to papa.

The doctor was in the house almost as soon as the stranger.

"Wants washing," he remarked, directly he saw him.

And that certainly was true,—I never saw a man who stood more obviously in need of the good offices of soap and water. Then he went

---

[1] Odd notions, whims, or fancies.

through the usual medical formula, I watching all the while. So far as I could see the man showed not the slightest sign of life.

"Is he dead?"

"He will be soon, if he doesn't have something to eat. The fellow's starving."

The doctor asked the policeman what he knew of him.

That sagacious officer's reply was vague. A boy had run up to him crying that a man was lying dead in the street. He had straightway followed the boy, and discovered the stranger. That was all he knew.

"What is the matter with the man?" I inquired of the doctor, when the constable had gone.

"Don't know.—It may be catalepsy, and it mayn't.—When I do know, you may ask again."

Dr. Cotes' manner was a trifle brusque,[1]—particularly, I believe, to me. I remember that once he threatened to box my ears. When I was a small child I used to think nothing of boxing his.

Realising that no satisfaction was to be got out of a speechless man—particularly as regards his mysterious references to Paul—I went upstairs. I found that papa was under the impression that he was suffering from a severe attack of gout.[2] But as he was eating a capital breakfast, and apparently enjoying it,—while I was still fasting—I ventured to hope that the matter was not so serious as he feared.

I mentioned nothing to him about the person whom I had found in the street,—lest it should aggravate his gout. When he is like that, the slightest thing does.

CHAPTER 26

A FATHER'S NO

Paul has stormed the House of Commons with one of the greatest speeches which even he has delivered, and I have quarrelled with papa. And, also, I have very nearly quarrelled with Sydney.

Sydney's little affair is nothing. He actually still persists, in thinking

---

[1] Abrupt.
[2] A disease characterized by the painful inflammation of smaller joints.

himself in love with me,—as if, since last night, when he what he calls "proposed" to me, he has not time to fall out of love, and in again, half a dozen times; and, on the strength of it, he seems to consider himself entitled to make himself as disagreeable as he can. That I should not mind,—for Sydney disagreeable is about as nice as Sydney any other way; but when it comes to his shooting poisoned shafts at Paul, I object. If he imagines that anything he can say, or hint, will lessen my estimation of Paul Lessingham by one hair's breadth, he has less wisdom even than I gave him credit for. By the way, Percy Woodville asked me to be his wife to-night,—which, also, is nothing; he has been trying to do it for the last three years,—though, under the circumstances, it is a little trying; but he would not spit venom merely because I preferred another man,—and he, I believe, does care for me.

Papa's affair is serious. It is the first clashing of the foils,—and this time, I imagine, the buttons are really off.[1] This morning he said a few words, not so much to, as at me. He informed me that Paul was expected to speak to-night,—as if I did not know it!—and availed himself of the opening to load him with the abuse which, in his case, he thinks is not unbecoming to a gentleman. I don't know—or, rather, I do know what he would think, if he heard another man use, in the presence of a woman, the kind of language which he habitually employs. However, I said nothing. I had a motive for allowing the chaff to fly before the wind.

But, to-night, issue was joined.[2]

I, of course, went to hear Paul speak, —as I have done over and over again before. Afterwards, Paul came and fetched me from the cage. He had to leave me for a moment, while he gave somebody a message; and in the lobby, there was Sydney,—all sneers! I could have pinched him. Just as I was coming to the conclusion that I should have to stick a pin into his arm, Paul returned,—and, positively, Sydney was rude to him. I was ashamed, if Mr. Atherton was not. As if it was not enough that he should be insulted by a mere popinjay,[3] at the very moment when he had been adding another stone to the fabric of his country's glory,— papa came up. He actually wanted to take me away from Paul. I should

---

[1] The allusion is to fencing; the buttons being off refers to the "safety" tips placed on the points of the foils in sport, suggesting that this is, figuratively, a fight to the death between the politicians.

[2] *Fig.* Battle commenced.

[3] Deriving originally from Arabic, then via the Spanish *papagayo* (parrot), the term refers in the nineteenth century to a vain and conceited person, usually a man.

have liked to see him do it. Of course I went down with Paul to the carriage, leaving papa to follow if he chose. He did not choose,—but, none the less, he managed to be home within three minutes after I had myself returned.

Then the battle began.

It is impossible for me to give an idea of papa in a rage. There may be men who look well when they lose their temper, but, if there are, papa is certainly not one. He is always talking about the magnificence, and the high breeding of the Lindons, but anything less high-bred than the head of the Lindons, in his moments of wrath, it would be hard to conceive. His language I will not attempt to portray,—but his observations consisted, mainly, of abuse of Paul, glorification of the Lindons, and orders to me.

"I forbid you—I forbid you—" when papa wishes to be impressive he repeats his own words three or four times over; I don't know if he imagines that they are improved by repetition; if he does, he is wrong— "I forbid you ever again to speak to that—that—that—"

Here followed language.

I was silent.

My cue was to keep cool. I believe that, with the exception, perhaps, of being a little white, and exceedingly sorry that papa should so forget himself, I was about the same as I generally am.

"Do you hear me?—do you hear what I say?—do you hear me, miss?"

"Yes, papa; I hear you."

"Then—then—then promise me!—promise that you will do as I tell you!—mark my words, my girl, you shall promise before you leave this room!"

"My dear papa!—do you intend me to spend the remainder of my life in the drawing-room?"

"Don't you be impertinent!—do-do-don't you speak to me like that!—I—won't have it!"

"I tell you what it is, papa, if you don't take care you'll have another attack of gout."

"Damn gout."

That was the most sensible thing he said; if such a tormentor as gout can be consigned to the nether regions by the mere utterance of a word, by all means let the word be uttered. Off he went again.

"The man's a ruffianly, rascally,—" and so on. "There's not such a villainous vagabond—" and all the rest of it. "And I order you,—I'm a Lindon, and I order you! I'm your father, and I order you!—I order you never to speak to such a—such a—"—various vain repetitions—"again, and—and—and I order you never to look at him!"

"Listen to me, papa. I will promise you never to speak to Paul Lessingham again, if you will promise me never to speak to Lord Cantilever again,—or to recognise him if you meet him in the street."

You should have seen how papa glared. Lord Cantilever is the head of his party. Its august, and, I presume, reverenced leader. He is papa's particular fetish. I am not sure that he does regard him as being any lower than the angels, but if he does it is certainly something in decimals. My suggestion seemed as outrageous to him as his suggestion seemed to me. But it is papa's misfortune that he can only see one side of a question,—and that's his own.

"You—you dare to compare Lord Cantilever to—to that—that— that —!"

"I am not comparing them. I am not aware of there being anything in particular against Lord Cantilever,—that is against his character. But, of course, I should not dream of comparing a man of his calibre, with one of real ability, like Paul Lessingham. It would be to treat his lordship with too much severity."

I could not help it,—but that did it. The rest of papa's conversation was a jumble of explosions. It was all so sad.

Papa poured all the vials of his wrath upon Paul,—to his own sore disfigurement. He threatened me with all the pains and penalties of the inquisition if I did not immediately promise to hold no further communication with Mr. Lessingham,—of course I did nothing of the kind. He cursed me, in default, by bell, book, and candle,[1]—and by ever so many other things beside. He called me the most dreadful names,—me! his only child. He warned me that I should find myself in prison before I had done,—I am not sure that he did not hint darkly at the gallows. Finally, he drove me from the room in a whirlwind of anathemas.[2]

[1] Referring to practices associated with Roman Catholic Mass, the phrase first appears in Shakespeare, *King John* (III.iii.12).
[2] Curses, condemnations.

CHAPTER 27

THE TERROR BY NIGHT

When I left papa,—or, rather, when papa had driven me from him—I went straight to the man whom I had found in the street. It was late, and I was feeling both tired and worried, so that I only thought of seeing for myself how he was. In some way, he seemed to be a link between Paul and myself, and as, at that moment, links of that kind were precious, I could not have gone to bed without learning something of his condition.

The nurse received me at the door.

"Well, nurse, how's the patient?"

Nurse was a plump, motherly woman, who had attended more than one odd protégé of mine, and whom I kept pretty constantly at my beck and call. She held out her hands.

"It's hard to tell. He hasn't moved since I came."

"Not moved?—Is he still insensible?"

"He seems to me to be in some sort of trance. He does not appear to breathe, and I can detect no pulsation, but the doctor says he's still alive,—it's the queerest case I ever saw."

I went farther into the room. Directly I did so the man in the bed gave signs of life which were sufficiently unmistakable. Nurse hastened to him.

"Why," she exclaimed, "he's moving!—he might have heard you enter!"

He not only might have done, but it seemed possible that that was what he actually had done. As I approached the bed, he raised himself to a sitting posture, as, in the morning, he had done in the street, and he exclaimed, as if he addressed himself to someone whom he saw in front of him,—I cannot describe the almost more than human agony which was in his voice,

"Paul Lessingham!—Beware!—The Beetle!"

What he meant I had not the slightest notion. Probably that was why what seemed more like a pronouncement of delirium than anything else had such an extraordinary effect upon my nerves. No sooner had he spoken than a sort of blank horror seemed to settle down upon my mind. I actually found myself trembling at the knees. I felt, all at once, as if I was standing in the immediate presence of something awful yet unseen.

As for the speaker, no sooner were the words out of his lips, than, as was the case in the morning, he relapsed into a condition of trance. Nurse, bending over him, announced the fact.

"He's gone off again!—What an extraordinary thing!—I suppose it is real." It was clear, from the tone of her voice, that she shared the doubt which had troubled the policeman. "There's not a trace of a pulse. From the look of things he might be dead. Of one thing I'm sure, that there's something unnatural about the man. No natural illness I ever heard of, takes hold of a man like this."

Glancing up, she saw that there was something unusual in my face; an appearance which startled her.

"Why, Miss Marjorie, what's the matter!—You look quite ill!"

I felt ill, and worse than ill; but, at the same time, I was quite incapable of describing what I felt to nurse. For some inscrutable reason I had even lost the control of my tongue,—I stammered.

"I—I—I'm not feeling very well, nurse; I—I—I think I'll be better in bed."

As I spoke, I staggered towards the door, conscious, all the while, that nurse was staring at me with eyes wide open. When I got out of the room, it seemed, in some incomprehensible fashion, as if something had left it with me, and that It and I were alone together in the corridor. So overcome was I by the consciousness of its immediate propinquity, that, all at once, I found myself cowering against the wall,—as if I expected something or someone to strike me.

How I reached my bedroom I do not know. I found Fanchette awaiting me. For the moment her presence was a positive comfort,— until I realised the amazement with which she was regarding me.

"Mademoiselle is not well?"

"Thank you, Fanchette, I—I am rather tired. I will undress myself tonight—you can go to bed."

"But if mademoiselle is so tired, will she not permit me to assist her?"

The suggestion was reasonable enough,—and kindly too; for, to say the least of it, she had as much cause for fatigue as I had. I hesitated. I should have liked to throw my arms about her neck, and beg her not to leave me; but, the plain truth is, I was ashamed. In my inner consciousness I was persuaded that the sense of terror which had suddenly come over me was so absolutely causeless, that I could not bear the notion of playing the craven in my maid's eyes. While I hesitated, something seemed to sweep past me through the air, and to brush against my cheek in passing. I caught at Fanchette's arm.

"Fanchette!—Is there something with us in the room?"

"Something with us in the room?—Mademoiselle?—What does mademoiselle mean?"

She looked disturbed,—which was, on the whole, excusable. Fanchette is not exactly a strong-minded person, and not likely to be much of a support when a support was most required. If I was going to play the fool, I would be my own audience. So I sent her off.

"Did you not hear me tell you that I will undress myself—you are to go to bed."

She went to bed,—with quite sufficient willingness.

The instant that she was out of the room I wished that she was back again. Such a paroxysm of fear came over me, that I was incapable of stirring from the spot on which I stood, and it was all I could do to prevent myself from collapsing in a heap on the floor. I had never, till then, had reason to suppose that I was a coward. Nor to suspect myself of being the possessor of "nerves." I was as little likely as anyone to be frightened by shadows. I told myself that the whole thing was sheer absurdity, and that I should be thoroughly ashamed of my own conduct when the morning came.

"If you don't want to be self-branded as a contemptible idiot, Marjorie Lindon, you will call up your courage, and these foolish fears will fly."

But it would not do. Instead of flying, they grew worse. I became convinced,—and the process of conviction was terrible beyond words!—that there actually was something with me in the room, some invisible horror,—which, at any moment, might become visible. I seemed to understand—with a sense of agony which nothing can describe!—that this thing which was with me was with Paul. That we were linked together by the bond of a common, and a dreadful terror. That, at that moment, that same awful peril which was threatening me, was threatening him, and that I was powerless to move a finger in his aid. As with a sort of second sight, I saw out of the room in which I was, into another, in which Paul was crouching on the floor, covering his face with his hands, and shrieking. The vision came again and again with a degree of vividness of which I cannot give the least conception. At last the horror, and the reality of it, goaded me to frenzy.

"Paul! Paul!" I screamed.

As soon as I found my voice, the vision faded. Once more I understood that, as a matter of simple fact, I was standing in my own bedroom; that the lights were burning brightly; that I had not yet commenced to remove a particle of dress.

"Am I going mad?" I wondered.

I had heard of insanity taking extraordinary forms, but what could have caused softening of the brain in me I had not the faintest notion. Surely that sort of thing does not come on one—in such a wholly unmitigated form!—without the slightest notice,—and that my mental faculties were sound enough a few minutes back I was certain. The first premonition of anything of the kind had come upon me with the melodramatic utterance of the man I had found in the street.

"Paul Lessingham!—Beware!—The Beetle!" *mantra*

The words were ringing in my ears.—What was that?—There was a buzzing sound behind me. I turned to see what it was. It moved as I moved, so that it was still at my back. I swung, swiftly, right round on my heels. It still eluded me,—it was still behind.

I stood and listened,—what was it that hovered so persistently at my back? *pursuit*

The buzzing was distinctly audible. It was like the humming of a bee. Or—could it be a beetle?

My whole life long I have had an antipathy to beetles,—of any sort or kind. I have objected neither to rats nor mice, nor cows, nor bulls, nor snakes, nor spiders, nor toads, nor lizards, nor any of the thousand and one other creatures, animate or otherwise, to which so many people have a rooted, and, apparently, illogical dislike. My pet—and only— horror has been beetles. The mere suspicion of a harmless, and, I am told, necessary cockroach, being within several feet has always made me seriously uneasy. The thought that a great, winged beetle—to me, a flying beetle is the horror of horrors!—was with me in my bedroom,— goodness alone knew how it had got there!—was unendurable. Anyone who had beheld me during the next few moments would certainly have supposed I was deranged. I turned and twisted, sprang from side to side, screwed myself into impossible positions, in order to obtain a glimpse of the detested visitant,—but in vain. I could hear it all the time; but see it—never! The buzzing sound was continually behind.

The terror returned,—I began to think that my brain must be softening. I dashed to the bed. Flinging myself on my knees, I tried to pray. But I was speechless,—words would not come; my thoughts would not take shape. I all at once became conscious, as I struggled to ask help of God, that I was wrestling with something evil,—that if I only could ask help of Him, evil would flee. But I could not. I was helpless,—over-mastered. I hid my face in the bedclothes, cramming my fingers into my ears. But the buzzing was behind me all the time.

I sprang up, striking out, blindly, wildly, right and left, hitting nothing,—the buzzing always came from a point at which, at the moment, I was not aiming.

I tore off my clothes. I had on a lovely frock which I had worn for the first time that night; I had had it specially made for the occasion of the Duchess' ball, and—more especially—in honour of Paul's great speech. I had said to myself, when I saw my image in a mirror, that it was the most exquisite gown I had ever had, that it suited me to perfection, and that it should continue in my wardrobe for many a day, if only as a souvenir of a memorable night. Now, in the madness of my terror, all reflections of that sort were forgotten. My only desire was to away with it. I tore it off anyhow, letting it fall in rags on the floor at my feet. All else that I had on I flung in the same way after it; it was a veritable holocaust of dainty garments,—I acting as relentless executioner who am, as a rule, so tender with my things. I leaped upon the bed, switched off the electric light, hurried into bed, burying myself, over head and all, deep down between the sheets.

I had hoped that by shutting out the light, I might regain my senses. That in the darkness I might have opportunity for sane reflection. But I had made a grievous error. I had exchanged bad for worse. The darkness lent added terrors. The light had not been out five seconds before I would have given all that I was worth to be able to switch it on again.

As I cowered beneath the bedclothes I heard the buzzing sound above my head,—the sudden silence of the darkness had rendered it more audible than it had been before. The thing, whatever it was, was hovering above the bed. It came nearer and nearer; it grew clearer and clearer. I felt it alight upon the coverlet;—shall I ever forget the sensations with which I did feel it? It weighed upon me like a ton of lead. How much of the seeming weight was real, and how much imaginary, I cannot pretend to say; but that it was much heavier than any beetle I have ever seen or heard of, I am sure.

For a time it was still,—and during that time I doubt if I even drew my breath. Then I felt it begin to move, in wobbling fashion, with awkward, ungainly gait, stopping every now and then, as if for rest. I was conscious that it was progressing, slowly, yet surely, towards the head of the bed. The emotion of horror with which I realised what this progression might mean, will be, I fear, with me to the end of my life,— not only in dreams, but too often, also, in my waking hours. My heart, as the Psalmist has it,[1] melted like wax within me. I was incapable of

---

[1]   Psalm 22:14: "My heart is like wax; it is melted in the midst of my bowels."

movement,—dominated by something as hideous as, and infinitely more powerful than, the fascination of the serpent.

When it reached the head of the bed, what I feared—with what a fear!—would happen, did happen. It began to find its way inside,—to creep between the sheets; the wonder is I did not die! I felt it coming nearer and nearer, inch by inch; I knew that it was upon me, that escape there was none; I felt something touch my hair.

And then oblivion did come to my aid. For the first time in my life I swooned. *physical, spiritual fear of disorder*

CHAPTER 28

THE STRANGE STORY OF THE MAN IN THE STREET

I have been anticipating for some weeks past, that things would become exciting,—and they have. But hardly in the way which I foresaw. It is the old story of the unexpected happening. Suddenly events of the most extraordinary nature have come crowding on me from the most unlooked-for quarters.

Let me try to take them in something like their proper order.

To begin with, Sydney has behaved very badly. So badly that it seems likely that I shall have to re-cast my whole conception of his character. It was nearly nine o'clock this morning when I,—I cannot say woke up, because I do not believe that I had really been asleep—but when I returned to consciousness. I found myself sitting up in bed, trembling like some frightened child. What had actually happened to me I did not know,—could not guess. I was conscious of an overwhelming sense of nausea, and, generally, I was feeling very far from well. I endeavoured to arrange my thoughts, and to decide upon some plan of action. Finally, I decided to go for advice and help where I had so often gone before,—to Sydney Atherton.

I went to him. I told him the whole gruesome story. He saw, he could not help but see what a deep impress the events of the night had made on me. He heard me to the end with every appearance of sympathy, —and then all at once I discovered that all the time papa had been concealed behind a large screen which was in the room, listening to every word I had been uttering. That I was dumfounded, goes without saying. It was bad enough in papa, but in Sydney it seemed, and it was, such treachery. He and I have told each other secrets all our lives; it has never entered my imagination, as he very well knows, to play him false, in one jot or tittle; and I have always understood that, in this sort of matter, men pride themselves on their sense of honour being so much keener than women's. I told them some plain truths; and I fancy that I left them both feeling heartily ashamed of themselves.

One result the experience had on me,—it wound me up. It had on me the revivifying effect of a cold douche. I realised that mine was a situation in which I should have to help myself.

When I returned home I learned that the man whom I had found in the street was himself again, and was as conscious as he was ever likely to be. Burning with curiosity to learn the nature of the connection which existed between Paul and him, and what was the meaning of his oracular apostrophes, I merely paused to remove my hat before hastening into his apartment.

When he saw me, and heard who I was, the expressions of his gratitude were painful in their intensity. The tears streamed down his cheeks. He looked to me like a man who had very little life left in him. He looked weak, and white, and worn to a shadow. Probably he never had been robust, and it was only too plain that privation had robbed him of what little strength he had ever had. He was nothing else but skin and bone. Physical and mental debility was written large all over him.

He was not bad-looking,—in a milk and watery sort of way. He had pale blue eyes and very fair hair, and, I daresay, at one time, had been a spruce enough clerk. It was difficult to guess his age, one ages so rapidly under the stress of misfortune, but I should have set him down as being about forty. His voice, though faint enough at first, was that of an educated man, and as he went on, and gathered courage, and became more and more in earnest, he spoke with a simple directness which was close akin to eloquence. It was a curious story which he had to tell.

So curious, so astounding indeed, that, by the time it was finished, I was in such a state of mind, that I could perceive no alternative but to forgive Sydney, and, in spite of his recent, and scandalous misbehaviour, again appeal to him for assistance. It seemed, if the story told by the man whom I had found in the street was true,—and incredible though it sounded, he spoke like a truthful man!—that Paul was threatened by some dreadful, and, to me, wholly incomprehensible danger; that it was a case in which even moments were precious; and I felt that, with the best will in the world, it was a position in which I could not move alone. The shadow of the terror of the night was with me still, and with that fresh in my recollection how could I hope, single-handed, to act effectually against the mysterious being of whom this amazing tale was told? No! I believed that Sydney did care for me, in his own peculiar way; I knew that he was quick, and cool, and fertile in resource, and that he showed to most advantage in a difficult situation; it was possible that he had a conscience, of a sort, and that, this time, I might not appeal to it in vain.

So I sent a servant off to fetch him, helter skelter.

As luck would have it, the servant returned with him within five minutes. It appeared that he had been lunching with Dora Grayling, who lives just at the end of the street, and the footman had met him coming down the steps. I had him shown into my own room.

"I want you to go to the man whom I found in the street, and listen to what he has to say."

"With pleasure."

"Can I trust you?"

"To listen to what he has to say?—I believe so."

"Can I trust you to respect my confidence?"

He was not at all abashed,—I never saw Sydney Atherton when he was abashed. Whatever the offence of which he has been guilty, he always seems completely at his ease. His eyes twinkled.

"You can,—I will not breathe a syllable even to papa."

"In that case, come! But, you understand, I am going to put to the test the affirmations which you have made during all these years, and to prove if you have any of the feeling for me which you pretend."

Directly we were in the stranger's room, Sydney marched straight up to the bed, stared at the man who was lying in it, crammed his hands into his trouser pockets, and whistled. I was amazed.

"So!" he exclaimed. "It's you!"

"Do you know this man?" I asked.

"I am hardly prepared to go so far as to say that I know him, but, I chance to have a memory for faces, and it happens that I have met this gentleman on at least one previous occasion. Perhaps he remembers me.—Do you?"

The stranger seemed uneasy,—as if he found Sydney's tone and manner disconcerting.

"I do. You are the man in the street."

"Precisely. I am that—individual. And you are the man who came through the window. And in a much more comfortable condition you appear to be than when first I saw you." Sydney turned to me. "It is just possible, Miss Lindon, that I may have a few remarks to make to this gentleman which would be better made in private,—if you don't mind."

"But I do mind,—I mind very much. What do you suppose I sent for you here for?"

Sydney smiled that absurd, provoking smile of his,—as if the occasion were not sufficiently serious.

"To show that you still repose in me a vestige of your confidence."

"Don't talk nonsense. This man has told me a most extraordinary story, and I have sent for you—as you may believe, not too willingly"— Sydney bowed—"in order that he may repeat it in your presence, and in mine."

"Is that so?—Well!—Permit me to offer you a chair,—this tale may turn out to be a trifle long."

To humour him I accepted the chair he offered, though I should have preferred to stand;—he seated himself on the side of the bed, fixing on the stranger those keen, quizzical, not too merciful, eyes of his. "Well, sir, we are at your service,—if you will be so good as to favour us with a second edition of that pleasant yarn you have been spinning. But—let us begin at the right end!—what's your name?"

"My name is Robert Holt."

"That so?—Then, Mr. Robert Holt,—let her go!"

Thus encouraged, Mr. Holt repeated the tale which he had told me, only in more connected fashion than before. I fancy that Sydney's glances exercised on him a sort of hypnotic effect, and this kept him to the point,—he scarcely needed a word of prompting from the first syllable to the last.

He told how, tired, wet, hungry, desperate, despairing, he had been refused admittance to the casual ward,—that unfailing resource, as one would have supposed, of those who had abandoned even hope. How he had come upon an open window in an apparently empty house, and, thinking of nothing but shelter from the inclement night, he had clambered through it. How he had found himself in the presence of an extraordinary being, who, in his debilitated and nervous state, had seemed to him to be only half human. How this dreadful creature had given utterance to wild sentiments of hatred towards Paul Lessingham,— my Paul! How he had taken advantage of Holt's enfeebled state to gain over him the most complete, horrible, and, indeed, almost incredible ascendency. How he actually had sent Holt, practically naked, into the storm-driven streets, to commit burglary at Paul's house,—and how he,—Holt,—had actually gone without being able to offer even a shadow of opposition. How Paul, suddenly returning home, had come upon Holt engaged in the very act of committing burglary, and how, on his hearing Holt make a cabalistic[1] reference to some mysterious beetle, the manhood had gone out of him, and he had suffered the intruder to make good his escape without an effort to detain him.

The story had seemed sufficiently astonishing the first time, it seemed still more astonishing the second,—but, as I watched Sydney listening, what struck me chiefly was the conviction that he had heard it all before. I charged him with it directly Holt had finished.

"This is not the first time you have been told this tale."

"Pardon me,—but it is. Do you suppose I live in an atmosphere of fairy tales?"

Something in his manner made me feel sure he was deceiving me.

"Sydney!—Don't tell me a story!—Paul has told you!"

"I am not telling you a story,—at least, on this occasion; and Mr. Lessingham has not told me. Suppose we postpone these details to a little later. And perhaps, in the interim, you will permit me to put a question or two to Mr. Holt."

I let him have his way,—though I knew he was concealing something from me; that he had a more intimate acquaintance with Mr. Holt's strange tale than he chose to confess. And, for some cause, his reticence annoyed me.

He looked at Mr. Holt in silence for a second or two. Then he said, with the quizzical little air of bland impertinence which is peculiarly his own,

"I presume, Mr. Holt, you have been entertaining us with a novelty in fables, and that we are not expected to believe this pleasant little yarn of yours."

"I expect nothing. But I have told you the truth. And you know it."

This seemed to take Sydney aback.

"I protest that, like Miss Lindon, you credit me with a more extensive knowledge than I possess. However, we will let that pass.—I take it that you paid particular attention to this mysterious habitant of this mysterious dwelling."

I saw that Mr. Holt shuddered.

"I am not likely ever to forget him."

"Then, in that case, you will be able to describe him to us."

---

[1] *Cabalistic*: referring to secret or mysterious practices.

"To do so adequately would be beyond my powers. But I will do my best."

If the original was more remarkable than the description which he gave of him, then he must have been remarkable indeed. The impression conveyed to my mind was rather of a monster than a human being. I watched Sydney attentively as he followed Mr. Holt's somewhat lurid language, and there was something in his demeanour which made me more and more persuaded that he was more behind the scenes in this strange business than he pretended, or than the speaker suspected. He put a question which seemed uncalled for by anything which Mr. Holt had said.

"You are sure this thing of beauty was a man?"

"No, sir, that is exactly what I am not sure."

There was a note in Sydney's voice which suggested that he had received precisely the answer which he had expected.

"Did you think it was a woman?"

"I did think so, more than once. Though I can hardly explain what made me think so. There was certainly nothing womanly about the face." He paused, as if to reflect. Then added, "I suppose it was a question of instinct."

"I see.—Just so.—It occurs to me, Mr. Holt, that you are rather strong on questions of instinct." Sydney got off the bed. He stretched himself, as if fatigued,—which is a way he has. "I will not do you the injustice to hint that I do not believe a word of your charming, and simple, narrative. On the contrary, I will demonstrate my perfect credence by remarking that I have not the slightest doubt that you will be able to point out to me, for my particular satisfaction, the delightful residence on which the whole is founded."

Mr. Holt coloured,—Sydney's tone could scarcely have been more significant.

"You must remember, sir, that it was a dark night, that I had never been in that neighbourhood before, and that I was not in a condition to pay much attention to locality!"

"All of which is granted, but—how far was it from Hammersmith Workhouse?"

"Possibly under half a mile."

"Then, in that case, surely you can remember which turning you took on leaving Hammersmith Workhouse,—I suppose there are not many turnings you could have taken."

"I think I could remember."

"Then you shall have an opportunity to try. It isn't a very far cry to Hammersmith,—don't you think you are well enough to drive there now, just you and I together in a cab?"

"I should say so. I wished to get up this morning. It is by the doctor's orders I have stayed in bed."

"Then, for once in a while, the doctor's orders shall be ignored,—I prescribe fresh air." Sydney turned to me. "Since Mr. Holt's wardrobe seems rather to seek, don't you think a suit of one of the men might fit him,—if Mr. Holt wouldn't mind making shift for the moment?— Then, by the time you've finished dressing, Mr. Holt, I shall be ready."

While they were ascertaining which suit of clothes would be best adapted to his figure, I went with Sydney to my room. So soon as we were in, I let him know that this was not a matter in which I intended to be trifled with.

"Of course you understand, Sydney, that I am coming with you."

He pretended not to know what I meant.

"Coming with me?—I am delighted to hear it,—but where?"

"To the house of which Mr. Holt has been speaking."

"Nothing could give me greater pleasure, but—might I point out?— Mr. Holt has to find it yet?"

"I will come to help you to help him find it."

Sydney laughed,—but I could see he did not altogether relish the suggestion.

"Three in a hansom?"

"There is such a thing as a four-wheeled cab,—or I could order a carriage if you'd like one."

Sydney looked at me out of the corners of his eyes; then began to walk up and down the room, with his hands in his trouser pockets. Presently he began to talk nonsense.

"I need not say with what a sensation of joy I should anticipate the delights of a drive with you,—even in a four-wheeled cab; but, were I in your place, I fancy that I should allow Holt and your humble servant to go hunting out this house of his alone. It may prove a more tedious business than you imagine. I promise that, after the hunt is over, I will describe the proceedings to you with the most literal accuracy."

"I daresay.—Do you think I don't know you've been deceiving me all the time?"

"Deceiving you?—I!"

"Yes,—you! Do you think I'm quite an idiot?"

"My dear Marjorie!"

"Do you think I can't see that you know all about what Mr. Holt has been telling us,—perhaps more about it than he knows himself."

"On my word!—With what an amount of knowledge you do credit me."

"Yes, I do,—or discredit you, rather. If I were to trust you, you would tell me just as much as you chose,—which would be nothing. I'm coming with you,—so there's an end."

"Very well.—Do you happen to know if there are any revolvers in the house?"

"Revolvers?—whatever for?"

"Because I should like to borrow one. I will not conceal from you— since you press me—that this is a case in which a revolver is quite likely to be required."

"You are trying to frighten me."

"I am doing nothing of the kind, only, under the circumstances, I am bound to point out to you what it is you may expect."

"Oh, you think that you're bound to point that out, do you,—then now your bounden duty's done. As for there being any revolvers in the house, papa has a perfect arsenal,—would you like to take them all?"

"Thanks, but I daresay I shall be able to manage with one,—unless you would like one too. You may find yourself in need of it."

"I am obliged to you, but, on this occasion, I don't think I'll trouble. I'll run the risk.—Oh, Sydney, what a hypocrite you are!"

"It's for your sake, if I seem to be. I tell you most seriously, that I earnestly advise you to allow Mr. Holt and I to manage this affair alone. I don't mind going so far as to say that this is a matter with which, in days to come, you will wish that you had not allowed yourself to be associated."

"What do you mean by that? Do you dare to insinuate anything against—Paul?"

"I insinuate nothing. What I mean, I say right out; and, my dear Marjorie, what I actually do mean is this,—that if, in spite of my urgent solicitations, you will persist in accompanying us, the expedition, so far as I am concerned, will be postponed."

"That is what you do mean, is it? Then that's settled." I rang the bell. The servant came. "Order a four-wheeled cab at once. And let me know the moment Mr. Holt is ready." The servant went. I turned to Sydney. "If you will excuse me, I will go and put my hat on. You are, of course, at liberty to please yourself as to whether you will or will not go, but, if you don't, then I shall go with Mr. Holt alone."

I moved to the door. He stopped me.

"My dear Marjorie, why will you persist in treating me with such injustice? Believe me, you have no idea what sort of adventure this is which you are setting out upon,—or you would hear reason. I assure you that you are gratuitously proposing to thrust yourself into imminent peril."

"What sort of peril? Why do you beat about the bush,—why don't you speak right out?"

"I can't speak right out, there are circumstances which render it practically impossible—and that's the plain truth,—but the danger is none the less real on that account. I am not jesting,—I am in earnest; won't you take my word for it?"

"It is not a question of taking your word only,—it is a question of something else beside. I have not forgotten my adventures of last night,—and Mr. Holt's story is mysterious enough in itself, but there is something more mysterious still at the back of it,—something which you appear to suggest points unpleasantly at Paul. My duty is dear, and nothing you can say will turn me from it. Paul, as you are very well aware, is already overweighted with affairs of state, pretty nearly borne down by them,—or I would take the tale to him, and he would talk to you after a fashion of his own. Things being as they are, I propose to show you that, although I am not yet Paul's wife, I can make his interests my own as completely as though I were. I can, therefore, only repeat that it is for you to decide what you intend to do; but, if you prefer to stay, I shall go with Mr. Holt,—alone."

"Understand that, when the time for regret comes—as it will come!—you are not to blame me for having done what I advised you not to do."

"My dear Mr. Atherton, I will undertake to do my utmost to guard your spotless reputation; I should be sorry that anyone should hold you responsible for anything I either said or did."

"Very well!—Your blood be on your own head!"

"My blood?"

"Yes,—your blood. I shouldn't be surprised if it comes to blood before we're through.—Perhaps you'll oblige me with the loan of one of that arsenal of revolvers of which you spoke."

I let him have his old revolver,—or, rather, I let him have one of papa's new ones. He put it in the hip pocket in his trousers. And the expedition started,—in a four-wheeled cab.

CHAPTER 29

THE HOUSE ON THE ROAD FROM THE WORKHOUSE

Mr. Holt looked as if he was in somebody else's garments. He was so thin, and worn, and wasted, that the suit of clothes which one of the men had lent him hung upon him as on a scarecrow. I was almost ashamed of myself for having incurred a share of the responsibility of taking him out of bed. He seemed so weak and bloodless that I should not have been surprised if he had fainted on the road. I had taken care that he should eat as much as he could eat before we started—the suggestion of starvation which he had conveyed to one's mind was dreadful!—and I had brought a flask of brandy in case of accidents, but, in spite of everything, I could not conceal from myself that he would be more at home in a sick-bed than in a jolting cab.

It was not a cheerful drive. There was in Sydney's manner towards me an air of protection which I instinctively resented,—he appeared to be regarding me as a careful, and anxious, nurse might regard a wrong-headed and disobedient child. Conversation distinctly languished. Since Sydney seemed disposed to patronise me, I was bent on snubbing him. The result was, that the majority of the remarks which were uttered were addressed to Mr. Holt.

The cab stopped,—after what had appeared to me to be an interminable journey. I was rejoiced at the prospect of its being at an end. Sydney put his head out of the window. A short parley with the driver ensued.

"This is 'Ammersmith Workhouse, it's a large place, sir,—which part of it might you be wanting?"

Sydney appealed to Mr. Holt. He put his head out of the window in his turn,—he did not seem to recognise our surroundings at all.

"We have come a different way,—this is not the way I went; I went through Hammersmith,—and to the casual ward; I don't see that here."

Sydney spoke to the cabman.

"Driver, where's the casual ward?"

"That's the other end, sir."

"Then take us there."

He took us there. Then Sydney appealed again to Mr. Holt.

"Shall I dismiss the cabman,—or don't you feel equal to walking."

"Thank you, I feel quite equal to walking,—I think the exercise will do me good."

So the cabman was dismissed,—a step which we—and I, in particular—had subsequent cause to regret. Mr. Holt took his bearings. He pointed to a door which was just in front of us.

"That's the entrance to the casual ward, and that, over it, is the window through which the other man threw a stone. I went to the right,—back the way I had come." We went to the right. "I reached this corner." We had reached a corner. Mr. Holt looked about him, endeavouring to recall the way he had gone. A good many roads appeared to converge at that point, so that he might have wandered in either of several directions.

Presently he arrived at something like a decision.

"I think this is the way I went,—I am nearly sure it is."

He led the way, with something of an air of dubitation, and we followed. The road he had chosen seemed to lead to nothing and nowhere. We had not gone many yards from the workhouse gates before we were confronted by something like chaos. In front and on either side of us were large spaces of waste land. At some more or less remote period attempts appeared to have been made at brickmaking,— there were untidy stacks of bilious-looking bricks in evidence. Here and there enormous weather-stained boards announced that "This Desirable Land was to be Let for Building Purposes." The road itself was unfinished. There was no pavement, and we had the bare uneven ground for sidewalk. It seemed, so far as I could judge, to lose itself in space, and to be swallowed up by the wilderness of "Desirable Land" which lay beyond. In the near distance there were houses enough, and to spare—of a kind. But they were in other roads. In the one in which we actually were, on the right, at the end, there was a row of unfurnished carcases, but only two buildings which were in anything like a fit state for occupation. One stood on either side, not facing each other,—there was a distance between them of perhaps fifty yards. The sight of them had a more exciting effect on Mr. Holt than it had on me. He moved rapidly forward,—coming to a standstill in front of the one upon our left, which was the nearer of the pair.

"This is the house!" he exclaimed.

He seemed almost exhilarated,—I confess that I was depressed. A more dismal-looking habitation one could hardly imagine. It was one of those dreadful jerry-built houses which, while they are still new, look old. It had quite possibly only been built a year or two, and yet, owing to neglect, or to poverty of construction, or to a combination of the two, it was already threatening to tumble down. It was a small place, a couple of storeys high, and would have been dear—I should think!—at thirty pounds a year. The windows had surely never been washed since the house was built,—those on the upper floor seemed all either cracked or broken. The only sign of occupancy consisted in the fact that a blind was down behind the window of the room on the ground floor. Curtains there were none. A low wall ran in front, which had apparently at one time been surmounted by something in the shape of an iron railing,—a rusty piece of metal still remained on one end; but, since there was only about a foot between it and the building, which was practically built upon the road,—whether the wall was intended to ensure privacy, or was merely for ornament, was not clear.

"This is the house!" repeated Mr. Holt, showing more signs of life than I had hitherto seen in him.

Sydney looked it up and down,—it apparently appealed to his aesthetic sense as little as it did to mine.

"Are you sure?"

"I am certain."

"It seems empty."

"It seemed empty to me that night,—that is why I got into it in search of shelter."

"Which is the window which served you as a door?"

"This one." Mr. Holt pointed to the window on the ground floor,—the one which was screened by a blind. "There was no sign of a blind when I first saw it, and the sash was up,—it was that which caught my eye."

Once more Sydney surveyed the place, in comprehensive fashion, from roof to basement,—then he scrutinisingly regarded Mr. Holt.

"You are quite sure this is the house? It might be awkward if you proved mistaken. I am going to knock at the door, and if it turns out that that mysterious acquaintance of yours does not, and never has lived here, we might find an explanation difficult."

"I am sure it is the house,—certain! I know it,—I feel it here,—and here."

Mr. Holt touched his breast, and his forehead. His manner was distinctly odd. He was trembling, and a fevered expression had come into his eyes. Sydney glanced at him, for a moment, in silence. Then he bestowed his attention upon me.

"May I ask if I may rely upon your preserving your presence of mind?"

The mere question ruffled my plumes.

"What do you mean?"

"What I say. I am going to knock at that door, and I am going to get through it, somehow. It is quite within the range of possibility that, when I am through, there will be some strange happenings,—as you have heard from Mr. Holt. The house is commonplace enough without; you may not find it so commonplace within. You may find yourself in a position in which it will be in the highest degree essential that you should keep your wits about you."

"I am not likely to let them stray."

"Then that's all right.—Do I understand that you propose to come in with me?"

"Of course I do,—what do you suppose I've come for? What nonsense you are talking."

"I hope that you will still continue to consider it nonsense by the time this little adventure's done."

That I resented his impertinence goes without saying—to be talked to in such a strain by Sydney Atherton, whom I had kept in subjection ever since he was in knickerbockers, was a little trying,—but I am forced to admit that I was more impressed by his manner, or his words, or by Mr. Holt's manner, or something, than I should have cared to own. I had not the least notion what was going to happen, or what horrors that woebegone-looking dwelling contained. But Mr. Holt's story had been of the most astonishing sort, my experiences of the previous night were still fresh, and, altogether, now that I was in such close neighbourhood with the Unknown—with a capital U!— although it was broad daylight, it loomed before me in a shape for which,—candidly!—I was not prepared.

A more disreputable-looking front door I have not seen,—it was in perfect harmony with the remainder of the establishment. The paint was off; the woodwork was scratched and dented; the knocker was red with rust. When Sydney took it in his hand I was conscious of quite a little thrill. As he brought it down with a sharp rat-tat, I half expected to see the door fly open, and disclose some gruesome object glaring out at us. Nothing of the kind took place; the door did not budge,— nothing happened. Sydney waited a second or two, then knocked again; another second or two, then another knock. There was still no sign of any notice being taken of our presence. Sydney turned to Mr. Holt.

"Seems as if the place was empty."

Mr. Holt was in the most singular condition of agitation,—it made me uncomfortable to look at him.

"You do not know,—you cannot tell; there may be someone there who hears and pays no heed."

"I'll give them another chance."

Sydney brought down the knocker with thundering reverberations. The din must have been audible half a mile away. But from within the house there was still no sign that any heard. Sydney came down the step.

"I'll try another way,—I may have better fortune at the back."

He led the way round to the rear, Mr. Holt and I following in single file. There the place seemed in worse case even than in the front. There were two empty rooms on the ground floor at the back,—there was no mistake about their being empty, without the slightest difficulty we could see right into them. One was apparently intended for a kitchen and wash-house combined, the other for a sitting-room. There was not a stick of furniture in either, nor the slightest sign of human habitation. Sydney commented on the fact.

"Not only is it plain that no one lives in these charming apartments, but it looks to me uncommonly as if no one ever had lived in them."

To my thinking Mr. Holt's agitation was increasing every moment. For some reason of his own, Sydney took no notice of it whatever,— possibly because he judged that to do so would only tend to make it worse. An odd change had even taken place in Mr. Holt's voice,—he spoke in a sort of tremulous falsetto.

"It was only the front room which I saw."

"Very good; then, before very long, you shall see that front room again."

Sydney rapped with his knuckles on the glass panels of the back door. He tried the handle; when it refused to yield he gave it a vigorous shaking. He saluted the dirty windows,—so far as succeeding in attracting attention was concerned, entirely in vain. Then he turned again to Mr. Holt,—half mockingly.

"I call you to witness that I have used every lawful means to gain the favourable notice of your mysterious friend. I must therefore beg to stand excused if I try something slightly unlawful for a change. It is true that you found the window already open; but, in my case, it soon will be."

He took a knife out of his pocket, and, with the open blade, forced back the catch,—as I am told that burglars do. Then he lifted the sash.

"Behold!" he exclaimed. "What did I tell you?—Now, my dear Marjorie, if I get in first and Mr. Holt gets in after me, we shall be in a position to open the door for you."

I immediately saw through his design.

"No, Mr. Atherton; you will get in first, and I will get in after you, through the window,—before Mr. Holt. I don't intend to wait for you to open the door."

Sydney raised his hands and opened his eyes, as if grieved at my want of confidence. But I did not mean to be left in the lurch, to wait their pleasure, while on pretence of opening the door, they searched the house. So Sydney climbed in first, and I second,—it was not a difficult operation, since the window-sill was under three feet from the ground—and Mr. Holt last. Directly we were in, Sydney put his hand up to his mouth, and shouted.

"Is there anybody in this house? If so, will he kindly step this way, as there is someone wishes to see him."

His words went echoing through the empty rooms in a way which was almost uncanny. I suddenly realised that if, after all, there did happen to be somebody in the house, and he was at all disagreeable, our presence on his premises might prove rather difficult to explain. However, no one answered. While I was waiting for Sydney to make the next move, he diverted my attention to Mr. Holt.

"Hollo, Holt, what's the matter with you? Man, don't play the fool like that!"

Something was the matter with Mr. Holt. He was trembling all over as if attacked by a shaking palsy. Every muscle in his body seemed twitching at once. A strained look had come on his face, which was not nice to see. He spoke as with an effort.

"I'm all right.—It's nothing."

"Oh, is it nothing? Then perhaps you'll drop it. Where's that brandy?" I handed Sydney the flask. "Here, swallow this."

Mr. Holt swallowed the cupful of neat spirit which Sydney offered without an attempt at parley. Beyond bringing some remnants of colour to his ashen cheeks it seemed to have no effect on him whatever. Sydney eyed him with a meaning in his glance which I was at a loss to understand.

"Listen to me, my lad. Don't think you can deceive me by playing any of your fool tricks, and don't delude yourself into supposing that I shall treat you as anything but dangerous if you do. I've got this." He showed the revolver of papa's which I had lent him. "Don't imagine that Miss Lindon's presence will deter me from using it."

Why he addressed Mr. Holt in such a strain surpassed my comprehension. Mr. Holt, however, evinced not the faintest symptoms of resentment,—he had become, on a sudden, more like an automaton than a man. Sydney continued to gaze at him as if he would have liked his glance to penetrate to his inmost soul.

"Keep in front of me, if you please, Mr. Holt, and lead the way to this mysterious apartment in which you claim to have had such a remarkable experience."

Of me he asked in a whisper,

"Did you bring a revolver?"

I was startled.

"A revolver?—The idea!—How absurd you are!"

Sydney said something which was so rude—and so uncalled for!—that it was worthy of papa in his most violent moments.

"I'd sooner be absurd than a fool in petticoats." I was so angry that I did not know what to say,—and before I could say it he went on. "Keep your eyes and ears well open; be surprised at nothing you see or hear. Stick close to me. And for goodness sake remain mistress of as many of your senses as you conveniently can."

I had not the least idea what was the meaning of it all. To me there seemed nothing to make such a pother about. And yet I was conscious of a fluttering of the heart as if there soon might be something. I knew Sydney sufficiently well to be aware that he was one of the last men in the world to make a fuss without reason,—and that he was as little likely to suppose that there was a reason when as a matter of fact there was none.

Mr. Holt led the way, as Sydney desired—or, rather, commanded, to the door of the room which was in front of the house. The door was closed. Sydney tapped on a panel. All was silence. He tapped again.

"Anyone in there?" he demanded.

As there was still no answer, he tried the handle. The door was locked.

"The first sign of the presence of a human being we have had,—doors don't lock themselves. It's just possible that there may have been someone or something about the place, at some time or other, after all."

Grasping the handle firmly, he shook it with all his might,—as he had done with the door at the back. So flimsily was the place constructed that he made even the walls to tremble.

"Within there!—if anyone is in there!—if you don't open this door, I shall."

There was no response.

"So be it!—I'm going to pursue my wild career of defiance of established law and order, and gain admission in one way, if I can't in another."

Putting his right shoulder against the door, he pushed with his whole force. Sydney is a big man, and very strong, and the door was weak. Shortly, the lock yielded before the continuous pressure, and the door flew open. Sydney whistled.

"So!—It begins to occur to me, Mr. Holt, that that story of yours may not have been such pure romance as it seemed."

It was plain enough that, at any rate, this room had been occupied, and that recently,—and, if his taste in furniture could be taken as a test, by an eccentric occupant to boot. My own first impression was that there was someone, or something, living in it still,—an uncomfortable odour greeted our nostrils, which was suggestive of some evil-smelling animal. Sydney seemed to share my thought.

"A pretty perfume, on my word! Let's shed a little more light on the subject, and see what causes it. Marjorie, stop where you are until I tell you."

I had noticed nothing, from without, peculiar about the appearance of the blind which screened the window, but it must have been made of some unusually thick material, for, within, the room was strangely dark. Sydney entered, with the intention of drawing up the blind, but he had scarcely taken a couple of steps when he stopped.

"What's that?"

"It's it," said Mr. Holt, in a voice which was so unlike his own that it was scarcely recognisable.

"It?—What do you mean by it?"

"The Beetle!"

Judging from the sound of his voice Sydney was all at once in a state of odd excitement.

"Oh, is it!—Then, if this time I don't find out the how and the why and the wherefore of that charming conjuring trick, I'll give you leave to write me down an ass,—with a great, big A."

He rushed farther into the room,—apparently his efforts to lighten it did not meet with the immediate success which he desired.

"What's the matter with this confounded blind? There's no cord! How do you pull it up?—What the—"

In the middle of his sentence Sydney ceased speaking. Suddenly Mr. Holt, who was standing by my side on the threshold of the door, was seized with such a fit of trembling, that, fearing he was going to fall, I caught him by the arm. A most extraordinary look was on his face. His eyes were distended to their fullest width, as if with horror at what they saw in front of them. Great beads of perspiration were on his forehead.

"It's coming!" he screamed.

Exactly what happened I do not know. But, as he spoke, I heard, proceeding from the room, the sound of the buzzing of wings. Instantly it recalled my experiences of the night before,—as it did so I was conscious of a most unpleasant qualm. Sydney swore a great oath, as if he were beside himself with rage.

"If you won't go up, you shall come down."

I suppose, failing to find a cord, he seized the blind from below, and dragged it down,—it came, roller and all, clattering to the floor. The room was all in light. I hurried in. Sydney was standing by the window, with a look of perplexity upon his face which, under any other circumstances, would have been comical. He was holding papa's revolver in his hand, and was glaring round and round the room, as if wholly at a loss to understand how it was he did not see what he was looking for.

"Marjorie!" he exclaimed. "Did you hear anything?"

"Of course I did. It was that which I heard last night,—which so frightened me."

"Oh, was it? Then, by—" in his excitement he must have been completely oblivious of my presence, for he used the most terrible language, "when I find it there'll be a small discussion. It can't have got out of the room,—I know the creature's here; I not only heard it, I felt it brush against my face.—Holt, come inside and shut that door."

Mr. Holt raised his arms, as if he were exerting himself to make a forward movement,—but he remained rooted to the spot on which he stood.

"I can't!" he cried.

"You can't!—Why?"

"It won't let me."

"What won't let you?"

"The Beetle!"

Sydney moved till he was close in front of him. He surveyed him with eager eyes. I was just at his back. I heard him murmur,—possibly to me.

"By George!—It's just as I thought!—The beggar's hypnotised!"

Then he said aloud,

"Can you see it now?"

"Yes."

"Where?"

"Behind you."

As Mr. Holt spoke, I again heard, quite close to me, that buzzing sound. Sydney seemed to hear it too,—it caused him to swing round so quickly that he all but whirled me off my feet.

"I beg your pardon, Marjorie, but this is of the nature of an unparalleled experience,—didn't you hear something then?"

"I did,—distinctly; it was close to me,—within an inch or two of my face."

We stared about us, then back at each other,—there was nothing else to be seen. Sydney laughed, doubtfully.

"It's uncommonly queer. I don't want to suggest that there are visions about, or I might suspect myself of softening of the brain. But—it's queer. There's a trick about it somewhere, I am convinced; and no doubt it's simple enough when you know how it's done,—but the difficulty is to find that out.—Do you think our friend over there is acting?"

"He looks to me as if he were ill."

"He does look ill. He also looks as if he were hypnotised. If he is, it must be by suggestion,—and that's what makes me doubtful, because it will be the first plainly established case of hypnotism by suggestion I've encountered.—Holt!"

"Yes."

"That," said Sydney in my ear, "is the voice and that is the manner of a hypnotised man, but, on the other hand, a person under influence generally responds only to the hypnotist,—which is another feature about our peculiar friend which arouses my suspicions." Then, aloud, "Don't stand there like an idiot,—come inside."

Again Mr. Holt made an apparently futile effort to do as he was bid. It was painful to look at him,—he was like a feeble, frightened, tottering child, who would come on, but cannot.

"I can't."

"No nonsense, my man! Do you think that this is a performance in a booth, and that I am to be taken in by all the humbug of the professional mesmerist? Do as I tell you,—come into the room."

There was a repetition, on Mr. Holt's part, of his previous pitiful struggle; this time it was longer sustained than before,—but the result was the same.

"I can't!" he wailed.

"Then I say you can,—and shall! If I pick you up, and carry you, perhaps you will not find yourself so helpless as you wish me to suppose."

Sydney moved forward to put his threat into execution. As he did so, a strange alteration took place in Mr. Holt's demeanour.

CHAPTER 30

THE SINGULAR BEHAVIOUR
OF MR. HOLT

I was standing in the middle of the room, Sydney was between the door and me; Mr. Holt was in the hall, just outside the doorway, in which he, so to speak, was framed. As Sydney advanced towards him he was seized with a kind of convulsion,—he had to lean against the side of the door to save himself from falling. Sydney paused, and watched. The spasm went as suddenly as it came,—Mr. Holt became as motionless as he had just now been the other way. He stood in an attitude of febrile expectancy,—his chin raised, his head thrown back, his eyes glancing upwards,—with the dreadful fixed glare which had come into them ever since we had entered the house. He looked to me as if his every faculty was strained in the act of listening,—not a muscle in his body seemed to move; he was as rigid as a figure carved in stone. Presently the rigidity gave place to what, to an onlooker, seemed causeless agitation.

"I hear!" he exclaimed, in the most curious voice I had ever heard. "I come!"

It was as though he was speaking to someone who was far away. Turning, he walked down the passage to the front door.

"Hollo!" cried Sydney. "Where are you off to?"

We both of us hastened to see. He was fumbling with the latch; before we could reach him, the door was open, and he was through it. Sydney, rushing after him, caught him on the step and held him by the arm.

"What's the meaning of this little caper?—Where do you think you're going now?"

Mr. Holt did not condescend to turn and look at him. He said in the same dreamy, faraway, unnatural tone of voice,—and he kept his unwavering gaze fixed on what was apparently some distant object which was visible only to himself.

"I am going to him. He calls me."

"Who calls you?"

"The Lord of the Beetle."

Whether Sydney released his arm or not I cannot say. As he spoke, he seemed to me to slip away from Sydney's grasp. Passing through the gateway, turning to the right, he commenced to retrace his steps in the direction we had come. Sydney stared after him in unequivocal amazement. Then he looked at me.

"Well!—this is a pretty fix!—now what's to be done?"

"What's the matter with him?" I inquired. "Is he mad?"

"There's method in his madness if he is. He's in the same condition in which he was that night I saw him come out of the Apostle's window." Sydney has a horrible habit of calling Paul "the Apostle"; I have spoken to him about it over and over again,—but my words have not made much impression. "He ought to be followed,—he may be sailing off to that mysterious friend of his this instant.—But, on the other hand, he mayn't, and it may be nothing but a trick of our friend the conjurer's to get us away from this elegant abode of his. He's done me twice already, I don't want to be done again,—and I distinctly do not want him to return and find me missing. He's quite capable of taking the hint, and removing himself into the *Ewigkeit*,[1]—when the clue to as pretty a mystery as ever I came across will have vanished."

"I can stay," I said.

"You?—Alone?"

He eyed me doubtingly,—evidently not altogether relishing the proposition.

"Why not? You might send the first person you meet,—policeman, cabman, or whoever it is—to keep me company. It seems a pity now that we dismissed that cab."

"Yes, it does seem a pity." Sydney was biting his lip. "Confound that fellow! how fast he moves."

Mr. Holt was already nearing the end of the road.

"If you think it necessary, by all means follow to see where he goes,—you are sure to meet somebody whom you will be able to send before you have gone very far."

"I suppose I shall.—You won't mind being left alone?"

"Why should I?—I'm not a child."

Mr. Holt, reaching the corner, turned it, and vanished out of sight. Sydney gave an exclamation of impatience.

"If I don't make haste I shall lose him. I'll do as you suggest—dispatch the first individual I come across to hold watch and ward with you."

"That'll be all right."

He started off at a run,—shouting to me as he went.

"It won't be five minutes before somebody comes!"

---

[1] Eternity (German).

I waved my hand to him. I watched him till he reached the end of the road. Turning, he waved his hand to me. Then he vanished, as Mr. Holt had done.

And I was alone.

CHAPTER 31

THE TERROR BY DAY

My first impulse, after Sydney's disappearance, was to laugh. Why should he display anxiety on my behalf merely because I was to be the sole occupant of an otherwise empty house for a few minutes more or less,—and in broad daylight too! To say the least, the anxiety seemed unwarranted.

I lingered at the gate, for a moment or two, wondering what was at the bottom of Mr. Holt's singular proceedings, and what Sydney really proposed to gain by acting as a spy upon his wanderings. Then I turned to re-enter the house. As I did so, another problem suggested itself to my mind,—what connection, of the slightest importance, could a man in Paul Lessingham's position have with the eccentric being who had established himself in such an unsatisfactory dwelling place? Mr. Holt's story I had only dimly understood,—it struck me that it would require a deal of understanding. It was more like a farrago of nonsense, an outcome of delirium, than a plain statement of solid facts. To tell the truth, Sydney had taken it more seriously than I expected. He seemed to see something in it which I emphatically did not. What was double Dutch to me, seemed clear as print to him. So far as I could judge, he actually had the presumption to imagine that Paul—my Paul!—Paul Lessingham!—the great Paul Lessingham!—was mixed up in the very mysterious adventures of poor, weak-minded, hysterical Mr. Holt, in a manner which was hardly to his credit.

Of course, any idea of the kind was purely and simply balderdash. Exactly what bee Sydney had got in his bonnet, I could not guess. But I did know Paul. Only let me find myself face to face with the fantastic author of Mr. Holt's weird tribulations, and I, a woman, single-handed, would do my best to show him that whoever played pranks with Paul Lessingham trifled with edged tools.

I had returned to that historical front room which, according to Mr. Holt, had been the scene of his most disastrous burglarious entry. Whoever had furnished it had had original notions of the resources of modern upholstery. There was not a table in the place,—no chair or couch, nothing to sit down upon except the bed. On the floor there was a marvellous carpet which was apparently of eastern manufacture. It was so thick, and so pliant to the tread, that moving over it was like walking on thousand-year-old turf. It was woven in gorgeous colours, and covered with—

When I discovered what it actually was covered with, I was conscious of a disagreeable sense of surprise.

It was covered with beetles!

All over it, with only a few inches of space between each, were representations of some peculiar kind of beetle,—it was the same beetle, over, and over, and over. The artist had woven his undesirable subject into the warp and woof of the material with such cunning skill that, as one continued to gaze, one began to wonder if by any possibility the creatures could be alive.

In spite of the softness of the texture, and the art—of a kind!—which had been displayed in the workmanship, I rapidly arrived at the conclusion that it was the most uncomfortable carpet I had ever seen. I wagged my finger at the repeated portrayals of the—to me!—unspeakable insect.

"If I had discovered that you were there before Sydney went, I think it just possible that I should have hesitated before I let him go."

Then there came a revulsion of feeling. I shook myself.

"You ought to be ashamed of yourself, Marjorie Lindon, to even think such nonsense. Are you all nerves and morbid imaginings,—you who have prided yourself on being so strong-minded! A pretty sort you are to do battle for anyone.—Why, they're only make-believes!"

Half involuntarily, I drew my foot over one of the creatures. Of course, it was nothing but imagination; but I seemed to feel it squelch beneath my shoe. It was disgusting.

"Come!" I cried. "This won't do! As Sydney would phrase it,—am I going to make an idiot of myself?"

I turned to the window,—looking at my watch.

"It's more than five minutes ago since Sydney went. That companion of mine ought to be already on the way. I'll go and see if he is coming."

I went to the gate. There was not a soul in sight. It was with such a distinct sense of disappointment that I perceived this was so, that I was in two minds what to do. To remain where I was, looking, with gaping eyes, for the policeman, or the cabman, or whoever it was Sydney was dispatching to act as my temporary associate, was tantamount to acknowledging myself a simpleton,—while I was conscious of a most unmistakable reluctance to return within the house.

Common sense, or what I took for common sense, however, triumphed, and, after loitering for another five minutes, I did go in again.

This time, ignoring, to the best of my ability, the beetles on the floor, I proceeded to expend my curiosity—and occupy my thoughts—in an examination of the bed. It only needed a very cursory examination, however, to show that the seeming bed was, in reality, none at all,—or if it was a bed after the manner of the Easterns it certainly was not after the fashion of the Britons. There was no framework,—nothing to represent the bedstead. It was simply a heap of rugs piled apparently indiscriminately upon the floor. A huge mass of them there seemed to be; of all sorts, and shapes, and sizes,—and materials too.

The top one was of white silk,—in quality, exquisite. It was of huge size, yet, with a little compression, one might almost have passed it through the proverbial wedding ring. So far as space admitted I spread it out in front of me. In the middle was a picture,—whether it was embroidered on the substance or woven in it, I could not quite make out. Nor, at first, could I gather what it was the artist had intended to depict,—there was a brilliancy about it which was rather dazzling. By degrees, I realised that the lurid hues were meant for flames,—and, when one had got so far, one perceived that they were by no means badly imitated either. Then the meaning of the thing dawned on me,—it was a representation of a human sacrifice. In its way, as ghastly a piece of realism as one could see.

On the right was the majestic seated figure of a goddess. Her hands were crossed upon her knees, and she was naked from her waist upwards. I fancied it was meant for Isis. On her brow was perched a gaily apparelled beetle—that ubiquitous beetle!—forming a bright spot of colour against her coppery skin,—it was an exact reproduction of the creatures which were imaged on the carpet. In front of the idol was an enormous fiery furnace. In the very heart of the flames was an altar. On the altar was a naked white woman being burned alive. There could be no doubt as to her being alive, for she was secured by chains in such a fashion that she was permitted a certain amount of freedom, of which she was availing herself to contort and twist her body into shapes which were horribly suggestive of the agony which she was enduring,—the artist, indeed, seemed to have exhausted his powers in his efforts to convey a vivid impression of the pains which were tormenting her.

"A pretty picture, on my word! A pleasant taste in art the garnitures of this establishment suggest! The person who likes to live with this kind of thing, especially as a covering to his bed, must have his own notions as to what constitute agreeable surroundings."

As I continued staring at the thing, all at once it seemed as if the woman on the altar moved. It was preposterous, but she appeared to gather her limbs together, and turn half over.

"What can be the matter with me? Am I going mad? She can't be moving!"

If she wasn't, then certainly something was,—she was lifted right into the air. An idea occurred to me. I snatched the rug aside.

The mystery was explained!

A thin, yellow, wrinkled hand was protruding from amidst the heap of rugs,—it was its action which had caused the seeming movement of the figure on the altar. I stared, confounded. The hand was followed by an arm; the arm by a shoulder; the shoulder by a head,—and the most awful, hideous, wicked-looking face I had ever pictured even in my most dreadful dreams. A pair of baleful eyes were glaring up at mine.

I understood the position in a flash of startled amazement.

Sydney, in following Mr. Holt, had started on a wild goose chase after all. I was alone with the occupant of that mysterious house,—the chief actor in Mr. Holt's astounding tale. He had been hidden in the heap of rugs all the while.

BOOK IV

IN PURSUIT

THE CONCLUSION OF THE MATTER IS EXTRACTED FROM THE CASE-BOOK OF THE HON. AUGUSTUS CHAMPNELL, CONFIDENTIAL AGENT

CHAPTER 32

A NEW CLIENT

On the afternoon of Friday, June 2, 18—, I was entering in my case-book some memoranda having reference to the very curious matter of the Duchess of Datchet's Deed-box. It was about two o'clock. Andrews came in and laid a card upon my desk. On it was inscribed "Mr. Paul Lessingham."

"Show Mr. Lessingham in."

Andrews showed him in. I was, of course, familiar with Mr. Lessingham's appearance, but it was the first time I had had with him any personal communication. He held out his hand to me.

"You are Mr. Champnell?"

"I am."

"I believe that I have not had the honour of meeting you before, Mr. Champnell, but with your father, the Earl of Glenlivet, I have the pleasure of some acquaintance."

I bowed. He looked at me, fixedly, as if he were trying to make out what sort of man I was.

"You are very young, Mr. Champnell."

"I have been told that an eminent offender in that respect once asserted that youth is not of necessity a crime."

"And you have chosen a singular profession,—one in which one hardly looks for juvenility."

"You yourself, Mr. Lessingham, are not old. In a statesman one expects grey hairs.—I trust that I am sufficiently ancient to be able to do you service."

He smiled.

"I think it possible. I have heard of you more than once, Mr.

Champnell, always to your advantage. My friend, Sir John Seymour, was telling me, only the other day, that you have recently conducted for him some business, of a very delicate nature, with much skill and tact; and he warmly advised me, if ever I found myself in a predicament, to come to you. I find myself in a predicament now."

Again I bowed.

["A predicament, I fancy, of an altogether unparalleled sort. I take it that anything I may say to you will be as though it were said to a father confessor." *father atonement*

"You may rest assured of that."

"Good.—Then, to make the matter clear to you I must begin by telling you a story—if I may trespass on your patience to that extent. I will endeavour not to be more verbose than the occasion requires." *voiced of the narrator*

I offered him a chair, placing it in such a position that the light from the window would have shone full upon his face. With the calmest possible air, as if unconscious of my design, he carried the chair to the other side of my desk, twisting it right round *reversal* before he sat on it,—so that now the light was at his back and on my face. Crossing his legs, clasping his hands about his knee, he sat in silence for some moments, as if turning something over in his mind. He glanced round the room.

"I suppose, Mr. Champnell, that some singular tales have been told in here."

"Some very singular tales indeed. I am never appalled by singularity. It is my normal atmosphere."

"And yet I should be disposed to wager that you have never listened to so strange a story as that which I am about to tell you now. So astonishing, indeed, is the chapter in my life which I am about to open out to you, that I have more than once had to take myself to task, and fit the incidents together with mathematical accuracy in order to assure myself of its perfect truth."

He paused. There was about his demeanour that suggestion of reluctance which I not uncommonly discover in individuals who are about to take the skeletons from their cupboards and parade them before my eyes. His next remark seemed to point to the fact that he perceived what was passing through my thoughts.

"My position is not rendered easier by the circumstance that I am not of a communicative nature. I am not in sympathy with the spirit of the age which craves for personal advertisement. I hold that the private life even of a public man should be held inviolate. I resent, with peculiar bitterness, the attempts of prying eyes to peer into matters which, as it seems to me, concern myself alone. You must, therefore, bear with me, Mr. Champnell, if I seem awkward in disclosing to you certain incidents in my career which I had hoped would continue locked in the secret depository of my own bosom, at any rate till I was carried to the grave. I am sure you will suffer me to stand excused if I frankly admit that it is only an irresistible chain of incidents which has constrained me to make of you a confidant."

"My experience tells me, Mr. Lessingham, that no one ever does come to me until they are compelled: In that respect I am regarded as something worse even than a medical man."

A wintry smile flitted across his features,—it was clear that he regarded me as a good deal worse than a medical man. Presently he began to tell me one of the most remarkable tales which even I had heard. As he proceeded I understood how strong, and how natural, had been his desire for reticence. On the mere score of credibility he must have greatly preferred to have kept his own counsel. For my part I own, unreservedly, that I should have deemed the tale incredible had it been told me by Tom, Dick, or Harry, instead of by Paul Lessingham.

CHAPTER 33

WHAT CAME OF LOOKING THROUGH A LATTICE

He began in accents which halted not a little. By degrees his voice grew firmer. Words came from him with greater fluency.

"I am not yet forty. So when I tell you that twenty years ago I was a mere youth I am stating what is a sufficiently obvious truth. It is twenty years ago since the events of which I was going to speak transpired.

"I lost both my parents when I was quite a lad, and by their death I was left in a position in which I was, to an unusual extent in one so young, my own master. I was ever of a rambling turn of mind, and when, at the mature age of eighteen, I left school, I decided that I should learn more from travel than from sojourn at a university. So, since there was no one to say me nay, instead of going either to Oxford or Cambridge, I went abroad. After a few months I found myself in Egypt,—I was down with fever at Shepheard's Hotel in Cairo.[1] I had caught it by drinking polluted water during an excursion with some Bedouins to Palmyra.[2]

"When the fever had left me I went out one night into the town in search of amusement. I went, unaccompanied, into the native quarter, not a wise thing to do, especially at night, but at eighteen one is not always wise, and I was weary of the monotony of the sick-room, and eager for something which had in it a spice of adventure. I found myself in a street which I have reason to believe is no longer existing. It had a French name, and was called the Rue de Rabagas,—I saw the name on the corner as I turned into it, and it has left an impress on the tablets of my memory which is never likely to be obliterated.

"It was a narrow street, and, of course, a dirty one, ill-lit, and, apparently, at the moment of my appearance, deserted. I had gone, perhaps, half-way down its tortuous length, blundering more than once into the kennel, wondering what fantastic whim had brought me into such unsavoury quarters, and what would happen to me if, as seemed extremely possible, I lost my way. On a sudden my ears were saluted by sounds which proceeded from a house which I was passing,—sounds of music and of singing.

"I paused. I stood awhile to listen.

"There was an open window on my right, which was screened by latticed blinds. From the room which was behind these blinds the sounds were coming. Someone was singing, accompanied by an instrument resembling a guitar,—singing uncommonly well."

Mr. Lessingham stopped. A stream of recollection seemed to come flooding over him. A dreamy look came into his eyes.

"I remember it all as clearly as if it were yesterday. How it all comes back,—the dirty street, the evil smells, the imperfect light, the girl's voice filling all at once the air. It was a girl's voice,—full, and round, and sweet; an organ seldom met with, especially in such a place as that. She sang a little *chansonnette*,[3] which, just then, half Europe was humming,—it occurred in an opera which they were acting at one of the Boulevard theatres,—'la P'tite Voyageuse!' The effect, coming so unexpectedly, was startling. I stood and heard her to an end.

"Inspired by I know not what impulse of curiosity, when the song

---

[1]   The hotel was the centre for English society in Cairo in the nineteenth century.
[2]   Ancient city in the middle of the Syrian desert, chiefly of interest to Victorian tourists for its amphitheatre and other ruins.
[3]   Literally, a little song, or a light-hearted tune.

was finished, I moved one of the lattice blinds a little aside, so as to enable me to get a glimpse of the singer. I found myself looking into what seemed to be a sort of cafe,—one of those places which are found all over the Continent, in which women sing in order to attract custom. There was a low platform at one end of the room, and on it were seated three women. One of them had evidently just been accompanying her own song,—she still had an instrument of music in her hands, and was striking a few idle notes. The other two had been acting as audience. They were attired in the fantastic apparel which the women who are found in such places generally—wear. An old woman was sitting knitting in a corner, whom I took to be the inevitable *patronne*.[1] With the exception of these four the place was empty.

"They must have heard me touch the lattice, or seen it moving, for no sooner did I glance within than the three pairs of eyes on the platform were raised and fixed on mine. The old woman in the corner alone showed no consciousness of my neighbourhood. We eyed one another in silence for a second or two. Then the girl with the harp,— the instrument she was manipulating proved to be fashioned more like a harp than a guitar—called out to me,

"'Entrez, monsieur!—Soyez le bienvenu!'[2]

"I was a little tired. Rather curious as to whereabouts I was,—the place struck me, even at that first momentary glimpse, as hardly in the ordinary line of that kind of thing. And not unwilling to listen to a repetition of the former song, or to another sung by the same singer.

"'On condition,' I replied, 'that you sing me another song.'

"'Ah, monsieur, with the greatest pleasure in the world I will sing you twenty.'

"She was almost, if not quite, as good as her word. She entertained me with song after song. I may safely say that I have seldom if ever heard melody more enchanting. All languages seemed to be the same to her. She sang in French and Italian, German and English,—in tongues with which I was unfamiliar. It was in these Eastern harmonies that she was most successful. They were indescribably weird and thrilling, and she delivered them with a verve and sweetness which was amazing. I sat at one of the little tables with which the room was dotted, listening entranced.

"Time passed more rapidly than I supposed. While she sang I sipped the liquor with which the old woman had supplied me. So enthralled

---

[1]   The owner of the establishment.
[2]   "Come in, sir!—Welcome!"

was I by the display of the girl's astonishing gifts that I did not notice what it was I was drinking. Looking back I can only surmise that it was some poisonous concoction of the creature's own. That one small glass had on me the strangest effect. I was still weak from the fever which I had only just succeeded in shaking off, and that, no doubt, had something to do with the result. But, as I continued to sit, I was conscious that I was sinking into a lethargic condition, against which I was incapable of struggling.

"After a while the original performer ceased her efforts and, her companions taking her place, she came and joined me at the little table. Looking at my watch I was surprised to perceive the lateness of the hour. I rose to leave. She caught me by the wrist.

"'Do not go,' she said;—she spoke English of a sort, and with the queerest accent. 'All is well with you. Rest awhile.'

"You will smile,—I should smile, perhaps, were I the listener instead of you, but it is the simple truth that her touch had on me what I can only describe as a magnetic influence. As her fingers closed upon my wrist, I felt as powerless in her grasp as if she held me with bands of steel. What seemed an invitation was virtually a command. I had to stay whether I would or wouldn't. She called for more liquor, and at what again was really her command I drank of it. I do not think that after she touched my wrist I uttered a word. She did all the talking. And, while she talked, she kept her eyes fixed on my face. Those eyes of hers! They were a devil's. I can positively affirm that they had on me a diabolical effect. They robbed me of my consciousness, of my power of volition, of my capacity to think,—they made me as wax in her hands. My last recollection of that fatal night is of her sitting in front of me, bending over the table, stroking my wrist with her extended fingers, staring at me with her awful eyes. After that, a curtain seems to descend. There comes a period of oblivion."

Mr. Lessingham ceased. His manner was calm and self-contained enough; but, in spite of that I could see that the mere recollection of the things which he told me moved his nature to its foundations. There was eloquence in the drawn lines about his mouth, and in the strained expression of his eyes.

So far his tale was sufficiently commonplace. Places such as the one which he described abound in the Cairo of to-day; and many are the Englishmen who have entered them to their exceeding bitter cost. With that keen intuition which has done him yeoman's service in the political arena, Mr. Lessingham at once perceived the direction my thoughts were taking.

"You have heard this tale before?—No doubt. And often. The traps are many, and the fools and the unwary are not a few. The singularity of my experience is still to come. You must forgive me if I seem to stumble in the telling. I am anxious to present my case as baldly, and with as little appearance of exaggeration as possible. I say with as little appearance, for some appearance of exaggeration I fear is unavoidable. My case is so unique, and so out of the common run of our every-day experience, that the plainest possible statement must smack of the sensational.

"As, I fancy, you have guessed, when understanding returned to me, I found myself in an apartment with which I was unfamiliar. I was lying, undressed, on a heap of rugs in a corner of a low-pitched room which was furnished in a fashion which, when I grasped the details, filled me with amazement. By my side knelt the Woman of the Songs. Leaning over, she wooed my mouth with kisses. I cannot describe to you the sense of horror and of loathing with which the contact of her lips oppressed me. There was about her something so unnatural, so inhuman, that I believe even then I could have destroyed her with as little sense of moral turpitude as if she had been some noxious insect.

"'Where am I?' I exclaimed.

"'You are with the children of Isis,' she replied. What she meant I did not know, and do not to this hour. 'You are in the hands of the great goddess,—of the mother of men!'

"'How did I come here?'

"'By the loving kindness of the great mother!'

"I do not, of course, pretend to give you the exact text of her words, but they were to that effect.

"Half raising myself on the heap of rugs, I gazed about me,—and was astounded at what I saw.

"The place in which I was, though the reverse of lofty, was of considerable size,—I could not conceive whereabouts it could be. The walls and roof were of bare stone,—as though the whole had been hewed out of the solid rock. It seemed to be some sort of temple, and was redolent with the most extraordinary odour. An altar stood about the centre, fashioned out of a single block of stone. On it a fire burned with a faint blue flame,—the fumes which rose from it were no doubt chiefly responsible for the prevailing perfumes. Behind it was a huge bronze figure, more than life size. It was in a sitting posture, and represented a woman. Although it resembled no portrayal of her I have seen either before or since, I came afterwards to understand that it was meant for

Isis. On the idol's brow was poised a beetle. That the creature was alive seemed clear, for, as I looked at it, it opened and shut its wings.

"If the one on the forehead of the goddess was the only live beetle which the place contained, it was not the only representation. It was modelled in the solid stone of the roof, and depicted in flaming colours on hangings which here and there were hung against the walls. Wherever the eye turned it rested on a scarab. The effect was bewildering. It was as though one saw things through the distorted glamour of a nightmare. I asked myself if I were not still dreaming; if my appearance of consciousness were not after all a mere delusion; if I had really regained my senses.

"And, here, Mr. Champnell, I wish to point out, and to emphasise the fact, that I am not prepared to positively affirm what portion of my adventures in that extraordinary, and horrible place, was actuality, and what the product of a feverish imagination. Had I been persuaded that all I thought I saw, I really did see, I should have opened my lips long ago, let the consequences to myself have been what they might. But there is the crux. The happenings were of such an incredible character, and my condition was such an abnormal one,—I was never really myself from the first moment to the last—that I have hesitated, and still do hesitate, to assert where, precisely, fiction ended and fact began.

"With some misty notion of testing my actual condition I endeavoured to get off the heap of rugs on which I reclined. As I did so the woman at my side laid her hand against my chest, lightly. But, had her gentle pressure been the equivalent of a ton of iron, it could not have been more effectual. I collapsed, sank back upon the rugs, and lay there, panting for breath, wondering if I had crossed the border line which divides madness from sanity,

"'Let me get up!—let me go!' I gasped.

"'Nay,' she murmured, 'stay with me yet awhile, o my beloved.'

"And again she kissed me."

Once more Mr. Lessingham paused. An involuntary shudder went all over him. In spite of the evidently great effort which he was making to retain his self-control his features were contorted by an anguished spasm. For some seconds he seemed at a loss to find words to enable him to continue.

When he did go on, his voice was harsh and strained.

"I am altogether incapable of even hinting to you the nauseous nature of that woman's kisses. They filled me with an indescribable repulsion. I look back at them with a feeling of physical, mental, and moral horror, across an interval of twenty years. The most dreadful part of it was that I was wholly incapable of offering even the faintest resistance to her caresses. I lay there like a log. She did with me as she would, and in dumb agony I endured."

He took his handkerchief from his pocket, and, although the day was cool, with it he wiped the perspiration from his brow.

"To dwell in detail on what occurred during my involuntary sojourn in that fearful place is beyond my power. I cannot even venture to attempt it. The attempt, were it made, would be futile, and, to me, painful beyond measure. I seem to have seen all that happened as in a glass darkly,[1]—with about it all an element of unreality. As I have already remarked, the things which revealed themselves, dimly, to my perception, seemed too bizarre, too hideous, to be true.

"It was only afterwards, when I was in a position to compare dates, that I was enabled to determine what had been the length of my imprisonment. It appears that I was in that horrible den more than two months,—two unspeakable months. And the whole time there were comings and goings, a phantasmagoric array of eerie figures continually passed to and fro before my hazy eyes. What I judge to have been religious services took place; in which the altar, the bronze image, and the beetle on its brow, figure largely. Not only were they conducted with a bewildering confusion of mysterious rites, but, if my memory is in the least degree trustworthy, they were orgies of nameless horrors. I seem to have seen things take place at them at the mere thought of which the brain reels and trembles.

"Indeed it is in connection with the cult of the obscene deity to whom these wretched creatures paid their scandalous vows that my most awful memories seem to have been associated. It may have been—I hope it was, a mirage born of my half delirious state, but it seemed to me that they offered human sacrifices."

When Mr. Lessingham said this, I pricked up my ears. For reasons of my own, which will immediately transpire, I had been wondering if he would make any reference to a human sacrifice. He noted my display of interest,—but misapprehended the cause.

"I see you start, I do not wonder. But I repeat that unless I was the victim of some extraordinary species of double sight—in which case the whole business would resolve itself into the fabric of a dream, and

---

[1]   The quotation, from I Corinthians 13:12, is partly incorrect, the proper wording being "For now we see through a glass, darkly."

I should indeed thank God!—I saw, on more than one occasion, a human sacrifice offered on that stone altar, presumably to the grim image which looked down on it. And, unless I err, in each case the sacrificial object was a woman, stripped to the skin, as white as you or I,—and before they burned her they subjected her to every variety of outrage of which even the minds of demons could conceive. More than once since then I have seemed to hear the shrieks of the victims ringing through the air, mingled with the triumphant cries of her frenzied murderers, and the music of their harps.

"It was the cumulative horrors of such a scene which gave me the strength, or the courage, or the madness, I know not which it was, to burst the bonds which bound me, and which, even in the bursting, made of me, even to this hour, a haunted man.

"There had been a sacrifice,—unless, as I have repeatedly observed, the whole was nothing but a dream. A woman—a young and lovely Englishwoman, if I could believe the evidence of my own eyes, had been outraged, and burnt alive, while I lay there helpless, looking on. The business was concluded. The ashes of the victim had been consumed by the participants. The worshippers had departed. I was left alone with the woman of the songs, who apparently acted as the guardian of that worse than slaughterhouse. She was, as usual after such an orgy, rather a devil than a human being, drunk with an insensate frenzy, delirious with inhuman longings. As she approached to offer to me her loathed caresses, I was on a sudden conscious of something which I had not felt before when in her company. It was as though something had slipped away from me,—some weight which had oppressed me, some bond by which I had been bound. I was aroused, all at once, to a sense of freedom; to a knowledge that the blood which coursed through my veins was after all my own, that I was master of my own honour.

"I can only suppose that through all those weeks she had kept me there in a state of mesmeric stupor. That, taking advantage of the weakness which the fever had left behind, by the exercise of her diabolical arts, she had not allowed me to pass out of a condition of hypnotic trance. Now, for some reason, the cord was loosed. Possibly her absorption in her religious duties had caused her to forget to tighten it. Anyhow, as she approached me, she approached a man, and one who, for the first time for many a day, was his own man. She herself seemed wholly unconscious of anything of the kind. As she drew nearer to me, and nearer, she appeared to be entirely oblivious of the fact that I was anything but the fibreless, emasculated creature which, up to that moment, she had made of me.

"But she knew it when she touched me,—when she stooped to press her lips to mine. At that instant the accumulating rage which had been smouldering in my breast through all those leaden torturing hours, sprang into flame. Leaping off my couch of rugs, I flung my hands about her throat,—and then she knew I was awake. Then she strove to tighten the cord which she had suffered to become unduly loose. Her baleful eyes were fixed on mine. I knew that she was putting out her utmost force to trick me of my manhood. But I fought with her like one possessed, and I conquered—in a fashion. I compressed her throat with my two hands as with an iron vice. I knew that I was struggling for more than life, that the odds were all against me, that I was staking my all upon the casting of a die,—I stuck at nothing which could make me victor.

"Tighter and tighter my pressure grew,—I did not stay to think if I was killing her—till on a sudden—"

Mr. Lessingham stopped. He stared with fixed, glassy eyes, as if the whole was being re-enacted in front of him. His voice faltered. I thought he would break down. But, with an effort, he continued.

"On a sudden, I felt her slipping from between my fingers. Without the slightest warning, in an instant she had vanished, and where, not a moment before, she herself had been, I found myself confronting a monstrous beetle,—a huge, writhing creation of some wild nightmare.

"At first the creature stood as high as I did. But, as I stared at it, in stupefied amazement,—as you may easily imagine,—the thing dwindled while I gazed. I did not stop to see how far the process of dwindling continued,—a stark raving madman for the nonce, I fled as if all the fiends in hell were at my heels."

CHAPTER 34

AFTER TWENTY YEARS

"How I reached the open air I cannot tell you,—I do not know. I have a confused recollection of rushing through vaulted passages, through endless corridors, of trampling over people who tried to arrest my passage,—and the rest is blank.

"When I again came to myself I was lying in the house of an American missionary named Clements. I had been found, at early dawn, stark naked, in a Cairo street, and picked up for dead. Judging from appearances I must have wandered for miles, all through the night. Whence I had come, or whither I was going, none could tell,—I could not tell myself. For weeks I hovered between life and death. The kindness of Mr. and Mrs. Clements was not to be measured by words. I was brought to their house a penniless, helpless, battered stranger, and they gave me all they had to offer, without money and without price,—with no expectation of an earthly reward. Let no one pretend that there is no Christian charity under the sun. The debt I owed that man and woman I was never able to repay. Before I was properly myself again, and in a position to offer some adequate testimony of the gratitude I felt, Mrs. Clements was dead, drowned during an excursion on the Nile, and her husband had departed on a missionary expedition into Central Africa, from which he never returned.

"Although, in a measure, my physical health returned, for months after I had left the roof of my hospitable hosts, I was in a state of semi-imbecility—I suffered from a species of aphasia. For days together I was speechless, and could remember nothing,—not even my own name. And, when that stage had passed, and I began to move more freely among my fellows, for years I was but a wreck of my former self. I was visited, at all hours of the day and night, by frightful—I know not whether to call them visions, they were real enough to me, but since they were visible to no one but myself, perhaps that is the word which best describes them. Their presence invariably plunged me into a state of abject terror, against which I was unable to even make a show of fighting. To such an extent did they embitter my existence, that I voluntarily placed myself under the treatment of an expert in mental pathology. For a considerable period of time I was under his constant supervision, but the visitations were as inexplicable to him as they were to me.

"By degrees, however, they became rarer and rarer, until at last I flattered myself that I had once more become as other men. After an interval, to make sure, I devoted myself to politics. Thenceforward I have lived, as they phrase it, in the public eye. Private life, in any peculiar sense of the term, I have had none."

Mr. Lessingham ceased. His tale was not uninteresting, and, to say the least of it, was curious. But I still was at a loss to understand what it had to do with me, or what was the purport of his presence in my room. Since he remained silent, as if the matter, so far as he was concerned, was at an end, I told him so.

"I presume, Mr. Lessingham, that all this is but a prelude to the play. At present I do not see where it is that I come in."

Still for some seconds he was silent. When he spoke his voice was grave and sombre, as if he were burdened by a weight of woe.

"Unfortunately, as you put it, all this has been but a prelude to the play. Were it not so I should not now stand in such pressing want of the services of a confidential agent,—that is, of an experienced man of the world, who has been endowed by nature with phenomenal perceptive faculties, and in whose capacity and honour I can place the completest confidence."

I smiled,—the compliment was a pointed one.

"I hope your estimate of me is not too high."

"I hope not,—for my sake, as well as for your own. I have heard great things of you. If ever man stood in need of all that human skill and acumen can do for him, I certainly am he."

His words aroused my curiosity. I was conscious of feeling more interested than heretofore.

"I will do my best for you. Man can do no more. Only give my best a trial."

"I will. At once."

He looked at me long and earnestly. Then, leaning forward, he said, lowering his voice perhaps unconsciously,

"The fact is, Mr. Champnell, that quite recently events have happened which threaten to bridge the chasm of twenty years, and to place me face to face with that plague spot of the past. At this moment I stand in imminent peril of becoming again the wretched thing I was when I fled from that den of all devils. It is to guard me against this that I have come to you. I want you to unravel the tangled thread which threatens to drag me to my doom,—and, when unravelled to sunder it—for ever, if God wills!—in twain."

"Explain."

To be frank, for the moment I thought him mad. He went on.

"Three weeks ago, when I returned late one night from a sitting in the House of Commons, I found, on my study table, a sheet of paper on which there was a representation—marvellously like!—of the creature into which, as it seemed to me, the woman of the songs was transformed as I clutched her throat between my hands. The mere sight of it brought back one of those visitations of which I have told you, and which I thought I had done with for ever,—I was convulsed by an agony of fear, thrown into a state approximating to a paralysis both of mind and body."

"But why?"

"I cannot tell you. I only know that—I have never dared to allow my thoughts to recur to that last dread scene, lest the mere recurrence should drive me mad."

"What was this you found upon your study table,—merely a drawing?"

"It was a representation, produced by what process I cannot say, which was so wonderfully, so diabolically, like the original, that for a moment I thought the thing itself was on my table."

"Who put it there?"

"That is precisely what I wish you to find out,—what I wish you to make it your instant business to ascertain. I have found the thing, under similar circumstances, on three separate occasions, on my study table,—and each time it has had on me the same hideous effect."

"Each time after you have returned from a late sitting in the House of Commons?"

"Exactly."

"Where are these—what shall I call them—delineations?"

"That, again, I cannot tell you."

"What do you mean?"

"What I say. Each time, when I recovered, the thing had vanished."

"Sheet of paper and all?"

"Apparently,—though on that point I could not be positive. You will understand that my study table is apt to he littered with sheets of paper, and I could not absolutely determine that the thing had not stared at me from one of those. The delineation itself, to use your word, certainly had vanished."

I began to suspect that this was a case rather for a doctor than for a man of my profession. And hinted as much.

"Don't you think it is possible, Mr. Lessingham, that you have been overworking yourself—that you have been driving your brain too hard, and that you have been the victim of an optical delusion?"

"I thought so myself; I may say that I almost hoped so. But wait till I have finished. You will find that there is no loophole in that direction."

He appeared to be recalling events in their due order. His manner was studiously cold,—as if he were endeavouring, despite the strangeness of his story, to impress me with the literal accuracy of each syllable he uttered.

"The night before last, on returning home, I found in my study a stranger."

"A stranger?"

"Yes.—In other words, a burglar."

"A burglar?—I see.—Go on."

He had paused. His demeanour was becoming odder and odder.

"On my entry he was engaged in forcing an entry into my bureau. I need hardly say that I advanced to seize him. But—I could not."

"You could not?—How do you mean you could not?"

"I mean simply what I say. You must understand that this was no ordinary felon. Of what nationality he was I cannot tell you. He only uttered two words, and they were certainly in English, but apart from that he was dumb. He wore no covering on his head or feet. Indeed, his only garment was a long dark flowing cloak which, as it fluttered about him, revealed that his limbs were bare."

"An unique costume for a burglar."

"The instant I saw him I realised that he was in some way connected with that adventure in the Rue de Rabagas. What he said and did, proved it to the hilt."

"What did he say and do?"

"As I approached to effect his capture, he pronounced aloud two words which recalled that awful scene the recollection of which always lingers in my brain, and of which I never dare to permit myself to think. Their very utterance threw me into a sort of convulsion."

"What were the words?"

Mr. Lessingham opened his mouth,—and shut it. A marked change took place in the expression of his countenance. His eyes became fixed and staring,—resembling the glassy orbs of the somnambulist. For a moment I feared that he was going to give me an object lesson in the "visitations" of which I had heard so much. I rose, with a view of offering him assistance. He motioned me back.

"Thank you.—It will pass away."

His voice was dry and husky,—unlike his usual silvern tones. After an uncomfortable interval he managed to continue.

"You see for yourself, Mr. Champnell, what a miserable weakling, when this subject is broached, I still remain. I cannot utter the words the stranger uttered, I cannot even write them down. For some inscrutable reason they have on me an effect similar to that which spells and incantations had on people in tales of witchcraft."

"I suppose, Mr. Lessingham, that there is no doubt that this mysterious stranger was not himself an optical delusion?"

"Scarcely. There is the evidence of my servants to prove the contrary!"

"Did your servants see him?"

"Some of them,—yes. Then there is the evidence of the bureau. The fellow had smashed the top right in two. When I came to examine the contents I learned that a packet of letters was missing. They were letters which I had received from Miss Lindon, a lady whom I hope to make my wife. This, also, I state to you in confidence."

"What use would he be likely to make of them?"

"If matters stand as I fear they do, he might make a very serious misuse of them. If the object of these wretches, after all these years, is a wild revenge, they would be capable, having discovered what she is to me, of working Miss Lindon a fatal mischief,—or, at the very least, of poisoning her mind."

"I see.—How did the thief escape,—did he, like the delineation, vanish into air?"

"He escaped by the much more prosaic method of dashing through the drawing-room window, and clambering down from the verandah into the street, where he ran right into someone's arms."

"Into whose arms,—a constable's?"

"No; into Mr. Atherton's,—Sydney Atherton's."

"The inventor?"

"The same.—Do you know him?"

"I do. Sydney Atherton and I are friends of a good many years standing.—But Atherton must have seen where he came from;—and, anyhow, if he was in the state of undress which you have described, why didn't he stop him?"

"Mr. Atherton's reasons were his own. He did not stop him, and, so far as I can learn, he did not attempt to stop him. Instead, he knocked at my hall door to inform me that he had seen a man climb out of my window."

"I happen to know that, at certain seasons, Atherton is a queer fish,—but that sounds very queer indeed."

"The truth is, Mr. Champnell, that, if it were not for Mr. Atherton, I doubt if I should have troubled you even now. The accident of his being an acquaintance of yours makes my task easier."

He drew his chair closer to me with an air of briskness which had been foreign to him before. For some reason, which I was unable to fathom, the introduction of Atherton's name seemed to have enlivened him. However, I was not long to remain in darkness. In half a dozen sentences he threw more light on the real cause of his visit to me than he had done in all that had gone before. His bearing, too, was more businesslike and to the point. For the first time I had some glimmerings of the politician,—alert, keen, eager,—as he is known to all the world.

"Mr. Atherton, like myself, has been a postulant for Miss Lindon's hand. Because I have succeeded where he has failed, he has chosen to be angry. It seems that he has had dealings, either with my visitor of Tuesday night, or with some other of his acquaintance, and he proposes to use what he has gleaned from him to the disadvantage of my character. I have just come from Mr. Atherton. From hints he dropped I conclude that, probably during the last few hours, he has had an interview with someone who was connected in some way with that lurid patch in my career; that this person made so-called revelations, which were nothing but a series of monstrous lies; and these so-called revelations Mr. Atherton has threatened, in so many words, to place before Miss Lindon. That is an eventuality which I wish to avoid. My own conviction is that there is at this moment in London an emissary from that den in the whilom Rue de Rabagas—for all I know it may be the Woman of the Songs herself. Whether the sole purport of this individual's presence is to do me injury, I am, as yet, in no position to say, but that it is proposed to work me mischief, at any rate, by the way, is plain. I believe that Mr. Atherton knows more about this person's individuality and whereabouts than he has been willing, so far, to admit. I want you, therefore, to ascertain these things on my behalf; to find out what, and where, this person is, to drag her!—or him;—out into the light of day. In short, I want you to effectually protect me from the terrorism which threatens once more to overwhelm my mental and my physical powers,—which bids fair to destroy my intellect, my career, my life, my all."

"What reason have you for suspecting that Mr. Atherton has seen this individual of whom you speak,—has he told you so?"

"Practically,—yes."

"I know Atherton well. In his not infrequent moments of excitement he is apt to use strong language, but it goes no further. I believe him to be the last person in the world to do anyone an intentional injustice, under any circumstances whatever. If I go to him, armed with credentials from you, when he understands the real gravity of the situation,—which it will be my business to make him do, I believe that, spontaneously, of his own accord, he will tell me as much about this mysterious individual as he knows himself."

"Then go to him at once."

"Good. I will. The result I will communicate to you."

I rose from my seat. As I did so, someone rushed into the outer office with a din and a clatter. Andrews' voice, and another, became distinctly audible,—Andrews' apparently raised in vigorous expostulation. Raised, seemingly, in vain; for presently the door of my own particular sanctum was thrown open with a crash, and Mr. Sydney Atherton himself came dashing in,—evidently conspicuously under the influence of one of those not infrequent "moments of excitement" of which I had just been speaking.

CHAPTER 35

A BRINGER OF TIDINGS

Atherton did not wait to see who might or might not be present, but, without even pausing to take breath, he broke into full cry on the instant,—as is occasionally his wont.

"Champnell!—Thank goodness I've found you in!—I want you!—At once!—Don't stop to talk, but stick your hat on, and put your best foot forward,—I'll tell you all about it in the cab."

I endeavoured to call his attention to Mr. Lessingham's presence,—but without success.

"My dear fellow—"

When I had got as far as that he cut me short.

"Don't 'dear fellow' me!—None of your jabber! And none of your excuses either! I don't care if you've got an engagement with the Queen, you'll have to chuck it. Where's that dashed hat of yours,—or are you going without it? Don't I tell you that every second put to waste may mean the difference between life and death?—Do you want me to drag you down to the cab by the hair of your head?"

"I will try not to constrain you to quite so drastic a resource,—and I was coming to you at once in any case. I only want to call your attention to the fact that I am not alone.—Here is Mr. Lessingham."

In his harum-scarum[1] haste Mr. Lessingham had gone unnoticed. Now that his observation was particularly directed to him, Atherton started, turned, and glared at my latest client in a fashion which was scarcely flattering.

"Oh!—It's you, is it?—What the deuce are you doing here?"

---

[1] Reckless, rash, hasty.

Before Lessingham could reply to this most unceremonious query, Atherton, rushing forward, gripped him by the arm.

"Have you seen her?"

Lessingham, not unnaturally nonplussed by the other's curious conduct, stared at him in unmistakable amazement.

"Have I seen whom?"

"Marjorie Lindon!"

"Marjorie Lindon?"

Lessingham paused. He was evidently asking himself what the inquiry meant.

"I have not seen Miss Lindon since last night. Why do you ask?"

"Then Heaven help us!—As I'm a living man I believe he, she, or it has got her!"

His words were incomprehensible enough to stand in copious need of explanation,—as Mr. Lessingham plainly thought.

"What is it that you mean, sir?"

"What I say,—I believe that that Oriental friend of yours has got her in her clutches,—if it is a 'her'; goodness alone knows what the infernal conjurer's real sex may be."

"Atherton!—Explain yourself!"

On a sudden Lessingham's tones rang out like a trumpet call.

"If damage comes to her I shall be fit to cut my throat,—and yours!"

Mr. Lessingham's next proceeding surprised me,—I imagine it surprised Atherton still more. Springing at Sydney like a tiger, he caught him by the throat.

"You—you hound! Of what wretched folly have you been guilty? If so much as a hair of her head is injured you shall repay it me ten thousand fold!—You mischief-making, intermeddling, jealous fool!"

He shook Sydney as if he had been a rat,—then flung him from him headlong on to the floor. It reminded me of nothing so much as Othello's treatment of Iago.[1] Never had I seen a man so transformed by rage. Lessingham seemed to have positively increased in stature. As he stood glowering down at the prostrate Sydney, he might have stood for a materialistic conception of human retribution.

Sydney, I take it, was rather surprised than hurt. For a moment or two he lay quite still. Then, lifting his head, he looked up at his assailant. Then, raising himself to his feet, he shook himself,—as if with a view

---

[1] At the end of Shakespeare's play, Othello rushes at Iago, wounding him. Perhaps Marsh is referring to a particularly violent dramatization.

of learning if all his bones were whole. Putting his hands up to his neck, he rubbed it, gently. And he grinned.

"By God, Lessingham, there's more in you than I thought. After all, you are a man. There's some holding power in those wrists of yours,—they've nearly broken my neck. When this business is finished, I should like to put on the gloves with you, and fight it out. You're clean wasted upon politics.—Damn it, man, give me your hand!"

Mr. Lessingham did not give him his hand. Atherton took it,—and gave it a hearty shake with both of his.

If the first paroxysm of his passion had passed, Lessingham was still sufficiently stern.

"Be so good as not to trifle, Mr. Atherton. If what you say is correct, and the wretch to whom you allude really has Miss Lindon at her mercy, then the woman I love—and whom you also pretend to love!—stands in imminent peril not only of a ghastly death, but of what is infinitely worse than death."

"The deuce she does!" Atherton wheeled round towards me. "Champnell, haven't you got that dashed hat of yours yet? Don't stand there like a tailor's dummy, keeping me on tenter-hooks,—move yourself! I'll tell you all about it in the cab.—And, Lessingham, if you'll come with us I'll tell you too."

CHAPTER 36

WHAT THE TIDINGS WERE

Three in a hansom cab is not, under all circumstances, the most comfortable method of conveyance,—when one of the trio happens to be Sydney Atherton in one of his "moments of excitement" it is distinctly the opposite; as, on that occasion, Mr. Lessingham and I both quickly found. Sometimes he sat on my knees, sometimes on Lessingham's, and frequently, when he unexpectedly stood up, and all but precipitated himself on to the horse's back, on nobody's. In the eagerness of his gesticulations, first he knocked off my hat, then he knocked off Lessingham's, then his own, then all three together,—once, his own hat rolling into the mud, he sprang into the road, without previously going through the empty form of advising the driver of his intention, to pick it up. When he turned to speak to Lessingham, he thrust his elbow into my eye; and when he turned to speak to me, he thrust it into Lessingham's. Never, for one solitary instant, was he at rest, or either of us at ease. The wonder is that the gymnastics in which he incessantly indulged did not sufficiently attract public notice to induce a policeman to put at least a momentary period to our progress. Had speed not been of primary importance I should have insisted on the transference of the expedition to the somewhat wider limits of a four-wheeler.

His elucidation of the causes of his agitation was apparently more comprehensible to Lessingham than it was to me. I had to piece this and that together under considerable difficulties. By degrees I did arrive at something like a dear notion of what had actually taken place.

He commenced by addressing Lessingham,—and thrusting his elbow into my eye.

"Did Marjorie tell you about the fellow she found in the street?" Up went his arm to force the trap-door open over-head,—and off went my hat. "Now then, William Henry!—let her go!—if you kill the horse I'll buy you another!"

We were already going much faster than, legally, we ought to have done,—but that, seemingly to him was not a matter of the slightest consequence. Lessingham replied to his inquiry.

"She did not."

"You know the fellow I saw coming out of your drawing-room window?"

"Yes."

"Well, Marjorie found him the morning after in front of her break-fast-room window—in the middle of the street. Seems he had been wandering about all night, unclothed,—in the rain and the mud, and all the rest of it,—in a condition of hypnotic trance."

"Who is the—gentleman you are alluding to?"

"Says his name's Holt, Robert Holt."

"Holt?—Is he an Englishman?"

"Very much so,—City quilldriver[1] out of a shop,—stony broke absolutely! Got the chuck from the casual ward,—wouldn't let him in,—house full, and that sort of thing,—poor devil! Pretty passes you politicians bring men to!"

"Are you sure?"

"Of what?"

---

[1] A clerk; the more modern phrase would be "pen-pusher."

"Are you sure that this man, Robert Holt, is the same person whom, as you put it, you saw coming out of my drawing-room window?"

"Sure!—Of course I'm sure!—Think I didn't recognise him?— Besides, there was the man's own tale,—owned to it himself,—besides all the rest, which sent one rushing Fulham way."

"You must remember, Mr. Atherton, that I am wholly in the dark as to what has happened. What has the man, Holt, to do with the errand on which we are bound?"—

"Am I not coming to it? If you would let me tell the tale in my own way I should get there in less than no time, but you will keep on cutting in,—how the deuce do you suppose Champnell is to make head or tail of the business if you will persist in interrupting?—Marjorie took the beggar in,—he told his tale to her,—she sent for me—that was just now; caught me on the steps after I had been lunching with Dora Grayling. Holt re-dished his yarn—I smelt a rat—saw that a connection possibly existed between the thief who'd been playing confounded conjuring tricks off on to me and this interesting party down Fulham way."

"What party down Fulham way?"

"This friend of Holt's—am I not telling you? There you are, you see,—won't let me finish! When Holt slipped through the window— which is the most sensible thing he seems to have done; if I'd been in his shoes I'd have slipped through forty windows!—dusky coloured charmer caught him on the hop,—doctored him—sent him out to commit burglary by deputy. I said to Holt, 'show us this agreeable little crib, young man.' Holt was game—then Marjorie chipped in—she wanted to go and see it too. I said, 'You'll be sorry if you do.'—that settled it! After that she'd have gone if she'd died,—I never did have a persuasive way with women. So off we toddled, Marjorie, Holt, and I, in a growler,—spotted the crib in less than no time,—invited ourselves in by the kitchen window—house seemed empty. Presently Holt became hypnotised before my eyes,—the best established case of hypno- tism by suggestion I ever encountered—started off on a pilgrimage of one. Like an idiot I followed, leaving Marjorie to wait for me—"

"Alone?"

"Alone!—Am I not telling you?—Great Scott, Lessingham, in the House of Commons they must be hazy to think you smart! I said, 'I'll send the first sane soul I meet to keep you company.' As luck would have it, I never met one,—only kids, and a baker, who wouldn't leave his cart, or take it with him either. I'd covered pretty nearly two miles before I came across a peeler,—and when I did the man was cracked—

and he thought me mad, or drunk, or both. By the time I'd got myself within nodding distance of being run in for obstructing the police in the execution of their duty without inducing him to move a single one of his twenty-four-inch feet, Holt was out of sight. So, since all my pains in his direction were clean thrown away, there was nothing left for me but to scurry back to Marjorie,—so I scurried, and I found the house empty, no one there, and Marjorie gone."

"But, I don't quite follow—"

Atherton impetuously declined to allow Mr. Lessingham to conclude.

"Of course you don't quite follow, and you'll follow still less if you will keep getting in front. I went upstairs and downstairs, inside and out—shouted myself hoarse as a crow—nothing was to be seen of Marjorie,—or heard; until, as I was coming down the stairs for about the five-and-fiftieth time, I stepped on something hard which was lying in the passage. I picked it up,—it was a ring, this ring. Its shape is not just what it was,—I'm not as light as gossamer, especially when I come jumping downstairs six at a time,—but what's left of it is here."

Sydney held something in front of him. Mr. Lessingham wriggled to one side to enable him to see. Then he made a snatch at it.

"It's mine!"

Sydney dodged it out of his reach.

"What do you mean, it's yours?"

"It's the ring I gave Marjorie for an engagement ring. Give it me, you hound!—unless you wish me to do you violence in the cab."

With complete disregard of the limitations of space,—or of my comfort,—Lessingham thrust him vigorously aside. Then gripping Sydney by the wrist, he seized the gaud,—Sydney yielding it just in time to save himself from being precipitated into the street. Ravished of his treasure, Sydney turned and surveyed the ravisher with something like a glance of admiration.

"Hang me, Lessingham, if I don't believe there is some warm blood in those fishlike veins of yours. Please the piper, I'll five to fight you after all,—with the bare ones, sir, as a gentleman should do."

Lessingham seemed to pay no attention to him whatever. He was surveying the ring, which Sydney had trampled out of shape, with looks of the deepest concern.

"Marjorie's ring!—The one I gave her! Something serious must have happened to her before she would have dropped my ring, and left it lying where it fell."

Atherton went on.

"That's it!—What has happened to her!—I'll be dashed if I know!—
When it was clear that there she wasn't, I tore off to find out where she
was. Came across old Lindon,—he knew nothing;—I rather fancy I startled him in the middle of Pall Mall, when I left he stared after me like
one possessed, and his hat was lying in the gutter. Went home,—she
wasn't there. Asked Dora Grayling,—she'd seen nothing of her. No one
had seen anything of her,—she had vanished into air. Then I said to
myself, 'You're a first-class idiot, on my honour! While you're looking for
her, like a lost sheep, the betting is that the girl's in Holt's friend's house
the whole jolly time. When you were there, the chances are that she'd
just stepped out for a stroll, and that now she's back again, and wondering where on earth you've gone!' So I made up my mind that I'd fly back
and see,—because the idea of her standing on the front doorstep looking for me, while I was going off my nut looking for her, commended
itself to what I call my sense of humour; and on my way it struck me that
it would be the part of wisdom to pick up Champnell, because if there
is a man who can be backed to find a needle in any amount of haystacks
it is the great Augustus.—That horse has moved itself after all, because
here we are. Now, cabman, don't go driving further on,—you'll have to
put a girdle round the earth if you do; because you'll have to reach this
point again before you get your fare.—This is the magician's house!"

CHAPTER 37

WHAT WAS HIDDEN UNDER THE FLOOR

The cab pulled up in front of a tumbledown cheap "villa" in an unfinished cheap neighbourhood,—the whole place a living monument of
the defeat of the speculative builder.

Atherton leaped out on to the grass-grown rubble which was meant
for a footpath.

"I don't see Marjorie looking for me on the doorstep."

Nor did I,—I saw nothing but what appeared to be an unoccupied
ramshackle brick abomination. Suddenly Sydney gave an exclamation.

"Hullo!—The front door's closed!"

I was hard at his heels.

"What do you mean?"

"Why, when I went I left the front door open. It looks as if I've made an idiot of myself after all, and Marjorie's returned,—let's hope to goodness that I have."

He knocked. While we waited for a response I questioned him.

"Why did you leave the door open when you went?"

"I hardly know,—I imagine that it was with some dim idea of Marjorie's being able to get in if she returned while I was absent,—but the truth is I was in such a condition of helter skelter that I am not prepared to swear that I had any reasonable reason."

"I suppose there is no doubt that you did leave it open?"

"Absolutely none,—on that I'll stake my life."

"Was it open when you returned from your pursuit of Holt?"

"Wide open,—I walked straight in expecting to find her waiting for me in the front room,—I was struck all of a heap when I found she wasn't there."

"Were there any signs of a struggle?"

"None,—there were no signs of anything. Everything was just as I had left it, with the exception of the ring which I trod on in the passage, and which Lessingham has."

"If Miss Lindon has returned, it does not look as if she were in the house at present."

It did not,—unless silence had such meaning. Atherton had knocked loudly three times without succeeding in attracting the slightest notice from within.

"It strikes me that this is another case of seeking admission through that hospitable window at the back."

Atherton led the way to the rear. Lessingham and I followed. There was not even an apology for a yard, still less a garden,—there was not even a fence of any sort, to serve as an enclosure, and to shut off the house from the wilderness of waste land. The kitchen window was open. I asked Sydney if he had left it so.

"I don't know,—I dare say we did; I don't fancy that either of us stood on the order of his coming."

While he spoke, he scrambled over the sill. We followed. When he was in, he shouted at the top of his voice,

"Marjorie! Marjorie! Speak to me, Marjorie,—it is I,—Sydney!"

The words echoed through the house. Only silence answered. He led the way to the front room. Suddenly he stopped.

"Hollo!" he cried. "The blind's down!" I had noticed, when we were outside, that the blind was down at the front room window. "It was up when I went, that I'll swear. That someone has been here is pretty plain, let's hope it's Marjorie."

He had only taken a step forward into the room when he again stopped short to exclaim.

"My stars!—here's a sudden clearance!—Why, the place is empty,—everything's clean gone!"

"What do you mean?—was it furnished when you left?"

The room was empty enough then.

"Furnished?—I don't know that it was exactly what you'd call furnished,—the party who ran this establishment had a taste in uphol-stery which was all his own,—but there was a carpet, and a bed, and—and lots of things,—for the most part, I should have said, distinctly Eastern curiosities. They seem to have evaporated into smoke,—which may be a way which is common enough among Eastern curiosities, though it's queer to me."

Atherton was staring about him as if he found it difficult to credit the evidence of his own eyes.

"How long ago is it since you left?"

He referred to his watch.

"Something over an hour,—possibly an hour and a half; I couldn't swear to the exact moment, but it certainly isn't more."

"Did you notice any signs of packing up?"

"Not a sign." Going to the window he drew up the blind,—speaking as he did so. "The queer thing about this business is that when we first got in this blind wouldn't draw up a little bit, so, since it wouldn't go up I pulled it down, roller and all, now it draws up as easily and smoothly as if it had always been the best blind that ever lived."

Standing at Sydney's back I saw that the cabman on his box was signalling to us with his outstretched hand. Sydney perceived him too. He threw up the sash.

"What's the matter with you?"

"Excuse me, sir, but who's the old gent?"

"What old gent?"

"Why the old gent peeping through the window of the room upstairs?"

The words were hardly out of the driver's mouth when Sydney was through the door and flying up the staircase. I followed rather more soberly,—his methods were a little too flighty for me. When I reached the landing, dashing out of the front room he rushed into the one at the back,—then through a door at the side. He came out shouting.

"What's the idiot mean!—with his old gent! I'd old gent him if I got him!—There's not a creature about the place!"

He returned into the front room,—I at his heels. That certainly was empty,—and not only empty, but it showed no traces of recent occupation. The dust lay thick upon the floor,—there was that mouldy, earthy smell which is so frequently found in apartments which have been long untenanted.

"Are you sure, Atherton, that there is no one at the back?"

"Of course I'm sure,—you can go and see for yourself if you like; do you think I'm blind? Jehu's drunk." Throwing up the sash he addressed the driver. "What do you mean with your old gent at the window?—what window?"

"That window, sir."

"Go to!—you're dreaming, man!—there's no one here."

"Begging your pardon, sir, but there was someone there not a minute ago."

"Imagination, cabman,—the slant of the light on the glass,—or your eyesight's defective."

"Excuse me, sir, but it's not my imagination, and my eyesight's as good as any man's in England,—and as for the slant of the light on the glass, there ain't much glass for the light to slant on. I saw him peeping through that bottom broken pane on your left hand as plainly as I see you. He must be somewhere about,—he can't have got away,—he's at the back. Ain't there a cupboard nor nothing where ere he could hide?"

The cabman's runner was so extremely earnest that I went myself to see. There was a cupboard on the landing, but the door of that stood wide open, and that obviously was bare. The room behind was small, and, despite the splintered glass in the window frame, stuffy. Fragments of glass kept company with the dust on the floor, together with a choice collection of stones, brickbats, and other missiles,—which not improbably were the cause of their being there. In the corner stood a cupboard,—but a momentary examination showed that that was as bare as the other. The door at the side, which Sydney had left wide open, opened on to a closet, and that was empty. I glanced up,—there was no trap door which led to the roof. No practicable nook or cranny, in which a living being could lie concealed, was anywhere at hand.

I returned to Sydney's shoulder to tell the cabman so.

"There is no place in which anyone could hide, and there is no one in either of the rooms,—you must have been mistaken, driver."

The man waxed wroth.

"Don't tell me! How could I come to think I saw something when I didn't?"

"One's eyes are apt to play us tricks;—how could you see what wasn't there?"

"That's what I want to know. As I drove up, before you told me to stop, I saw him looking through the window,—the one at which you are. He'd got his nose glued to the broken pane, and was staring as hard as he could stare. When I pulled up, off he started,—I saw him get up off his knees, and go to the back of the room. When the gentleman took to knocking, back he came,—to the same old spot, and flopped down on his knees. I didn't know what caper you was up to,—you might be bum bailiffs for all I knew!—and I supposed that he wasn't so anxious to let you in as you might be to get inside, and that was why he didn't take no notice of your knocking, while all the while he kept a eye on what was going on. When you goes round to the back, up he gets again, and I reckoned that he was going to meet yer, and perhaps gave yer a bit of his mind, and that presently I should hear a shindy, or that something would happen. But when you pulls up the blind down-stairs, to my surprise back he come once more. He shoves his old nose right through the smash in the pane, and wags his old head at me like a chattering magpie. That didn't seem to me quite the civil thing to do,—I hadn't done no harm to him; so I gives you the office, and lets you know that he was there. But for you to say that he wasn't there, and never had been,—blimey! that cops the biscuit.[1] If he wasn't there, all I can say is I ain't here, and my 'orse ain't the biscuit and my cab ain't neither,—damn it!—the house ain't here, and nothing ain't!"

He settled himself on his perch with an air of the most extreme ill usage,—he had been standing up to tell his tale. That the man was serious was unmistakable. As he himself suggested, what inducement could he have had to tell a lie like that? That he believed himself to have seen what he declared he saw was plain. But, on the other hand, what could have become—in the space of fifty seconds!—of his "old gent?"

Atherton put a question.

"What did he look like,—this old gent of yours?"

"Well, that I shouldn't hardly like to say. It wasn't much of his face I could see, only his face and his eyes,—and they wasn't pretty. He kept a thing over his head all the time, as if he didn't want too much to be seen."

---

[1] An alternative version of this phrase is "that takes the cake," meaning that something is beyond belief.

"What sort of a thing?"

"Why,—one of them cloak sort of things, like them Arab blokes used to wear what used to be at Earl's Court Exhibition,—you know!"

This piece of information seemed to interest my companions more than anything he had said before.

"A burnoose do you mean?"

"How am I to know what the thing's called? I ain't up in foreign languages,—'tain't likely! All I know that them Arab blokes what was at Earl's Court used to walk about in them all over the place,—sometimes they wore them over their heads, and sometimes they didn't. In fact if you'd asked me, instead of trying to make out as I sees double, or things what was only inside my own noddle, or something or other, I should have said this here old gent what I've been telling you about was a Arab bloke,—when he gets off his knees to sneak away from the window, I could see that he had his cloak thing, what was over his head, wrapped all round him."

Mr. Lessingham turned to me, all quivering with excitement.

"I believe that what he says is true!"

"Then where can this mysterious old gentleman have got to,—can you suggest an explanation? It is strange, to say the least of it, that the cabman should be the only person to see or hear anything of him."

"Some devil's trick has been played,—I know it, I feel it!—my instinct tells me so!"

I stared. In such a matter one hardly expects a man of Paul Lessingham's stamp to talk of "instinct." Atherton stared too. Then, on a sudden, he burst out,

"By the Lord, I believe the Apostle's right,—the whole place reeks to me of hankey-pankey,—it did as soon as I put my nose inside. In matters of prestidigitation, Champnell, we Westerns are among the rudiments,—we've everything to learn,—Orientals leave us at the post. If their civilisation's what we're pleased to call extinct, their conjuring—when you get to know it!—is all alive oh!"

He moved towards the door. As he went he slipped, or seemed to, all but stumbling on to his knees.

"Something tripped me up,—what's this?" He was stamping on the floor with his foot. "Here's a board loose. Come and lend me a hand, one of you fellows, to get it up. Who knows what mystery's beneath?"

I went to his aid. As he said, a board in the floor was loose. His stepping on it unawares had caused his stumble. Together we prised it out of its place,—Lessingham standing by and watching us the while. Having removed it, we peered into the cavity it disclosed.

There was something there.

"Why," cried Atherton, "it's a woman's clothing!"

CHAPTER 38

THE REST OF THE FIND

It was a woman's clothing, beyond a doubt, all thrown in anyhow,—as if the person who had placed it there had been in a desperate hurry. An entire outfit was there, shoes, stockings, body linen, corsets, and all,— even to hat, gloves, and hairpins;—these latter were mixed up with the rest of the garments in strange confusion. It seemed plain that whoever had worn those clothes had been stripped to the skin.

Lessingham and Sydney stared at me in silence as I dragged them out and laid them on the floor. The dress was at the bottom,—it was an alpaca, of a pretty shade in blue, bedecked with lace and ribbons, as is the fashion of the hour, and lined with sea-green silk. It had perhaps been a "charming confection" once—and that a very recent one!—but now it was all soiled and creased and torn and tumbled. The two spectators made a simultaneous pounce at it as I brought it to the light.

"My God!" cried Sydney, "it's Marjorie's!—she was wearing it when I saw her last!"

"It's Marjorie's!" gasped Lessingham,—he was clutching at the ruined costume, staring at it like a man who has just received sentence of death. "She wore it when she was with me yesterday,—I told her how it suited her, and how pretty it was!"

There was silence,—it was an eloquent find; it spoke for itself. The two men gazed at the heap of feminine glories,—it might have been the most wonderful sight they ever had seen. Lessingham was the first to speak,—his face had all at once grown grey and haggard.

"What has happened to her?"

I replied to his question with another.

"Are you sure this is Miss Lindon's dress?"

"I am sure,—and were proof needed, here it is."

He had found the pocket, and was turning out the contents. There was a purse, which contained money and some visiting cards on which were her name and address; a small bunch of keys, with her nameplate attached; a handkerchief, with her initials in a corner. The question of ownership was placed beyond a doubt.

"You see," said Lessingham, exhibiting the money which was in the purse, "it is not robbery which has been attempted. Here are two ten-pound notes, and one for five, besides gold and silver,—over thirty pounds in all."

Atherton, who had been turning over the accumulation of rubbish between the joists, proclaimed another find.

"Here are her rings, and watch, and a bracelet,—no, it certainly does not look as if theft had been an object."

Lessingham was glowering at him with knitted brows.

"I have to thank you for this."

Sydney was unwontedly meek.

"You are hard on me, Lessingham, harder than I deserve,—I had rather have thrown away my own life than have suffered misadventure to have come to her."

"Yours are idle words. Had you not meddled this would not have happened. A fool works more mischief with his folly than of malice prepense.[1] If hurt has befallen Marjorie Lindon you shall account for it to me with your life's blood."

"Let it be so," said Sydney. "I am content. If hurt has come to Marjorie, God knows that I am willing enough that death should come to me."

While they wrangled, I continued to search. A little to one side, under the flooring which was still intact, I saw something gleam. By stretching out my hand, I could just manage to reach it,—it was a long plait of woman's hair. It had been cut off at the roots,—so close to the head in one place that the scalp itself had been cut, so that the hair was dotted with blood.

They were so occupied with each other that they took no notice of me. I had to call their attention to my discovery.

"Gentlemen, I fear that I have here something which will distress you,—is not this Miss Lindon's hair?"

They recognised it on the instant. Lessingham, snatching it from my hands, pressed it to his lips.

"This is mine,—I shall at least have something." He spoke with a grimness which was a little startling. He held the silken tresses at arm's

---

[1] A legal term, the alternative version being "malice aforethought," used to describe a crime that has been planned.

length. "This points to murder,—foul, cruel, causeless murder. As I live, I will devote my all,—money, time, reputation!—to gaining vengeance on the wretch who did this deed."

Atherton chimed in.

"To that I say, Amen!" He lifted his hand. "God is my witness!"

"It seems to me, gentlemen, that we move too fast,—to my mind it does not by any means of necessity point to murder. On the contrary, I doubt if murder has been done. Indeed, I don't mind owning that I have a theory of my own which points all the other way."

Lessingham caught me by the sleeve.

"Mr. Champnell, tell me your theory."

"I will, a little later. Of course it may be altogether wrong;—though I fancy it is not; I will explain my reasons when we come to talk of it. But, at present, there are things which must be done."

"I vote for tearing up every board in the house!" cried Sydney. "And for pulling the whole infernal place to pieces. It's a conjurer's den.—I shouldn't be surprised if cabby's old gent is staring at us all the while from some peephole of his own."

We examined the entire house, methodically, so far as we were able, inch by inch. Not another board proved loose,—to lift those which were nailed down required tools, and those we were without. We sounded all the walls,—with the exception of the party walls they were the usual lath and plaster constructions, and showed no signs of having been tampered with. The ceilings were intact; if anything was concealed in them it must have been there some time,—the cement was old and dirty. We took the closet to pieces; examined the chimneys; peered into the kitchen oven and the copper;—in short, we pried into everything which, with the limited means at our disposal, could be pried into,— without result. At the end we found ourselves dusty, dirty, and discomfited. The cabman's "old gent" remained as much a mystery as ever, and no further trace had been discovered of Miss Lindon.

Atherton made no effort to disguise his chagrin.

"Now what's to be done? There seems to be just nothing in the place at all, and yet that there is, and that it's the key to the whole confounded business I should be disposed to swear."

"In that case I would suggest that you should stay and look for it. The cabman can go and look for the requisite tools, or a workman to assist you, if you like. For my part it appears to me that evidence of another sort is, for the moment, of paramount importance; and I propose to commence my search for it by making a call at the house which is over the way."

I had observed, on our arrival, that the road only contained two houses which were in anything like a finished state,—that which we were in, and another, some fifty or sixty yards further down, on the opposite side. It was to this I referred. The twain immediately proffered their companionship.

"I will come with you," said Mr. Lessingham.

"And I," echoed Sydney. "We'll leave this sweet homestead in charge of the cabman,—I'll pull it to pieces afterwards." He went out and spoke to the driver. "Cabby, we're going to pay a visit to the little crib over there,—you keep an eye on this one. And if you see a sign of anyone being about the place,—living, or dead, or anyhow—you give me a yell. I shall be on the lookout, and I'll be with you before you can say Jack Robinson."

"You bet I'll yell,—I'll raise the hair right off you." The fellow grinned. "But I don't know if you gents are hiring me by the day,—I want to change my horse; he ought to have been in his stable a couple of hours ago."

"Never mind your horse,—let him rest a couple of hours extra tomorrow to make up for those he has lost to-day. I'll take care you don't lose anything by this little job,—or your horse either.—By the way, look here,—this will be better than yelling."

Taking a revolver out of his trousers' pocket he handed it up to the grinning driver.

"If that old gent of yours does appear, you have a pop at him,—I shall hear that easier than a yell. You can put a bullet through him if you like,—I give you my word it won't be murder."

"I don't care if it is," declared the cabman, handling the weapon like one who was familiar with arms of precision. "I used to fancy my revolver shooting when I was with the colours,[1] and if I do get a chance I'll put a shot through the old hunks, if only to prove to you that I'm no liar."

Whether the man was in earnest or not I could not tell,—nor whether Atherton meant what he said in answer.

"If you shoot him I'll give you fifty pounds."

"All right!" The driver laughed. "I'll do my best to earn that fifty!"

---

[1] Colloquial reference to the regiment in which the cabman served.

CHAPTER 39

MISS LOUISA COLEMAN

That the house over the way was tenanted was plain to all the world,—
at least one occupant sat gazing through the window of the first floor
front room. An old woman in a cap,—one of those large old-fashioned
caps which our grandmothers used to wear, tied with strings under the
chin. It was a bow window, and as she was seated in the bay looking
right in our direction she could hardly have failed to see us as we
advanced,—indeed she continued to stare at us all the while with placid
calmness. Yet I knocked once, twice, and yet again without the slightest notice being taken of my summons.

Sydney gave expression to his impatience in his own peculiar vein.

"Knockers in this part of the world seem intended for ornament only,—
nobody seems to pay any attention to them when they're used. The old
lady upstairs must be either deaf or dotty." He went out into the road to
see if she still was there. "She's looking at me as calmly as you please,—
what does she think we're doing here, I wonder; playing a tune on her front
door by way of a little amusement?—Madam!" He took off his hat and
waved it to her. "Madam! might I observe that if you won't condescend to
notice that we're here your front door will run the risk of being severely
injured!—She don't care for me any more than if I was nothing at all,—
sound another tattoo upon that knocker. Perhaps she's so deaf that nothing short of a cataclysmal uproar will reach her auditory nerves."

She immediately proved, however, that she was nothing of the sort.
Hardly had the sounds of my further knocking died away than, throwing
up the window, she thrust out her head and addressed me in a fashion
which, under the circumstances, was as unexpected as it was uncalled for.

"Now, young man, you needn't be in such a hurry!"

Sydney explained.

"Pardon me, madam, it's not so much a hurry we're in as pressed for
time,—this is a matter of life and death."

She turned her attention to Sydney,—speaking with a frankness for
which, I imagine, he was unprepared.

"I don't want none of your imperence,[1] young man. I've seen you

---

[1] Slang for impertinence.

before,—you've been hanging about here the whole daylong!—and I don't like the looks of you, and so I'll let you know. That's my front door, and that's my knocker,—I'll come down and open when I like, but I'm not going to be hurried, and if the knocker's so much as touched again, I won't come down at all."

She closed the window with a bang. Sydney seemed divided between mirth and indignation.

"That's a nice old lady, on my honour,—one of the good old crusty sort. Agreeable characters this neighbourhood seems to grow,—a sojourn hereabouts should do one good. Unfortunately I don't feel disposed just now to stand and kick my heels in the road." Again saluting the old dame by raising his hat he shouted to her at the top of his voice. "Madam, I beg ten thousand pardons for troubling you, but this is a matter in which every second is of vital importance,—would you allow me to ask you one or two questions?"

Up went the window; out came the old lady's head.

"Now, young man, you needn't put yourself out to holler at me,—I won't be hollered at! I'll come down and open that door in five minutes by the clock on my mantelpiece, and not a moment before."

The fiat delivered, down came the window. Sydney looked rueful,—he consulted his watch.

"I don't know what you think, Champnell, but I really doubt if this comfortable creature can tell us anything worth waiting another five minutes to hear. We mustn't let the grass grow under our feet, and time is getting on."

I was of a different opinion,—and said so.

"I'm afraid, Atherton, that I can't agree with you. She seems to have noticed you hanging about all day; and it is at least possible that she has noticed a good deal which would be well worth our hearing. What more promising witness are we likely to find?—her house is the only one which overlooks the one we have just quitted. I am of opinion that it may not only prove well worth our while to wait five minutes, but also that it would be as well, if possible, not to offend her by the way. She's not likely to afford us the information we require if you do."

"Good. If that's what you think I'm sure I'm willing to wait,—only it's to be hoped that that clock upon her mantelpiece moves quicker than its mistress."

Presently, when about a minute had gone, he called to the cabman.

"Seen a sign of anything?"

The cabman shouted back.

"Never a sign,—you'll hear a sound of popguns when I do."

Those five minutes did seem long ones. But at last Sydney, from his post of vantage in the road, informed us that the old lady was moving.

"She's getting up;—she's leaving the window;—let's hope to goodness she's coming down to open the door. That's been the longest five minutes I've known."

I could hear uncertain footsteps descending the stairs. They came along the passage. The door was opened—"on the chain." The old lady peered at us through an aperture of about six inches.

"I don't know what you young men think you're after, but have all three of you in my house I won't. I'll have him and you"—a skinny finger was pointed to Lessingham and me; then it was directed towards Atherton—"but have him I won't. So if it's anything particular you want to say to me, you'll just tell him to go away."

On hearing this Sydney's humility was abject. His hat was in his hand,—he bent himself double.

"Suffer me to make you a million apologies, madam, if I have in any way offended you; nothing, I assure you, could have been farther from my intention, or from my thoughts."

"I don't want none of your apologies, and I don't want none of you neither; I don't like the looks of you, and so I tell you. Before I let anybody into my house you'll have to sling your hook."

The door was banged in our faces. I turned to Sydney.

"The sooner you go the better it will be for us. You can wait for us over the way."

He shrugged his shoulders, and groaned,—half in jest, half in earnest.

"If I must I suppose I must,—it's the first time I've been refused admittance to a lady's house in all my life! What have I done to deserve this thing?—If you keep me waiting long I'll tear that infernal den to pieces!"

He sauntered across the road, viciously kicking the stones as he went. The door reopened.

"Has that other young man gone?"

"He has."

"Then now I'll let you in. Have him inside my house I won't."

The chain was removed. Lessingham and I entered. Then the door was refastened and the chain replaced. Our hostess showed us into the front room on the ground floor; it was sparsely furnished and not too clean,—but there were chairs enough for us to sit upon; which she insisted on our occupying.

"Sit down, do,—I can't abide to see folks standing; it gives me the fidgets."

So soon as we were seated, without any overture on our parts she plunged *in medias res.*[1]

"I know what it is you've come about,—I know! You want me to tell you who it is as lives in the house over the road. Well, I can tell you,—and I dare bet a shilling that I'm about the only one who can."

I inclined my head.

"Indeed. Is that so, madam?"

She huffed at once.

"Don't madam me,—I can't bear none of your lip service. I'm a plainspoken woman, that's what I am, and I like other people's tongues to be as plain as mine. My name's Miss Louisa Coleman; but I'm generally called Miss Coleman,—I'm only called Louisa by my relatives."

Since she was apparently between seventy and eighty—and looked every year of her apparent age—I deemed that possible. Miss Coleman was evidently a character. If one was desirous of getting information out of her it would be necessary to allow her to impart it in her own manner,—to endeavour to induce her to impart it in anybody else's would be time clean wasted. We had Sydney's fate before our eyes.

She started with a sort of roundabout preamble.

"This property is mine; it was left me by my uncle, the late George Henry Jobson,—he's buried in Hammersmith Cemetery just over the way,—he left me the whole of it. It's one of the finest building sites near London, and it increases in value every year, and I'm not going to let it for another twenty, by which time the value will have more than trebled,—so if that is what you've come about, as heaps of people do, you might have saved yourselves the trouble. I keep the boards standing, just to let people know that the ground is to let,—though, as I say, it won't be for another twenty years, when it'll be for the erection of high-class mansions only, same as there is in Grosvenor Square,—no shops or public houses, and none of your shanties. I live in this place just to keep an eye upon the property,—and as for the house over the way, I've never tried to let it, and it never has been let, not until a month ago, when, one morning, I had this letter. You can see it if you like."

She handed me a greasy envelope which she ferreted out of a capacious pocket which was suspended from her waist, and which she had to lift up her skirt to reach. The envelope was addressed, in unformed

---

[1] "in the middle of things" (Latin), i.e., not starting at the beginning.

characters, "Miss Louisa Coleman, The Rhododendrons, Convolvulus Avenue, High Oaks Park, West Kensington."—I felt, if the writer had not been of a humorous turn of mind, and drawn on his imagination, and this really was the lady's correct address, then there must be something in a name.

The letter within was written in the same straggling, characterless calligraphy,—I should have said, had I been asked offhand, that the whole thing was the composition of a servant girl. The composition was about on a par with the writing.

"The undersigned would be oblidged if Miss Coleman would let her empty house. I do not know the rent but send fifty pounds. If more will send. Please address, Mohamed el Kheir, Post Office, Sligo Street, London."

It struck me as being as singular an application for a tenancy as I remembered to have encountered. When I passed it on to Lessingham, he seemed to think so too.

"This is a curious letter, Miss Coleman."

"So I thought,—and still more so when I found the fifty pounds inside. There were five ten-pound notes, all loose, and the letter not even registered. If I had been asked what was the rent of the house, I should have said, at the most, not more than twenty pounds,—because, between you and me, it wants a good bit of doing up, and is hardly fit to live in as it stands."

I had had sufficient evidence of the truth of this altogether apart from the landlady's frank admission.

"Why, for all he could have done to help himself I might have kept the money, and only sent him a receipt for a quarter. And some folks would have done,—but I'm not one of that sort myself, and shouldn't care to be. So I sent this here party,—I never could pronounce his name, and never shall—a receipt for a year."

Miss Coleman paused to smooth her apron, and consider.

"Well, the receipt should have reached this here party on the Thursday morning, as it were,—I posted it on the Wednesday night, and on the Thursday, after breakfast, I thought I'd go over the way to see if there was any little thing I could do,—because there wasn't hardly a whole pane of glass in the place,—when I all but went all of a heap. When I looked across the road, blessed if the party wasn't in already,—at least as much as he ever was in, which, so far as I can make out, never has been anything particular,—though how he had got in, unless it was through a window in the middle of the night, is more than I should care to say,—there was nobody in the house when I went to bed, that I could pretty nearly take my Bible oath,—yet there was the blind up at the parlour, and, what's more, it was down, and it's been down pretty nearly ever since.

"'Well,' I says to myself, 'for right down imperence this beats anything,—why he's in the place before he knows if I'll let him have it. Perhaps he thinks I haven't got a word to say in the matter,—fifty pounds or no fifty pounds, I'll soon show him.' So I slips on my bonnet, and I walks over the road, and I hammers at the door.

"Well, I have seen people hammering since then, many a one, and how they've kept it up has puzzled me,—for an hour, some of them,— but I was the first one as begun it. I hammers, and I hammers, and I kept on hammering, but it wasn't no more use than if I'd been hammering at a tombstone. So I starts rapping at the window, but that wasn't no use neither. So I goes round behind, and I hammers at the back door,—but there, I couldn't make anyone hear nohow. So I says to myself, 'Perhaps the party as is in, ain't in, in a manner of speaking; but I'll keep an eye on the house, and when he is in I'll take care that he ain't out again before I've had a word to say.'

"So I come back home, and as I said I would, I kept an eye on the house the whole of that livelong day, but never a soul went either out or in. But the next day, which it was a Friday, I got out of bed about five o'clock, to see if it was raining, through my having an idea of taking a little excursion if the weather was fine, when I see a party coming down the road. He had on one of them dirty-coloured bedcover sort of things, and it was wrapped all over his head and round his body, like, as I have been told, them there Arabs wear,—and, indeed, I've seen them in them myself at West Brompton,[1] when they was in the exhibition there. It was quite fine, and broad day and I see him as plainly as I see you,—he comes skimming along at a tear of a pace, pulls up at the house over the way, opens the front door, and lets himself in.

"'So,' I says to myself, 'there you are. Well, Mr. Arab, or whatever, or whoever, you may be, I'll take good care that you don't go out again before you've had a word from me. I'll show you that landladies have their rights, like other Christians, in this country, however it may be in yours!' So I kept an eye on the house, to see that he didn't go out again, and nobody never didn't, and between seven and eight I goes and I

---

[1]   District of West London.

knocks at the door,—because I thought to myself that the earlier I was the better it might be.

"If you'll believe me, no more notice was taken of me than if I was one of the dead. I hammers, and I hammers, till me wrist was aching, I daresay I hammered twenty times,—and then I went round to the back door, and I hammers at that,—but, it wasn't the least good in the world. I was that provoked to think I should be treated as if I was nothing and nobody, by a dirty foreigner, who went about in a bed gown through the public streets, that it was all I could do to hold myself.

"I comes round to the front again, and I starts hammering at the window, with every knuckle on my hands, and I calls out, 'I'm Miss Louisa Coleman, and I'm the owner of this house, and you can't deceive me,—I saw you come in, and you're in now, and if you don't come and speak to me this moment I'll have the police.'

"All of a sudden, when I was least expecting it, and was hammering my very hardest at the pane, up goes the blind, and up goes the window too, and the most awful-looking creature ever I heard of, not to mention seeing, puts his head right into my face,—he was more like a hideous baboon than anything else, let alone a man. I was struck all of a heap, and plumps down on the little wall, and all but tumbles head over heels backwards. And he starts shrieking, in a sort of a kind of English, and in such a voice as I'd never heard the like,—it was like a rusty steam engine.

"'Go away! go away! I don't want you! I will not have you,—never! You have your fifty pounds,—you have your money,—that is the whole of you,—that is all you want! You come to me no more!—never!—never no more!—or you be sorry!—Go away!'

"I did go away, and that as fast as over my legs would carry me,— what with his looks, and what with his voice, and what with the way that he went on, I was nothing but a mass of trembling. As for answering him back, or giving him a piece of my mind, as I had meant to, I wouldn't have done it not for a thousand pounds. I don't mind confessing, between you and me, that I had to swallow four cups of tea, right straight away, before my nerves was steady.

"'Well,' I says to myself, when I did feel, as it might be, a little more easy, 'you never have let that house before, and now you've let it with a vengeance,—so you have. If that there new tenant of yours isn't the greatest villain that ever went unhung it must be because he's got near relations what's as bad as himself,—because two families like his I'm sure there can't be. A nice sort of Arab party to have sleeping over the road he is!'

"But after a time I cools down, as it were,—because I'm one of them sort as likes to see on both sides of a question. 'After all,' I says to myself, 'he has paid his rent, and fifty pounds is fifty pounds,—I doubt if the whole house is worth much more, and he can't do much damage to it whatever he does.'

"I shouldn't have minded, so far as that went, if he'd set fire to the place, for, between ourselves, it's insured for a good bit over its value. So I decided that I'd let things be as they were, and see how they went on. But from that hour to this I've never spoken to the man, and never wanted to, and wouldn't, not of my own free will, not for a shilling a time,—that face of his will haunt me if I live till Noah, as the saying is.[1] I've seen him going in and out at all hours of the day and night,—that Arab party's a mystery if ever there was one,—he always goes tearing along as if he's flying for his life. Lots of people have come to the house, all sorts and kinds, men and women—they've been mostly women, and even little children. I've seen them hammer and hammer at that front door, but never a one have I seen let in,—or yet seen taken any notice of, and I think I may say, and yet tell no lie, that I've scarcely took my eye off the house since he's been inside it, over and over again in the middle of the night have I got up to have a look, so that I've not missed much that has took place.

"What's puzzled me is the noises that's come from the house. Sometimes for days together there's not been a sound, it might have been a house of the dead; and then, all through the night, there've been yells and screeches, squawks and screams,—I never heard nothing like it. I have thought, and more than once, that the devil himself must be in that front room, let alone all the rest of his demons. And as for cats!— where they've come from I can't think. I didn't use to notice hardly a cat in the neighbourhood till that there Arab party came,—there isn't much to attract them; but since he came there's been regiments. Sometimes at night there's been troops about the place, screeching like mad,—I've wished them farther, I can tell you. That Arab party must be fond of 'em. I've seen them inside the house, at the windows, upstairs and downstairs, as it seemed to me, a dozen at a time."

---

[1] If someone were to live to the age of six hundred—Noah's age given in Genesis 7:11.

CHAPTER 40

WHAT MISS COLEMAN SAW
THROUGH THE WINDOW

As Miss Coleman had paused, as if her narrative was approaching a conclusion, I judged it expedient to make an attempt to bring the record as quickly as possible up to date.

"I take it, Miss Coleman, that you have observed what has occurred in the house to-day."

She tightened her nut-cracker jaws and glared at me disdainfully,—her dignity was ruffled.

"I'm coming to it, aren't I?—if you'll let me. If you've got no manners I'll learn you some. One doesn't like to be hurried at my time of life, young man."

I was meekly silent;—plainly, if she was to talk, every one else must listen.

"During the last few days there have been some queer goings on over the road,—out of the common queer, I mean, for goodness knows that they always have been queer enough. That Arab party has been flitting about like a creature possessed,—I've seen him going in and out twenty times a day. This morning—"

She paused,—to fix her eyes on Lessingham. She apparently observed his growing interest as she approached the subject which had brought us there,—and resented it.

"Don't look at me like that, young man, because I won't have it. And as for questions, I may answer questions when I'm done, but don't you dare to ask me one before, because I won't be interrupted."

Up to then Lessingham had not spoken a word,—but it seemed as if she was endowed with the faculty of perceiving the huge volume of the words which he had left unuttered.

"This morning—as I've said already,—" she glanced at Lessingham as if she defied his contradiction—"when that Arab party came home it was just on the stroke of seven. I know what was the exact time because, when I went to the door to the milkman, my clock was striking the half hour, and I always keep it thirty minutes fast. As I was taking the milk, the man said to me, 'Hollo, Miss Coleman, here's your friend coming along.' 'What friend?' I says,—for I ain't got no friends, as I know, round here, nor yet, I hope, no enemies neither.

"And I looks round, and there was the Arab party coming tearing down the road, his bedcover thing all flying in the wind, and his arms straight out in front of him,—I never did see anyone go at such a pace. 'My goodness,' I says, 'I wonder he don't do himself an injury!' 'I wonder someone else don't do him an injury,' says the milkman. 'The very sight of him is enough to make my milk go sour!' And he picked up his pail and went away quite grumpy,—though what that Arab party's done to him is more than I can say.—I have always noticed that milkman's temper's short like his measure. I wasn't best pleased with him for speaking of that Arab party as my friend, which he never has been, and never won't be, and never could be neither.

"Five persons went to the house after the milkman was gone, and that there Arab party was safe inside,—three of them was commercials, that I know, because afterwards they came to me. But of course they none of them got no chance with that there Arab party except of hammering at his front door, which ain't what you might call a paying game, nor nice for the temper, but for that I don't blame him, for if once those commercials do begin talking they'll talk for ever.

"Now I'm coming to this afternoon."

I thought it was about time,—though for the life of me, I did not dare to hint as much.

"Well, it might have been three, or it might have been half past, anyhow it was thereabouts, when up there comes two men and a woman, which one of the men was that young man what's a friend of yours. 'Oh,' I says to myself, 'here's something new in callers, I wonder what it is they're wanting.' That young man what was a friend of yours, he starts hammering, and hammering, as the custom was with every one who came, and, as usual, no more notice was taken of him than nothing,—though I knew that all the time the Arab party was indoors."

At this point I felt that at all hazards I must interpose a question.

"You are sure he was indoors?"

She took it better than I feared she might.

"Of course I'm sure,—hadn't I seen him come in at seven, and he never hadn't gone out since, for I don't believe that I'd taken my eyes off the place not for two minutes together, and I'd never had a sight of him. If he wasn't indoors, where was he then?"

For the moment, so far as I was concerned, the query was unanswerable. She triumphantly continued:

"Instead of doing what most did, when they'd had enough of hammering, and going away, these three they went round to the back, and I'm blessed if they mustn't have got through the kitchen window, woman and all, for all of a sudden the blind in the front room was pulled not up, but down—dragged down it was, and there was that young man what's a friend of yours standing with it in his hand.

"'Well,' I says to myself, 'if that ain't cool I should like to know what is. If, when you ain't let in, you can let yourself in, and that without so much as saying by your leave, or with your leave, things is coming to a pretty pass. Wherever can that Arab party be, and whatever can he be thinking of, to let them go on like that because that he's the sort to allow a liberty to be took with him, and say nothing, I don't believe.'

"Every moment I expects to hear a noise and see a row begin, but, so far as I could make out, all was quiet and there wasn't nothing of the kind. So I says to myself, 'There's more in this than meets the eye, and them three parties must have right upon their side, or they wouldn't be doing what they are doing in the way they are, there'd be a shindy!'[1]

"Presently, in about five minutes, the front door opens, and a young man—not the one what's your friend, but the other—comes sailing out, and through the gate, and down the road, as stiff and upright as a grenadier,—I never see anyone walk more upright, and few as fast. At his heels comes the young man what is your friend, and it seems to me that he couldn't make out what this other was a-doing of. I says to myself, 'There's been a quarrel between them two, and him as has gone has hooked it!' This young man what is your friend he stood at the gate, all of a fidget, staring after the other with all his eyes, as if he couldn't think what to make of him, and the young woman, she stood on the doorstep, staring after him too.

"As the young man what had hooked it turned the corner, and was out of sight, all at once your friend he seemed to make up his mind, and he started off running as hard as he could pelt,—and the young woman was left alone. I expected, every minute, to see him come back with the other young man, and the young woman, by the way she hung about the gate, she seemed to expect it too. But no, nothing of the kind. So when, as I expect, she'd had enough of waiting, she went into the house again, and I see her pass the front room window. After a while, back she comes to the gate, and stands looking and looking, but nothing was to be seen of either of them young men. When she'd been at the gate, I daresay five minutes, back she goes into the house,—and I never saw nothing of her again."

---

[1] A commotion or upset, trouble.

"You never saw anything of her again?—Are you sure she went back into the house?"

"As sure as I am that I see you."

"I suppose that you didn't keep a constant watch upon the premises?"

"But that's just what I did do. I felt something queer was going on, and I made up my mind to see it through. And when I make up my mind to a thing like that I'm not easy to turn aside. I never moved off the chair at my bedroom window, and I never took my eyes off the house, not till you come knocking at my front door."

"But, since the young lady is certainly not in the house at present, she must have eluded your observation, and, in some manner, have left it without your seeing her."

"I don't believe she did, I don't see how she could have done,—there's something queer about that house, since that Arab party's been inside it. But though I didn't see her, I did see someone else."

"Who was that?"

"A young man."

"A young man?"

"Yes, a young man, and that's what puzzled me, and what's been puzzling me ever since, for see him go in I never did do."

"Can you describe him?"

"Not as to the face, for he wore a dirty cloth cap pulled down right over it, and he walked so quickly that I never had a proper look. But I should know him anywhere if I saw him, if only because of his clothes and his walk."

"What was there peculiar about his clothes and his walk?"

"Why, his clothes were that old, and torn, and dirty, that a ragman wouldn't have given a thank you for them,—and as for fit,—there wasn't none, they hung upon him like a scarecrow—he was a regular figure of fun; I should think the boys would call after him if they saw him in the street. As for his walk, he walked off just like the first young man had done, he strutted along with his shoulders back, and his head in the air, and that stiff and straight that my kitchen poker would have looked crooked beside of him."

"Did nothing happen to attract your attention between the young lady's going back into the house and the coming out of this young man?"

Miss Coleman cogitated.

"Now you mention it there did,—though I should have forgotten all about it if you hadn't asked me,—that comes of your not letting me tell the tale in my own way. About twenty minutes after the young woman had gone in someone put up the blind in the front room, which that young man had dragged right down, I couldn't see who it was for the blind was between us, and it was about ten minutes after that that young man came marching out."

"And then what followed?"

"Why, in about another ten minutes that Arab party himself comes scooting through the door."

"The Arab party?"

"Yes, the Arab party! The sight of him took me clean aback. Where he'd been, and what he'd been doing with himself while them there people played hi-spy-hi about his premises I'd have given a shilling out of my pocket to have known, but there he was, as large as life, and carrying a bundle."

"A bundle?"

"A bundle, on his head, like a muffin-man carries his tray. It was a great thing, you never would have thought he could have carried it, and it was easy to see that it was as much as he could manage; it bent him nearly double, and he went crawling along like a snail,—it took him quite a time to get to the end of the road."

Mr. Lessingham leaped up from his seat, crying,

"Marjorie was in that bundle!"

"I doubt it," I said.

He moved about the room distractedly, wringing his hands.

"She was! she must have been! God help us all!"

"I repeat that I doubt it. If you will be advised by me you will wait awhile before you arrive at any such conclusion."

All at once there was a tapping at the window pane. Atherton was staring at us from without.

He shouted through the glass,

"Come out of that, you fossils!—I've news for you!"

CHAPTER 41

THE CONSTABLE,—HIS CLUE,
—AND THE CAB

Miss Coleman, getting up in a fluster, went hurrying to the door.

"I won't have that young man in my house. I won't have him! Don't let him dare to put his nose across my doorstep."

I endeavoured to appease her perturbation.

"I promise you that he shall not come in, Miss Coleman. My friend here, and I, will go and speak to him outside."

She held the front door open just wide enough to enable Lessingham and me to slip through, then she shut it after us with a bang. She evidently had a strong objection to any intrusion on Sydney's part.

Standing just without the gate he saluted us with a characteristic vigour which was scarcely flattering to our late hostess. Behind him was a constable.

"I hope you two have been mewed in with that old pussy long enough. While you've been tittle-tattling I've been doing,—listen to what this bobby's got to say."

The constable, his thumbs thrust inside his belt, wore an indulgent smile upon his countenance. He seemed to find Sydney amusing. He spoke in a deep bass voice,—as if it issued from his boots.

"I don't know that I've got anything to say."

It was plain that Sydney thought otherwise.

"You wait till I've given this pretty pair of gossips a lead, officer, then I'll trot you out." He turned to us.

"After I'd poked my nose into every dashed hole in that infernal den, and been rewarded with nothing but a pain in the back for my trouble, I stood cooling my heels on the doorstep, wondering if I should fight the cabman, or get him to fight me, just to pass the time away,—for he says he can box, and he looks it,—when who should come strolling along but this magnificent example of the metropolitan constabulary." He waved his hand towards the policeman, whose grin grew wider. "I looked at him, and he looked at me, and then when we'd had enough of admiring each other's fine features and striking proportions, he said to me, 'Has he gone?' I said, 'Who?—Baxter?—or Bob Brown?' He said, 'No, the Arab.' I said, 'What do you know about any

Arab?' He said, 'Well, I saw him in the Broadway about three-quarters of an hour ago, and then, seeing you here, and the house all open, I wondered if he had gone for good.' With that I almost jumped out of my skin, though you can bet your life I never showed it. I said, 'How do you know it was he?' He said, 'It was him right enough, there's no doubt about that. If you've seen him once, you're not likely to forget him.' 'Where was he going?' 'He was talking to a cabman,—four-wheeler. He'd got a great bundle on his head,—wanted to take it inside with him. Cabman didn't seem to see it!' That was enough for me,—I picked this most deserving officer up in my arms, and carried him across the road to you two fellows like a flash of lightning."

Since the policeman was six feet three or four, and more than sufficiently broad in proportion, his scarcely seemed the kind of figure to be picked up in anybody's arms and carried like a "flash of lightning," which,—as his smile grew more indulgent, he himself appeared to think.

Still, even allowing for Atherton's exaggeration, the news which he had brought was sufficiently important. I questioned the constable upon my own account.

"There is my card, officer, probably, before the day is over, a charge of a very serious character will be preferred against the person who has been residing in the house over the way. In the meantime it is of the utmost importance that a watch should be kept upon his movements. I suppose you have no sort of doubt that the person you saw in the Broadway was the one in question?"

"Not a morsel. I know him as well as I do my own brother,—we all do upon this beat. He's known amongst us as the Arab. I've had my eye on him ever since he came to the place. A queer fish he is. I always have said that he's up to some game or other. I never came across one like him for flying about in all sorts of weather, at all hours of the night, always tearing along as if for his life. As I was telling this gentleman I saw him in the Broadway,—well, now it's about an hour since, perhaps a little more. I was coming on duty when I saw a crowd in front of the District Railway Station,—and there was the Arab, having a sort of argument with the cabman. He had a great bundle on his head, five or six feet long, perhaps longer. He wanted to take this great bundle with him into the cab, and the cabman, he didn't see it."

"You didn't wait to see him drive off."

"No,—I hadn't time. I was due at the station,—I was cutting it pretty fine as it was."

"You didn't speak to him,—or to the cabman?"

"No, it wasn't any business of mine you understand. The whole thing just caught my eye as I was passing."

"And you didn't take the cabman's number?"

"No, well, as far as that goes it wasn't needful. I know the cabman, his name and all about him, his stable's in Bradmore."

I whipped out my note-book.

"Give me his address."

"I don't know what his Christian name is, Tom, I believe, but I'm not sure. Anyhow his surname's Ellis and his address is Church Mews, St John's Road, Bradmore,—I don't know his number, but any one will tell you which is his place, if you ask for Four-Wheel Ellis,—that's the name he's known by among his pals because of his driving a four-wheeler."

"Thank you, officer. I am obliged to you." Two half-crowns changed hands. "If you will keep an eye on the house and advise me at the address which you will find on my card, of any thing which takes place there during the next few days, you will do me a service."

We had clambered back into the hansom, the driver was just about to start, when the constable was struck by a sudden thought.

"One moment, sir,—blessed if I wasn't going to forget the most important bit of all. I did hear him tell Ellis where to drive him to,—he kept saying it over and over again, in that queer lingo of his. 'Waterloo Railway Station, Waterloo Railway Station!' 'All right,' said Ellis, 'I'll drive you to Waterloo Railway Station right enough, only I'm not going to have that bundle of yours inside my cab. There isn't room for it, so you put it on the roof.' 'To Waterloo Railway Station,' said the Arab, 'I take my bundle with me to Waterloo Railway Station,—I take it with me!' 'Who says you don't take it with you?' said Ellis. 'You can take it, and twenty more besides, for all I care, only you don't take it inside my cab,—put it on the roof.' 'I take it with me to Waterloo Railway Station,' said the Arab, and there they were, wrangling and jangling, and neither seeming to be able to make out what the other was after, and the people all laughing."

"Waterloo Railway Station,—you are sure that was what he said?"

"I'll take my oath to it, because I said to myself, when I heard it, 'I wonder what you'll have to pay for that little lot, for the District Railway Station's outside the four-mile radius.'"

As we drove off I was inclined to ask myself, a little bitterly—and perhaps unjustly—if it were not characteristic of the average London policeman to almost forget the most important part of his information,—at any rate to leave it to the last and only to bring it to the front on having his palm crossed with silver.

As the hansom bowled along we three had what occasionally approached a warm discussion.

"Marjorie was in that bundle," began Lessingham, in the most lugubrious of tones, and with the most woe-begone of faces.

"I doubt it," I observed.

"She was,—I feel it,—I know it. She was either dead and mutilated, or gagged and drugged and helpless. All that remains is vengeance."

"I repeat that I doubt it."

Atherton struck in.

"I am bound to say, with the best will in the world to think otherwise, that I agree with Lessingham."

"You are wrong."

"It's all very well for you to talk in that cock-sure way, but it's easier for you to say I'm wrong than to prove it. If I am wrong, and if Lessingham's wrong, how do you explain his extraordinary insistence on taking it inside the cab with him, which the bobby describes? If there wasn't something horrible, awful in that bundle of his, of which he feared the discovery, why was he so reluctant to have it placed upon the roof?"

"There probably was something in it which he was particularly anxious should not be discovered, but I doubt if it was anything of the kind which you suggest."

"Here is Marjorie in a house alone—nothing has been seen of her since,—her clothing, her hair, is found hidden away under the floor. This scoundrel sallies forth with a huge bundle on his head,—the bobby speaks of it being five or six feet long, or longer,—a bundle which he regards with so much solicitude that he insists on never allowing it to go, for a single instant, out of his sight and reach. What is in the thing? don't all the facts most unfortunately point in one direction?"

Mr. Lessingham covered his face with his hands, and groaned.

"I fear that Mr. Atherton is right."

"I differ from you both."

Sydney at once became heated.

"Then perhaps you can tell us what was in the bundle?"

"I fancy I could make a guess at the contents."

"Oh you could, could you, then, perhaps, for our sakes, you'll make it,—and not play the oracular owl!—Lessingham and I are interested in this business, after all."

"It contained the bearer's personal property: that, and nothing more. Stay! before you jeer at me, suffer me to finish. If I am not mistaken as to the identity of the person whom the constable describes as the Arab,

I apprehend that the contents of that bundle were of much more importance to him than if they had consisted of Miss Lindon, either dead or living. More. I am inclined to suspect that if the bundle was placed on the roof of the cab, and if the driver did meddle with it, and did find out the contents, and understand them, he would have been driven, out of hand, stark staring mad."

Sydney was silent, as if he reflected. I imagine he perceived there was something in what I said.

"But what has become of Miss Lindon?"

"I fancy that Miss Lindon, at this moment, is—somewhere; I don't, just now, know exactly where, but I hope very shortly to be able to give you a clearer notion,—attired in a rotten, dirty pair of boots; a filthy, tattered pair of trousers; a ragged, unwashed apology for a shirt; a greasy, ancient, shapeless coat; and a frowsy peaked cloth cap."

They stared at me, opened-eyed. Atherton was the first to speak.

"What on earth do you mean?"

"I mean that it seems to me that the facts point in the direction of my conclusions rather than yours—and that very strongly too. Miss Coleman asserts that she saw Miss Lindon return into the house; that within a few minutes the blind was replaced at the front window; and that shortly after a young man, attired in the costume I have described, came walking out of the front door. I believe that young man was Miss Marjorie Lindon."

Lessingham and Atherton both broke out into interrogations, with Sydney, as usual, loudest.

"But—man alive! what on earth should make her do a thing like that? Marjorie, the most retiring, modest girl on all God's earth, walk about in broad daylight, in such a costume, and for no reason at all! my dear Champnell, you are suggesting that she first of all went mad."

"She was in a state of trance."

"Good God!—Champnell!"

"Well?"

"Then you think that—juggling villain did get hold of her?"

"Undoubtedly. Here is my view of the case, mind it is only a hypothesis and you must take it for what it is worth. It seems to me quite clear that the Arab, as we will call the person for the sake of identification, was somewhere about the premises when you thought he wasn't."

"But—where? We looked upstairs, and downstairs, and everywhere—where could he have been?"

"That, as at present advised, I am not prepared to say, but I think you may take it for granted that he was there. He hypnotised the man Holt, and sent him away, intending you to go after him, and so being rid of you both—"

"The deuce he did, Champnell! You write me down an ass!"

"As soon as the coast was clear he discovered himself to Miss Lindon, who, I expect, was disagreeably surprised, and hypnotised her."

"The hound!"

"The devil!"

The first exclamation was Lessingham's, the second Sydney's.

"He then constrained her to strip herself to the skin—"

"The wretch!"

"The fiend!"

"He cut off her hair; he hid it and her clothes under the floor where we found them—where I think it probable that he had already some ancient masculine garments concealed—"

"By Jove! I shouldn't be surprised if they were Holt's. I remember the man saying that that nice joker stripped him of his duds,—and certainly when I saw him,—and when Marjorie found him!—he had absolutely nothing on but a queer sort of cloak. Can it be possible that that humorous professor of hankey-pankey—may all the maledictions of the accursed alight upon his head!—can have sent Marjorie Lindon, the daintiest damsel in the land!—into the streets of London rigged out in Holt's old togs!"

"As to that, I am not able to give an authoritative opinion, but, if I understand you aright, it at least is possible. Anyhow I am disposed to think that he sent Miss Lindon after the man Holt, taking it for granted that he had eluded you.—"

"That's it. Write me down an ass again!"

"That he did elude you, you have yourself admitted."

"That's because I stopped talking with that mutton-headed bobby,—I'd have followed the man to the ends of the earth if it hadn't been for that."

"Precisely; the reason is immaterial, it is the fact with which we are immediately concerned. He did elude you. And I think you will find that Miss Lindon and Mr. Holt are together at this moment."

"In men's clothing."

"Both in men's clothing, or, rather, Miss Lindon is in a man's rags."

"Great Potiphar![1] To think of Marjorie like that!"

---

[1] The phrase, here intended as a mild oath or exclamation, is ironic in the context of the novel's colonial sentiments regarding Egypt, Potiphar being an officer of the Pharaoh, who, in Genesis 39:1-20, owned Joseph as a slave.

"And where they are, the Arab is not very far off either."

Lessingham caught me by the arm.

"And what diabolical mischief do you imagine that he proposes to do to her?"

I shirked the question.

"Whatever it is, it is our business to prevent his doing it."

"And where do you think they have been taken?"

"That it will be our immediate business to endeavour to discover,— and here, at any rate, we are at Waterloo."

CHAPTER 42

THE QUARRY DOUBLES

I turned towards the booking-office on the main departure platform. As I went, the chief platform inspector, George Bellingham, with whom I had some acquaintance, came out of his office. I stopped him.

"Mr. Bellingham, will you be so good as to step with me to the booking-office, and instruct the clerk in charge to answer one or two questions which I wish to put to him. I will explain to you afterwards what is their exact import, but you know me sufficiently to be able to believe me when I say that they refer to a matter in which every moment is of the first importance."

He turned and accompanied us into the interior of the booking-office.

"To which of the clerks, Mr. Champnell, do you wish to put your questions?"

"To the one who issues third-class tickets to Southampton."

Bellingham beckoned to a man who was counting a heap of money, and apparently seeking to make it tally with the entries in a huge ledger which lay open before him,—he was a short, slightly-built young fellow, with a pleasant face and smiling eyes.

"Mr. Stone, this gentleman wishes to ask you one or two questions."

"I am at his service."

I put my questions.

"I want to know, Mr. Stone, if, in the course of the day, you have issued any tickets to a person dressed in Arab costume?"

His reply was prompt.

"I have—by the last train, the 7.25,—three singles."

Three singles! Then my instinct had told me rightly.

"Can you describe the person?"

Mr. Stone's eyes twinkled.

"I don't know that I can, except in a general way,—he was uncommonly old and uncommonly ugly, and he had a pair of the most extraordinary eyes I ever saw,—they gave me a sort of all-overish feeling when I saw them glaring at me through the pigeon-hole. But I can tell you one thing about him, he had a great bundle on his head, which he steadied with one hand, and as it bulged out in all directions its presence didn't make him popular with other people who wanted tickets too."

Undoubtedly this was our man.

"You are sure he asked for three tickets?"

"Certain. He said three tickets to Southampton; laid down the exact fare,—nineteen and six—and held up three fingers—like that. Three nasty looking fingers they were, with nails as long as talons."

"You didn't see who were his companions?"

"I didn't,—I didn't try to look. I gave him his tickets and off he went,—with the people grumbling at him because that bundle of his kept getting in their way."

Bellingham touched me on the arm.

"I can tell you about the Arab of whom Mr. Stone speaks. My attention was called to him by his insisting on taking his bundle with him into the carriage,—it was an enormous thing, he could hardly squeeze it through the door; it occupied the entire seat. But as there weren't as many passengers as usual, and he wouldn't or couldn't be made to understand that his precious bundle would be safe in the luggage van along with the rest of the luggage, and as he wasn't the sort of person you could argue with to any advantage, I had him put into an empty compartment, bundle and all."

"Was he alone then?"

"I thought so at the time, he said nothing about having more than one ticket, or any companions, but just before the train started two other men—English men—got into his compartment; and as I came down the platform, the ticket inspector at the barrier informed me that these two men were with him, because he held tickets for the three, which, as he was a foreigner, and they seemed English, struck the inspector as odd."

"Could you describe the two men?"

"I couldn't, not particularly, but the man who had charge of the barrier might. I was at the other end of the train when they got in. All

I noticed was that one seemed to be a commonplace looking individual and that the other was dressed like a tramp, all rags and tatters, a disreputable looking object he appeared to be."

"That," I said to myself, "was Miss Marjorie Lindon, the lovely daughter of a famous house; the wife-elect of a coming statesman."

To Bellingham I remarked aloud:

"I want you to strain a point, Mr. Bellingham, and to do me a service which I assure you you shall never have any cause to regret. I want you to wire instructions down the line to detain this Arab and his companions and to keep them in custody until the receipt of further instructions. They are not wanted by the police as yet, but they will be as soon as I am able to give certain information to the authorities at Scotland Yard,—and wanted very badly. But, as you will perceive for yourself, until I am able to give that information every moment is important.—Where's the Station Superintendent?"

"He's gone. At present I'm in charge."

"Then will you do this for me? I repeat that you shall never have any reason to regret it."

"I will if you'll accept all responsibility."

"I'll do that with the greatest pleasure."

Bellingham looked at his watch.

"It's about twenty minutes to nine. The train's scheduled for Basingstoke at 9.6. If we wire to Basingstoke at once they ought to be ready for them when they come."

"Good!"

The wire was sent.

We were shown into Bellingham's office to await results. Lessingham paced agitatedly to and fro; he seemed to have reached the limits of his self-control, and to be in a condition in which movement of some sort was an absolute necessity. The mercurial Sydney, on the contrary, leaned back in a chair, his legs stretched out in front of him, his hands thrust deep into his trouser pockets, and stared at Lessingham, as if he found relief to his feelings in watching his companion's restlessness. I, for my part, drew up as full a précis of the case as I deemed advisable, and as time permitted, which I despatched by one of the company's police to Scotland Yard.

Then I turned to my associates.

"Now, gentlemen, it's past dinner time. We may have a journey in front of us. If you take my advice you'll have something to eat."

Lessingham shook his head.

"I want nothing."

"Nor I," echoed Sydney.

I started up.

"You must pardon my saying nonsense, but surely you of all men, Mr. Lessingham, should be aware that you will not improve the situation by rendering yourself incapable of seeing it through. Come and dine."

I hauled them off with me, willy nilly, to the refreshment room. I dined,—after a fashion; Mr. Lessingham swallowed with difficulty, a plate of soup; Sydney nibbled at a plate of the most unpromising looking "chicken and ham."—he proved, indeed, more intractable than Lessingham, and was not to be persuaded to tackle anything easier of digestion.

I was just about to take cheese after chop when Bellingham came hastening in, in his hand an open telegram.

"The birds have flown," he cried.

"Flown!—How?"

In reply he gave me the telegram. I glanced at it. It ran:

"Persons described not in the train. Guard says they got out at Vauxhall. Have wired Vauxhall to advise you."

"That's a level-headed chap," said Bellingham. "The man who sent that telegram. His wiring to Vauxhall should save us a lot of time,—we ought to hear from there directly. Hollo! what's this? I shouldn't he surprised if this is it."

As he spoke a porter entered,—he handed an envelope to Bellingham. We all three kept our eyes fixed on the inspector's face as he opened it. When he perceived the contents he gave an exclamation of surprise.

"This Arab of yours, and his two friends, seem rather a curious lot, Mr. Champnell."

He passed the paper—on to me. It took the form of a report. Lessingham and Sydney, regardless of forms and ceremonies, leaned over my shoulder as I read it.

"Passengers by 7.30 Southampton, on arrival of train, complained of noises coming from a compartment in coach 8964. Stated that there had been shrieks and yells ever since the train left Waterloo, as if someone was being murdered. An Arab and two Englishmen got out of the compartment in question, apparently the party referred to in wire just to hand from Basingstoke. All three declared that there was nothing the matter. That they had been shouting for fun. Arab gave up three third singles for Southampton, saying, in reply to questions, that they had changed their minds, and did not want to go any farther. As there were no signs of a struggle or of violence, nor, apparently, any definite cause for detention, they were allowed to pass. They took a fourwheeler, No. 09435. The Arab and one man went inside, and the other man on the box. They asked to be driven to Commercial Road, Limehouse. The cab has since returned. Driver says put the three men down, at their request, in Commercial Road, at the corner of Sutcliffe Street, near the East India Docks.[1] They walked up Sutcliffe Street, the Englishmen in front, and the Arab behind, took the first turning to the right, and after that he saw nothing of them. The driver further states that all the way the Englishman inside, who was so ragged and dirty that he was reluctant to carry him, kept up a sort of wailing noise which so attracted his attention that he twice got off his box to see what was the matter, and each time he said it was nothing. The cabman is of opinion that both the Englishmen were of weak intellect. We were of the same impression here. They said nothing, except at the seeming instigation of the Arab, but when spoken to stared and gaped like lunatics.

"It may be mentioned that the Arab had with him an enormous bundle, which he persisted, in spite of all remonstrances, on taking with him inside the cab."

As soon as I had mastered the contents of the report, and perceived what I believed to be—unknown to the writer himself—its hideous inner meaning, I turned to Bellingham.

"With your permission, Mr. Bellingham, I will keep this communication,—it will be safe in my hands, you will be able to get a copy, and it may be necessary that I should have the original to show to the police. If any inquiries are made for me from Scotland Yard, tell them that I have gone to the Commercial Road, and that I will report my movements from Limehouse Police Station."

In another minute we were once more traversing the streets of London,—three in a hansom cab.

---

[1] Always the places where ships docked and unloaded goods, the various areas along the Thames, east of the City of London, such as Blackwall, Wapping, Limehouse, and the Isle of Dogs were the sites for the development of major docks receiving produce from the countries of the British Empire and other locations, from the late eighteenth century onwards. In 1803 the East India Dock Act established a company to develop the East India Dock, which was opened in 1806, to great national interest and a crowd of more than 10,000 spectators.

CHAPTER 43

THE MURDER AT MRS. 'ENDERSON'S

It is something of a drive from Waterloo to Limehouse,—it seems longer when all your nerves are tingling with anxiety to reach your journey's end; and the cab I had hit upon proved to be not the fastest I might have chosen. For some time after our start, we were silent. Each was occupied with his own thoughts.

Then Lessingham, who was sitting at my side, said to me,

"Mr. Champnell, you have that report."

"I have."

"Will you let me see it once more?"

I gave it to him, He read it once, twice,—and I fancy yet again. I purposely avoided looking at him as he did so. Yet all the while I was conscious of his pallid cheeks, the twitched muscles of his mouth, the feverish glitter of his eyes,—this Leader of Men, whose predominate characteristic in the House of Commons was immobility, was rapidly approximating to the condition of a hysterical woman. The mental strain which he had been recently undergoing was proving too much for his physical strength. This disappearance of the woman he loved bade fair to be the final straw. I felt convinced that unless something was done quickly to relieve the strain upon his mind he was nearer to a state of complete mental and moral collapse than he himself imagined. Had he been under my orders I should have commanded him to at once return home, and not to think; but conscious that, as things were, such a direction would be simply futile, I decided to do something else instead. Feeling that suspense was for him the worst possible form of suffering I resolved to explain, so far as I was able, precisely what it was I feared, and how I proposed to prevent it.

Presently there came the question for which I had been waiting, in a harsh, broken voice which no one who had heard him speak on a public platform, or in the House of Commons, would have recognised as his.

"Mr. Champnell,—who do you think this person is of whom the report from Vauxhall Station speaks as being all in rags and tatters?"

He knew perfectly well,—but I understood the mental attitude which induced him to prefer that the information should seem to come from me.

"I hope that it will prove to be Miss Lindon."

"Hope!" He gave a sort of gasp.

"Yes, hope,—because if it is I think it possible, nay probable, that within a few hours you will have her again enfolded in your arms."

"Pray God that it may be so! pray God!—pray the good God!"

I did not dare to look round for, from the tremor which was in his tone, I was persuaded that in the speaker's eyes were tears. Atherton continued silent. He was leaning half out of the cab, staring straight ahead, as if he saw in front a young girl's face, from which he could not remove his glance, and which beckoned him on.

After a while Lessingham spoke again, as if half to himself and half to me.

"This mention of the shrieks on the railway, and of the wailing noise in the cab,—what must this wretch have done to her? How my darling must have suffered!"

That was a theme on which I myself scarcely ventured to allow my thoughts to rest. The notion of a gently-nurtured girl being at the mercy of that fiend incarnate, possessed—as I believed that so-called Arab to be possessed—of all the paraphernalia of horror and of dread, was one which caused me tangible shrinkings of the body. Whence had come those shrieks and yells, of which the writer of the report spoke, which had caused the Arab's fellow-passengers to think that murder was being done? What unimaginable agony had caused them? what speech-less torture? And the "wailing noise," which had induced the prosaic, indurated[1] London cabman to get twice off his box to see what was the matter, what anguish had been provocative of that? The helpless girl who had already endured so much, endured, perhaps, that to which death would have been preferred!—shut up in that rattling, jolting box on wheels, alone with that diabolical Asiatic, with the enormous bundle, which was but the lurking place of nameless terrors,—what might she not, while being borne through the heart of civilised London, have been made to suffer? What had she not been made to suffer to have kept up that continued "wailing noise"?

It was not a theme on which it was wise to permit one's thoughts to linger,—and particularly was it clear that it was one from which Lessingham's thoughts should have been kept as far as possible away.

"Come, Mr. Lessingham, neither you nor I will do himself any good by permitting his reflections to flow in a morbid channel. Let

---

[1]   Emotionally hard, callous, indifferent, and uncaring.

us talk of something else. By the way, weren't you due to speak in the House tonight?"

"Due!—Yes, I was due,—but what does it matter?"

"But have you acquainted no one with the cause of your non-attendance?"

"Acquaint!—whom should I acquaint?"

"My good sir! Listen to me, Mr. Lessingham. Let me entreat you very earnestly, to follow my advice. Call another cab,—or take this! and go at once to the House. It is not too late. Play the man, deliver the speech you have undertaken to deliver, perform your political duties. By coming with me you will be a hindrance rather than a help, and you may do your reputation an injury from which it never may recover. Do as I counsel you, and I will undertake to do my very utmost to let you have good news by the time your speech is finished."

He turned on me with a bitterness for which I was unprepared.

"If I were to go down to the House, and try to speak in the state in which I am now, they would laugh at me, I should be ruined."

"Do you not run an equally great risk of being ruined by staying away?"

He gripped me by the arm.

"Mr. Champnell, do you know that I am on the verge of madness? Do you know that as I am sitting here by your side I am living in a dual world? I am going on and on to catch that—that fiend, and I am back again in that Egyptian den, upon that couch of rugs, with the Woman of the Songs beside me, and Marjorie is being torn and tortured, and burnt before my eyes! God help me! Her shrieks are ringing in my ears!"

He did not speak loudly, but his voice was none the less impressive on that account. I endeavoured my hardest to be stern.

"I confess that you disappoint me, Mr. Lessingham. I have always understood that you were a man of unusual strength; you appear instead, to be a man of extraordinary weakness; with an imagination so ill-governed that its ebullitions remind me of nothing so much as feminine hysterics. Your wild language is not warranted by circumstances. I repeat that I think it quite possible that by to-morrow morning she will be returned to you."

"Yes,—but how? as the Marjorie I have known, as I saw her last,—or how?"

That was the question which I had already asked myself, in what condition would she be when we had succeeded in snatching her from her captor's grip? It was a question to which I had refused to supply an answer. To him I lied by implication.

"Let us hope that, with the exception of being a trifle scared, she will be as sound and hale and hearty as ever in her life."

"Do you yourself believe that she'll be like that,—untouched, unchanged, unstained?"

Then I lied right out,—it seemed to me necessary to calm his growing excitement.

"I do."

"You don't!"

"Mr. Lessingham!"

"Do you think that I can't see your face and read in it the same thoughts which trouble me? As a man of honour do you care to deny that when Marjorie Lindon is restored to me,—if she ever is!—you fear she will be but the mere soiled husk of the Marjorie whom I knew and loved?"

"Even supposing that there may be a modicum of truth in what you say,—which I am far from being disposed to admit—what good purpose do you propose to serve by talking in such a strain?"

"None,—no good purpose,—unless it be the desire of looking the truth in the face. For, Mr. Champnell, you must not seek to play with me the hypocrite, nor try to hide things from me as if I were a child. If my life is ruined—it is ruined,—let me know it, and look the knowledge in the face. That, to me, is to play the man."

I was silent.

The wild tale he had told me of the Cairene inferno, oddly enough—yet why oddly, for the world is all coincidence!—had thrown a flood of light on certain events which had happened some three years previously and which ever since had remained shrouded in mystery. The conduct of the business afterwards came into my hands,—and briefly, what had occurred was this:

Three persons,—two sisters and their brother, who was younger than themselves, members of a decent English family, were going on a trip round the world. They were young, adventurous, and—not to put too fine a point on it—foolhardy. The evening after their arrival in Cairo, by way of what is called "a lark," in spite of the protestations of people who were better informed than themselves, they insisted on going, alone, for a ramble through the native quarter.

They went,—but they never returned. Or, rather the two girls never returned. After an interval the young man was found again,—what was left of him. A fuss was made when there were no signs of their reappearance, but as there were no relations, nor even friends of theirs, but only casual acquaintances on board the ship by which they had travelled, perhaps not so great a fuss as might have been was made. Anyhow, nothing was discovered. Their widowed mother, alone in England, wondering how it was that beyond the receipt of a brief wire, acquainting her with their arrival at Cairo, she had heard nothing further of their wanderings, placed herself in communication with the diplomatic people over there,—to learn that, to all appearances, her three children had vanished from off the face of the earth.

Then a fuss was made,—with a vengeance. So far as one can judge the whole town and neighbourhood was turned pretty well upside down. But nothing came of it,—so far as any results were concerned, the authorities might just as well have left the mystery of their vanishment alone. It continued where it was in spite of them.

However, some three months afterwards a youth was brought to the British Embassy by a party of friendly Arabs who asserted that they had found him naked and nearly dying in some remote spot in the Wady Halfa desert.[1] It was the brother of the two lost girls. He was as nearly dying as he very well could be without being actually dead when they brought him to the Embassy,—and in a state of indescribable mutilation. He seemed to rally for a time under careful treatment, but he never again uttered a coherent word. It was only from his delirious ravings that any idea was formed of what had really occurred.

Shorthand notes were taken of some of the utterances of his delirium. Afterwards they were submitted to me. I remembered the substance of them quite well, and when Mr. Lessingham began to tell me of his own hideous experiences they came back to me more clearly still. Had I laid those notes before him I have little doubt but that he would have immediately perceived that seventeen years after the adventure which had left such an indelible scar upon his own life, this youth—he was little more than a boy—had seen the things which he had seen, and suffered the nameless agonies and degradations which he had suffered. The young man was perpetually raving about some indescribable den of horror which was own brother to Lessingham's temple and about some female monster, whom he regarded with such fear and horror that every allusion he made to her was followed by a convulsive paroxysm which taxed all the ingenuity of his medical attendants to bring him out of. He frequently called upon his sisters by name, speaking of them in a manner

---

[1]   A town on the Nile, crucial in the battles between the Madhi's troops and the British army.

which inevitably suggested that he had been an unwilling and helpless witness of hideous tortures which they had undergone; and then he would rise in bed, screaming, "They're burning them! they're burning them! Devils! devils!" And at those times it required all the strength of those who were in attendance to restrain his maddened frenzy.

The youth died in one of these fits of great preternatural excitement, without, as I have previously written, having given utterance to one single coherent word, and by some of those who were best able to judge it was held to have been a mercy that he did die without having been restored to consciousness. And, presently, tales began to be whispered, about some idolatrous sect, which was stated to have its headquarters somewhere in the interior of the country—some located it in this neighbourhood, and some in that—which was stated to still practise, and to always have practised, in unbroken historical continuity, the debased, unclean, mystic, and bloody rites, of a form of idolatry which had had its birth in a period of the world's story which was so remote, that to all intents and purposes it might be described as prehistoric.

While the ferment was still at its height, a man came to the British Embassy who said that he was a member of a tribe which had its habitat on the banks of the White Nile. He asserted that he was in association with this very idolatrous sect,—though he denied that he was one of the actual sectaries. He did admit, however, that he had assisted more than once at their orgies, and declared that it was their constant practice to offer young women as sacrifices—preferably white Christian women, with a special preference, if they could get them, to young English women. He vowed that he himself had seen with his own eyes, English girls burnt alive. The description which he gave of what preceded and followed these foul murders appalled those who listened. He finally wound up by offering, on payment of a stipulated sum of money, to guide a troop of soldiers to this den of demons, so that they should arrive there at a moment when it was filled with worshippers, who were preparing to participate in an orgy which was to take place during the next few days.

His offer was conditionally accepted. He was confined in an apartment with one man on guard inside and another on guard outside the room. That night the sentinel without was startled by hearing a great noise and frightful screams issuing from the chamber in which the native was interned. He summoned assistance. The door was opened. The soldier on guard within was stark, staring mad,—he died within a few months, a gibbering maniac to the end. The native was dead. The window, which was a very small one, was securely fastened inside and strongly barred without. There was nothing to show by what means entry had been gained. Yet it was the general opinion of those who saw the corpse that the man had been destroyed by some wild beast. A photograph was taken of the body after death, a copy of which is still in my possession. In it are distinctly shown lacerations about the neck and the lower portion of the abdomen, as if they had been produced by the claws of some huge and ferocious animal. The skull is splintered in half-a-dozen places, and the face is torn to rags.

That was more than three years ago. The whole business has remained as great a mystery as ever. But my attention has once or twice been caught by trifling incidents, which have caused me to more than suspect that the wild tale told by that murdered native had in it at least the elements of truth; and which have even led me to wonder if the trade in kidnapping was not being carried on to this very hour, and if women of my own flesh and blood were not still being offered up on that infernal altar. And now, here was Paul Lessingham, a man of world-wide reputation, of great intellect, of undoubted honour, who had come to me with a wholly unconscious verification of all my worst suspicions!

That the creature spoken of as an Arab,—and who was probably no more an Arab than I was, and whose name was certainly not Mohamed el Kheir!—was an emissary from that den of demons, I had no doubt. What was the exact purport of the creature's presence in England was another question. Possibly part of the intention was the destruction of Paul Lessingham, body, soul and spirit; possibly another part was the procuration of fresh victims for that long-drawn-out holocaust. That this latter object explained the disappearance of Miss Lindon I felt persuaded. That she was designed by the personification of evil who was her captor, to suffer all the horrors at which the stories pointed, and then to be burned alive, amidst the triumphant yells of the attendant demons, I was certain. That the wretch, aware that the pursuit was in full cry, was tearing, twisting, doubling, and would stick at nothing which would facilitate the smuggling of the victim out of England, was clear.

My interest in the quest was already far other than a merely professional one. The blood in my veins tingled at the thought of such a woman as Miss Lindon being in the power of such a monster. I may assuredly claim that throughout the whole business I was urged forward by no thought of fee or of reward. To have had a share in rescuing that unfortunate girl, and in the destruction of her noxious persecutor, would have been reward enough for me.

One is not always, even in strictly professional matters, influenced by strictly professional instincts.

The cab slowed. A voice descended through the trap door.

"This is Commercial Road, sir,—what part of it do you want?"

"Drive me to Limehouse Police Station."

We were driven there. I made my way to the usual inspector behind the usual pigeon-hole.

"My name is Champnell. Have you received any communication from Scotland Yard to-night having reference to a matter in which I am interested?"

"Do you mean about the Arab? We received a telephonic message about half an hour ago."

"Since communicating with Scotland Yard this has come to hand from the authorities at Vauxhall Station. Can you tell me if anything has been seen of the person in question by the men of your division?"

I handed the Inspector the "report." His reply was laconic.

"I will inquire."

He passed through a door into an inner room and the "report" went with him.

"Beg pardon, sir, but was that a Harab you was a-talking about to the Hinspector?"

The speaker was a gentleman unmistakably of the guttersnipe[1] class. He was seated on a form.[2] Close at hand hovered a policeman whose special duty it seemed to be to keep an eye upon his movements.

"Why do you ask?"

"I beg your pardon, sir, but I saw a Harab myself about a hour ago, leastways he looked like as if he was a Harab."

"What sort of a looking person was he?"

"I can't 'ardly tell you that, sir, because I didn't never have a proper look at him,—but I know he had a bloomin' great bundle on 'is 'ead.... It was like this, 'ere. I was comin' round the corner, as he was passin', I never see 'im till I was right atop of 'im, so that I haccidentally run agin 'im,—my heye! didn't 'e give me a downer! I was down on the back of my 'ead in the middle of the road before I knew where I was and 'e was at the other end of the street. If 'e 'adn't knocked me more'n 'arf silly I'd been after 'im, sharp,—I tell you! and hasked 'im what 'e

---

[1] Someone who lives on the streets or, otherwise, ill-bred or boorish, as in this usage. The term comes from the practice of gathering rags and scraps of paper and other waste from the gutters, in order to sell it.

[2] A bench.

thought 'e was a-doin' of, but afore my senses was back agin 'e was out o' sight,—clean!"

"You are sure he had a bundle on his head?"

"I noticed it most particular."

"How long ago do you say this was? and where?"

"About a hour ago,—perhaps more, perhaps less."

"Was he alone?"

"It seemed to me as if a cove[1] was a follerin' 'im, leastways there was a bloke as was a-keepin' close at 'is 'eels,—though I don't know what 'is little game was, I'm sure. Ask the pleesman—he knows, he knows everythink, the pleesman do."

I turned to the "pleesman."

"Who is this man?"

The "pleesman" put his hands behind his back, and threw out his chest. His manner was distinctly affable.

"Well,—he's being detained upon suspicion. He's given us an address at which to make inquiries, and inquiries are being made. I shouldn't pay too much attention to what he says if I were you. I don't suppose he'd be particular about a lie or two."

This frank expression of opinion re-aroused the indignation of the gentleman on the form.

"There you hare! at it again! That's just like you peelers,—you're all the same! What do you know about me?—Nuffink! This gen'leman ain't got no call to believe me, not as I knows on,—it's all the same to me if 'e do or don't, but it's trewth what I'm sayin', all the same."

At this point the Inspector re-appeared at the pigeon-hole. He cut short the flow of eloquence.

"Now then, not so much noise outside there!" He addressed me. "None of our men have seen anything of the person you're inquiring for, so far as we're aware. But, if you like, I will place a man at your disposal, and he will go round with you, and you will be able to make your own inquiries."

A capless, wildly excited young ragamuffin came dashing in at the street door. He gasped out, as clearly as he could for the speed which he had made:

"There's been murder done, Mr. Pleesman,—a Harab's killed a bloke."

"Mr. Pleesman" gripped him by the shoulder.

"What's that?"

---

[1] Slang for "person."

The youngster put up his arm, and ducked his head, instinctively, as if to ward off a blow.

"Leave me alone! I don't want none of your 'andling!—I ain't done nuffink to you! I tell you 'e 'as!"

The Inspector spoke through the pigeon-hole.

"He has what, my lad? What do you say has happened?"

"There's been murder done—it's right enough!—there 'as!—up at Mrs. 'Enderson's, in Paradise Place,—a Harab's been and killed a bloke!"

CHAPTER 44

THE MAN WHO WAS MURDERED

The Inspector spoke to me.

"If what the boy says is correct it sounds as if the person whom you are seeking may have had a finger in the pie."

I was of the same opinion, as, apparently, were Lessingham and Sydney. Atherton collared the youth by the shoulder which Mr. Pleesman had left disengaged.

"What sort of looking bloke is it who's been murdered?"

"I dunno! I 'aven't seen 'im! Mrs. 'Enderson, she says to me! "Gustus Barley,' she says, 'a bloke's been murdered. That there Harab what I chucked out 'alf a hour ago been and murdered 'im, and left 'im behind up in my back room. You run as 'ard as you can tear and tell them there dratted pleese what's so fond of shovin' their dirty noses into respectable people's 'ouses.' So I comes and tells yer. That's all I knows about it."

We went four in the hansom which had been waiting in the street to Mrs. Henderson's in Paradise Place,—the Inspector and we three. "Mr. Pleesman" and "'Gustus Barley" followed on foot. The Inspector was explanatory.

"Mrs. Henderson keeps a sort of lodging-house,—a 'Sailors' Home' she calls it, but no one could call it sweet. It doesn't bear the best of characters, and if you asked me what I thought of it, I should say in plain English that it was a disorderly house."[1]

---

[1] Slang for an unlicensed bar or pub, or possibly brothel, possibly also used for fencing stolen items or as an opium den.

Paradise Place proved to be within three or four hundred yards of the Station House. So far as could be seen in the dark it consisted of a row of houses of considerable dimensions,—and also of considerable antiquity. They opened on to two or three stone steps which led directly into the street. At one of the doors stood an old lady with a shawl drawn over her head. This was Mrs. Henderson. She greeted us with garrulous volubility.

"So you 'ave come, 'ave you? I thought you never was a-comin', that I did." She recognised the Inspector. "It's you, Mr. Phillips, is it?" Perceiving us, she drew a little back. "Who's them 'ere parties? They ain't coppers?"

Mr. Phillips dismissed her inquiry, curtly.

"Never you mind who they are. What's this about someone being murdered?"

"Ssh!" The old lady glanced round. "Don't you speak so loud, Mr. Phillips. No one don't know nothing about it as yet. The parties what's in my 'ouse is most respectable,—most! and they couldn't abide the notion of there being police about the place."

"We quite believe that, Mrs. Henderson."

The Inspector's tone was grim.

Mrs. Henderson led the way up a staircase which would have been distinctly the better for repairs. It was necessary to pick one's way as one went, and as the light was defective stumbles were not infrequent.

Our guide paused outside a door on the topmost landing. From some mysterious recess in her apparel she produced a key.

"It's in 'ere. I locked the door so that nothing mightn't be disturbed. I knows 'ow particular you pleesmen is."

She turned the key. We all went in—we, this time, in front, and she behind.

A candle was guttering on a broken and dilapidated single wash hand stand. A small iron bedstead stood by its side, the clothes on which were all tumbled and tossed. There was a rush-seated chair with a hole in the seat,—and that, with the exception of one or two chipped pieces of stoneware, and a small round mirror which was hung on a nail against the wall, seemed to be all that the room contained. I could see nothing in the shape of a murdered man. Nor, it appeared, could the Inspector either.

"What's the meaning of this, Mrs. Henderson? I don't see anything here."

"It's be'ind the bed, Mr. Phillips. I left 'im just where I found 'im, I wouldn't 'ave touched 'im not for nothing, nor yet 'ave let nobody else

I 'ave touched 'im neither, because, as I say, I know 'ow particular you pleesmen is."

We all four went hastily forward. Atherton and I went to the head of the bed, Lessingham and the Inspector, leaning right across the bed, peeped over the side. There, on the floor in the space which was between the bed and the wall, lay the murdered man.

At the sight of him an exclamation burst from Sydney's lips.

"It's Holt!"

"Thank God!" cried Lessingham. "It isn't Marjorie!"

The relief in his tone was unmistakable. That the one was gone was plainly nothing to him in comparison with the fact that the other was left.

Thrusting the bed more into the centre of the room I knelt down beside the man on the floor. A more deplorable spectacle than he presented I have seldom witnessed. He was decently clad in a grey tweed suit, white hat, collar and necktie, and it was perhaps that fact which made his extreme attenuation the more conspicuous. I doubt if there was an ounce of flesh on the whole of his body. His cheeks and the sockets of his eyes were hollow. The skin was drawn tightly over his cheek bones,—the bones themselves were staring through. Even his nose was wasted, so that nothing but a ridge of cartilage remained. I put my arm beneath his shoulder and raised him from the floor; no resistance was offered by the body's gravity,—he was as light as a little child.

"I doubt," I said, "if this man has been murdered. It looks to me like a case of starvation, or exhaustion,—possibly a combination of both."

"What's that on his neck?" asked the Inspector,—he was kneeling at my side.

He referred to two abrasions of the skin,—one on either side of the man's neck.

"They look to me like scratches. They seem pretty deep, but I don't think they're sufficient in themselves to cause death."

"They might be, joined to an already weakened constitution. Is there anything in his pockets?—let's lift him on to the bed."

We lifted him on to the bed,—a featherweight he was to lift. While the Inspector was examining his pockets—to find them empty—a tall man with a big black beard came bustling in. He proved to be Dr. Glossop, the local police surgeon, who had been sent for before our quitting the Station House.

His first pronouncement, made as soon as he commenced his examination, was, under the circumstances, sufficiently startling.

"I don't believe the man's dead. Why didn't you send for me directly you found him?"

The question was put to Mrs. Henderson.

"Well, Dr. Glossop, I wouldn't touch 'im myself, and I wouldn't 'ave 'im touched by no one else, because, as I've said afore, I know 'ow particular them pleesmen is."

"Then in that case, if he does die you'll have had a hand in murdering him,—that's all."

The lady sniggered. "Of course Dr. Glossop, we all knows that you'll always 'ave your joke."

"You'll find it a joke if you have to hang, as you ought to, you—"

The doctor said what he did say to himself, under his breath. I doubt if it was flattering to Mrs. Henderson. "Have you got any brandy in the house?"

"We've got everythink in the 'ouse for them as likes to pay for it,— everythink." Then, suddenly remembering that the police were present, and that hers were not exactly licensed premises, "Leastways we can send out for it for them parties as gives us the money, being, as is well known, always willing to oblige."

"Then send for some,—to the tap downstairs, if that's the nearest. If this man dies before you've brought it I'll have you locked up as sure as you're a living woman."

The arrival of the brandy was not long delayed,—but the man on the bed had regained consciousness before it came. Opening his eyes he looked up at the doctor bending over him.

"Hollo, my man! that's more like the time of day! How are you feeling?"

The patient stared hazily up at the doctor, as if his sense of perception was not yet completely restored,—as if this big bearded man was something altogether strange. Atherton bent down beside the doctor.

"I'm glad to see you looking better, Mr. Holt. You know me don't you? I've been running about after you all day long."

"You are—you are—." The man's eyes closed, as if the effort at recollection exhausted him. He kept them closed as he continued to speak.

"I know who you are. You are—the gentleman."

"Yes, that's it, I'm the gentleman,—name of Atherton.—Miss Lindon's friend. And I daresay you're feeling pretty well done up, and in want of something to eat and drink,—here's some brandy for you."

The doctor had some in a tumbler. He raised the patient's head, allowing it to trickle down his throat. The man swallowed it mechanically, motionless, as if unconscious what it was that he was doing. His cheeks flushed, the passing glow of colour caused their condition of extraordinary, and, indeed, extravagant attenuation, to be more prominent than ever. The doctor laid him back upon the bed, feeling his pulse with one hand, while he stood and regarded him in silence.

Then, turning to the Inspector, he said to him in an undertone: you want him to make a statement he'll have to make it now, he's going fast. You won't be able to get much out of him,—he's too far gone, and I shouldn't bustle him, but get what you can."

The Inspector came to the front, a notebook in his hand.

"I understand from this gentleman—" signifying Atherton—"that your name's Robert Holt. I'm an Inspector of police, and I want you to tell me what has brought you into this condition. Has anyone been assaulting you?"

Holt, opening his eyes, glanced up at the speaker mistily, as if he could not see him clearly,—still less understand what it was that he was saying. Sydney, stooping over him, endeavoured to explain.

"The Inspector wants to know how you got here, has anyone been doing anything to you? Has anyone been hurting you?"

The man's eyelids were partially closed. Then they opened wider and wider. His mouth opened too. On his skeleton features there came a look of panic fear. He was evidently struggling to speak. At last words came.

"The beetle!" He stopped. Then, after an effort, spoke again. "The beetle!"

"What's he mean?" asked the Inspector.

"I think I understand," Sydney answered; then turning again to the man in the bed. "Yes, I hear what you say,—the beetle. Well, has the beetle done anything to you?"

"It took me by the throat!"

"Is that the meaning of the marks upon your neck?"

"The beetle killed me."

The lids closed. The man relapsed into a state of lethargy. The Inspector was puzzled;—and said so.

"What's he mean about a beetle?"

Atherton replied.

"I think I understand what he means,—and my friends do too. We'll explain afterwards. In the meantime I think I'd better get as much out of him as I can,—while there's time."

"Yes," said the doctor, his hand upon the patient's pulse, "while there's time. There isn't much—only seconds."

Sydney endeavoured to rouse the man from his stupor.

"You've been with Miss Lindon all the afternoon and evening, haven't you, Mr. Holt?"

Atherton had reached a chord in the man's consciousness. His lips moved,—in painful articulation.

"Yes—all the afternoon—and evening—God help me!"

"I hope God will help you my poor fellow; you've been in need of His help if ever man was. Miss Lindon is disguised in your old clothes, isn't she?"

"Yes,—in my old clothes. My God!"

"And where is Miss Lindon now?"

The man had been speaking with his eyes closed. Now he opened them, wide; there came into them the former staring horror. He became possessed by uncontrollable agitation,—half raising himself in bed. Words came from his quivering lips as if they were only drawn from him by the force of his anguish.

"The beetle's going to kill Miss Lindon."

A momentary paroxysm seemed to shake the very foundations of his being. His whole frame quivered. He fell back on to the bed,—ominously. The doctor examined him in silence—while we too were still.

"This time he's gone for good, there'll be no conjuring him back again."

I felt a sudden pressure on my arm, and found that Lessingham was clutching me with probably unconscious violence. The muscles of his face were twitching. He trembled. I turned to the doctor.

"Doctor, if there is any of that brandy left will you let me have it for my friend?"

Lessingham disposed of the remainder of the "shillingsworth." I rather fancy it saved us from a scene.

The Inspector was speaking to the woman of the house.

"Now, Mrs. Henderson, perhaps you'll tell us what all this means. Who is this man, and how did he come in here, and who came in with him, and what do you know about it altogether? If you've got anything to say, say it, only you'd better be careful, because it's my duty to warn you that anything you do say may be used against you."

CHAPTER 45

ALL THAT MRS. 'ENDERSON KNEW

Mrs. Henderson put her hands under her apron and smirked.

"Well, Mr. Phillips, it do sound strange to 'ear you talkin' to me like that. Anybody'd think I'd done something as I didn't ought to 'a' done to 'ear you going on. As for what's 'appened, I'll tell you all I know with the greatest willingness on earth. And as for bein' careful, there ain't no call for you to tell me to be that, for that I always am, as by now you ought to know."

"Yes,—I do know. Is that all you have to say?"

"Rilly, Mr. Phillips, what a man you are for catching people up, you rilly are. O'course that ain't all I've got to say,—ain't I just a-comin' to it?"

"Then come."

"If you presses me so you'll muddle of me up, and then if I do 'appen to make a herror, you'll say I'm a liar, when goodness knows there ain't no more truthful woman not in Limehouse."

Words plainly trembled on the Inspector's lips,—which he refrained from uttering. Mrs. Henderson cast her eyes upwards, as if she sought for inspiration from the filthy ceiling.

"So far as I can swear it might 'ave been a hour ago, or it might 'ave been a hour and a quarter, or it might 'ave been a hour and twenty minutes—"

"We're not particular as to the seconds."

"When I 'ears a knockin' at my front door, and when I comes to open it, there was a Harab party, with a great bundle on 'is 'ead, bigger nor 'isself, and two other parties along with him. This Harab party says, in that queer foreign way them Harab parties 'as of talkin', 'A room for the night, a room.' Now I don't much care for foreigners, and never did, especially them Harabs, which their 'abits ain't my own,—so I as much 'ints the same. But this 'ere Harab party, he didn't seem to quite foller of my meaning, for all he done was to say as he said afore, 'A room for the night, a room.' And he shoves a couple of 'arf crowns[1] into my 'and. Now it's always been a motter o' mine, that money is money, and one

---

[1] A half-crown was one of the coins in the duodecimal monetary system. The half-crown was a coin worth two shillings and sixpence, and therefore was 1/8th of a pound.

man's money is as good as another man's. So, not wishing to be disagreeable—which other people would have taken 'em if I and't, I shows 'em up 'ere. I'd been downstairs it might 'ave been 'arf a hour, when I 'ears a shindy a-coming from this room."

"What sort of a shindy?"

"Yelling and shrieking—oh my gracious, it was enough to set your blood all curdled,—for ear-piercingness I never did 'ear nothing like it. We do 'ave troublesome parties in 'ere, like they do elsewhere, but I never did 'ear nothing like that before. I stood it for about a minute, but it kep' on, and kep' on, and every moment I expected as the other parties as was in the 'ouse would be complainin', so up I comes and I thumps at the door, and it seemed that thump I might for all the notice that was took of me."

"Did the noise keep on?"

"Keep on! I should think it did keep on! Lord love you! shriek after shriek, I expected to see the roof took off."

"Were there any other noises? For instance, were there any sounds of struggling, or of blows?"

"There weren't no sounds except of the party hollering."

"One party only?"

"One party only. As I says afore, shriek after shriek,—when you put your ear to the panel there was a noise like some other party blubbering, but that weren't nothing, as for the hollering you wouldn't have thought that nothing what you might call 'umin could 'ave kep' up such a screechin'. I thumps and thumps and at last when I did think that I should 'ave to 'ave the door broke down, the Harab says to me from inside, 'Go away! I pay for the room! go away!' I did think that pretty good, I tell you that. So I says, 'Pay for the room or not pay for the room, you didn't pay to make that shindy!' And what's more I says, 'If I 'ear it again,' I says, 'out you goes! And if you don't go quiet I'll 'ave somebody in as'll pretty quickly make you!'"

"Then was there silence?"

"So to speak there was,—only there was this sound as if some party was a-blubbering, and another sound as if a party was a-panting for his breath."

"Then what happened?"

"Seeing that, so to speak, all was quiet, down I went again. And in another quarter of a hour, or it might 'ave been twenty minutes, I went to the front door to get a mouthful of hair. And Mrs. Barker, what lives over the road, at No. 24, she comes to me and says, 'That there Arab party of yours didn't stop long.' I looks at 'er, 'I don't quite foller you.' I says,—which I didn't. 'I saw him come in,' she says, 'and then, a few minutes back, I see 'im go again, with a great bundle on 'is 'ead he couldn't 'ardly stagger under!' 'Oh,' I says, 'that's news to me, I didn't know 'e'd gone, nor see him neither—' which I didn't. So, up I comes again, and, sure enough, the door was open, and it seems to me that the room was empty, till I come upon this pore young man what was lying be'ind the bed."

There was a growl from the doctor.

"If you'd had any sense, and sent for me at once, he might have been alive at this moment."

"'Ow was I to know that, Dr. Glossop? I couldn't tell. My finding 'im there murdered was quite enough for me. So I runs downstairs, and I nips 'old of 'Gustus Barley, what was leaning against the wall, and I says to him, "Gustus Barley, run to the station as fast as you can and tell 'em that a man's been murdered,—that Harab's been and killed a bloke.' And that's all I know about it, and I couldn't tell you no more, Mr. Phillips, not if you was to keep on asking me questions not for hours and hours."

"Then you think it was this man"—with a motion towards the bed—"who was shrieking?"

"To tell you the truth. Mr. Phillips, about that I don't 'ardly know what to think. If you 'ad asked me I should 'ave said it was a woman. I ought to know a woman's holler when I 'ear it, if any one does, I've 'eard enough of 'em in my time, goodness knows. And I should 'ave said that only a woman could 'ave hollered like that and only 'er when she was raving mad. But there weren't no woman with him. There was only this man what's murdered, and the other man,—and as for the other man I will say this, that 'e 'adn't got twopennyworth of clothes to cover 'im. But, Mr. Phillips, howsomever that may be, that's the last Harab I'll 'ave under my roof, no matter what they pays, and you may mark my words I'll 'ave no more."

Mrs. Henderson, once more glancing upward, as if she imagined herself to have made some declaration of a religious nature, shook her head with much solemnity.

CHAPTER 46

THE SUDDEN STOPPING

As we were leaving the house a constable gave the Inspector a note. Having read it he passed it to me. It was from the local office.

> "Message received that an Arab with a big bundle on his head has been noticed loitering about the neighbourhood of St Pancras Station.[1] He seemed to be accompanied by a young man who had the appearance of a tramp. Young man seemed ill. They appeared to be waiting for a train, probably to the North. Shall I advise detention?"

I scribbled on the flyleaf of the note.

> "Have them detained. If they have gone by train have a special in readiness."

In a minute we were again in the cab I endeavoured to persuade Lessingham and Atherton to allow me to conduct the pursuit alone,—in vain. I had no fear of Atherton's succumbing, but I was afraid for Lessingham. What was more almost than the expectation of his collapse was the fact that his looks and manner, his whole bearing, so eloquent of the agony and agitation of his mind, was beginning to tell upon my nerves. A catastrophe of some sort I foresaw. Of the curtain's fall upon one tragedy we had just been witnesses. That there was worse—much worse, to follow I did not doubt. Optimistic anticipations were out of the question,—that the creature we were chasing would relinquish the prey uninjured, no one, after what we had seen and heard, could by any possibility suppose. Should a necessity suddenly arise for prompt and immediate action, that

---

[1] The St. Pancras Station and the Midland Grand Hotel, which abutts the station and serves in part as the entrance to the terminus, were designed by architect Gilbert George Scott in Gothic revival style, popular in the mid-Victorian period, and built between 1868 and 1877. Along with King's Cross Station, adjacent to St. Pancras, the station serves towns and cities such as Sheffield (mentioned here) in the North of England. St. Alban's, Bedford, and Luton, all mentioned in this chapter, are small towns to the North of London, the furthest being Luton, which is approximately 30 miles away.

Lessingham would prove a hindrance rather than a help I felt persuaded.

But since moments were precious, and Lessingham was not to be persuaded to allow the matter to proceed without him, all that remained was to make the best of his presence.

The great arch of St Pancras was in darkness. An occasional light seemed to make the darkness still more visible. The station seemed deserted. I thought, at first, that there was not a soul about the place, that our errand was in vain, that the only thing for us to do was to drive to the police station and to pursue our inquiries there. But as we turned towards the booking-office, our footsteps ringing out clearly through the silence and the night, a door opened, a light shone out from the room within, and a voice inquired:

"Who's that?"

"My name's Champnell. Has a message been received from me from the Limehouse Police Station?"

"Step this way."

We stepped that way,—into a snug enough office, of which one of the railway inspectors was apparently in charge. He was a big man, with a fair beard. He looked me up and down, as if doubtfully. Lessingham he recognised at once. He took off his cap to him.

"Mr. Lessingham, I believe?"

"I am Mr. Lessingham. Have you any news for me?"

I fancy, by his looks,—that the official was struck by the pallor of the speaker's face,—and by his tremulous voice.

"I am instructed to give certain information to a Mr. Augustus Champnell."

"I am Mr. Champnell. What's your information?"

"With reference to the Arab about whom you have been making inquiries. A foreigner, dressed like an Arab, with a great bundle on his head, took two single thirds for Hull by the midnight express."

"Was he alone?"

"It is believed that he was accompanied by a young man of very disreputable appearance. They were not together at the booking-office, but they had been seen together previously. A minute or so after the Arab had entered the train this young man got into the same compartment—they were in the front waggon."

"Why were they not detained?"

"We had no authority to detain them, nor any reason. Until your message was received a few minutes ago we at this station were not aware that inquiries were being made for them."

"You say he booked to Hull,—does the train run through to Hull?"

"No—it doesn't go to Hull at all. Part of it's the Liverpool and Manchester Express, and part of it's for Carlisle. It divides at Derby. The man you're looking for will change either at Sheffield or at Cudworth junction and go on to Hull by the first train in the morning. There's a local service."

I looked at my watch.

"You say the train left at midnight. It's now nearly five-and-twenty past. Where's it now?"

"Nearing St Albans, it's due there 12.35."

"Would there be time for a wire to reach St Albans?"

"Hardly,—and anyhow there'll only be enough railway officials about the place to receive and despatch the train. They'll be fully occupied with their ordinary duties. There won't be time to get the police there."

"You could wire to St Albans to inquire if they were still in the train?"

"That could be done,—certainly. I'll have it done at once if you like."

"Then where's the next stoppage?"

"Well, they're at Luton at 12.51. But that's another case of St Albans. You see there won't be much more than twenty minutes by the time you've got your wire off, and I don't expect there'll be many people awake at Luton. At these country places sometimes there's a policeman hanging about the station to see the express go through, but, on the other hand, very often there isn't, and if there isn't, probably at this time of night it'll take a good bit of time to get the police on the premises. I tell you what I should advise."

"What's that?"

"The train is due at Bedford at 1.29—send your wire there. There ought to be plenty of people about at Bedford, and anyhow there'll be time to get the police to the station."

"Very good. I instructed them to tell you to have a special ready,— have you got one?"

"There's an engine with steam up in the shed,—we'll have all ready for you in less than ten minutes. And I tell you what,—you'll have about fifty minutes before the train is due at Bedford. It's a fifty mile run. With luck you ought to get there pretty nearly as soon as the express does.—Shall I tell them to get ready?"

"At once."

While he issued directions through a telephone to what, I presume, was the engine shed, I drew up a couple of telegrams. Having completed his orders he turned to me.

"They're coming out of the siding now—they'll be ready in less than ten minutes. I'll see that the line's kept clear. Have you got those wires?"

"Here is one,—this is for Bedford."

It ran:

"Arrest the Arab who is in train due at 1.29. When leaving St Pancras he was in a third-class compartment in front waggon. He has a large bundle, which detain. He took two third singles for Hull. Also detain his companion, who is dressed like a tramp. This is a young lady whom the Arab has disguised and kidnapped while in a condition of hypnotic trance. Let her have medical assistance and be taken to a hotel. All expenses will be paid on the arrival of the undersigned who is following by special train. As the Arab will probably be very violent a sufficient force of police should be in waiting. "AUGUSTUS CHAMPNELL."

"And this is the other. It is probably too late to be of any use at St Albans,—but send it there, and also to Luton."

"Is Arab with companion in train which left St Pancras at 12.0? If so, do not let them get out till train reaches Bedford, where instructions are being wired for arrest."

The Inspector rapidly scanned them both.

"They ought to do your business, I should think. Come along with me—I'll have them sent at once, and we'll see if your train's ready."

The train was not ready,—nor was it ready within the prescribed ten minutes. There was some hitch, I fancy, about a saloon. Finally we had to be content with an ordinary old-fashioned first-class carriage. The delay, however, was not altogether time lost. Just as the engine with its solitary coach was approaching the platform someone came running up with an envelope in his hand.

"Telegram from St Albans."

I tore it open. It was brief and to the point.

"Arab with companion was in train when it left here. Am wiring Luton."

"That's all right. Now unless something wholly unforeseen takes place, we ought to have them."

That unforeseen!

I went forward with the Inspector and the guard of our train to exchange a few final words with the driver. The Inspector explained what instructions he had given.

"I've told the driver not to spare his coal but to take you into Bedford within five minutes after the arrival of the express. He says he thinks that he can do it."

The driver leaned over his engine, rubbing his hands with the usual oily rag. He was a short, wiry man with grey hair and a grizzled moustache, with about him that bearing of semi-humorous, frank-faced resolution which one notes about engine-drivers as a class.

"We ought to do it, the gradients are against us, but it's a clear night and there's no wind. The only thing that will stop us will be if there's any shunting on the road, or any luggage trains; of course, if we are blocked, we are blocked, but the Inspector says he'll clear the way for us."

"Yes," said the Inspector, "I'll clear the way. I've wired down the road already."

Atherton broke in.

"Driver, if you get us into Bedford within five minutes of the arrival of the mail there'll be a five-pound note to divide between your mate and you."

The driver grinned.

"We'll get you there in time, sir, if we have to go clear through the shunters. It isn't often we get a chance of a five-pound note for a run to Bedford, and we'll do our best to earn it."

The fireman waved his hand in the rear.

"That's right, sir!" he cried. "We'll have to trouble you for that five-pound note."

So soon as we were clear of the station it began to seem probable that, as the fireman put it, Atherton would be "troubled." Journeying in a train which consists of a single carriage attached to an engine which is flying at topmost speed is a very different business from being an occupant of an ordinary train which is travelling at ordinary express rates. I had discovered that for myself before. That night it was impressed on me more than ever. A tyro[1]—or even a nervous "season"[2]—might have been excused for expecting at every moment we were going to be derailed. It was hard to believe that the carriage had any springs,—

---

[1] A novice or beginner.
[2] Someone who is inexperienced in the ways of the world.

it rocked and swung, and jogged and jolted. Of smooth travelling had we none. Talking was out of the question;—and for that, I, personally, was grateful. Quite apart from the difficulty we experienced in keeping our seats—and when every moment our position was being altered and we were jerked backwards and forwards up and down, this way and that, that was a business which required care,—the noise was deafening. It was as though we were being pursued by a legion of shrieking, bellowing, raging demons.

"George!" shrieked Atherton, "he does mean to earn that fiver. I hope I'll be alive to pay it him!"

He was only at the other end of the carriage, but though I could see by the distortion of his visage that he was shouting at the top of his voice,—and he has a voice,—I only caught here and there a word or two of what he was saying. I had to make sense of the whole.

Lessingham's contortions were a study. Few of that large multitude of persons who are acquainted with him only by means of the portraits which have appeared in the illustrated papers, would then have recognised the rising statesman. Yet I believe that few things could have better fallen in with his mood than that wild travelling. He might have been almost shaken to pieces,—but the very severity of the shaking served to divert his thoughts from the one dread topic which threatened to absorb them to the exclusion of all else beside. Then there was the tonic influence of the element of risk. The pick-me-up effect of a spice of peril. Actual danger there quite probably was none; but there very really seemed to be. And one thing was absolutely certain, that if we did come to smash while going at that speed we should come to as everlasting smash as the heart of man could by any possibility desire. It is probable that the knowledge that this was so warmed the blood in Lessingham's veins. At any rate as—to use what in this case, was simply a form of speech—I sat and watched him, it seemed to me that he was getting a firmer hold of the strength which had all but escaped him, and that with every jog and jolt he was becoming more and more of a man.

On and on we went dashing, crashing, smashing, roaring, rumbling. Atherton, who had been endeavouring to peer through the window, strained his lungs again in the effort to make himself audible.

"Where the devil are we?"

Looking at my watch I screamed back at him.

"It's nearly one, so I suppose we're somewhere in the neighbourhood of Luton.—Hollo! What's the matter?"

That something was the matter seemed certain. There was a shrill whistle from the engine. In a second we were conscious—almost too conscious—of the application of the Westinghouse brake. Of all the jolting that was ever jolted! the mere reverberation of the carriage threatened to resolve our bodies into their component parts. Feeling what we felt then helped us to realise the retardatory force which that vacuum brake must be exerting,—it did not seem at all surprising that the train should have been brought to an almost instant standstill.

Simultaneously all three of us were on our feet. I let down my window and Atherton let down his,—he shouting out,

"I should think that Inspector's wire hasn't had its proper effect, looks as if we're blocked—or else we've stopped at Luton. It can't be Bedford."

It wasn't Bedford—so much seemed clear. Though at first from my window I could make out nothing. I was feeling more than a trifle dazed,—there was a singing in my ears,—the sudden darkness was impenetrable. Then I became conscious that the guard was opening the door of his compartment. He stood on the step for a moment, seeming to hesitate. Then, with a lamp in his hand, he descended on to the line.

"What's the matter?" I asked.

"Don't know, sir. Seems as if there was something on the road. What's up there?"

This was to the man on the engine. The fireman replied:

"Someone in front there's waving a red light like mad,—lucky I caught sight of him, we should have been clean on top of him in another moment. Looks as if there was something wrong. Here he comes."

As my eyes grew more accustomed to the darkness I became aware that someone was making what haste he could along the six-foot way, swinging a red light as he came. Our guard advanced to meet him, shouting as he went:

"What's the matter! Who's that?"

A voice replied,

"My God! Is that George Hewett? I thought you were coming right on top of us!"

Our guard again.

"What! Jim Branson! What the devil are you doing here, what's wrong? I thought you were on the twelve out, we're chasing you."

"Are you? Then you've caught us. Thank God for it!—We're a wreck."

I had already opened the carriage door. With that we all three clambered out on to the line.

CHAPTER 47

THE CONTENTS OF THE
THIRD-CLASS CARRIAGE

I moved to the stranger who was holding the lamp. He was in official uniform.

"Are you the guard of the 12.0 out from St Pancras?"

"I am."

"Where's your train? What's happened?"

"As for where it is, there it is, right in front of you, what's left of it. As to what's happened, why, we're wrecked."

"What do you mean by you're wrecked?"

"Some heavy loaded trucks broke loose from a goods in front and came running down the hill on top of us."

"How long ago was it?"

"Not ten minutes. I was just starting off down the road to the signal box, it's a good two miles away, when I saw you coming. My God! I thought there was going to be another smash."

"Much damage done?"

"Seems to me as if we're all smashed up. As far as I can make out they're matchboxed up in front. I feel as if I was all broken up inside of me. I've been in the service going on for thirty years, and this is the first accident I've been in."

It was too dark to see the man's face, but judging from his tone he was either crying or very near to it.

Our guard turned and shouted back to our engine,

"You'd better go back to the box and let 'em know!"

"All right!" came echoing back.

The special immediately commenced retreating, whistling continually as it went. All the countryside must have heard the engine shrieking, and all who did hear must have understood that on the line something was seriously wrong.

The smashed train was all in darkness, the force of the collision had put out all the carriage lamps. Here was a flickering candle, there the glimmer of a match, these were all the lights which shone upon the scene. People were piling up debris by the side of the line, for the purpose of making a fire,—more for illumination than for warmth.

Many of the passengers had succeeded in freeing themselves, and were moving hither and thither about the line. But the majority appeared to be still imprisoned. The carriage doors were jammed. Without the necessary tools it was impossible to open them. Every step we took our ears were saluted by piteous cries. Men, women, children, appealed to us for help.

"Open the door, sir!" "In the name of God, sir, open the door!"

Over and over again, in all sorts of tones, with all degrees of violence, the supplication was repeated.

The guards vainly endeavoured to appease the, in many cases, half-frenzied creatures.

"All right, sir! If you'll only wait a minute or two, madam! We can't get the doors open without tools, a special train's just started off to get them. If you'll only have patience there'll be plenty of help for every-one of you directly. You'll be quite safe in there, if you'll only keep still."

But that was just what they found it most difficult to do—keep still!

In the front of the train all was chaos. The trucks which had done the mischief—there were afterwards shown to be six of them, together with two guards' vans—appeared to have been laden with bags of Portland cement. The bags had burst, and everything was covered with what seemed gritty dust. The air was full of the stuff, it got into our eyes, half blinding us. The engine of the express had turned a complete somersault. It vomited forth smoke, and steam, and flames,—every moment it seemed as if the woodwork of the carriages immediately behind and beneath would catch fire.

The front coaches were, as the guard had put it, "matchboxed." They were nothing but a heap of débris,—telescoped into one another in a state of apparently inextricable confusion. It was broad daylight before access was gained to what had once been the interiors. The condition of the first third-class compartment revealed an extraordinary state of things.

Scattered all over it were pieces of what looked like partially burnt rags, and fragments of silk and linen. I have those fragments now. Experts have assured me that they are actually neither silk nor linen! but of some material—animal rather than vegetable—with which they are wholly unacquainted. On the cushions and woodwork—especially on the woodwork of the floor—were huge blotches,—stains of some sort. When first noticed they were damp, and gave out a most unpleas-ant smell. One of the pieces of woodwork is yet in my possession,—with the stain still on it. Experts have pronounced upon it too,—with the result that opinions are divided. Some maintain that the stain was produced by human blood, which had been subjected to a great heat, and, so to speak, parboiled. Others declare that it is the blood of some wild animal,—possibly of some creature of the cat species. Yet others affirm that it is not blood at all, but merely paint. While a fourth describes it as—I quote the written opinion which lies in front of me— "caused apparently by a deposit of some sort of viscid matter, probably the excretion of some variety of lizard."

In a corner of the carriage was the body of what seemed a young man costumed like a tramp. It was Marjorie Lindon. *] fall from grace*

So far as a most careful search revealed, that was all the compartment contained.

CHAPTER 48

THE CONCLUSION OF THE MATTER

It is several years since I bore my part in the events which I have rapidly sketched,—or I should not have felt justified in giving them publicity. Exactly how many years, for reasons which should be sufficiently obvious, I must decline to say.

Marjorie Lindon still lives. The spark of life which was left in her, when she was extricated from among the débris of the wrecked express, was fanned again into flame. Her restoration was, however, not merely an affair of weeks or months, it was a matter of years. I believe that, even after her physical powers were completely restored—in itself a tedious task—she was for something like three years under medical supervision as a lunatic. But all that skill and money could do was done, and in course of time—the great healer—the results were entirely satisfactory.

Her father is dead,—and has left her in possession of the family estates. She is married to the individual who, in these pages, has been known as Paul Lessingham. Were his real name divulged she would be recognised as the popular and universally reverenced wife of one of the greatest statesmen the age has seen.

Nothing has been said to her about the fateful day on which she was—consciously or unconsciously—paraded through London in the tattered masculine habiliments of a vagabond. She herself has never once alluded to it. With the return of reason the affair seems to have passed from her memory as wholly as if it had never been, which, although she may not know it, is not the least cause she has for thankfulness. Therefore what actually transpired will never, in all human probability, be certainly known and particularly what precisely occurred in the railway carriage during that dreadful moment of sudden passing from life unto death. What became of the creature who all but did her to death; who he was—if it was a "he," which is extremely doubtful; whence he came; whither he went; what was the purport of his presence here,—to this hour these things are puzzles.

Paul Lessingham has not since been troubled by his old tormentor. He has ceased to be a haunted man. None the less he continues to have what seems to be a constitutional disrelish for the subject of beetles, nor can he himself be induced to speak of them. Should they be mentioned in a general conversation, should he be unable to immediately bring about a change of theme, he will, if possible, get up and leave the room. More, on this point he and his wife are one.

The fact may not be generally known, but it is so. Also I have reason to believe that there still are moments in which he harks back, with something like physical shrinking, to that awful nightmare of the past, and in which he prays God, that as it is distant from him now so may it be kept far off from him for ever.

Before closing, one matter may be casually mentioned. The tale has never been told, but I have unimpeachable authority for its authenticity.

During the recent expeditionary advance towards Dongola,[1] a body of native troops which was encamped at a remote spot in the desert was aroused one night by what seemed to be the sound of a loud explosion. The next morning, at a distance of about a couple of miles from the camp, a huge hole was discovered in the ground,—as if blasting operations, on an enormous scale, had recently been carried on. In the hole itself, and round about it, were found fragments of what seemed bodies; credible witnesses have assured me that they were bodies neither of men nor women, but of creatures of some monstrous growth. I prefer to believe, since no scientific examination of the remains took place, that these witnesses ignorantly, though innocently, erred.

One thing is sure. Numerous pieces, both of stone and of metal, were seen, which went far to suggest that some curious subterranean building had been blown up by the force of the explosion. Especially were

---

[1]   Town on the western bank of the Sudanese Nile. Like Wady Halfa, one of the towns involved in the British fight with the Mahdi's Sudanese troops.

there portions of moulded metal which seemed to belong to what must have been an immense bronze statue. There were picked up also, more than a dozen replicas in bronze of the whilom sacred scarabaeus.

That the den of demons described by Paul Lessingham, had, that night, at last come to an end, and that these things which lay scattered, here and there, on that treeless plain, were the evidences of its final destruction, is not a hypothesis which I should care to advance with any degree of certainty. But, putting this and that together, the facts seem to point that way,—and it is a consummation devoutly to be desired.

By-the-bye, Sydney Atherton has married Miss Dora Grayling. Her wealth has made him one of the richest men in England. She began, the story goes, by loving him immensely; I can answer for the fact that he has ended by loving her as much. Their devotion to each other contradicts the pessimistic nonsense which supposes that every marriage must be of necessity a failure. He continues his career of an inventor. His investigations into the subject of aerial flight, which have brought the flying machine within the range of practical politics, are on everybody's tongue.

The best man at Atherton's wedding was Percy Woodville, now the Earl of Barnes. Within six months afterwards he married one of Mrs. Atherton's bridesmaids.

It was never certainly shown how Robert Holt came to his end. At the inquest the coroner's jury was content to return a verdict of "Died of exhaustion." He lies buried in Kensal Green Cemetery;[1] under a handsome tombstone, the cost of which, had he had it in his pockets, might have indefinitely prolonged his days.

It should be mentioned that that portion of this strange history which purports to be The Surprising Narration of Robert Holt was compiled from the statements which Holt made to Atherton, and to Miss Lindon, as she then was, when, a mud-stained, shattered derelict he lay at the lady's father's house.

Miss Lindon's contribution towards the elucidation of the mystery was written with her own hand. After her physical strength had come back to her, and, while mentally, she still hovered between the darkness and the light, her one relaxation was writing. Although she would never speak of what she had written, it was found that her theme was always

---

[1] One of seven major Victorian cemeteries in London, the most famous being Highgate, the burial ground of, amongst others, Karl Marx, George Eliot, and Charles Dickens. Wilkie Collins is buried at Kensal Green.

the same. She confided to pen and paper what she would not speak of with her lips. She told, and re-told, and re-told again, the story of her love, and of her tribulation so far as it is contained in the present volume. Her MSS. invariably began and ended at the same point. They have all of them been destroyed, with one exception. That exception is herein placed before the reader.

On the subject of the Mystery of the Beetle I do not propose to pronounce a confident opinion. Atherton and I have talked it over many and many a time, and at the end we have got no "forrarder." So far as I am personally concerned, experience has taught me that there are indeed more things in heaven and earth than are dreamed of in our philosophy,[1] and I am quite prepared to believe that the so-called Beetle, which others saw, but I never, was—or is, for it cannot be certainly shown that the Thing is not still existing—a creature born neither of God nor man.

· psychological horror that will always exist

- compare w/ end of The Master & Margarita

---

[1] "There are more things in heaven and earth, Horatio, / Than are dreamt of in our philosophy." *Hamlet* (I.v. 168–69).

Appendix A: London in the fin de siècle

[London is its own singular, often monstrous, character in the fiction of the
last two decades of the nineteenth century, and, as the opening chapters and
final book of *The Beetle* demonstrate, Marsh is all too aware of the modes
of urban representation then prevalent in which he is situating his own
novel. The following extracts from various novels, many of which have
enjoyed better fortunes than *The Beetle* throughout the twentieth century,
are intended to suggest the extent to which Marsh's novel belongs to, and
is very much a manifestation of, *fin de siècle* urban anxiety. There is, without
doubt, a language or discourse of the city at the end of the century which
grips the literary imagination, and of which Marsh partakes readily.]

1. From Walter Besant, *All Sorts and Conditions of Men*, introd. Helen Small (1882; Oxford: OUP, 1997) 28–29

The situation of this boarding-house, poetically described ... as in the midst
of the gaiety of London, was in the East, in that region of London which
is less known to Englishmen than if it were situated in the wildest parts of
Colorado, or among the pine forests of British Columbia....

Two millions of people, or thereabouts, live in the East End of London.
That seems a good size population for an utterly unknown town. They have
no institutions of their own to speak of, no public buildings of any importance, no municipality, no gentry, no carriages, no soldiers, no picture-
galleries, no theatres, no opera—they have nothing. It is the fashion to
believe that they are all paupers, which is a foolish and mischievous
belief.... Probably there is no such spectacle in the whole world as that of
this immense, neglected, forgotten great city of East London. It is even
neglected by its own citizens, who have never yet perceived their abandoned condition. They are Londoners, it is true, but they have no part or
share of London; its wealth, its splendours, its honours exist not for them.
They see nothing of any splendours ... the city lies between them and the
greatness of England. They are beyond the wards, and cannot become alder-
men; the rich London merchants go north and south and west; but they
do not go east. Nobody goes east, no one wants to see the place; no one is
curious about the way of life in the east. Books on London pass it over; it
has little or no history; great men are not buried in its churchyards, which
are not even ancient, and crowded by citizens as obscure as those who now
breathe the upper airs about them. If anything happens in the east, people

at the other end have to stop and think before they can remember where the place may be. (Chapter 1)

2. From Robert Louis Stevenson, *The Strange Case of Dr Jekyll and Mr Hyde* (1886), in *The Strange Case of Dr. Jekyll and Mr. Hyde and Other Strange Tales of Terror*, ed. Robert Mighall (London: Penguin, 2002) 2–70, 6, 23

It chanced on one of these rambles that their way led them down a bystreet in a busy quarter of London. The street was small and what is called quiet, but it drove a thriving trade on the weekdays....

Two doors from one corner, on the left hand going east, the line was broken by the entry of a court; and just at that point, a certain sinister block of building thrust forward its gable on the street. It was two storeys high; showed no window, nothing but a door on the lower storey and a blind forehead of discoloured wall on the upper; and bore in every feature, the marks of prolonged and sordid negligence, blistered and distained. ("Story of the Door")

It was by this time about nine in the morning, and the first fog of the season. A great chocolate-coloured pall lowered over heaven, but the wind was continually charging and routing these embattled vapours; so that as the cab crawled from street to street, Mr Utterson beheld a marvellous number of degrees and hues of twilight; for here it would be dark like the back-end of evening; and there would be a glow of a rich, lurid brown, like the light of some strange conflagration; and here, for a moment, the fog would be quite broken up, and a haggard shaft of daylight would glance in between the swirling wreaths. The dismal quarter of Soho[1] seen under these changing glimpses, with its muddy ways, and slatternly passengers, and its lamps, which had never been extinguished or had been kindled afresh to combat this mournful reinvasion of darkness, seemed, in the lawyer's eyes, like a district of some city in a nightmare....

As the cab drew up before the address indicated, the fog lifted a little and showed him a dingy street, a gin palace, a low French eating house, a shop for the retail of penny numbers and twopenny salads, many ragged children

---

[1]   Soho is a district in central London adjacent to Piccadilly and south of Oxford Street. During the late seventeenth century, Soho was the settling place of French immigrants fleeing religious persecution, but later became known principally as an area of criminality and the sex trade.

huddled in the doorways, and many women of many different nationalities passing out, key in hand, to have a morning glass; and the next moment the fog settled down again upon that part, as brown as umber, and cut him off from his blackguardly surroundings. ("The Carew Murder Case")

3. From Henry James, "London" (1888), in *London Stories and Other Writings*, ed. David Kynaston (Padstow: Tabb House, 1989) 241–70, 241, 244–45

There is a certain evening that I count as virtually a first impression—the end of a wet, black Sunday, twenty years ago, about the first of March. There had been an earlier vision, but it had turned to grey, like faded ink, and the occasion I speak of was a fresh beginning. No doubt I had mystic prescience of how fond of the murky modern Babylon I was one day to become....
[...]
   A day or two later, in the afternoon, I found myself staring at my fire, in a lodging of which I had taken possession on foreseeing that I should spend some weeks in London. I had just come in, and, having attended to the distribution of my luggage, sat down to consider my habituation. It was on the ground floor, and the fading daylight reached it in a sadly damaged condition. It struck me as stuffy and unsocial, with its mouldy smell and its decoration of lithographs and wax-flowers—an impersonal black hole in the huge general blackness. The uproar of Piccadilly hummed away at the end of the street, and the rattle of a heartless hansom passed close to my ears. A sudden horror of the whole place came over me, like a tiger-pounce of homesickness which had been watching its moment. London was hideous, vicious, cruel, and above all overwhelming; whether or no she was 'careful of the type', she was as indifferent as Nature herself to the single life.... It appeared to me that I would rather remain dinnerless, would rather even starve, than sally forth into the infernal town, where the natural fate of an obscure stranger would be trampled to death in Piccadilly and have his carcass thrown into the Thames. I did not starve, however, and I eventually attached myself by a hundred human links to the dreadful, delightful city....
   It is, no doubt, not the taste of every one, but for the real London-lover the mere immensity of the place is a large part of its savour. A small London would be an abomination, as it fortunately is an impossibility, for the idea and the name are beyond everything an expression of extent and number.

4. From Arthur Conan Doyle, *The Sign of Four*, introd. Peter Ackroyd (1890; London: Penguin, 2001) 21

It was a September evening and not yet seven o'clock, but the day had been a dreary one, and a dense drizzly fog lay low upon the great city. Mud-coloured clouds drooped sadly over the muddy streets. Down the Strand the lamps were but misty splotches of diffused light which threw a feeble circular glimmer upon the slimy pavement. The yellow glare from the shop-windows streamed out into the steamy, vaporous air and threw a murky, shifting radiance across the crowded thoroughfare. There was ... something eerie and ghostlike in the endless procession of faces which flitted across these narrow bars of light—sad faces and glad, haggard and merry. Like all humankind, they flitted from the gloom into the light and so back into the gloom once more....

At the Lyceum Theatre the crowds were already thick at the side-entrances. In front a continuous stream of hansoms[1] and four-wheelers were rattling up, discharging their cargoes of shirt-fronted men and beshawled, be-diamonded women.

[...]

We had ... reached a questionable and forbidding neighbourhood. Long lines of dull brick houses were only relieved by the coarse glare and tawdry brilliancy of public-houses at the corner. Then came rows of two-storeyed villas, each with a fronting of miniature garden, and then again interminable lines of new, staring brick buildings—the monster tentacles which the giant city was throwing out into the country. At last the cab drew up at the third house in a new terrace. None of the other houses was inhabited, and that at which we stopped was as dark as its neighbours, save for a single glimmer in the kitchen-window. On our knocking, however, the door was instantly thrown open by a Hindoo servant, clad in a yellow turban, white loose-fitting clothes, and a yellow sash. There was something strangely incongruous in this Oriental figure framed in the commonplace door-way of a third-rate suburban dwelling-house. (Chapter 3)

---

[1]   Popular form of public cab throughout the nineteenth century, patented by Joseph Hansom in 1834, and undergoing several design changes in the century, the cab's distinguishing feature is that the driver stands behind the cab.

5. From Oscar Wilde, *The Picture of Dorian Gray*, ed. Peter Ackroyd (1891; London: Penguin, 1988) 73

"As I lounged in the Park or strolled down Piccadilly, I used to look at every one who passed me, and wonder, with a mad curiosity, what sort of lives they led. Some of them fascinated me. Others filled me with terror. There was an exquisite poison in the air. I had a passion for sensations.... Well, one evening about seven o'clock, I determined to go out in search of some adventure. I felt that this grey, monstrous London of ours, with its myriads of people, its sordid sinners, and its splendid sins, as you once phrased it, must have something in store for me. I fancied a thousand things. The mere danger gave me a sense of delight.... I don't know what I expected, but I went out and wandered eastward, soon losing my way in a labyrinth of grimy streets and black, grassless squares. About half past eight I passed by an absurd little theatre, with great flaring gas-jets and gaudy play-bills. A hideous Jew, in the most amazing waistcoat I ever beheld in my life, was standing at the entrance smoking a vile cigar. He had greasy ringlets, and an enormous diamond glazed in the centre of a soiled shirt."

6. From Arthur Machen, *The Three Impostors*, ed. David Trotter (1895; London: J.M. Dent, 1995) 9, 10

The flushing twilight of a summer evening vied with the gas-lamps in the square, had fashioned a chiaroscuro that had in it something unearthly; and the children, racing to and fro upon the pavement, the lounging idlers by the public, and the casual passers-by rather flickered and hovered in the play of lights than stood out substantial things. By degrees in the houses opposite one window after another leapt out a square of light; now and again a figure would shape itself against a blind and vanish, and to all this semi-theatrical magic the runs and flourishes of brave Italian opera played a little distance off on a piano-organ seemed an appropriate accompaniment, while the deep-muttered bass of the traffic of Holborn[1] never ceased. [...]

I got into one of those quiet places to the north of Oxford Street as you go west, the genteel residential neighbourhood of stucco and prosperity. I turned east again without knowing it, and it was quite dark when I passed

---

[1] Holborn is an area of central London east of Tottenham Court Road and south of Bloomsbury, between the West End, the traditional area of theatres, shopping, and entertainment, and the City, where the Bank of England and St. Paul's Cathedral are located.

along a sombre little by-street, ill-lighted and empty. I did not know at the time in the least where I was, but I found out afterwards that it was not very far from Tottenham Court Road. I strolled idly along, enjoying the stillness; on one side there seemed to be the back premises of some great shop; tier after tier of dusty windows lifted up into the night, with gibbet-like contrivances for raising heavy goods, and below large doors, fast closed and bolted, all dark and desolate. Then there came a huge pantechnicon warehouse; and over the way a grim blank wall, as forbidding as the wall of a gaol, and then the headquarters of some volunteer regiment, and afterwards a passage leading to a court where wagons were standing to be hired; it was, one might almost say, a street devoid of inhabitants, and scarce a window showed the glimmer of light. I was wondering at the strange peace and dimness there, where it must be close to some roaring main artery of London life, when suddenly I heard the noise of dashing feet tearing along the pavement at full speed, and from a narrow passage, a mews or something of that kind, a man was discharged as from a catapult under my very nose, and rushed past me, flinging something as he ran.

7. From Arthur Morrison, *A Child of the Jago*, ed. Peter Miles (1896; London: J.M. Dent, 1996) 11–12

It was past the mid of a summer night in the Old Jago.[1] The narrow street was all the blacker for the lurid sky; for there was a fire in a farther part of Shoreditch, and the welkin was an infernal coppery glare. Below, the hot, heavy air lay, a rank oppression, on the contorted forms of those who made for sleep on the pavement: and in it, and through it all, there rose from the foul earth and the grimed walls a close, mingled stink—the odour of the Jago.

From where, off Shoreditch High Street, a narrow passage, set across with posts,[2] gave menacing entrance on one end of Old Jago Street, to where it ended north at Honey Lane—there the Jago, for one hundred years the blackest pit in London, lay and festered; and half way along Old Jago Street a narrow archway gave upon Jago Court, the blackest hole in all that pit.

A square of two hundred and fifty yards or less—that was all there was of the Jago. But in that Square the human population swarmed in thou-

---

[1]   Morrison invents the fictional area of the Jago but locates it in Shoreditch, a district in the East End of London. The various streets and areas with which Morrison draws comparison to the Jago in this extract are all known for their association with crime and poverty.
[2]   Posts were set across narrow alleyways to prohibit access to horses and carts.

sands. Old Jago Street, New Jago Street, Half Jago Street lay parallel, east and west: Jago Row at one end and Edge Lane at the other lay parallel also, stretching north and south: foul ways all. What was too vile for Kate Street, Seven Dials, and Ratcliff Highway in its worst day, what was too useless, incapable and corrupt—all that teemed in the Old Jago....

...the sky, flickering and brightening no longer, settled to a sullen flush. On the pavement some writhed wearily, longing for sleep; others, despairing of it, sat and lolled, and a few talked. They were not there for lack of shelter, but because in this weather repose was less unlikely in the street than within doors; and the lodgings of the few who nevertheless abode at home were marked here and there by the lights visible from the windows. For in this place none ever slept without a light, because of three sorts of vermin that light in some sort keeps at bay: vermin which added to existence here a terror not to be guessed by the unafflicted: who object to being told of it. For on them that lay writhen and gasping on the pavement; on them that sat among them; on them that rolled and blasphemed in the lighted rooms; on every moving creature in this, the Old Jago, day and night, sleeping and walking, the third plague of Egypt,[1] and more, lay unceasing.

---

[1]   In Exodus, the third plague is that of flies, fleas, and lice.

Appendix B: The New Woman

[The phrase "New Woman" came into popular use in the 1890's, even though the notion of new women had already been around for some time. What was new about new women was a strongly voiced desire for greater economic freedom and educational opportunities, and for a recognition politically and socially of women's equality with men. Both the subject of cultural fear and comic satire, the New Woman as idea, as fictional form, and as reality aroused strong emotions and opinions for and against greater emancipation and autonomy for women. The New Woman was opinionated, educated, well-read, liberal in her beliefs, physically active. Perhaps the greatest fear for the more conservative members of late-Victorian society, however, was that the New Woman was also sexually active. Novels such as Grant Allen's *The Woman Who Did* (1895) presented heroines who enter into relationships outside marriage, while Ménie Muriel Dowie's novel, *Gallia* (1895), presents its protagonist who embraces education and the rational life at the expense of emotional fulfilment, in the quest for modern self-fulfilment.]

1. From Ouida, "The New Woman," *North American Review* (May 1894) 610–19

It can scarcely be disputed, I think, that in the English language there are conspicuous at the present moment two words which designate two unmitigated bores: The Workingman and the Woman. The Workingman and the Woman, the New Woman, be it remembered, meet us at every page of literature written in the English tongue; and each is convinced that on its own especial W hangs the future of the world. Both he and she want to have their values artificially raised and rated, and a status given to them by favor in lieu of dessert. In an age in which persistent clamor is generally crowned by success they have both obtained considerable attention; is it offensive to say much more of it than either deserves? Your contributor avers that the Cow-Woman and the Scum-Woman, man understands; but that the New Woman is above him.

[...]

Woman, whether new or old, has immense fields of culture untilled, immense areas of influence wholly neglected. She does almost nothing with the resources she possesses, because her whole energy is concentrated on desiring and demanding those she has not. She can write and print anything she chooses; and she scarcely ever takes the pains to acquire correct grammar or elegance of style before wasting ink and paper. She can paint and model any subjects she chooses, but she imprisons herself in men's *ateliers*[1] to endeavor to steal their technique and their methods, and thus loses any originality she might possess. Her influence on children might be so great that through them she would practically rule the future of the world; but she delegates her influence to the vile school boards if she be poor, and if she be rich to governesses and tutors; nor does she in ninety-nine cases out of a hundred ever attempt to educate or control herself into fitness from the personal exercise of such influence.

[…]

The error of the New Woman (as of many an old one) lies in speaking of women as the victims of men, and entirely ignoring the frequency with which men are the victims of women. In nine cases out of ten the first to corrupt the youth is the woman. In nine cases out of ten also she becomes corrupt herself because she likes it.

[…]

The New Woman reminds me of an agriculturist who, discarding a fine farm of his own, and leaving it to nettles, stones, thistles, and wire-worms, should spend his whole time in demanding neighboring fields which are not his. The New Woman will not even look at the extent of ground indisputably her own, which she leaves unweeded and untilled.

2. From Sarah Grand, "The New Aspect of the Woman Question," *North American Review* (March 1894) 270–76

It is amusing as well as interesting to note the pause which the new aspect of the woman question has given to the Bawling Brothers[2] who have hitherto tried to howl down every attempt on the part of our sex to make the world a pleasanter place to live in. That woman should ape man and desire to change places with him was conceivable to him as he stood on the hearth-rug in his lord-and-master-monarch-of-all-I-survey attitude, well inflated with his own conceit; but that she should be content to develop the good material which she finds in herself and be only dissatisfied with the poor quality of that which his being offered to her in man, her mate, must appear to him to be a thing as monstrous as it is unaccountable. "If women don't want to be men, what do they want?" asked the Bawling

---

[1]   An artist's attic or loft; literally, "workshop" or "studio" (French).
[2]   A derogatory metaphor for those men who opposed the goals and ideals of the New Woman.

Brotherhood when the first misgiving of the truth flashed upon them; and then, to reassure themselves, they pointed to a certain sort of woman in proof of the contention that we were all unsexing ourselves.

It would be as rational for us now to declare that men generally are Bawling Brothers or to adopt the hasty conclusion which makes all men out to be fiends on the one hand, and all women fools on the other. We have our Shrieking Sisterhood, as the counterpart of the Bawling Brotherhood.... Both the cow-woman and the scum-woman are well within the range of the comprehension of the Bawling Brotherhood, but the new woman is a little above him, and he never even thought of looking up to where she has been sitting apart in silent contemplation all these years, thinking and thinking, until at last she solved the problem and proclaimed for herself what was wrong with Home-is-the-Woman's-Sphere, and prescribed the remedy.

What she perceived at the outset was the sudden and violent upheaval of the suffering sex in all parts of the world. Women were awaking from their long apathy, and, as they awoke, like healthy hungry children unable to articulate, they began to whimper for they knew not what. They might have been easily satisfied at that time had not society, like an ill-conditioned and ignorant nurse, instead of finding out what they lacked, shaken them and beaten them and stormed at them until what was once a little wail became convulsive shrieks and roused up the whole human household. [...]

Woman may be foolish, but her folly has never been greater than man's conceit, and the one is not more disastrous to the understanding than the other.... Of old if a woman ventured to be at all unconventional, man was allowed to slander her with the imputation that she must be abandoned, and he really believed it because with him liberty meant license. [...]

True womanliness is not in danger, and the sacred duties of wife and mother will be all the more honourably performed when women have a reasonable hope of becoming wives and mothers of *men*. But there is the difficulty. The trouble is not because women are mannish, but because men grow ever more effeminate. [...]

There are upwards of a hundred thousand women in London doomed to damnation by the written law of man if they dare to die, and to infamy for a livelihood if they must live; yet the man at the head of affairs wonders what it is that we with the power are protesting against in the name of our sex. But *is* there any wonder we women wail for the dearth of manliness when we find men from end to end of their rotten social system forever doing the most cowardly deed in their own code, striking at the defenceless woman, especially when she is down?

The Bawling Brotherhood have been seeing reflections of themselves lately which did not flatter them, but their conceit survives, and they cling confidently to the delusion that they are truly all that is admirable, and it is the mirror that is in fault. Mirrors may be either a distorting or a flattering medium, but women do not care to see life any longer in a glass darkly. Let there be light. We suffer in the first shock of it. We shriek in horror at what we discover when it is turned on that which was hidden away in dark corners; but the first principle of good housekeeping is to have no dark corners, and as we recover ourselves we got to work with a will to sweep them out. It is for us to set the human household in order to see to it that all is clean and sweet and comfortable for the men who are fit to help us to make home in it. We are bound to raise the dust while we are at work, but only those who are in it will suffer any inconvenience from it, and the self-sufficing and self-supporting are not afraid. For the rest it will be all benefits. The Woman Question is the Marriage Question... .

3. From Nat Arling, "What is the Rôle of the 'New Woman?'," *Westminster Review* (November 1898) 576–87

Letters on the subject of women's emancipation have lately been taking up the pages of the *Cambrian News*,[1] whose editor is strongly in sympathy with the movement that is bringing on itself the derision of the bigoted and the superficial, who cannot discern the signs of the times, and drawing to conversion that portion of humanity for whom the morality and progress of the race is the question of supreme importance. The new woman (as she is styled) takes the form which a concourse of atoms, intangible at present to many as colour or sound, must take—*i.e.* that of the personality through which she is viewed. According to the materialists, she is a presentment of simulated mannishness; to religionists of Pharisaical type,[2] a monstrosity to be condemned and defeated; to unthinking male youth, a creature who seeks to usurp their hitherto undisturbed royalty of arrogance and selfishness; to the frivolous of her own sex, as an absurdity to be laughed at in the company of the men they affect, who enjoy the society of women lacking self-respect, and with whom they can often take liberties, short only of

---

1   Newspaper, published in Aberystwyth, Wales.
2   Rigid observance of forms of religion without genuine belief.

those they reserve for the more lowly of condition. In the eyes of, alas! many well-meaning and virtuous of both sexes, she takes the form of an interloper into matters beyond and outside her stereotyped "sphere." Those who have an intimate acquaintance with the real new woman, have come into touch with their subject, see her under a very different aspect.

By them she is known as the woman who, with a strong sense of her own importance, usefulness, and responsibility, longs to strengthen the cause of right and justice, to make head against evil, to help the fallen, to raise her own sex to the highest level it can attain, and the other to a nobler ideal, which an age of money-making is hampering with low aims and luxurious tastes. She wishes to make marriage no longer an auction of sale to the highest bidder, or an exercise in tyranny on one side and subjection on the other, but a covenant of mutual help and service; and motherhood, not dreaded, despised, and a hindrance to self-fulfilment and rights of citizenship, but a state of recognition and honour. The desire of the new woman is to make lives of children more sanitary and joyous, more fit not only for the battle but the service of life, and the lives of all men and women purer, better, and more pleasureful. These are the aims of the new woman solidarised in the flesh, however short she may come in the carrying of them out.

[...]

In uncivilised nations still women are made beasts of burden; in countries under the sway of Christianity, and European, a beast of draught to take the place of or assist the dog; and in some primitive but prosperous highlands she attains a noble development and takes part in agriculture. Whatever gave the first impetus to the feebleness of women, it is quite certain that man by various means fostered it for his own benefit, and erected helplessness, timidity and dependence into feminine virtues, by which it should be maintained.

[...]

...though much rests with women, all does not; men are the force they have to reckon with, and at present it is too strong for them. The few opportunities already yielded, the few advantages allowed, are even now banding men against women and kindling their jealousy. They say women are "cheapening the market," though only by this cheapening have they been able to get a run of the ladder to stand upon. "Women are throwing men out of work"; it is idle to reply you have introduced machinery, which has turned women out of industries they have long maintained to the satisfaction of the public, earning thereby the respect and consideration which being of use to the community brings. It is vain to say that men in shops are doing what women could do, if the former would fill the ranks of the army and navy or return to the plough.

[...]

Believing that humanity is not two, but one, that no moral being has a right to oppress another or forbid its use of natural powers, we cannot go so far as to say we recognise no difference at all of sex, of condition, of position in the world we know, whatever may be the case in one whose circumstances are to us unthinkable, anyhow foreign to our present constitution, as is shown in the weakness of every Utopia formulated by men.

In the very classifying of these distinctions together, though it may at first seem we point a moral from the Catechism to women who wish to alter their standing, we in reality produce an argument on their side. No one thinks it impious to seek to rise from his own sphere into a higher one; condition and position are alterable at will—the one is retrievable, the other attainable, but the hardship of sex classification is that its condition is irretrievable, its higher position unattainable.

Women have been lumped together in one indistinguishable mass. In the midst of change woman must be inert, in the progressions of the State, a fixture, if not an unconsidered nonentity; and this, no matter how keen her interest and intelligence, how active her sympathy, how great her capacity, how wide her interests. Was ever a bondage equal to this bondage?...When we admit, as we do, a physical difference between men and women, we allow no inferiority of one to the other in the aggregate, and we believe the difference is needed for the improvement of the race, and because the side this difference initiates has not been properly represented in the State and the world, the consummation desired has been, and is, delayed.

[...]

The "new woman" has no desire to imitate the bad points of the other sex: she sees no shame in womanliness; but, unfortunately, neither men nor women exactly agree in their definitions of womanliness. Men, and the women who follow their lead, think it exists in timidity, self-depreciation and effacement, and deference to the views and opinions covered by a coat and trousers, and doubtless because of the last, they load with opprobrium and regard jealously the unfortunate individuals who seek safety and health in some scheme of rational dress which will suit active healthy human beings who have ceased to shun exercise and mud as did their grandmothers...

A womanly woman, to our thinking, should have courage; in fact, courage is an integral part of woman's condition; without it she could not face her life; she should have self-respect, humility—equally with men—deference to the opinions of those older or wiser, men or women, modesty in setting out her own, but independence enough to have them, and truth enough not to hide them.

[...]

Too long have women been lulled by songs of love, so called, to rest in a gilded cage, or where limited income takes the place of luxury, been the hewers of wood and drawers of water that men might be free to follow their leanings. Where would have been the men who... "have done and do all the important work of the world," but for the women who bore them, reared them, and in most cases of success, by men's own acknowledgement, laid its foundation-stone by the pains they bestowed on the cultivation of character? Where would have been the means found for men's education and opportunities if women had not been sacrificed, or laboured at distasteful occupations, that the men might learn, or be free to follow their bent?

[...]

The elevation of responsibility is what women need to check the impulsiveness that produces results grievous to the world at large, and the superficiality of ignorance that equally ends in disaster. Experience shows us that women will have power and exercise influence, and it were wiser that they used both more advisedly. They are the best women who take up professions and claim loudest the vote; they are not the women who lead aimless lives of selfish indulgence, exist to pose as leaders of fashion, neglect homes and children for the sake of amusement, bring disgrace on themselves and families or ruin on their husbands. They are not the fast women who copy men's failings, live for sport, or swagger about in imitation of the worst types of the male species. They form the real basis of the "new woman," ennobling their smallest duties with understanding, calling nothing small, indeed that can benefit in the slightest degree the individual or the race.

[...]

...[the] deprecation of woman is at the root of the greater evils of every State, and it is only by putting her in her right place as companion, friend, and helpmeet, not making her the toy or drudge of man, that the race can be exalted.

Pagans admitted her to the ranks of their gods, the Egyptian mythology, that of a highly civilised period, included her in a divine triad of father, mother, son. Heathen philosophers, not knowing how to raise her, suggested her being trained as men were, not to be even trammelled in her higher form by motherhood... Christians of later times, feeling the blank of the feminine in the aspect of God, have formed a reason for worshipping her as the mother of God, and seeking her merciful existence; Positivists make her a priestess of humanity; yet none of these accord women in general a place as man's equal, and this illogicality has resulted in the annulment of their good endeavours....

When women, untrammelled by unjust laws, with their intellects cultivated, their views enlarged by civic and political responsibility, are treated with respect *as women*, with their work, whatever it be, held in like esteem as that of men; when they are enfranchised, because either unmarried or as mothers, they, equally with men, support the State, or imperil their lives for its well-being, and because, though equally concerned in its prosperity, and affected by its laws, they hold views tinctured by their own woman's nature, which are valuable and necessary of consideration, as long as humanity is made up of male and female, then we shall hear no more of women wishing to be men, or holding marriage and motherhood, as they are accused of doing, in contempt or abhorrence.

4. From Kathleen Caffe, "A Reply from Daughters," *The Nineteenth Century* (March 1894) 438–42

[...]

Surely the modern damsel ought to be sufficiently mistress of her pen and her grammar to be able to break a lance in her own cause. It is a cruel fate that has caused us to be painted in glaring colours, and held up to ... ridicule and ... horror ... so will you allow me to put the subject before you as *we* look upon it?

When I say "we," I do not mean the highly educated, examination-passing, Girton girl, with her vast schemes for regenerating mankind, or ousting our lords and masters from the paths where women are at present not allowed to follow. Nor do I mean the happy few whose talents for music, drawing, or any other art open out to them vistas of endless occupation and happiness. I want to speak in the name of the average more or less unemployed, tea-drinking, lawn-tennis playing, ball-going damsel, whose desire for greater emancipation does not run in the same lines as those of the independent shop-girl, or of the young woman with a mission.

I should not like to assert that, were we given the free use of latchkeys and the entrée of music-halls, we should not avail ourselves of, and at the moment enjoy, these prerogatives keenly. But we do not adopt as our highest ideals these very frivolous and evanescent pleasures of the average hobbledehoy;[1] nor do we imagine that by so doing we should be most likely to gain that freedom and emancipation so many of us long for,

---

[1] Awkward or ungainly boy; an adolescent between boyhood and manhood.

though we do consider ourselves bound by many senseless prejudices, meaningless restrictions, and annoying trammels.... How many girls are not at this moment whose position in life is best described by the old simile of a round peg in a square hole?

[...]

Far be it from me to say that it is essential to every young woman's welfare or happiness that she should be pursuing some vague ideal— whether amusing or instructive—at the greatest possible distance from her home. I only think that there are many cases in which a girl might, at the expense merely of a few malicious words, and that only in the first instances, be allowed to do a lot of things which she is not permitted to do now, which would make all the difference in the world to her and could harm no one. At least in my eyes and those of my contemporary friends they do not appear capable of harming anyone, and we do think there is harm in the present system.

For example, it has always struck me that there is an increase in the number of unhappy marriages; and I cannot resist the conclusion that they arise often from girls plunging into matrimony simply and solely to escape from a home life whose restrictions they imagine less endurable than a loveless marriage of convenience. The novelty of the situation for a time makes things go smoothly, but the awakening comes all too surely, and two wrecked lives are the result.

Now we say that if a girl were, whilst at home, of course within reasonable bounds, permitted to follow the natural bent of her mind, she would not be impelled by her boredom and discontent into marrying the first person, whether congenial or not, who appeared on her limited horizon.

Set down in plain black and white, her requirements may appear very trifling.... What she wants, first of all, is the abolition of chaperons on all possible occasions. This at once results in a deadlock between the modern mother and her yet more modern daughter: ...she considers it hard that she cannot walk the length of two or three—even five or six—streets to visit a friend, without having first provided herself with an unhappy maid or attendant of some description, presumably to prevent her from losing her way or getting run over.... So it is in everything. No early morning stroll in the Park, or afternoon tea-party, may be undertaken without the same faithful domestic walking gloomily by her side, or waiting drearily for her in alien front halls.

A young married woman does not wear her wedding-ring in her nose or other prominent spot to assure the passer-by of her social status; and, owing to prevailing fashions, her clothes do little to distinguish her from her unwedded sister. Yet she can walk through the streets alone, and drive in hansoms alone. Why cannot the girl?

[...]

There is another point to mention: the question of friendship between men and girls, as distinguished from flirtation. It does indeed seem a mistaken system which prevents a man and a girl knowing anything in reality of each other's characters until they are engaged, when, unless they be people unusually indifferent to gossip and kindred annoyances, it is too late to make any alterations or repair mistaken impressions.

Inter-feminine conversation has never been famed for its depth of ideas or intellect: why may not the girls enjoy a little of the superior article from masculine lips without being suspected of ulterior designs in their hearts, if the men be poor, or on their fortunes, if they be rich? They never get a chance of finding out what a man thinks; and the married woman in the ball-room routs them with ignominy, simply because with her the unmarried man can chat at his ease, secure of not being angled for if he be rich, or warned off the premises if he be poor.

The so-called revolting maiden only asks for a small amount of liberty. The average girl, as Mr. Besant[1] might call her, does not want it for any of the weird and wild purposes set forth to the world of late. She does not want to read the books forbidden by her parents, or to see the plays they prefer she should not see. She only wishes to enjoy the minor pleasures and duties of life without the now inevitable bored and wearied chaperon. She does not want anything very startling or very important. And as things are now, if she wanted to be great, how could she? ...The refusal of parents and guardians to grant these desires, or even to sympathise with them, probably arises from the fact that in their young days—those times to modern minds so terribly dull and unenterprising—such sentiments were as unknown as the electric light. But they have admitted the practicability of the latter, and it is to be trusted that they may eventually acknowledge the advisability of the former.

---

[1] Walter Besant (1836-1901), novelist, historian, social reformer, and member of the Fabian Society.

Appendix C: English Interest and Involvement in Egypt

[English involvement in Egypt has a long and complex history, as I discuss in the Introduction. As the extracts below demonstrate, Egypt was a source of constant cultural fascination for the Victorians, whether through travel, research, or the opportunities afforded by that curious offshoot of Victorian colonialism and imperialism, the exhibition, of which there were many in London, and elsewhere, especially throughout the second half of the nineteenth century. The appeal of, and interest in, Egypt may perhaps have lain in the fact that Egypt, so different culturally from Northern Europe, nonetheless had a history and culture older than that of European countries; hence the fascination expressed in certain of the articles with what are called the occult sciences, with ancient Egyptian mythology and religion, with Egypt's architecture and rites, and forms of knowledge. At the same time, however, Egypt in the late Victorian period was, for a number of years, a source of anxiety as a result of rebellions and uprisings, also detailed in the Introduction.]

1. From Georgia Louise Leonard, "The Occult Sciences in the Temples of Ancient Egypt," *The Open Court*, 1 & 2 (1887): 470–72, 496–98

...Scientists, historians, archaeologists, even Egyptologists themselves, ignore all mention of the occult, or speak of it only with derision. To them, the idea of a religion, the highest aspect of which was essentially esoteric, presided over by priests who were not only the possessors of dead secrets, but the accredited workers of wonders, has in it something manifestly absurd.

Where then are we to look for the treasures of which we are in search? The avenues are not many where seeking leads to finding....

To unravel the *history* of the occult sciences of Egypt, is nearly as difficult as to *rediscover* the *sciences themselves*. True it is that dozens of old papyrus rolls have been brought forth from dark tombs to the light of day; true that all the monuments of her land were once a pictured glory—her history and her religion chiselled deep into every fragment of her mighty pylons or the massive columns of her vast sanctuaries. True again, that these writings have been translated to the world; but the task has been accomplished by those of alien race, of foreign tongue, and a hostile faith. Honest and patient, then, as these scholars may be, it is not singular they have failed to comprehend the full significance of ideas veiled in obscure or mystical language, and have stigmatized many a precious Egyptian scroll as childish and absurd. And yet—those who *will* may discover in them priceless germs of truth half hid 'midst the clumsy modern renderings of a speech long dead.…

Many historians, from the old Greek and Roman to the Arab writers of the Middle Ages, have discoursed of Egypt, her manners and customs, laws, religion, and sacred mysteries; while scores of exhaustive modern works treat of her ancient grandeur. The chief difficulty to be met in any search into her more secret history, lies in the fact that her vast learning was zealously guarded and revealed only to those who by long and faithful devotion and rigid purity of life had rendered themselves its fitting depositories; and upon the most binding assurances that it should never be divulged.
[…]

Upon the very threshold of their history—under Menes the first king[1]—we find them in full possession of the practical sciences of hydrostatics and hydraulic engineering and mechanical construction. Already had they turned the course of the Nile, and reared the city of Memphis with its gigantic temples and palace. We learn that even at this early day there were from thirty to forty colleges of priests who studied the occult sciences and practical magic.…

The cities of Memphis, Heliopolis, Thebes and later, Saïs, became the great centers of Egyptian learning. Their splendid temples formed the nuclei around which clustered schools, universities, observatories and priestly habitations.

There were many different orders of the priests, ranging from the simple scribe to the high-priest himself; but it was only those of the highest degree who were permitted to become the repositories of that occult lore which had come down from the remotest ages. In the silence and obscurity of the lowest crypts of the temples these priestly sages conducted their ceremonies and magical operations, and hither, doubtless, were brought the candidates for initiation into the greater mysteries.

Among the branches of learning pursued by them were mathematics, astronomy, astrology, metallurgy, chemistry and alchemy, all of which bore an occult aspect.
[…]

---

[1] Menes, King of Egypt, conquered Lower Egypt, c. 3100 BC, and united the country for the first time. He founded the city of Memphis as Egypt's first capital, which was located near the site of present-day Cairo.

The most *conservative* Egyptologists *admit* that this ancient people possessed a very *considerable* knowledge of both mathematics and astronomy.... Upon the ceiling of the beautiful temple of Denderah there is a representation of the zodiac. It is claimed that this is the work of the Ptolemaic period;[1] but an inscription found at Denderah distinctly states that the building has been restored in accordance with a plan discovered in the writings of the Khufu,[2] or Cheops, who belonged to the fourth dynasty....

In considering the amount of mathematical and astronomical knowledge possessed by the Egyptian priests, we must remember that they kept their cyclic notations in the profoundest mystery, as their calculations applied equally to the spiritual as to the physical progress of mankind.

The "Sacred Books" of the Egyptians were ascribed to Hermes Trismegistus,[3] and ante-dated Menes. They were 1,100 in number, we are told by Jamblicus,[4] and forty-two were still extant in the time of Clement of Alexandria.[5] They contained an epitome of the secret knowledge, and treated of many different subjects. The majority of those books are now lost to us, and of them we know only what has been preserved in the works of later writers. Diogenes Laërtius[6] makes a statement, probably derived from these lost books, that the Egyptians possessed records of 373 solar eclipses [sic.] and 832 lunar; and he carries back these observations to the period of 48,863 years before Alexander....

That portion of their calculations which was regarded as the most secret, undoubtedly related to the evolution of our planet, both physically and spiritually—such evolution proceeding in cycle, of greater and lesser duration. They taught that the close of the "great year" was attended by destructive cataclysms either of fire or water....

Astrology was pursued hand in hand with the higher mathematics and astronomy. Professor Proctor seeks to prove in his work on the great pyramid that the monument was reared not alone as a tomb for Khufu, but for

---

[1] Though disputed, it is generally agreed that Ptolemy (c.100-165 AD) made his significant astronomical observations in Alexandria, Egypt, in 150 AD.

[2] Khufu, King of Egypt, c. 2600 BC; his tomb is the Great Pyramid at Giza (Al-Jizah); also known as Cheops by the Greeks.

[3] Supposedly the originator of Hermetic thought and alchemy, Hermes Trismegistus is the name given to the Egyptian deity Thoth, who is regarded as being more or less synonymous with the Greek god Hermes; "Trismegistus" means "thrice great."

[4] Jamblicus, a Neoplatonist and biographer of Pythagoras, born in Syria, particularly versed in mystical numerology and principles of universal harmony central to Masonic thought.

[5] An early Greek Theologian, St. Clement is believed to have been born in Athens, and to have died c. 215 AD.

[6] Biographer of ancient Greek philosophers, Diogenes Laertius' dates are unknown.

astronomical and astrological purposes as well. Very likely this was so, but is it not possible that there were also *other* reasons? Why was it oriented with wonderful exactness? Why, of necessity, constructed in the pyramidal form, with its apex pointing toward heaven? What meant the long secret passages, and the seven impenetrable chambers, one succeeding another? And what purpose did the great sarcophagus serve…?

Mystery surrounds us upon every side as we seek to solve these problems of the past.

Astrology was believed in implicitly by the Egyptians, and they considered unquestioned the influence of the planets upon the destines both of individuals and the human race collectively…. The Egyptians took careful note of all singular or unusual occurrences, whether related to the heavenly bodies or to themselves, and observed omens connected with everything they undertook. They even watched the day when any one was born.

Perhaps in no branches of their science was their knowledge more conspicuously apparent than in those of chemistry or alchemy. It has been vigorously denied that they understood anything more than the rudiments of chemistry—and as for alchemy! The idea has been treated with derision. A few instances will show their superiority to modern achievements, and inference may be left to do the rest. In the perfect imitation of precious stones we have never even approached them. Many splendid imitations of emeralds, amethysts, and other gems of rich and varied hues, have been found in the tombs of Thebes…. It is useless to deny to these strange dwellers in the old temples, a skill and knowledge far beyond our own, and which we can only wonder at and imitate, not equal.

Magic in its highest sense was a part of the daily life of the Egyptian priests…. This magic was practiced by the priests in divers ways, some of which we can only guess at. They were seers, clairvoyants, diviners and dreamers of dreams. They understood and manipulated the subtlest properties of matter. No wonder they were not astonished at the exhibitions of Moses, who had learned all he knew in their own temples!

In their religious works, veiled as they are in symbolism, we discover the belief in an all-pervading, universal essence—call it the astral ether, or psychic force, or *od,* or *biogen,* or *akas,* or what you will—from which emanated all things, and which could be controlled and directed by those who were instructed and otherwise properly qualified. They believed in ghosts, and that the living under certain well-known conditions could communicate with the souls of the departed….

No one who impartially examines the mass of evidence derived from Egyptian and classic sources, can fail to be impressed with the belief that the Egyptian priests were perfectly familiar with all classes of psychic phenomena, characterized as modern, and that they were also in possession of secrets pertaining to the so-called exact sciences, as well as of the occult, of which we to-day have no knowledge or conception....

They were worshippers of one only God, whose very name was so sacred it was ... unlawful to utter; and their various divinities but personified some form of the divine attributes. Inter-blended and inter-dependent we find Egyptian science and religion. To understand one we cannot remain ignorant of the other. To the Egyptian his religion was everything. He regarded his abode upon earth as but a short journey upon the pathway of eternal life. To the future which stretched before him he turned with hope and longing. He did not believe that when his short life closed, physical existence was ended. Again and again, his religion taught, he would return to earth, to work out in higher forms his spiritual salvation. (This doctrine of re-incarnation, often called transmigration or metempsychosis, has been grossly misunderstood by writers who have attempted to explain it). With this belief was connected the doctrine of the "cycle of necessity." Can our Egyptologists say what this cycle was? or what it signified? and can they further tell what the winged scarabaei of Egypt symbolized? which are found by the hundreds in the tombs of Thebes! They cannot, I fear, tell us these things any more than they can explain the septenary composition of man or his triune character.... Egypt is dead. Her priests have passed away, and buried with them in the recesses of impenetrable tombs lie her wisdom, her magic, and her glory.

2. From J. Norman Lockyer, "The Astronomy and Mythology of the Ancient Egyptians," *The Nineteenth Century* (July 1892): 29–51

[...]
I know of no more striking proof of the wit of man than the gradual unravelling of the strange hieroglyphic signs in which the learning of the ancient Egyptians was enshrined, and there are few things more remarkable in the history of scientific investigation than the way in which a literature has been already brought together which is appalling in its extent; and yet it may well be that, vast as this present literature is at present, it is but the vanguard of a much more stupendous one to follow; for we are dealing with a nation which we now know existed completely equipped in many ways at least six or seven thousand years ago.

Let us, to approach the subject-matter of the present article, go back to the year 1820.... From my point of view it may be said that the new discoveries might be arranged into three different groups. First of all the land had been found full of temples, vast and majestic beyond imagination; among these the temples at Karnak were supreme, but there were others on a par with them in points of architectural detail. But besides these, then as now, above ground and inviting inspection, there were many others which were ... more or less buried in the sand; some of these have since been unearthed to reveal the striking features of their structure.

The second revelation was that the walls of these temples, and of many funereal buildings, were, for the most part, covered with inscriptions in the language which was then but gradually emerging from the unknown, its very alphabet and syllabary being still incomplete. Hence there was not only a great wealth of temple buildings, but a still more wonderful wealth of temple inscriptions.

There was even more than this, and something more germane to our present purpose. In several temples which were examined, zodiacs ... were discovered; these, also, accompanied by inscriptions of an obviously astronomical nature.

[...]

It is little to be wondered at that, when these revelations first burst upon the scientific world, great excitement was produced. It was obvious that we had to do with a nation which had very definite ideas of astronomy, and that the astronomy was very closely connected with worship. It was also suggested by so many animal forms, that we also had to do with a people whose condition was not unlike that of the American Indians at the beginning of this century ... one in which each tribe, or clan, or locality had chosen a special animal totem.

...With all this new work before them,... it was not long before the French ... compelled the hieroglyphics to give up some of their secrets. First one word gave two or three letters, then another two or three more, and finally an alphabet and syllabary were constructed. So it was not long before some of the inscriptions at Denderah were read.... [In] 700 B.C. in Egypt the solstice was recognised; a means of determining the instant of midnight with more or less precision was known; observations of the stars were regularly made; the risings of some of them were associated with the rising of the sun, and many of them had been collected into groups or constellations .... almost every detail seen in the zodiac of Denderah reproduces inscriptions or astronomical figures unearthed ... must be referred to the time of the Eighteenth Dynasty—that is, 1700 B.C., or thereabouts....

The next point to notice is connected with the astronomical drawings which have been found in the Ramesseum at Thebes—drawings which also have very obvious connections with the zodiac of Denderah. On these we find the hieroglyphics for the different months; the constellations Orion, Hippopotamus, and Jackal, as we saw them at Denderah, and another form of the constellation of the Thigh. There is obviously the closest connection between the two sets of delineations....

We know several points regarding Egyptian customs quite independently of the astronomical inscriptions, properly so called, to which I have called attention. We know that there were sacrifices at daybreak; we know that stars were watched rising heliacally, that is, before sunrise, and heralding the dawn; we know that such observations were among the chief duties of the sacrificial priests, and it is obvious that a knowledge of star-places, as well as star-names, must have been imperative to these morning watchers....

We next come to the complex phenomenon of day and night .... the difference between night and day was to the ancient Egyptians almost the difference between death and life. We can imagine that darkness thus considered by a mythologically-thinking people was regarded as the work of an enemy, and hence, in time, their natural enemies were represented as being the friends of darkness.

[...]

Let us now turn to the associated mythology. We see that the astronomical ideas have a most definite character; we learn also, from the inscriptions dating from the eighteenth dynasty, that the Egyptians at that time recognised three different risings. There was the rising at sunset, the rising at midnight, and the rising at dawn. Plutarch says that the Hippopotamus was certainly one of the forms of Typhon, and a reference to the myth of Horus....

In the inscriptions at Denderah we find the star Sirius represented by a cow in a boat. In the circular zodiac we have the cow in the boat, the point of the beginning of the year, and the constellation Orion so located as to indicate clearly that, at that time, the beginning of the year fell between the heliacal rising of Sirius and of the stars in Orion. Sirius was Isis-Sothis.

If we go to Thebes we pass, there, from the cow Isis-Sothis to Isis-Hathor, and there we find that mythology retains the idea of the cow, the cow gradually appearing from behind the western hills. There is not a doubt, I think, that the basis of this mythological representation was, that the temple which was built to observe the rising of the star ... was situated in the western hills of Thebes, so that Hathor, the goddess on which the light was to fall in the sanctuary, was imaged as dwelling in the western hills. At Philae we get no longer either Isis-Sothis or Isis-Hathor, but Isis-Sati. Here we get a first glimpse at the personification of a star.

[...]

Next, to attempt to get a step further in the domain of mythology, I assume that it is agreed that we have arrived at the certain conclusion that the goddess Hathor personified a star, Sirius, rising at the dawn.

I will begin by taking a certain group of goddesses.

1. *There is evidence that many of the goddesses under discussion personified stars in exactly the same way that Hathor personified Sirius.* There is the well-known temple at Thebes, the temple of Mut, from the orientation of which we know that Sirius was not in question. We do not know exactly, but it looks very much as if the temple of Mut was really aligned to the same star that the old temple of Hathor at Denderah was pointed to.

If we leave Thebes for the moment and consider the pyramid region of Ghizeh, we find that the temples there, which are associated with each of the pyramids, are also not oriented to Sirius; but yet they are temples of Isis, pointing due east; therefore they could not have pointed to the same Isis worshipped at Denderah. Quite recently there has been excavated near the sphinx a temple undoubtedly of Osiris, pointed due west, and built just as strictly in relation to the second pyramid as the temple of Isis. The temple of Isis is in an exact line running through the centre of the pyramid. The temple of Osiris is built so that its axis prolonged passes along the face of the pyramid, so that the sunset could be seen without being interfered with by the pyramid. Of course the sunrise could be seen from the temple of Isis, because the temple was built on the east side of the pyramid. There has been a covered way found connecting the temple of Isis with the temple of Osiris. Thus, in the case of the temple of Mut at Thebes, and the temple of Isis at the pyramids, obviously different stars were in question, whatever the mythology may be.

2. *There is evidence that many of the names of these goddesses are pure synonyms.* That is to say, we have the same goddess (or the same star) called by different names in different places, and associated with different animal emblems, in consequence of the existence of different totems in different names. For instance, let us take the goddess Mut and note how she is symbolized. In one form she is a hippopotamus; in another she has a cow's horns and disc. The temple of Hathor at Denderah was probably associated with the crocodile or the hippopotamus, so that, from the symbolism referred to, we get the suggestion that the goddess Mut was really the Theban form of the goddess Hathor at Denderah. There is another delineation which shows that even more clearly. It is a drawing of the goddess with both the lion's and crocodile's head. One of the most wonderful things seen at Thebes is that marvellous collection of the statues of Sekhet in the temple of Mut, all of them lion-headed. From the evidence of this kind we

get a clear indication of the fact that Apet, Mut, Taurt, Sekhet, were the same goddesses under different names, and I may add that they, in all probability symbolized the star Draconis.

3. *All these goddesses have a special symbol.* Hathor wears the cow's head and the horns with the disc. Taurt, the hippopotamus goddess, is also represented with horns and disc. The horns and disc are also worn by Sati and Ra-t, the wife of the sun-god Ra, and other goddesses might be added to the list.

The suggestion is that Isis is, *par excellence*, the goddess represented in this way, and that she symbolised generically a rising star; therefore all the goddesses so symbolised are either different forms of Isis or represent goddesses who personify or bring before us mythologically other stars, the rising of which was observed at the dawn at some time of the year or another.

4. *Many of the goddesses are represented as Isis nursing Horus.* It is very important not to forget that stars were chiefly observed rising in the dawn, and that mythologically such an event was represented by the Egyptians as Isis, the rising star, nursing Horus, the rising sun. The sun was supposed to be the youth of the morning; to be very young, therefore, at the moment of rising, and the goddess Isis was supposed to be then nursing him. Many of the goddesses are thus portrayed. I may mention Renent, Selk, Ra-t, Ament, as instances. Thus I hold that we get in this series of goddesses the statement put mythologically that certain stars to which the goddesses were sacred rose heliacally at some time of the year or another. Of course the record is far from complete when inquiries are made from this point of view. The original symbolism is that Isis is a star rising in the dawn, watching over the sun or taking him from his cradle, and the young Horus, the rising sun, is, of course, the son of Isis. We have here a very early edition of the Virgin and Child.

3. From "Egypt," *London Quarterly Review* 2:3 (April 1884): 136–51

…Just now the eyes of all Europe are fixed on our conduct of affairs in Egypt, and especially in its outlying dependencies grouped under the generic term "the Soudan." Whatever were the real motives of Ismail Pasha[1] in annexing the wilder and remote parts of "the Country of the Blacks," there can be but little doubt that a great blow was thereby struck at the slave-trade, and under

---

[1] Ismail Pasha (1830–95), ruler of Egypt 1863–79, was responsible for the building of the Suez Canal, but was forced to sell his shares to the British in 1875.

the governorship of the brave and genial Gordon[1] the tide of slavery was driven back, humanity enlarged its borders, and civilization was making its way to the very heart of Africa. But soon Ismail was deposed, Gordon resigned his charge, and, after a while, Mahomet Achmet,[2] the Mahdi, arose and profited by the misgovernment of Sheikhs and Pashas to rally men to his standard of slavery and fanaticism. Already had his troops penetrated into Sennaar, and were getting nearer and nearer to Khartoum, when the Egyptian Government, in order to make that city secure, and to free the province of Sennaar from the dangerous invader, sent a small army against him under Hicks Pasha,[3] who soon expelled him and his rebel rout from the district. Unfortunately the Egyptian cabinet was not content with this success, but sent the bold Englishman across an inhospitable desert to attack the Mahdi at Kordofan, the stronghold of his power; and this ill-advised move—which the English Government should not have permitted to be made, knowing as it did the inadequacy of the means and the hopelessness of the undertaking—led to the sad catastrophe of the destruction of General Hicks and his gallant officers and black troops. And this was the very same which our Government had chosen for withdrawing British troops from Cairo! After the calamity to Hicks it did indeed cancel the absurd order; but even then it did not awake to dangers that were patent to every intelligent observer.

In January the English Ministry came to the resolution that the Soudan must be given up, *in toto*,[4] by Egypt. Anxious only to get rid of any foreign affair which caused the smallest trouble of thought or action, they quite ignored the probability that the abandonment of Khartoum would raise the *prestige* of the false Prophet, and bring him in dangerous proximity to Upper Egypt; as well as the fact that Khartoum and Berber and Dongola and Sennaar are important parts of the Egyptian dominions, which should not lightly be thrown away, and which under proper management would materially help the Egyptian revenue. In any case the order for the evacuation of the Soudan should not have been promulgated till proper precautions had been taken for

---

1   Charles George Gordon (1833–85), British Soldier and colonial administrator. Gordon was sent to the Sudan by the British Government, where Muhammad Ahmad (Mahomet Achmet), the Mahdi, had control. Despite orders to evacuate the garrison at Khartoum, Gordon took it on himself to defeat the Mahdi. Gordon held the Garrison under siege for ten months, until it was stormed and he was killed.

2   Muhammad Ahmad (1844–85) declared himself to be Mahdi (Arabic for "he who is divinely guided"). In Sunni Islam, the Mahdi will be sent to earth to restore the Islamic faith. Ahmad defeated Gordon at Khartoum, dying shortly thereafter.

3   Major-General William "Billy" Hicks, having led several successful campaigns in the Sudan against the Mahdi, was defeated on 5th November, 1883.

4   *in toto*: completely.

the relief and rescue of the Egyptian garrisons scattered through that long stretch of country. But, in spite of the most urgent appeals, the starving garrison of Sinkat, under the brave Tewfik Bey,[1] was left to perish; and at last, when the news of their sally, and consequent massacre, and of the piteous slaughter of women and children, spread horror all over England, our Ministers—roused to some manhood by the storm of indignation which shook the country— took the very steps which had for months been urged upon them, and sent English troops to the Red Sea Coast. And now, instead of recalling our soldiers from Cairo, we are sending reinforcements there. Surely it is the duty of a Government, in managing the foreign policy of a nation, to look ahead and avert disaster, instead of waiting till it sees whether the news communicated by the daily press has any effect on the public mind, and whether constituencies or caucuses are pressing certain views on their representatives. "Let us but keep always in time with the mood of popular feeling for the hour, and the rest of the world may take its chance," should not be the ruling principle for any English Ministry; nor should it, again and again, by its sluggish indecision, earn the ominous sentence, "Too late, too late!" A firm and outspoken adherence to that policy of protection which Egypt needs from us would have rendered unnecessary a costly expedition and prevented the painful sacrifice of life which has attended our recent victories.

[…]

Egypt is a land that needs, and that will repay, the best efforts of our best men. It demands not a Gordon only, but a Dufferin;[2] and evil for it was the day when that enlightened statesman had to return to Constantinople. His was the "masterful hand" that was needed, at once to guide the internal affairs of Egypt, and to influence the wavering minds of Ministers at home to a steady, consistent policy, which should commend itself alike to the commercial and to the philanthropic world: —redressing the wrongs of the Fellahs,[3]

---

1 Muhammed Tewfik (1852-92), son of Ismail Pasha and khedive of Egypt (1879-92).

2 Frederick Temple Hamilton-Temple-Blackwood, 1st Marquess of Dufferin and Ava (1826-1902), commissioner to Egypt (1882-83).

3 Fellahs, or Fellaheen, constituted the majority of the agrarian population of Egypt at the end of the nineteenth century. Mostly farmers, they profited from the American Civil War as a result of the interruption caused by that war in the cotton trade. Cotton, also grown in Egypt, provided an alternative source, until the end of the war and the resumption of the American source. The author of the article attributes the majority of Egypt's problems in the late 1880s to them. Earlier in the same article, the author describes the Fellahs in the following manner: "The Fellahs may be regarded as genuine Egyptians, sons of the soil, but intermixed with the Arabs, sons of the desert, who have from time to time settled down to agriculture…. Most of the Fellahs are, or have been landowners in a small way …. though his wants are few, and he is a born proprietor, or quasi-freeholder, the poor Fellah sinks very low in the struggle for existence, being heavily weighted in his efforts by the evil custom of polygamy and early marriage."

freeing the finances from embarrassment, developing the resources of the soil, and avoiding the infantile impatience which is continually pulling up the plant of progress to see how it grows, or to throw it away as an ungrateful weed.

As we revise these last paragraphs, we have the news of General Graham's victories. Gordon and Graham seem, for the present, to have saved Egypt and also to have saved the English Ministry. That Ministry, not long ago, was strong in the magic of a great statesman's name, and in the support of a large majority within and without the House. But its lamentable imbecility, first in the affairs of South Africa and then of Egypt, has done much to weaken its position alike in England and in the councils of the world.

4. From "Our Position in Egypt," *The Speaker* (19 October 1891): 427–28

We do not propose to follow those rabid scribes, like Sir Lepel Griffin,[1] who have plunged into angry disquisitions against Mr. Gladstone[2] because in a few pregnant words at Newcastle he called the attention of his fellow-countrymen to the truth regarding our occupation of Egypt. We would rather rejoice that, speaking with an authority superior to that of any other member of the Liberal party, he should not have omitted the Egyptian Question from his recent survey of public affairs. There are certain facts connected with our occupation of that country to which, apparently, a portion of the public habitually shuts its eyes, yet they are facts which cannot be ignored without grave danger. Nothing can be more satisfactory to our national pride than the manner in which, under English auspices, civilisation is flourishing apace in the Delta of the Nile. It is delightful to think that we are in a measure accomplishing there the great work which we have already done in India, and the Chauvinist feeling which is strong in most men cannot but be stimulated by our knowledge of this fact. That we should scuttle out of Egypt leaving our work undone, our pledges unfulfilled, is what no man amongst us can desire. But that we should stay there indefinitely in the hope that sooner or later Europe will be induced to acquiesce in the transformation of our present temporary occupancy of the country into a real and permanent conquest, is another thing, about which it is necessary that there should be very plain speaking on the part of Liberals at all events.

---

[1] Sir Lepel Griffin, an Anglo-Indian official and Lieutenant-Governor of the Punjab in the 1880s.

[2] William Ewart Gladstone (1809-98), served as British Liberal Prime Minister four times (1868–74, 1880–85, 1886, and 1892–94).

Fate may determine that Egypt shall be ours, that having established our soldiers in that country we shall never again withdraw them from it; but if that is to be the case, it is to be hoped that the furious Jingoes who reproach Mr. Gladstone for having ventured to touch upon the question at all, will bear one fact at least in mind. That is, that we are pledged in honour to leave the country as soon as our work there is done, and that the only honourable manner ... in which we can evade the pledge is by asserting our right to do so by the sword. If we are prepared frankly to face Europe and say, "We withdraw from our promise to quit Egyptian territory, and are prepared to abide the consequences," we may then satisfy at once our own sense of honour and our national covetousness. But in that case we must be prepared to assert our right to Egypt at the point of the sword—in other words, we must go to war with France in order to cover our retreat from our own pledges.... There is no sane man, even among the Tory party, who would venture to assert that our trade with Egypt would be worth a war with Portugal, much less a war with France. The desire to hold the country in perpetuity is nothing more than an outburst of the maddest Chauvinism, and when we remember that its gratification would mean not only that war with a great Continental Power of which we have spoken, but the loss of the advantages we enjoy from our own insular position, and our embroilment in every Continental quarrel and intrigue, however desperate or however foolish, we are at a loss to understand by what process of reasoning any responsible body of men can have brought themselves to believe that the game would be worth the candle. Egypt must be permitted to secure under our fostering care a reasonable degree of national security and self-reliance, and when that end has been attained it must be placed under the protection, not of a single Power, but of Europe as a whole. This is the true and only solution of the Egyptian question. To wish for any other solution is to desire the embroilment of England in dangers and difficulties which it would be impossible to exaggerate. Fortunately the voice of patriotism is in this matter identical with the voice of honour and of prudence, and this fact, we cannot doubt, will ere long be recognised by the country as a whole.

Appendix D: Mesmerism and Animal Magnetism

[Discovered by Austrian physician Franz Anton Mesmer (1734-1815) and given the name of animal magnetism, mesmerism was first used by Mesmer and other physicians in medical practice. However, its uses spread rapidly throughout Europe in the first half of the nineteenth century, becoming a widespread source of entertainment. When *Tait's Edinburgh Magazine* described mesmerism as "the prevailing popular frenzy of the hour" in 1843, this was no exaggeration. Its scientific value always hotly contended, its more unscrupulous practitioners brought mesmerism into disrepute, as it came to occupy the shady territory between science and pseudo-science in the nineteenth century, along with the the practice of other cultural pseudo-sciences, such as phenology and clairvoyance. Nevertheless, from the 1830s to the 1860s the practice of animal magnetism extended well beyond a few medical institutions, theatres, and music halls, mesmeric séances being held throughout Great Britain, at every level of society, on an almost daily basis, whether in public spaces, such as public houses, or in the drawing rooms of middle-class Victorians.]

1. From Joseph W. Haddock, *Somnolism & Psycheism; or, the Science of the Soul and the Phenomena of Nervation, as Revealed by Vital Magnetism or Mesmerism, Considered Physiologically and Philosophically, with Notes of Mesmeric and Psychical Experience* (1851)

In the records of past ages, we have many statements of remarkable mental or psychical manifestations, and also of the performance of remarkable cures, by mental or moral agency, which ignorance and superstition have ascribed to *miracle* or *magic*; and scepticism, to collusion and deception. The more extended knowledge, and juster philosophy which is progressing in the present generation, has admitted the possibility and probability of many things which were ridiculed in the middle of the eighteenth century; some of these, as the fall of large masses of iron,—meteorites, as they are termed,—from the atmosphere, are now admitted as established verities; and the more recent observation of what is called mesmeric phenomena, has gone far to establish the veracity of ancient writers on other disputed matters, and to afford a reasonable explanation of otherwise mysterious, and apparently impossible, events.

Ancient history speaks of the mysterious doings, oracular sayings, prophetic forebodings, and apparently miraculous performances of the

Egyptian Priests; of the Delphian Oracle[1] among the Greeks, and of the Sybils[2] among the Romans....

[...]

Mesmer's theory is as follows. "Animal magnetism is a fluid universally diffused: it is the medium of a mutual influence between the heavenly bodies, the earth, and animated bodies; it is continuous, so as to leave no void; its subtlety admits of no comparison; it is capable of receiving, propagating, communicating all the impressions of motion; it is susceptible of flux and reflux. The animal body experiences the effects of this agent: by insinuating itself into the substance of the nerves, it affects them immediately. There are observed, particularly in the human body, properties analogous to those of the magnet, and in it are discerned poles, equally different and opposite. The action and the virtues of animal magnetism may be communicated from one body to other bodies, animate and inanimate. This action takes place at a remote distance without the aid of any intermediate body; it is increased, reflected by mirrors; communicated, augmented, and propagated by sound; its virtues may be accumulated, concentrated, transported. Although this fluid is universal, all animal bodies are not equally susceptible of it; there are even some, though a very small number, which have properties so opposite, that their very presence destroys all the effects of this fluid on other bodies. Animal magnetism is capable of healing diseases of the nerves immediately, and others mediately. It perfects the action of medicines; it excites and directs salutary *crises* in such a manner, that the physician may render himself master of them; by its means he knows the state of the health of each individual, and judges with certainty of the origin, the nature, and the progress of the most complicated in healing them, without at any time exposing his patient to dangerous effects or troublesome consequences. In animal magnetism nature presents a universal method of healing and preserving mankind."[3] (Ch. 2, 6, 13–14)

A very slight practical acquaintance with the phenomena associated with the name of MESMERISM, will be sufficient to manifest, that although one common character of somnolency is always more or less apparent, still there are a variety of states, and widely differing manifestations, included in one

---

[1] The word Oracle refers to both the shrine and prophet in ancient Greece, from whom advice was sought. The most important Greek Oracle was located in Delphi, in central Greece, and was dedicated to the God Apollo.

[2] Virgin priestesses endowed with the gift of prophecy, devoted to Apollo.

[3] Haddock's source is a translation and paraphrase of Mesmer's twenty-seven propositions on animal magnetism, taken from his *Mémoire sur la découverte du magnétisme animal* (1779).

generic term. One person who is truly *mesmerized* as it is called, may evince only symptoms of slight drowsiness or inability to open the eyes; while another, with the same amount of manipulation, will display the higher faculties of lucidity or clairvoyance. It is necessary, therefore, for a clear apprehension of the phenomena, to have some classification of the different states. Judging from my own experience, these states may be classified as follows. First, SIMPLE MESMERIC DROWSINESS OR SLEEP; secondly, COMA, or more profound sleep; thirdly, ANAESTHESIA, or insensibility to pain, occasioned by general want of feeling. This last mentioned characteristic is a result of the *full* establishment of the mesmeric coma, and by this means, the *entire* closure of the external consciousness; for a person may *appear to be* insensible to, or unconscious of outward objects, and yet upon receiving a sudden prick or pinch, startle, or draw back the limb; plainly shewing that sensibility is not entirely deadened. These three stages comprise all that are required to manifest the various phenomena, arising from the partial and entire closure of the outward consciousness. The next stages display the opening of an *inner* consciousness, which has given rise to the phrase of *double-consciousness*, employed by some physiological writers. A subject may not progress further than the state of coma, but it will, I believe mostly happen, that when coma is really established, the other states will follow. On the other hand, some subjects appear to possess the state of inner-consciousness, without passing properly into the state of coma. Perhaps the first or lowest state of inner-consciousness, may be classified as PHRENO-MESMERISM, or the manifestation of the phrenological sentiments and feelings, which is but a form of simple imaginative action. Next in order, is PHANTASY, or that state in which the mesmerized person takes the mere suggestions of the operator to be realities. TRANSFER of STATE and FEELING, or that imaginative and sympathetic action, which causes the subject to feel what is done to the operator, as if it were done to himself, which is in reality but another phrase of phantasy, but having a real base. MENTAL or VITAL MAGNETIC ATTRACTION, by which the subject is irresistibly drawn, even contrary to his inclination, towards the operator. And lastly, the still higher faculties of CEREBRAL LUCIDITY, or apparent illumination of the brain, by which objects are seen without the use of the eye; together with those other forms of *distant perception*, commonly known by the name of CLAIRVOYANCE, or clear-seeing; all which would perhaps, be better stressed as INNER VISION, or INTERNAL, or SPIRITUAL SIGHT. These various phenomena exhibit a series of great and interesting facts, which cannot be set aside, neither by argument nor ridicule, whatever medical or literary critics may affect to say to the contrary;…

[...]

PHANTASY and TRANSFER of STATE and FEELING, which I have classified after phreno-mesmerism, may, I think, be considered, but as more advanced stages of the same *imaginative* action. By *phantasy*, is meant such an action on the mind of the mesmerized party, that the mere *suggestions* of the mesmeriser, or, it may be, of some other person, sometimes even, not audibly expressed, but merely silently willed, are taken for *realities*. Thus, a handkerchief being thrown into the lap of a susceptible subject, and at the same time the operator *thinking* of any harmless or pleasing living object, such as a rabbit, a guinea-pig, or a child, or even of disagreeable objects, as a snake, or other reptile, and at the same time *willing* that the mesmerized party shall fancy the handkerchief to be the animal which is the subject of the operator's thoughts, and directing the patient's attention to it, it will be taken for the animal or reptile, and the language and action will soon evince that it is really considered to be such; and, in some cases, the subjects of such experiments, cannot, by any means in their own power, divest themselves of the phantasy. These are surprising instances of the effect of *merely excited imagination*, scarcely conceivable, and yet not uncommon....
[...]

By TRANSFER of STATE or FEELING, is meant, that curious effect of *reflected action*, which is exhibited by good mesmeric subjects, in feeling whatever is done to the mesmeriser *as done to themselves*....
[...]

CEREBRAL LUCIDITY and CLAIRVOYANCE complete our classification. These states are so purely psychological, that they belong rather to the subject of the next chapter; but as they also have a physiological character, I will briefly note them here. By CEREBRAL LLUCIDITY, I mean, that peculiar condition of the mind and brain, by which the lucid subjects see objects that are around or near them, by light, or an element analogous to light, which they perceive as issuing from the brain, and quite independent of the usual visual organ—the eye.... The human body seems as if transparent to the truly lucid subject; ...CLAIRVOYANCE I would restrict to the perception of *distant objects* or to *spiritual matters*. (Ch. 3, 20-21, 50-51, 52-53)

2. From James Esdaile, *Natural and Mesmeric Clairvoyance, with the Practical Application of Mesmerism in Surgery and Medicine* (1852) 56–57

In fact, we can now imitate perhaps all that was true and useful in the ancient temples in our modern hospitals, by the use of opium, hemp, ether, chloroform, different gases, and especially by *Mesmerism*, which is the safest and most effectual stimulant of the brain we are acquainted with.

Everything goes to prove that the oracles received in dreams, and the cures which followed them, were the consequences of what we now call the mesmeric exaltation of the nervous system, variously brought about, no doubt, but frequently by the modern method of manipulations, assisted by breathing.

Indeed, it is impossible that, in the long course of ages, this faculty in man should not have been observed. It was so, in fact, and the pagan priests explored it to their own advantage by giving the credit to the Temples of Isis, Serapis, and Esculapius. Knowing how to produce and direct somnambulism, they placed the person whom they knew to be gifted with the power of distant vision and of prevision in the sanctuary of the temple to be the organ of the god, who, it was pretended, possessed him. Another, in his state of exaltation, felt the diseases of those who approached him, perceived the state of their organs, indicating the accessions of their complaints, and prescribed remedies....

Prosper Albinus says, in his Treatise on the Medicine of the Egyptians,— "After numerous ceremonies, the sick were wrapped up in the skins of goats, and carried within the sanctuary of the temple, where the god appeared to them in dreams, and revealed the remedies that ought to be resorted to for their cure. When the patients received no communication from the divinity, then priests, called *oneiropoles*, slept in their places, and the god no longer withheld the hoped-for boon."

3. From "Magic and Mesmerism," *Tait's Edinburgh Magazine*, 50 (1843): 484–92

Mesmerism and Phreno-Mesmerism, seem the prevailing popular frenzy of the hour. The epidemic is, we presume, on the decline in America, where it broke out fiercely about four years back; but it has had a powerful revival in France, where the belief in Mesmerism has languished on for sixty years; while in Britain, in every town, village, and hamlet, adepts of both sexes, professional and amateur, are mesmerizing, and being mesmerized, hypnotizing, or being hypnotized; lecturing (for money) and exhibiting, in illustration of their lectures, the varied phenomena of Animal Magnetism, from the simple rigidity of a finger or a limb up to the highest achievements of phreno-magnetism, ecstatic delirium, and *clairvoyance*. Tailors, hand-loom weavers, sempstresses, and females of no ostensible calling, are all (for money) exhibiting the Mesmeric phenomena in various degrees of perfection, to select private circles—consisting of ladies, idlers, and men of science; while the less profoundly initiated, or the less enterprising, are content to perform before thin or crowded audiences, as it may happen, and generally at very moderate rates. The first crop of these itinerant lecturers and exhibitors in this quarter have been peculiarly unfortunate in their staff; that is, in the adepts who accompany them; clumsy, ill-trained, maladroit rogues, whose bungling performances were enough to ruin any professor, if the great majority of the audiences had not been in the humour of being gulled, while the minority viewed the thing in the light of a broad, acted piece of farce, too absurd to require exposure, and which served to laugh out the hour as well as anything else. It is not easy to say which class of society has been the most tickled with the excitement and palpable humbug of these edifying exhibitions. We restrict these remarks to the platform and private exhibitions in Edinburgh and the neighbouring towns; pronouncing no opinion upon genuine Mesmeric phenomena; a matter for grave and searching investigation, and one quite unconnected with the tom-fooleries and egregious humbug to which we allude. Meanwhile, we have reached a stage in Scotland which may well make England envious. If *clairvoyance* arose in France, and has made a distinguished progress in America, it ought to be remembered that second-sight, and second-hearing, though extinct for generations, was an exclusive attribute of the Scottish Highlanders, and chiefly of the Hebrideans; and, consequently, that modern *clairvoyance* is, in Scotland, a recovered faculty. Scotland, also, has a prior claim to "The Tongues," though there were powerful "manifestations" both in London and Oxford. The only remarkable difference is, that science now pretends to explain the phenomena which formerly were said to be produced by supernatural influence or the agency of the Devil. *Clairvoyance* is, we understand, at present as fashionable in Paris as ever was fortune-telling ... and *clairvoyance*, we prophesy, will get fast ahead at home.... We therefore apprehend that anything we have yet witnessed in *clairvoyance* will be utterly eclipsed by what is to come hereafter, if proper encouragement be given....

4. From Romulus Katscher, "Mesmerism, Spiritualism and Hypnotism," *The Literary Digest*, II:17 (21 February 1891): 460–61

While the pursuit of the subject of animal magnetism has landed the spiritualists in a realm of phantasy wholly without scientific support, and has been made the basis of an almost unparalleled amount of charlatanism, it has, nevertheless, on the other hand, guided to positive demonstration of the undeniable phenomena of artificially induced somnambulism, which, during the past decade, have been made the subject of earnest investigation by some of the leading medical authorities of nearly all lands, so that there is a reasonable hope of an early and exhaustive explanation of remarkable phenomena. To the English Surgeon, James Braid,[1] of Manchester, belongs the credit of first discarding the untenable theories of Mesmer, and pursuing his researches in the direction of physiological investigation.

Braid published the results of his investigations in numerous papers, one of which, entitled Neurypnolopy,[2] or the rationale of nervous sleep, published in 1853, is especially worthy of recall, as in it he endeavoured to formulate his theory of hypnotism, laying down the proposition that hypnotism and its phenomena are purely subjective, having their seat in the nervous system of the person under treatment. "Strictly speaking," he wrote, "hypnotism is not a specific condition but a whole class of conditions, which vary in every conceivable degree between the simple dream state and deep coma, attended with the complete abnegation of self-consciousness and will on the one hand, and an almost incredible exaltation of the functions of special sense organs, of intellectual capacity and of will power in another direction. The phenomena are partly mental, partly physical, voluntary, involuntary or mixed, according to the state of the sleeper."

At the outset, Braid's views found very slow acceptance,.... But the Faculty and the public began to array themselves in favour of hypnotism, when the celebrated physiologist Richet,[3] in 1875, gave scientific demonstration of the phenomena of somnambulism. Three years later, Charcot,[4] at the Salpêtrière, took up the study of artificially induced somnambulism on hysterical patients.... The learned in Austria, Germany, Italy and other countries have also taken an active part in the investigation of the remarkable phenomena.

---

[1] James Braid (1795-1860), was not English, as the article claims, but Scottish, born in Fife. A surgeon, he coined the term "hypnotism."

[2] Braid published Neurypnolopy, the Rationale of Nervous Sleep Considered in Relation with Animal Magnetism in 1853.

[3] Charles Richet (1850-1935), Professor of Physiology, won the Nobel Prize in 1913 for his discovery of anaphylaxis, a heightened sensitivity to usually nontoxic proteins, resulting in shock or, occasionally, death. He was honorary president of the Paris-based Institut Métapsychique International (1919). He also pursued experiments in telepathy, psychokinesis, and ectoplasm (he was the first to use this word), which he used to define a supposed emanation or residue from a medium's body when in a trance.

[4] Jean-Martin Charcot (1825-1893), a Professor at the University of Paris for over thirty years, his research focused on neurology, and he established a neurological clinic at the Salpêtrière Hospital, using hypnosis on the hysterics under his care. Sigmund Freud was amongst his students.

The first question which naturally occurs to the investigator in this department is, who and what persons are susceptible to the hypnotic influence? On this point, ... investigations ... furnish conclusive evidence that all persons are hypnotizable, but that the measure of susceptibility varies greatly with the age, pursuits, state of health and temperament of the person operated on. Children and young persons with greater physical than mental activity, nervous, hypochondriac, hysterical and epileptic subjects, fall most readily under its influence. Women, too, are, as a rule, easier to hypnotise than men, and the people of the South, easier than those of the North. But success is impossible, where the person experimented on exerts his will-power to negate the efforts of the experimenter. The result is further hindered by weariness of body or mind, by excess of stimulating food or drink.... Persons who have been frequently hypnotized yield to the influence readily....

Hypnotizers differ in their methods, some adopting physical, some psychical means, and some a mixture of both; but consciously or unconsciously all these methods rest on the influence of suggestion, that is to say, on the uncomprehended but indisputable capacity of the operator to transmit his thoughts at will, to arouse him to act upon the impressions thus transmitted, and to guide to specific action by suggestion. It is the expressed, or it may be even the mere unconscious, wish of the operator that suffices to induce the hypnotic sleep, unless the patient strive against it. The physical means resorted to, the instructions to fix the eyes on a bright object for example, serve only to withdraw the mind from external distractions and guide it to a contemplation of the end sought. That suggestion alone is the operative force, appears to be proved by the fact, that the hypnotic condition frequently follows immediately on the operator, too, generally suffices to arouse the patient from sleep, requiring at most to be aided by breathing on the face.

The cataleptic state, (the first stage of Charcot), is distinguished by the open staring eyes, and rigidity of limbs. These last remain fixed in any position, no matter how difficult, in which the operator disposes them; the patient making little or no opposition to change of posture, being, in fact, like lifeless, pliable material in the hands of the operator; the faculty of sensibility to external influences, as heat or cold, appears to be entirely in abeyance, and can only be aroused by suggestion. The breathing in this state is slow and irregular.

In the lethargic state, the eyes are closed, the muscles are contracted by the slightest mechanical stimulus, the mere touch of the finger on any muscle sufficing to arouse it to action. The breathing is regular and deep. [...]

Passing now to the extraordinary mental phenomena of hypnotism, the first psychical phenomenon which invites our attention, is the ability of the somnambulistic subject to recall clearly the past occurrences of his life, even in the long forgotten past, and that not only of his waking moments, but also of his intervals of sleep; and that on awaking, he has no recollection of what transpired during the hypnotic sleep, unless instructed by the operator to remember all the circumstances after awaking.

The second psychical phenomenon, the *rapport*, consists in the complete subjection of the patient to the will of the operator. He has no longer any relations with the outside world, except through the medium of the operator; he hears only his voice, obeys only his will, sees things only as he presents them. To the voice of a third person he is deaf, unless the operator transfers his power, by suggesting the presence of the third party and instructing the subject to hear and obey him. Innumerable hypotheses have been advanced to account for this phenomena of *rapport*, but the problem is still unsolved.

There appears no reasonable doubt that hypnotism is destined to become an important factor in the treatment of disease, and the relief of both mental and physical suffering. It will be an important factor, too, in the science of jurisprudence. The fear of perversion of hypnotism to improper purposes will be found groundless, as its practice becomes fenced about with laws and regulations, and we have no doubt that, sooner or later, it will take the position to which it is entitled.

Works Cited and Recommended Reading

Biographical and Literary Criticism on Richard Marsh and *The Beetle*

Baker, William. "Introduction" *The Beetle*. Phoenix Mill: Alan Sutton, 1994. 3–7.

Greene, Hugh. "Introduction." *Victorian Villainies*. Selection by Graham Greene and Hugh Greene. Harmondsworth: Penguin, 1984. 7–10.

Hurley, Kelly. *The Gothic Body: Sexuality, Materialism, and Degeneration at the Fin de Siècle*. Cambridge: Cambridge UP, 1996. 125.

Luckhurst, Roger. "Trance-Gothic, 1882–1897." *Victorian Gothic: Literary and Cultural Manifestations in the Nineteenth Century*. Ed. Ruth Robbins and Julian Wolfreys. Basingstoke: Palgrave, 2000. 148–67.

Taylor, Michael Rupert. "G. A. Henty, Richard Marsh and Bernard Heldmann." *Antiquarian Book Monthly* 3 (August/September 1997): 10–19.

Historical Background

Hall, Catherine, Keith McClelland, and Jane Rendall. *Defining the Victorian Nation: Class, Race, Gender and the Reform Act of 1867*. Cambridge: Cambridge UP, 2000.

Hobsbawm, Eric. *The Age of Capital 1848–1875*. New York: Vintage, 1996.

Hoppen, K. Theodore. *The Mid-Victorian Generation 1846–1886*. Oxford: Oxford UP, 1998.

Rubenstein, W.D. *Britain's Century: A Political and Social History 1815–1905*. London: Arnold, 1998.

Other Critical Works

Benjamin, Walter. "Theses on the Philosophy of History." *Illuminations*. (1955) Ed. and int. Hannah Arendt. Trans. Harry Zohn. New York: Schocken Books, 1969.

Bivona, Daniel. *Desire and Contradiction: Imperial Visions and Domestic Debates in Victorian Literature*. Manchester: Manchester UP, 1990.

Daly, Nicholas. *Modernism, Romance, and the* Fin de Siècle: *Popular Fiction and British Culture, 1880–1914*. Cambridge: Cambridge UP, 1999.

Chrisman, Laura. "Empire, 'Race' and Feminism at the *Fin de Siècle*: The Work of George Egerton and Olive Schreiner." *Cultural Politics at the Fin de Siècle*. Ed. Sally Ledger and Scott McCracken. Cambridge: Cambridge UP, 1995. 45–65.

Derrida, Jacques. *Dissemination*. 1972 Trans. Barbara Johnson. Chicago: U of Chicago P, 1981.

Derrida, Jacques. "*Fors*: the Anglish Words of Nicolas Abraham and Maria Torok." Trans. Barbara Johnson. *The Wolf Man's Magic Word*. Nicolas Abraham and Maria Torok. 1976 Trans. Nicholas Rand. Minneapolis: U of Minnesota P. 1986. xi–il; xxviii.

Derrida, Jacques. *Specters of Marx: The State of the Debt, the Work of Mourning, & the New International*. 1993 Trans. Peggy Kamuf. Int. Bernd Magnus and Stephen Cullenberg. New York: Routledge, 1994.

Ellis, Havelock. *The Criminal*. Montclair: Patterson Smith, 1973.

Flint, Kate. "Literature, Music, and the Theatre." *The Nineteenth Century: The British Isles 1815–1901*. Ed. Colin Matthew. Cambridge: Cambridge UP, 2000. 229–54.

Freud, Sigmund. "The 'Uncanny.'" *The Standard Edition of the Complete Psychological Works of Sigmund Freud*. 24 vols. Ed. James Strachey. London: Hogarth, 1953–74. Vol. 17. 219–56.

Greenslade, William. *Degeneration, Culture and the Novel*. Cambridge: Cambridge UP, 1994.

Halberstam, Judith. "Technologies of Monstrosity: Bram Stoker's *Dracula*." *Cultural Politics at the Fin de Siècle*. Ed. Sally Ledger and Scott McCracken. Cambridge: Cambridge UP, 1995. 248–67.

Kestner, Joseph A. *The Edwardian Detective, 1901–1915*. Aldershot: Ashgate, 2000.

Larson, Jil. *Ethics and Narrative in the English Novel, 1880–1914*. Cambridge: Cambridge UP, 2001.

Ledger, Sally. "The New Woman and the Crisis of Victorianism." *Cultural Politics at the Fin de Siècle*. Ed. Sally Ledger and Scott McCracken, Cambridge: Cambridge UP, 1995. 22–44.

Lombroso-Ferrero, Gina. *Criminal Man According to the Classification of Cesare Lombroso, with an Introduction by Cesare Lombroso*. Montclair: Patterson Smith, 1972.

Mighall, Robert. *A Geography of Victorian Gothic Fiction: Mapping History's Nightmares*. Oxford: Oxford UP, 1999.

Miller, J. Hillis. *On Literature*. London: Routledge, 2002.

Rand, Nicholas. "Translator's Introduction: Toward a Cryptonymy of Literature." *The Wolf Man's Magic Word*. Nicolas Abraham and Maria

Torok. 1976 Trans. Nicholas Rand. Minneapolis: U of Minnesota P, 1986. li–lxx; lii.

Said, Edward W. *The World, the Text, and the Critic.* Cambridge: Harvard UP, 1983.

Said, Edward W. *Orientalism.* London: Penguin, 1985.

Schmitt, Cannon. *Alien Nation: Nineteenth-Century Gothic Fictions and English Nationality.* Philadelphia: U of Pennsylvania P, 1997.

Showalter, Elaine. "Syphilis, Sexuality, and the Fiction of the Fin de Siècle." *Sex, Politics, and Science in the Nineteenth-Century Novel: Selected Papers from the English Institute, 1983–84.* Ed. Ruth Bernard Yeazell. Baltimore: The Johns Hopkins UP, 1986. 88–115.

Winter, Alison. *Mesmerized: Powers of Mind in Victorian Britain.* Chicago: U of Chicago P, 1998.